The stirring story of the life and times
Alexander Kent's bestselling novels.

A TRADITION OF VICTORY

Alexander Kent

arrow books

First Published by Arrow Books in 1982
This edition published by Arrow Books in 2006

11

Copyright © Highseas Authors Ltd 1981

Alexander Kent has asserted his right under the Copyright, Designs and Patents Act, 1988 to
be identified as the author of this work

First published in the United Kingdom in 1981 by Hutchinson

Arrow Books
The Random House Group Limited
20 Vauxhall Bridge Road, London SW1V 2SA

www.randomhouse.co.uk

Addresses for companies within The Random House Group Limited can be found at:
www.randomhouse.co.uk/offices.htm

The Random House Group Limited Reg. No. 954009

A CIP catalogue record for this book
is available from the British Library

The Random House Group Limited supports The Forest Stewardship
Council® (FSC®), the leading international forest-certification organisation.
Our books carrying the FSC label are printed on FSC®-certified paper.
FSC is the only forest-certification scheme supported by the leading
environmental organisations, including Greenpeace. Our
paper procurement policy can be found at
www.randomhouse.co.uk/environment

ISBN 9780099591658

Printed and bound in Great Britain by Clays Ltd, St Ives plc

For Winifred,
with my love

Contents

God and the Sailor we alike adore
But only when in danger, not before:
The danger o'er, both are alike requited,
God is forgotten and the sailor slighted.

JOHN OWEN

I

A Touch of Land

Even for the West Country of England the summer of 1801 was rare with its cloudless blue skies and generous sunlight. In Plymouth, on this bustling July forenoon, the glare was so bright that the ships which seemed to cover the water from the Hamoaze to the Sound itself danced and shimmered to lessen the grimness of their gundecks and the scars of those which had endured the fury of battle.

A smart gig pulled purposefully beneath the stern of a tall three-decker and skilfully avoided a cumbersome lighter loaded almost to the gills with great casks and barrels of water. The gig's pale oars rose and fell together, and her crew in their checkered shirts and tarred hats were a credit to her ship and coxswain. The latter was gauging the comings and goings of other harbour craft, but his mind was firmly on the gig's passenger, Captain Thomas Herrick, whom he had just carried from the jetty.

Herrick was well aware of his coxswain's apprehension, just as he could sense the tension from the way his gig's crew carefully avoided his eye as they feathered their blades and made the boat scud across the water like a bright beetle.

It had been a long, tiresome journey from Kent, Herrick's home, and as the distance from Plymouth had fallen away he had started to fret over what he would discover.

His ship, the seventy-four-gun *Benbow*, had arrived in Plymouth barely a month back. It was incredible to believe that it was less than three months since the bloody fight itself, the one which was now called the Battle of

Copenhagen. The small Inshore Squadron, of which *Benbow* was the flagship, had fought with distinction. Everyone had said so, and the *Gazette* had hinted that but for their efforts 'things' might have gone very differently.

Herrick shifted on his thwart and frowned. He did not notice the stroke oarsman flinch under his stare, nor was he conscious of seeing him at all. Herrick was forty-four years old, and had made the hard and treacherous climb to his present appointment with neither influence nor patronage. He had heard it all before, and despised those who spoke of a sea-fight as if it were a kind of umpired contest.

Those sort of folk never saw the carnage, the broken bodies and minds which went with each encounter. The tangle of cordage and splintered timbers and spars which had to be put to rights without so much as a by-your-leave so that the ruin could be restored into a fighting ship and sent where she could be best used.

He glanced around the busy anchorage. Ships taking on stores, others being refitted. His eye rested on a lithe frigate, mastless and riding high above her reflection, uncluttered by guns and men, as she swung to her warps from a slipway. *Just launched*. He saw the waving hats and arms, the bright flags curling along her empty gunports, her growing confidence like that of a newly dropped colt.

Herrick frowned again. After eight years of constant war with France and her allies they were still short of frigates. Where would this one go? Who would command her and find glory or ignominy?

Herrick turned and looked at the young lieutenant who had come out to collect him with the gig. He must have arrived during his seven precious days in Kent. He was so pale and young, so unsure of himself that Herrick could barely see him as a newly joined midshipman, let alone a lieutenant. But the war had taken so many that the whole fleet seemed to be manned by boys and old men.

It was useless to ask *him* anything. He was scared of his own shadow.

Herrick glanced up at his square-shouldered coxswain as he steered the boat beneath another tapering bowsprit and glaring figurehead.

This shivering boy posing as a lieutenant had met him at the jetty, doffed his hat and had stammered in one breath, 'The first lieutenant's respects, sir, and the admiral is come aboard.'

Thank God the first lieutenant had been there to greet him, Herrick thought grimly. But what was Rear-Admiral Bolitho, an officer he had served in many parts of the world, a man whom he loved more than any other, doing aboard *Benbow* now?

It was easy to see him in those last moments outside Copenhagen. The smoke, the terrible din of falling spars and the jarring crash of cannon fire, and always Bolitho had been there. Waving them on. Driving them, leading them with all the reckless determination only he could use. Except that Herrick, who carried the pride deep within him of being his greatest friend, knew the real man underneath. The doubts and the fears, the excitement at a challenge, the despair at the waste of life if wrongly cast away.

Their homecoming should have been different for him above all others. This time there was a woman waiting. A beautiful girl who could and would be a reprieve from all which Bolitho had held dear and had previously lost. Bolitho had been going to London, to the Admiralty, and then back again to his home in Cornwall, that big grey house in Falmouth.

The gig straightened up on the last leg of the journey, and Herrick held his breath as he saw his ship stand out from the other anchored vessels, her black and buff tumblehome shining in the sunlight as a personal welcome. Only a professional seaman, and above all her captain, would see beyond the fresh paint and pitch, the blacked-down rigging and neatly furled canvas. The *Benbow*'s fat hull was almost hemmed in by lighters and moored platforms. The air vibrated with the din of hammers and saws, and even as he watched another great bundle of new cordage was being swayed aloft to the mizzen topmast, the one which had been shot away in battle. But *Benbow* was a new ship and had the strength of two older consorts. She had suffered badly, but was out of dock, and within months would be at sea again with her squadron. In spite of his usual caution, Herrick was pleased and proud with what they had done. Being Herrick, it never occurred to him that much of the success had been due to his own inspiration and his tireless efforts to get *Benbow* ready for sea.

His eyes rested on the mizzen mast and the flag which flapped only occasionally from its truck. The flag of a Rear-Admiral of the Red, but to Herrick it meant so much more. At least he had been able to share it with his new wife, Dulcie. Herrick had been married such a short time, and yet as he had given his sister away in marriage to the beanpole Lieutenant George Gilchrist, just four days back in Maidstone, he had felt like a husband of long years standing. He smiled, his round, homely face losing its sternness as he thought about it. His own ability to offer advice on marriage!

The bowman stood up with his boathook at the ready.

Benbow had risen right above the gig as Herrick's mind had drifted away. Close alongside he could see the repaired timbers, the paint which now hid the blood from the scuppers. As if the ship and not her people had been bleeding to death.

The oars were tossed and Tuck, the coxswain, removed his hat. Their eyes met and Herrick gave a quick smile. 'Thank you, Tuck. Smart turnout.'

They understood each other.

Herrick looked up at the entry port and prepared himself for the thousandth time. Once he had never believed he would ever hold his rank of lieutenant. The step from wardroom to quarterdeck, and now to being the flag-captain to one of the finest sea-officers alive, was even harder to accept.

Like the new house in Kent. Not a cottage, but a real house, with a full admiral living nearby and several rich merchants too. Dulcie had assured him, 'Nothing is too good for you, dear Thomas. You've worked for it, you deserve far more.'

Herrick sighed. Most of the money had been hers anyway. How had he ever managed to be so lucky, to find his Dulcie?

'Marines! At*ten*-shun!'

A cloud of pipeclay floated above the stolid faces and black shakoes as the muskets banged to the present, and, as the air cringed to the twitter of the boatswains' calls, Herrick removed his hat to the quarterdeck and to Wolfe, his towering first lieutenant, the most ungainly, but certainly one of the best seamen Herrick had ever met.

The din faded away, and Herrick looked at the side party with sadness. So many new faces to learn. But now he only saw the others who had died in the battle or were suffering the pain and humiliation of some naval hospital.

But Major Clinton of the marines was still here. And beyond his scarlet shoulder Herrick saw old Ben Grubb, the sailing master. He was lucky to have so many seasoned hands to weld the recruits and pressed men into some kind of company.

'Well, Mr Wolfe, maybe *you* can tell me why the admiral's flag is aloft?'

He fell in step with the lieutenant with the two wings of bright ginger hair poking from beneath his hat like studding sails. It was as if he had never been away. As if the ship had swallowed him up and the distant shore with its shimmering houses and embrazured batteries was of no importance.

Wolfe said in his flat, harsh voice, 'The admiral came off shore yesterday afternoon, sir.' He shot out a massive fist and pointed at some newly coiled halliards. 'What's that lot? Bloody birds'-nests?' He swung away from the transfixed sailor and bellowed, 'Mr Swale, take this idiot's name! He should be a damned weaver, not a seaman!'

Wolfe added, breathing hard, 'Most of the new hands are like that. The sweepings of the assizes, with a sprinkling of trained ones.' He tapped his big nose. 'Got *them* off an Indiaman. They said they were free from service in a King's ship. They *said* they had the papers to prove it too.'

Herrick gave a wry smile. 'But their ship had sailed by the time you sorted things out, Mr Wolfe?'

Like his first lieutenant, Herrick had little sympathy with all the prime seamen who were exempt from naval service merely because they were employed by John Company or some harbour authority. England was at war. They needed seamen, not cripples and criminals. Every day it got harder. Herrick had heard that the press gangs and undaunted recruiting parties were working many miles from the sea now.

He glanced up at the towering mainmast and its imposing spread of rigging and crossed yards. It was not difficult to remember the smoke and the punctured sails. The marines in the maintop yelling and cheering, firing swivels and muskets in a world gone mad.

They walked into the coolness of the poop, each ducking between the heavy deckhead beams.

Wolfe said, 'The admiral came alone, sir.' He hesitated, as if to test their relationship. 'I thought he might bring his lady.'

Herrick eyed him gravely. Wolfe was huge and violent and had seen service in everything from a slaver to a collier brig. He was not the kind of man to be patient with a laggard or allow time for personal weaknesses. But neither was he a gossip.

Herrick said simply, 'I had hopes too. By God, if ever a man deserved or needed —'

The rest of his words were cut dead as the marine sentry outside the great cabin tapped his musket smartly on the deck and shouted, 'Flag-Captain, *sah*!'

Wolfe grinned and turned aside. 'Damned bullocks!'

The door was opened swiftly by little Ozzard, Bolitho's personal servant. He was an oddity. Although a good servant, he was said to have been an even better lawyer's clerk, but had fled to the Navy rather than face trial or, as some had unkindly hinted, a quick end on a hangman's halter.

The great cabin, divided by white screens from the dining and sleeping quarters, had been freshly painted, and the deck was once more covered by checkered canvas with no hint of the battle scars underneath.

Bolitho had been leaning out of a stern window, and as he turned to greet his friend, Herrick felt relieved that there was apparently no change. His gold-laced rear-admiral's coat lay carelessly across a chair, and he wore only his shirt and breeches. His black hair, with the one loose lock above his right eye, and his ready smile made him seem more like a lieutenant than a flag-officer.

They held hands momentarily, compressing the memories and the pictures into a few seconds.

Bolitho said, 'Some hock, Ozzard.' He pulled a chair for Herrick. 'Sit you down, Thomas. It is *good* to see you.'

His level grey eyes held on to his friend for a moment longer. Herrick was sturdier, his face a mite rounder, but that would be his new wife's care and cooking. There were a few touches of grey on his brown hair, like frost on a strong bush. But the clear blue eyes which could be so stubborn and so hurt were the same.

They touched their goblets and Bolitho added, 'What is your state of readiness, Thomas?'

Herrick almost choked on his wine. *Readiness?* A month in port, and two of the squadron's strength lost forever during the battle! Even their smallest two-decker, the sixty-four-gun *Odin*, under the command of Captain Inch, had barely reached safety at the Nore, so deep by the bows had she been. Here in Plymouth, the *Indomitable* and the *Nicator*, seventy-fours like *Benbow*, were in the throes of repair.

He said carefully, '*Nicator* will be ready for sea soon, sir. The rest of the squadron should be reporting readiness by September, if we can bribe some help from these dockyard thieves!'

'And *Styx*, what of her?'

Even as he asked of the squadron's one surviving frigate, Bolitho saw the faraway look in his friend's eyes. They had lost their other frigate and a sloop-of-war. Wiped away, like footprints on a beach at high water.

Herrick allowed Ozzard to refill the goblet before answering, '*Styx* is working night and day, sir. Captain Neale seems able to inspire miracles from his people.' He added apologetically, 'I have only just returned from Kent, sir, but I shall be able to give you a full report by the end of the day.'

Bolitho had risen to his feet, as if the chair could no longer contain his restlessness.

'Kent?' He smiled. 'Forgive me, Thomas. I forgot. I am too full of my own problems to ask about your visit. How did the wedding go?'

As Herrick related the events which culminated in the marriage of his sister to his one-time first lieutenant, Bolitho found his mind moving away again.

When he had returned to Falmouth after the battle at Copenhagen he had been happier, more content than he could believe possible. To have survived had been one thing. To arrive at the Bolitho home with his nephew, Adam Pascoe, and his coxswain and friend, John Allday, had been crowned by the girl who had been waiting there for him. Belinda; he still found it hard to speak her name without fear that it was another dream, a ruse to taunt him back to hard reality.

The squadron, the battle, everything had seemed to fade as they had explored the old house like strangers. Made plans together. Had vowed not to waste a single minute while Bolitho was released from duty.

There was even a rumour of peace in the air. After all the years of war, blockade and violent death, it was said that secret negotiations were being made in London and Paris to stop the fighting, to gain a respite without loss of honour to either side. Even that had seemed possible in Bolitho's new dreamlike world.

But within two weeks a courier had come from London with orders for Bolitho to report to the Admiralty to visit his old superior and mentor, Admiral Sir George Beauchamp, who had given him command of the Baltic Inshore Squadron in the first place.

Even then Bolitho had seen the courier's dramatic despatch as nothing more than a necessary interruption.

Belinda had walked with him to the carriage, her eyes laughing, her body warm against his as she had told him of her plans, what she would do to prepare for their marriage while he was in London. She would be staying at the squire's house until they were finally married, for there were always loose tongues in a seaport like Falmouth, and Bolitho wanted nothing to spoil it. He disliked Lewis Roxby, the squire, intensely, and could not imagine what his sister Nancy had seen in him when she had married him. But he could be relied on to keep her entertained and occupied with his horses and his spreading empire of farms and villages.

Behind his back, Roxby's servants called him the King of Cornwall.

The shock had really hit Bolitho when he had been ushered into Admiral Beauchamp's chambers. He had always been a small, frail man, seemingly weighed down as much by his epaulettes and gold lace as the tremendous responsibility he held and the interest he retained wherever a British man-of-war sailed on the King's service. Hunched at his littered table, Beauchamp had been unable to rise and greet him. In his sixties, he had looked a hundred years old, and only his eyes had held their fire and alertness.

'I will not waste time, Bolitho. You have little to squander, I daresay. I have none left at all.'

He was dying with each hour and every tight breath, and Bolitho had been both moved and fascinated by the intensity of the little man's words, the enthusiasm which had always been his greatest quality.

'Your squadron performed with excellence.' A hand like a claw had dragged blindly over the litter of papers on the table. 'Good men lost, but others rising to replace them.' He had nodded as if the words were too heavy for him. 'I am asking a lot of you. Probably too much, I don't know. You have heard about the peace proposals?' His deepset eyes had caught the reflected sunlight from the tall windows. Like lights in a skull. 'The rumours are true. We need peace, a peace moulded within the necessity of hyprocrisy, to give us time, a breathing space before the final encounter.'

Bolitho had asked quietly, 'You do not trust them, sir?'

'*Never!*' The word had drained the strength from him, and it had taken several moments before Beauchamp had continued, 'The French will force the most advantageous terms for a settlement. To obtain them they are already filling their channel ports with invasion craft and barges, and the troops and artillery to fill them. Bonaparte hopes to frighten our people into a covenant advantageous only to him. When his wounds are healed, his ships and regiments replenished, he will tear up the treaty and attack us. There will be no second chance this time.'

After another pause, Beauchamp had said in a dull voice, 'We *must* give our people confidence. Show them we can still attack as well as defend. It is the only way we'll even the odds at the tables. For years we've driven the French back into their ports or fought them to surrender. Blockade and patrol, line-of-battle or single ship actions, it is what has made our Navy *great*. Bonaparte is a soldier, he does not understand these matters, and will take no advice from those who know better, thank God.'

His voice had grown weaker, and Bolitho had almost decided to call for assistance for the small, limp figure at the table.

Then Beauchamp had jerked his body upright and had snapped, 'We need a gesture. Of all the young officers I have watched and guided up the ladder of advancement, you have never failed me.' A wizened finger had wagged at him, like part of a memory of the man Bolitho had recalled so vividly from their first meeting. 'Well, not in matters of duty anyway.'

'Thank you, sir.'

Beauchamp had not heard him. 'Get as many of your ships

to sea as soon as possible. I have written instructions that you are to assume overall command of the blockading squadron off Bell Ile. Further vessels will be obtained for your convenience just as soon as my despatches are delivered to the port admirals.' He had fixed Bolitho with an unwinking stare. 'I need you at sea. In Biscay. I know I am asking everything, but then, I have given all *I* have to offer.'

The picture of the high-ceilinged room at the Admiralty, the view from the windows of bright carriages, colourful gowns and scarlet uniforms seemed to blur as Bolitho's mind came back to the cabin in *Benbow*.

He said, 'Admiral Sir George Beauchamp is ordering me to sea, Thomas. No arguments, minimum delays. Unfinished repairs, short-handed, outstanding powder and shot, I shall need to know everything to the last detail. I suggest a conference of all the captains, and I shall draft a letter to Captain Inch which must be sent immediately by courier to his ship at Chatham.'

Herrick stared at him. 'It sounds urgent, sir.'

'I – I am not sure.' Bolitho recalled Beauchamp's words. *I need you at sea*. He looked at Herrick's troubled face. 'I am sorry to burst into your new happiness like this.' He shrugged. 'And to Biscay of all places.'

Herrick asked gently, 'When you went back to Falmouth, sir . . .'

Bolitho looked through the stern windows and watched a local bumboat edging towards the *Benbow*'s counter. Food and drink to be examined and bartered for. The small luxuries in a sailor's life.

He replied, 'The house was empty. It was as much my fault as anyone's. Belinda had gone away with my sister and her husband. My brother-in-law wanted to show her a newly purchased estate in Wales.'

He swung round, unable to conceal the bitterness, the despair.

'After the Baltic and that hell at Copenhagen, who would have expected I should be sent to sea again within weeks?'

He looked around the quiet cabin as if listening for those lost sounds of battle. The despairing cries of the wounded, the jubilant cheers of the Danish boarders as they had swarmed up through these very stern windows to die on Major Clinton's bloodied bayonets.

'How will she see it, Thomas? What use are words like *duty* and *honour* to a lady who has already given and lost so much?'

Herrick watched him, scarcely daring to breathe. He could see it all exactly. Bolitho hurrying back to Falmouth, preparing his explanations, how he would describe his obligations to Beauchamp even if it turned out to be a fruitless gesture.

Beauchamp had given his health in the war against France. He had selected young men to replace older ones whose minds had been left behind by a war which had expanded beyond their imagination.

He had offered Bolitho his first chance to command a squadron. Now he was dying, his work still unfinished.

Herrick knew Bolitho better than himself. So that was why Bolitho had come to the ship. The house had been empty and with no way of telling Belinda Laidlaw what had been decided.

'She'll despise me, Thomas. Someone else should have gone in my place. Rear-admirals, especially junior ones, are two a penny. What am I? Some kind of god?'

Herrick smiled. 'She'll not think anything like that, and you know it! We both do.'

'Do we?' Bolitho walked past him, his hand brushing his shoulder as if to reassure himself. 'I *wanted* to stay. But I needed to do Beauchamp's bidding. I owe him that much.'

It had been like that old dream again. The house empty but for the servants, the wall above the sea lined with wild flowers and humming with insects. But the principal players were not there to enjoy it. Not even Pascoe, and that was almost as unnerving. He had received a letter of appointment to another ship within hours of Bolitho leaving for London.

He smiled even as he fretted about it. The Navy was

desperate for experienced officers, and Adam Pascoe was equally eager to take the first opportunity which would carry him to his goal, a command of his own. Bolitho pushed the anxiety from his mind. Adam was just twenty-one. He was ready. He must stop worrying about him.

The sentry's muffled voice came through the door. Admiral's coxswain, *sah!*'

Allday stepped into the cabin and smiled broadly at Bolitho. To Herrick he gave a cheerful nod. 'Captain Herrick, sir.' He laid a large canvas bag on the deck.

Bolitho slipped into his uniform coat and allowed Ozzard to pull his queue over the gold-edged collar. Only one good thing had happened, and he had almost forgotten it.

'I shall shift my flag to *Styx*, Thomas. The sooner I contact my other ships off Belle Ile the better, I think.' He dragged a long envelope from inside his coat and handed it to the astonished Herrick. 'From their lordships, Thomas. To take effect as from noon tomorrow.' He nodded to Allday who tipped a great scarlet broad-pendant on to the deck like a carpet. 'You, Captain Thomas Herrick of His Britannic Majesty's Ship *Benbow* at Plymouth will take upon yourself and assume the appointment of Acting-Commodore of this squadron with all direct responsibilities thereof.' He thrust the envelope into Herrick's hard palm and wrung the other one warmly. 'My God, Thomas, I feel a mite better to see you so miserable!'

Herrick swallowed hard. 'Me, sir? *Commodore?*'

Allday was grinning. 'Well *done*, sir!'

Herrick was still staring, his eyes on the red pendant at his feet.

'With my own flag-captain? Who, I mean what . . .'

Bolitho signalled for some more wine. His heart still ached as painfully as before and his sense of failure no less evident, but the sight of his friend's confusion had helped considerably. This was their world. That other existence of marriage plans and security, talk of peace and future stability were alien here.

'I am certain all will be explained in your despatches from London, Thomas.' He watched Herrick's mind grappling with it and then accepting it as a reality. The Navy taught you that if nothing else. Or you went under. 'Think how proud Dulcie will be!'

Herrick nodded slowly. 'I suppose so.' He shook his head. 'All the same. Commodore.' He looked steadily at Bolitho, his eyes very blue. 'I hope it'll not steer us too far apart, sir.'

Bolitho was moved and turned away to hide his emotion. How typical of Herrick to think of that first. Not of his right and just promotion, long overdue, but of what it might mean to each of them. Personally.

Allday sauntered to the two swords on the cabin bulkhead, suddenly engrossed in their appearance and condition. The brilliant presentation sword from the people of Falmouth as recognition of Bolitho's achievements in the Mediterranean and at the Nile. The other sword, without shine or lustre, outdated but finely balanced, seemed shabby by comparison. But neither the presentation blade, with all its gold and silver, nor a hundred like it, could equal the value of the older one. The Bolitho sword which appeared in several of those family portraits at Falmouth, and which Allday had seen in the press of many a battle, was beyond price.

For once even Allday was unable to accept the sudden orders for sea with his usual philosophy. He had not stepped on shore this time for more than a dog watch, and now they were off again. He had already been fuming at the unfairness and stupidity which had prevented Bolitho from receiving a proper reward after Copenhagen. *Sir* Richard Bolitho. It would have just the right ring to it, he thought.

But no, those buggers at the Admiralty had deliberately avoided doing what was proper. He clenched his big fists as he looked at the swords. It was buzzing through the fleet that Nelson had received much the same treatment, so that was some consolation. Nelson had raised all their hearts when he had pretended not to see his superior officer's signal to break off the action. It was so like the man, what made the Jacks love him and the admirals who never went to sea loathe his very name.

Allday sighed and thought of the girl he had helped to rescue from the wrecked carriage just a few months ago. To think that Bolitho might still lose her because of a few stupid written orders was beyond his understanding.

'A toast to our new commodore.' Bolitho glanced at the goblets. The first lieutenant had come aft, his head bowed beneath the deckhead, while Grubb, the master, feet well apart to proportion his considerable weight, was already contemplating the goblet which looked like a thimble in his hand.

Herrick said, 'Allday, come here. Under the cirumstances, I'd like you to join us.'

Allday wiped his hands on his smart nankeen breeches and mumbled, 'Well, thankee, sir.'

Bolitho raised his goblet. 'To you, Thomas. To old friends, and old ships.'

Herrick smiled gravely. 'It's a good toast, that one.'

Allday drank the wine and withdrew into the shadows of the great cabin. Herrick had wanted him to share it. More than that, he had wanted the others to know it.

Allday slipped out of a small screen door and made his way forward towards the sunshine of the upper deck.

They had come a long way together, while others had been less fortunate. As their numbers grew fewer so the tasks seemed to get harder, he thought. Now Bolitho's flag would soon be in the Bay of Biscay. A new collection of ships, a different puzzle for the rear-admiral to unravel.

But why the Bay? There were ships and men a-plenty who had been doing that bloody blockade for years, until their hulls had grown weed as long as snakes. No, for Beauchamp to order it, and for Richard Bolitho to be selected for the work, it had to be *hard*, there was no second way round it.

Allday walked into the sunlight and squinted up at the flag which curled from the mizzen.

'I still say he should be *Sir* Richard!'

The young lieutenant on watch considered ordering him about his affairs and then recalled what he had been told of the admiral's coxswain. Instead, he moved to the opposite side of the quarterdeck.

When the anchorage was eventually plunged into darkness, with only the riding lights and occasional beam from the shore to divide sea from land, even the *Benbow* felt to be resting. Exhausted from their constant work aloft and below, her people lay packed in their hammocks like pods in some sealed cavern. Beneath the lines of hammocks the guns stood quietly behind their ports, dreaming perhaps of those times when they had shaken the life from the air and made the world cringe with their fury.

Right aft in the great cabin Bolitho sat at his desk, a lantern spiralling gently above him as the ship pulled and tested her cables.

To most of the squadron, and to many of *Benbow*'s people, he was a name, a leader, whose flag they obeyed. Some had served with him before and were proud of it, proud to be able to give him his nickname which none of the new hands would know. *Equality Dick*. There were others who had created their own image of the young rear-admiral, as if by expanding it they would increase their own immortality and fame. There were a few, a very few, like the faithful Ozzard who was dozing like a mouse in his pantry, who saw Bolitho's moods in the early morning or at the end of a great storm or sea-chase. Or Allday, who had been drawn to him when on the face of things he should have had their first meeting marred by the hatred and humiliation of a press gang. Herrick, who had fallen asleep over the last pile of signed reports from the other captains, had known him at the height of excitement and at the depths of despair. Perhaps he better than any other would have recognized the Richard Bolitho who sat poised at his desk, the pen held deliberately above the paper, his mind lost to everything but the girl he was leaving behind.

Then with great care he began. '*My dearest Belinda . . .*'

2

No Looking Back

Richard Bolitho lay back in a chair and waited for Allday to finish shaving him. Herrick was standing by the screen door, just out of his line of sight, while around and above them the *Benbow*'s hull and decks quivered and echoed to the clatter of repairs.

Herrick was saying, 'I've informed Captain Neale that you will be shifting your flag to *Styx* this forenoon, sir. He seems uncommon pleased about it.'

Bolitho glanced at Allday's engrossed features as he worked the razor skilfully around his chin. Poor Allday, he obviously disapproved of the move to a cramped frigate after the comparative luxury of the flagship, just as Herrick mistrusted any other captain's ability to conduct his affairs.

It was strange how the Navy always managed to weave the threads so finely together. Captain John Neale of the thirty-two-gun *Styx* had served as a chubby midshipman under Bolitho in his first frigate, in another war. Like Captain Keen who was anchored less than a cable away in the third-rate *Nicator*, he too had been a midshipman in one of Bolitho's commands.

He frowned, and wondered when he would hear how Adam Pascoe was progressing, what his appointment was, what manner of captain he now served.

Allday wiped his face carefully and nodded. 'All done, sir.'

Bolitho washed from a bowl which Allday had placed near the stern windows. No word was said, it was something they had formed over the years. At sea or in harbour, Bolitho disliked wasting time staring at a blank piece of timber while he was preparing himself for another day.

There was so much to do, orders to sign for individual captains, a report of readiness for the Admiralty, approval for the squadron's mounting dockyard expenses, new appointments to be settled. It would be unfair to leave Herrick with too much unfinished business, he decided.

Herrick remarked, 'The mail-boat took your despatches ashore, sir. She's just returned to her boom.'

'I see.' It was Herrick's way of telling him that there was no letter from Belinda.

He glanced through one of the windows. The sky was as clear as yesterday's, but the sea was livelier. He would use the wind to seek out the ships of the blockading squadron where he was to assume control. Off Belle Ile, a key point in a chain of patrols and squadrons which stretched from Gibraltar to the Channel ports. Beauchamp certainly intended that he should be in the centre of things. This particular sector would cover the approaches to Lorient in the north and the vital routes to and from the Loire Estuary to the east. But if it was a stranglehold on the enemy's trade and resources it could also be a hazard for an unwary British frigate or sloop should she be caught on a lee shore or too interested in a French harbour to notice the swift approach of an attacker.

Bolitho was no stranger to *Styx*. He had been aboard her several times, and in the Baltic had seen her young captain engage the enemy with the coolness of a veteran.

Bolitho threw down his towel, angry with himself for his dreaming. *He must stop going over past events.* Think only of what lay ahead, and the ships which would soon be depending on him. He was a flag-officer now and, like Herrick, he had to accept that promotion was an honour, not some god-given right.

He smiled awkwardly as he realized the others were staring at him.

Allday asked mildly, 'Second thoughts, mebbee, sir?'

'About what, damn you?'

Allday rolled his eyes around the big cabin. 'Well, I mean, sir, after this the *Styx* will seem more like a pot o' paint than a *ship*!'

Herrick said, 'You get away with murder, Allday. One day you'll overstep the mark, my lad!' He looked at Bolitho. 'All the same, he has a point. You *could* shift flag to *Nicator*, and I could take command until —'

Bolitho eyed him impassively. 'Old friend, it is no use. For either of us. Today you assume the appointment of commodore and will hoist your broad-pendant accordingly. You will eventually have to select your own flag-captain and attend to the appointment of a new one for *Indomitable*.'

He tried to parry the thought aside. Another memory. *Indomitable* had been in the thick of it at Copenhagen, and it was not until after the order to cease fire that Bolitho had learned that her captain, Charles Keverne, had fallen in the fighting. Keverne had been Bolitho's first lieutenant when *he* had been a flag-captain like Herrick. Links in a chain. As each one broke, the chain got shorter and tighter.

Bolitho continued sharply, 'And I cannot moon about here like a sixth lieutenant. The decisions are not ours.'

Feet clattered in the passageway, and he knew that, like himself, Herrick was very conscious of these precious moments. Soon there would be the busy comings and goings of officers for orders, senior officials from Plymouth to be flattered and coaxed into greater efforts to finish the repairs. Yovell, his clerk, would have more letters to copy and be signed, Ozzard would need to be told what to pack, what to leave aboard the *Benbow* until . . . he frowned. Until when?

Herrick turned quickly as the sentry shouted the arrival of the first lieutenant.

'I am needed, sir.' He sounded wretched.

Bolitho gripped his hand. 'I am sorry I'll not be here when your broad-pendant breaks. But if I have to go, I'd like to go with haste.'

Wolfe appeared in the doorway. 'Beg pardon, sir, but there's a visitor coming aboard.' He was looking at Bolitho who felt his heart give a great leap. It fell just as quickly as Wolfe said flatly, 'Your flag-lieutenant is here, sir.'

Herrick exclaimed, 'Browne?'

Allday hid a grin. 'Browne with an "e".'

'Send him aft.' Bolitho sat down again.

Lieutenant the Honourable Oliver Browne had been thrust upon him as flag-lieutenant by Beauchamp. Instead of the empty-minded aide he had appeared at first meeting, Browne had proved himself invaluable as adviser to a newly appointed rear-admiral, and later as a friend. When the battered ships had returned from the Baltic, Bolitho had allowed Browne a choice. Return to his more civilized surroundings and duties in London, or resume as his flag-lieutenant.

When Browne entered the cabin he looked unusually dishevelled and weary.

Herrick and Wolfe hastily left the cabin, and Bolitho said, 'This is unexpected.'

The lieutenant sank down into a proferred chair, and as his cloak fell aside Bolitho saw the dark stains on his breeches, sweat and leather. He must have ridden like a madman.

Browne said huskily, 'Sir George Beauchamp died last night, sir. He completed his orders for your squadron and then . . .' He gave a shrug. 'He was at his table with his maps and charts.' He shook his head. 'I thought you should know, sir. Before you sail for Belle Ile.'

Bolitho had learned never to question Browne's knowledge of things which were supposed to be secret.

'Ozzard. Make some fresh coffee for my flag-lieutenant.' He saw Browne's tired features light up slightly. 'If that is what you intend to be?'

Browne released the cloak from his throat and shook himself. 'Indeed, I was praying for that, sir. I wish nothing more than to get away from London, from the carrion!'

Overhead, calls trilled and tackles creaked as more stores and equipment were hoisted up from the lighters alongside.

But down in the cabin it was different. Very still, as Browne described how Beauchamp had died at his table, his signature barely dry on his last despatches.

Browne said evenly, 'I have brought those orders direct to you, sir. Had you sailed before I arrived here, it is likely they would never have been put aboard a courier-brig and sent after you.'

'You are saying that Sir George's plan would have been cancelled?'

Browne held a cup of coffee in both hands, his face thoughtful. 'Postponed indefinitely. There are, I fear, too many in high places who can see nothing but a treaty with France. Not as the respite which Lord St Vincent and some of the others see it, but as a means to profit and exploit the plunder which an armistice will bring. Any attack on French harbours and shipping with peace so near would be seen by them as a handicap not an advantage.'

'Thank you for telling me.'

Bolitho looked past him at the two swords on the bulkhead. What did men such as Browne had described know of honour?

Browne smiled. 'I thought it was important you should know. With Sir George Beauchamp alive and in control of future events, your activities on the new station would have made no difference to your security, no matter what hornets' nest you disturbed.' He looked at Bolitho steadily, his youthful face suddenly mature. 'But with Sir George dead there is nobody to defend you if things go wrong. His record of achievements and service will give weight to your instructions and nobody will question them. But should you fail, it will be a scapegoat not a blameless commander who returns here.'

Bolitho nodded. 'Not for the first time.'

Browne smiled. 'After Copenhagen I can believe anything of you, sir, but I am uneasy about the risk this time. Your name is known and toasted from Falmouth to the ale houses of Whitechapel. And so is Nelson's, but their lordships are not so impressed that they could not hurt him for his impudence at Copenhagen.'

'Tell me.' Bolitho stared at the young lieutenant. His was another world. Intrigue and scheming, influence of fortune and family. No wonder Browne was glad to be quitting the land. The *Benbow* had given him a taste for excitement.

Browne sounded bitter. 'Nelson. Victor of the Nile, hero of Copenhagen, the public's darling. And now, their lord-ships intend that he should be appointed to take charge of a new force of recruited landsmen to defend the Channel coast against possible invaders!' He spat out the words angrily. 'A set of drunken, good-for-nothing rascals to all accounts! A fine reward for Our Nel!'

Bolitho was appalled. He had heard plenty of gossip about Nelson's contempt for authority, his incredible luck which had so far saved him when others might have expected ruin at a court martial. Browne was only trying to protect him. He had no chance at all if he failed to execute Beauchamp's plan with complete success.

Bolitho said quietly, 'If you *are* coming with me, I intend to sail on the tide. Tell Allday what you need and he will have it sent over to *Styx*. Anything else you require will doubtless catch up with you later. With influential friends like yours, it should be easy to arrange.' He held out his hand. 'Tell me. What *are* these orders?'

Browne said, 'The French have been gathering invasion craft along their northern ports for months, as you know, sir. By way of intelligence obtained from the Portuguese, it appears that many of the invasion craft are being built, armed and stored in harbours along the coastline of Biscay.' He smiled wryly. 'Your new sector, sir. I did not always see eye to eye with Sir George, but he had *style*, sir, and this plan to destroy an invasion fleet before it can be moved to the Channel has his touch, the mark of the master!' He flushed. 'I do beg your pardon, sir. But I still cannot accept he is dead.'

Bolitho turned the heavy folder of instructions over in his hands. Beauchamp's last strategy worked out to the final detail. All it needed was the man to translate it into action. Bolitho was moved to realize that Beauchamp must have considered him from the very beginning. There was no choice at all, and never had been.

He said quietly, 'I have another letter to write.'

He looked around the cabin, the shimmering reflections of the sea along the white deckhead. To trade this for the dash and excitement of a small frigate, to set his collection of vessels against the stronghold of France itself was no mere gesture. Perhaps it was intended for him, like a part of fate. At the beginning of the war, as a very young captain, Bolitho had taken part in the ill-fated attack on Toulon, the attempt by the French royalists to overturn the revolution and reverse the course of history. They had made history well enough, Bolitho thought grimly, but it had ended in bloody disaster.

Bolitho felt a chill at his spine. Maybe everything was decided by fate. Belinda may have thought he was coming back to Falmouth for several months, perhaps longer if peace was indeed signed. In fact, he stared through the stern windows at the anchored ships, she was being protected from further pain. *He was not coming back*. It had to happen one day. He touched his left thigh, expecting to feel the pain where the musket ball had cut him down. So soon after that? Not a respite, not even a warning.

Bolitho said abruptly, 'On second thoughts, I'll not write a letter. I shall shift to *Styx* directly. Tell my cox'n, will you?'

Alone at last, Bolitho sat on the bench below the windows and kneaded his eyes with his knuckles until the pain steadied him.

Fate had been kind to him, had even allowed him the touch and the sight of love, something he would hold on to until it was decided even that should vanish.

Herrick appeared in the doorway. 'Boat's alongside, sir.'

By the entry port with its side party and scarlet-coated marines Bolitho paused and stared across at the rakish frigate. Her sails were already loosely brailed, and figures moved about her spars and ratlines like insects, impatient to be off, to seek the unreachable horizon.

Herrick said, 'The squadron will be ready to proceed in

weeks not months, sir. I'll not be satisfied until *Benbow*'s under your orders again.'

Bolitho smiled, the wind plucking at his coat as if to tug him away, and lifting the lock of hair to reveal the livid scar beneath.

'If you should see her, Thomas . . .' He gripped his friend's hand, unable to continue.

Herrick returned the grasp firmly. 'I'll tell her, sir. You just take care of yourself. Lady Luck can't be expected to solve everything!'

They stood back from each other and allowed formality to separate them.

As the *Benbow*'s barge pulled smartly away from the seventy-four's tall side, Bolitho turned and raised his hand, but Herrick had already merged with the men around him and the ship which had meant so much to both of them.

Bolitho climbed through the companionway and paused to gain his bearings as the frigate took another violent plunge beneath him. All day long it had been the same. Once clear of Plymouth Sound, the *Styx* had set every stitch of canvas to take full advantage of a stiffening north-easterly. Although Bolitho had remained for most of the day in the frigate's cabin going carefully through his written orders and making notes for later use, he had been constantly reminded of the agility and the exuberance of a small ship.

Captain Neale had used the friendly wind under his coat tails to put his people through every kind of sail drill. All afternoon the decks had quivered to the slap and bang of bare feet, the urgent voices of petty officers and lieutenants rising above the din to create order out of chaos. Neale was no better off than any other captain. Many of his trained men had been promoted and moved to other vessels. The remaining skilled hands had been thinly spread amongst the new ones, some of whom were still so shocked at being snatched by the press or hauled from the comparative safety of the local jails that they were too terrified to venture up the madly vibrating ratlines without a few blows to encourage them.

He saw Neale with his taciturn first lieutenant leaning at the weather side of the quarterdeck, their hair plastered across their faces, their eyes everywhere as they searched for flaws in the patterns of sail-handling and quickness to respond to orders. Later on such failings could lose lives, even the ship. Neale had grown well with his profession, although it was not difficult to see him as the thirteen-year-old midshipman Bolitho had once discovered under his command. He saw Bolitho and hurried to greet him.

'I shall be shortening sail presently, sir!' He had to shout above the hiss and surge of sea alongside. 'But we've made a good run today!'

Bolitho walked to the nettings and held on firmly as the ship plunged forward and down, her tapering jib boom slicing at the drifting spray like a lance. No wonder Adam yearned so much for a command of his own. *As I once did.* Bolitho looked up at the bulging canvas, the spread legs of some seamen working out along the swaying length of the mainyard. It was what he missed most. The ability to hold and tame the power of a ship like *Styx*, to match his skill with rudder and sail against her own wanton desire to be free.

Neale watched him and asked, 'I hope we are not disturbing you, sir?'

Bolitho shook his head. It was a tonic, one to drive the anxieties away, to make nonsense of anything beyond here and now.

'Deck there!' The masthead lookout's voice was shredded by the wind. 'Land on th' weather bow!'

Neale grinned impetuously and snatched a telescope from its rack by the wheel. He trained it over the nettings and then handed it to Bolitho.

'There, sir. France.'

Bolitho waited for the deck to lurch up again from a long line of white horses and then steadied the glass on the bearing. It was getting dark already, but not so much that he could not see the dull purple blur of land. Ushant, with Brest somewhere beyond. Names carved into the heart of any sailor who had sweated out the months in a blockading squadron.

Soon they would alter course and run south-east, deeper and deeper into the Bay of Biscay. That was Neale's problem, but it was nothing compared with the task he must order his ships to do.

Within a week Beauchamp's orders would have been acknowledged by the flag-officers concerned. Captains would be rousing their men, laying off courses to rendezvous with their new rear-admiral. A cross on a chart near Belle Ile. And within a month Bolitho would be expected to act, to catch the enemy off balance inside his own defences.

Browne was obviously awed by his ability to discuss the proposed tactics as if success was already an accepted fact. But Browne had been appointed to his position of personal aide in London through his father's influence, and knew little of the Navy's harsh methods of training for command. Like most sea-officers, Bolitho had gone to his first ship at the age of twelve. Within a very short time he had been made to learn how to take charge of a longboat and discover an authority he had not known he had possessed. Laying out a great anchor for kedging, carrying passengers and stores between ship and land, and later leading a boat's crew in hand-to-hand attacks against pirates and privateers, all had been part of a very thorough schooling for the young officer.

Lieutenant, captain and now rear-admiral, Bolitho felt little different, but accepted that everything had been changed for him. Now it was not just a question of momentary courage or madness, the ability to risk life and limb rather than reveal fear to the men you led. Nor was it a case of obeying orders, no matter what was happening or how horrible were the scenes of hell around you. Now he must decide the destiny of others, who would live or die depended on his skill, his understanding of the rough facts at his disposal. And there were many more who might depend on that first judgement, even, as Beauchamp had made clear, the country itself.

It was a harsh school, right enough, Bolitho thought. But a lot of good had come from it. The petty tyrants and bullies were fewer now, for braggarts had little to sustain them in the face of an enemy broadside. Adroit young leaders were emerging daily. He glanced at Neale's profile. Men like him, who could rouse that vital loyalty when it was most needed.

Apparently unaware of his superior's scrutiny, Neale said, 'We shall change tack at midnight, sir. Close-hauled, it's likely to be a bit lively.'

Bolitho smiled. Browne was already as sick as a dog in his borrowed cabin.

'We should sight some of our ships tomorrow then.'

'Aye, sir.' Neale turned as a young midshipman struggled across the spray-dashed planking and scribbled quickly on the slate by the wheel. 'Oh, this is Mr Kilburne, sir, my signals midshipman.'

The youth, aged about sixteen, froze solid and stared at Bolitho as if he was having a seizure.

Bolitho smiled. 'I am pleased to meet you.'

As the midshipman still seemed unable to move, Neale added, 'Mr Kilburne has a question for you, sir.'

Bolitho grinned. 'Don't play with the boy, Neale. Is your memory so short?' He turned to the midshipman. 'What is it?'

Kilburne, astonished that he was still alive after being brought face-to-face with his admiral, a young one or not, stammered, 'W – well, sir, we were all so excited when we were told about your coming aboard . . .'

By *all* he probably meant the ship's three other midshipmen, Bolitho thought.

Kilburne added, 'Is it true, sir, that the first frigate you commanded was the *Phalarope*?'

Neale said abruptly, 'That's enough, Mr Kilburne!' He turned apologetically to Bolitho. 'I am sorry, sir. I thought the idiot was going to ask you something different.'

Bolitho could feel the sudden tension. 'What is it, Mr

Kilburne? I am still all attention.'

Kilburne said wretchedly, 'I was correcting the signals book, sir.' He darted a frightened glance at his captain, wondering what had suddenly changed everything into a nightmare. '*Phalarope* is joining the squadron, sir. Captain Emes.'

Bolitho tightened his hold of the nettings, his mind wrestling with Kilburne's words.

Surely he was wrong. But how could he be? There had been nothing published about a new vessel named *Phalarope*. He looked at Neale. And he had just been remembering him aboard that very ship. It was unnerving.

Neale said awkwardly, 'I was surprised too, sir. But I didn't want to dampen your first night aboard. My officers were looking forward to having you as their honoured guest, although the fare is hardly a banquet.'

Bolitho nodded. 'I shall be honoured, Captain Neale.' But his mind still clung to the *Phalarope*. She must be all of twenty-five years old by now. She had been about six years old when he had taken command of her at Spithead. A ship cursed by cruelty and despair, whose people had been so abused by her previous captain they were ripe for mutiny.

He could remember it all. The topsails and pendants of the French fleet rising above the horizon like mounted knights about to charge. The Battle of the Saintes it was called, and when it had ended in victory *Phalarope* had been a barely-floating wreck.

'Are you all right, sir?' Neale was looking at him anxiously, his own ship momentarily forgotten.

Bolitho said quietly, 'She's too old for this kind of work. I thought she was finished. The honourable way, not left to rot as a prison hulk or storeship in some dismal harbour.' The Navy was desperately short of frigates, but surely not that desperate?

Neale said helpfully, 'I did hear she had been fitting out in Ireland, sir. But I imagined it was for use as guardship or accommodation vessel.'

Bolitho stared out at the advancing lines of jagged whitecaps. *Phalarope*. After all this time, so many miles, so many ships and faces. Herrick may have seen the signals book by now. It would mean so much to him too. Bolitho took a sharp breath. And Allday, who had been brought aboard *Phalarope* as a pressed man like a felon.

He realized that the midshipman was still watching him, his eyes filling his face.

Bolitho touched his arm. 'You have nothing to worry about, Mr Kilburne. It was just a shock, that is all. She was a fine ship; we made her something special.'

Neale said, 'With respect, sir, *you* made her that.'

Bolitho descended the ladder again and then strode aft towards the marine sentry by the cabin door.

He saw a figure squatting on one of the *Styx*'s twelve-pounders. It was gloomy between decks and still too early for wasting lanterns where they were not needed. Had it been pitch dark Bolitho would have known Allday's sturdy figure. Like an oak. Always nearby when he was needed. Ready to use his cheek when his courage was to no avail.

He made to stand but Bolitho said quietly, 'Rest easy. You've heard then?'

'Aye, sir.' Allday nodded heavily. 'It's not right. Not fair.'

'Don't be an old woman, Allday. You've been at sea long enough to know better. Ships come and go. One you served in last year might lie alongside you tomorrow. Another you may have seen in a dozen different ports, or fighting in a hundred fights, yet never set foot aboard, may well be your next appointment.'

Allday persisted stubbornly. 'S'not that, sir. She were different. They've no *right* to put her in the Bay, she's too old, an' I doubt if she ever got over the Saintes. God knows, I never did.'

Bolitho watched him, suddenly uneasy. 'There's nothing I can do. She will be under my command, like the others.'

Allday stood up and turned beside the cannon, his head bowed between the beams.

'But she's not *like* the others!'

Bolitho bit back the sharp retort as quickly as it had formed. Why take it out on Allday? Like the midshipman on the quarterdeck who had unwittingly broken the news, he was not to blame.

Bolitho said quietly, 'No, Allday, she's not. I won't deny it. But it rests between us. You know how sailors love to create mystery when there is none. We'll need all our wits about us in the next month or so without lower-deck gossip. We cannot *afford* to look back.'

Allday sighed. The sound seemed to rise right up from his shoes.

'I expect you're right, sir.' He tried to shake himself free of it. 'Anyway, I must get you ready for the wardroom. It'll be something for 'em to remember.' But his usual humour evaded him.

Bolitho walked to the cabin door. 'Well, let's be about it then, shall we?'

Allday followed him, deep in thought. Nineteen years ago it was. When Bolitho had not been much older than his nephew, Mr Pascoe. There had been plenty of danger and cut-and-thrust since then, and all the while they had stayed together. A pressed seaman and a youthful captain who had somehow turned a ship blackened by every sort of tyranny into one to win the hearts and pride of her company. Now she was coming back down the years, like a phantom ship. To help or to haunt, he wondered?

He saw Bolitho standing by the stern windows watching the light dying across the frothing water beneath the frigate's counter.

He cares all right. Most likely more than I do.

Under shortened canvas the frigate turned on to her new course and pointed her bowsprit towards the Bay, and a rendezvous.

3

Return of a Veteran

Captain John Neale of the frigate *Styx* broke off his morning discussion with his first lieutenant and waited for Bolitho to leave the companionway. This was their seventh day out of Plymouth, and Neale was still surprised at his admiral's unflagging energy.

Bolitho had certainly taken a good keen look at the enemy shoreline, and the ships at his disposal. That had been the first shock, when they had made contact with the inshore patrol, the frigate *Sparrowhawk*, a day after sighting Belle Ile. Apart from a speedy brig, aptly named *Rapid*, there had been one other frigate in the sector, the *Unrivalled*. Neale grimaced. *Had been*. Her captain had been beating close inshore when he had made the fatal mistake of not leaving himself enough sea-room to claw into open waters. Two enemy ships had run down on him from windward, and only *Unrivalled* captain's skill had enabled him to escape capture or destruction. As far as Bolitho's small force was concerned, it might just as well have been either, for, pitted with shot holes and under jury-rig, the *Unrivalled* had crawled for home and the security of a dockyard.

Neale glanced at the masthead pendant. The wind had shifted to the north again. It was lively and gusty. He hoped that the battered survivor reached port intact.

Bolitho nodded as Neale touched his hat. No matter what time he chose to come on deck, even before daylight, Neale always seemed to be there ahead of him. If there was anything wrong with his ship, he wanted to see it for himself first and not be told by his admiral. He had learned well.

Bolitho had been thinking about his thinly-stretched force while Allday had been pouring coffee for him. Until reinforcements arrived, he now had but two frigates on the station, with the brig for keeping contact with the bigger squadrons to north and south. It looked very manageable on a wall chart in Whitehall. Out here, with dawn touching the endless ranks of wave crests in a dirty yellow glow, it was a desert.

But shortly they would see the pyramid of sails far abeam where *Sparrowhawk* cruised within sight of Belle Ile and any local shipping which might be hugging the coast en route for Nantes or northward to Lorient.

How they must hate us, he thought. The dogged, storm-dashed ships which were always there at the break of every day. Waiting to dash in and seize a prize under the enemy's nose, or scurry to rouse the main fleet if the French admirals dared to present a challenge.

What he had seen of his small force he liked. He had boarded both the brig and the other frigate, getting drenched on each occasion as he had been forced to leap unceremoniously while his boat had poised on a passing crest.

He had seen the grins, and had known that his small bravado had been appreciated.

They had to know him, like one of their own. Not as an aloof flag-officer on the poop of some great three-decker, but as the man who would be amongst them when danger came.

He remarked, 'Wind's shifted.'

Neale watched his foretopmen dashing aloft yet again to reset the topgallant.

'Aye, sir. The master states it'll back still further before nightfall.'

Bolitho smiled. The sailing master would know. His breed always seemed to understand the wind before it knew its own mind.

Seven days out of Plymouth. It was like a dirge in his thoughts. And with little to show for it. Even if his whole squadron arrived, what should he do or say?

Only one chink had shown itself. Each of the captains, Duncan, a bluff, red-faced youngster of the *Sparrowhawk*, and, still younger, Lapish of the *Rapid*, had mentioned the ease with which the enemy seemed able to foretell their movements. In the past year raids had been mounted on nearby ports by heavier ships of the line, and on each occasion the French had been prepared, with their own vessels and shore batteries ready to make a full attack pointless.

And yet the squadrons to north and south stopped and searched every so-called neutral and warned them away from any area where they might discover the true strength of the British patrols. Or the lack of it, more likely, he thought wryly.

He began to pace the side of the quarterdeck, his hands behind him, as he toyed with this tiny fragment of intelligence. The French might have been using small boats at night. No, they would be too slow, and incapable of escaping if they were sighted. Fast horsemen along the coast, ready to ride as Browne had done, to carry their news to the local commanders. Possible. But still unlikely. The poor roads and long distances between harbours would make for serious delays.

In spite of his guard, Bolitho felt his mind slip back to Falmouth. Belinda would be there again. Visiting the empty house, where Ferguson, his one-armed steward, would try his best to explain and to console her. What would she think? How could she know the ways of the Navy?

She was thirty-four, ten years his junior. She would not wait, should not be made to suffer as she had done with her late husband.

Bolitho stopped and gripped the nettings tightly. Even now she might be with someone else. Younger perhaps, with his feet firmly set on the land.

Browne joined him by the nettings and offered weakly, 'Good morning, sir.'

Browne had rarely been seen since leaving Plymouth, although his fight with the frigate's lively movements and the smells which were constant reminders of his sea-sickness was spoken of with awe even by the older hands.

He looked a little stronger, Bolitho thought. It was ironic, for whereas he himself was beset with problems both personal and tactical, he had never felt in better health. The ship, the constant comings and goings of faces which were already familiar, were ready reminders of his own days as a frigate captain.

There was a kind of hardness to his body, and a swiftness of thought which could soon be lost in a ponderous ship of the line.

'I must make contact with *Rapid* today, Browne. I intend to stand her closer inshore, unless the master is wrong about the change of wind.'

Browne watched him thoughtfully. Having to think again was bringing the colour back to his face. So how did Bolitho manage it, he wondered? Boarding the other ships, discussing details of local trade and coastal craft with Neale, he never appeared to tire.

He was driving himself like this to hold his other thoughts at bay. At least he had learned that much about Bolitho.

'Deck there!'

Browne looked aloft and winced as he saw the tiny figure perched on the cross-trees high above the deck.

'Sail on th' starboard quarter!'

Neale came hurrying across the deck, and as Bolitho gave him a curt nod, shouted, 'All hands, Mr Pickthorn! We shall wear ship at once and beat to wind'rd!'

Before his first lieutenant had even time to snatch up his speaking trumpet, or the boatswain's mates had run below with their calls trilling to rouse the hands, Neale was already calculating and scheming, even though he could not yet see the newcomer.

Bolitho watched the seamen and marines flooding up through the hatches and along both gangways, to be stemmed and mustered into their stations by petty officers and master's mates.

Neale said, 'The light is better, sir. In a moment or so—'

'Man the braces there! Stand by to wear ship!'

'Put up the helm!'

With yards and canvas banging in confusion and blocks shrieking like live things as the cordage raced through the sheaves, *Styx* leaned heavily towards the sea, spray climbing the gangways and pattering across the straining seamen at the braces like pellets.

'Full an' bye, sir! Sou'-west by west!'

Neale moved a pace this way and that, watching as his command came under control again, her lee gunports almost awash.

'Aloft with you, Mr Kilburne, and take a glass.' To the quarterdeck at large he said, 'If she's a Frenchie, we'll dish her up before she stands inshore.'

Browne murmured, 'Such confidence.'

Bolitho sensed, rather than felt, Allday at his side, and held up his arms so that the burly coxswain could clip the sword to his belt.

Allday looked suddenly older, although he and Bolitho were of the same age. The lower deck was insensitive when it came to the smallest comfort.

Even as an admiral's personal coxswain, life was not that easy. Allday would be the first to deny it, just as he would be angry and hurt if Bolitho suggested he took himself to Falmouth to enjoy the comfort and security which were his right.

Allday saw his gaze and gave his lazy grin. 'I can still give some o' these mothers' boys a run for their money, sir!'

Bolitho nodded slowly. When it came, it would be on a day like this. Like all the others when Allday had fetched the old sword and they had shared some stupid joke together.

Perhaps it was because of Neale, or the fact he was made to be an onlooker.

He lifted his eyes to the mizzen truck where his flag stood out in the wind like painted metal.

Then he shook himself angrily. If Beauchamp had

appointed another junior admiral for this work he would have been equally unsettled.

Allday moved away, satisfied with what he had seen.

Several telescopes rose like swivels, and Bolitho waited until Midshipman Kilburne's voice floated thinly from the masthead.

'Deck, sir! She's British!'

A small pause while he endeavoured to cling to his precarious perch and open his signal book with the other hand.

'She's *Phalarope*, thirty-two, Captain Emes, sir!'

Allday muttered, 'Holy God!'

Bolitho folded his arms and waited for the bows to rise again, the horizon appearing to tilt as if to rid itself of the two converging pyramids of sails.

Bolitho had known she would come today. Even as *Styx*'s people had run to halliards and braces, he had *known*.

Neale watched him warily. 'What orders, sir?'

Bolitho turned to see the bright signal flags break from *Styx*'s yard. Numbers exchanged, two ships meeting on a pinpoint. To most of the hands it was a welcome diversion, as well as a sight of some additional fire power.

'Heave to when convenient, if you please. Make to——' his tongue faltered over her name, 'to *Phalarope* that I shall be coming aboard.'

Neale nodded. 'Aye, sir.'

Bolitho took a telescope from the midshipman of the watch and walked up the deck to the weather side.

He was conscious of each move and every heartbeat, like an actor about to make an entrance.

He held his breath and waited for the sea to smooth itself. There she was. With her yards already swinging, her topgallants and main-course being manhandled into submission, she was heeling on to a fresh tack. Bolitho moved the glass just a fraction more. Before that bowsprit plunged down again in a welter of flying spindrift he saw that familiar figurehead, the gilded bird riding on a dolphin.

The same and yet different. He was frowning as he moved

the glass again, seeing the insect-like figures on the ratlines and gangways, the blues and whites of the officers aft by the wheel.

Outdated, that was it. The weak sunlight touched the frigate's poop, and Bolitho recalled the fineness of her gingerbread, carved by experts in the trade. That had been another war. Newer frigates like *Styx* had fewer embellishments, less dignity, honed down to the demands of chase and battle.

Neale lowered his telescope and said huskily, 'Hell's teeth, sir, it's like yesterday. Like watching myself.'

Bolitho looked past him at Allday by the hammock nettings. He was opening and closing his large fists, staring at the fast-running frigate until his eyes watered. So that he looked as if he was weeping.

He made himself raise the telescope once again. She was smart for her age, and was reacting to the sight of a rear-admiral's flag just as Bolitho had once done when he had taken *Phalarope* to Antigua.

Neale called, 'Heave to, Mr Pickthorn! Have the gig swayed out.'

Browne asked, 'Will you require me, sir?'

'If you want to come, please do.' Bolitho saw the uncertainty, the need to understand. He added, 'If you can trust your stomach during the crossing.'

Allday walked to the entry port and waited for the gig to be pulled round to the main chains. Neale's own coxswain nodded to Allday and allowed him to take his place at the tiller without comment.

Bolitho noticed all and none of these things. So it was right through *Styx* already, probably every vessel under his flag.

He touched his hat to the officers and marines at the entry port, and to Neale said quietly, 'I will renew the acquaintanceship for all of us.'

Who did he mean? Allday and Neale, Herrick back in Plymouth, or Ferguson, his steward, who had lost his arm at the Saintes. Or perhaps he was speaking for the others who would never come home.

Then he was settled in the sternsheets and the oars were already thrashing at the tossing water to take the gig clear of the side.

Allday called, 'Give way, all!'

Bolitho glanced up at him. But Allday kept his eyes fixed on the ship. Perhaps they had both known this would happen, but now that it had, could no longer share it.

Bolitho unclipped the boatcloak from about his neck and threw it clear of the bright gold epaulettes, each with its new silver star.

It was just another ship in a desperately depleted squadron, and he was their admiral.

He glanced again at Allday's rigid shoulders and knew it was a lie.

After the creak of oars and the sting of spray it seemed suddenly subdued on the *Phalarope*'s deck. Bolitho replaced his hat and nodded briefly to the ship's marine officer who had arranged his men in two scarlet ranks to receive him.

'Captain Emes?' Bolitho held out his hand as the slightly built figure stepped forward. He had a swift impression of alert wariness, a youthful face, but with a mouth hardened by the rigours of command.

Emes said, 'I am honoured to receive you aboard, sir.' Again there was a sharpness to his voice, a man on guard, one who had been practising for this very moment. 'Although I fear you must know *Phalarope* better than I do.' A shutter seemed to drop behind his level gaze, as if he had already said too much. He half turned, but although he was about to present his officers, his eyes were elsewhere, seeking flaws to the pattern, anything which might make a poor showing.

Bolitho could well understand any captain being eager to make a good impression on his new flag-officer, the man who could fulfil or shatter his hopes for any kind of future. But he had gleaned enough about Emes to doubt if that was the full story. A post-captain at twenty-nine was a record to be proud of, and should have given him a confidence to go with it.

Emes said crisply, 'My senior you will also know better than I, sir.' Emes stood aside as if to watch for reactions.

Bolitho exclaimed, 'Adam! Of all things!'

Lieutenant Adam Pascoe, looking even younger than his twenty-one years, was both relieved and pleased.

'I – I am sorry, Unc—' he flushed, 'sir, I had no way of letting you know. The appointment came without warning and I had to leave for Ireland by the first packet.'

They examined each other, more like brothers than uncle and nephew.

Pascoe added uncertainly, 'When I heard what my appointment was to be, I am afraid I thought of little else.'

Bolitho moved on and shook hands with the second and third lieutenants, the sailing master, ship's surgeon, and the captain of marines. Beyond them, the midshipmen and other warrant officers were backed by crowds of curious seamen, who were too surprised at this unexpected visit on their first commission to be aware of the more personal emotions by the entry port.

Bolitho looked slowly along the gundeck, at the neatly flaked lines and taut rigging. He could even remember the way she had felt that first time when he had stepped aboard.

He cleared his throat. 'Dismiss the hands, Captain Emes, and take station to windward of *Styx*.' He did not see the astonishment in Emes' eyes. 'Allday, send back the gig.' He hesitated. 'You remain with me.'

The mass of seamen and marines broke into orderly confusion as the call to get under way was piped around the deck. Within fifteen minutes Emes had reset the courses and topgallants, and although some of the hands were slow and even clumsy as they ran to obey his commands, it was obvious they had been training hard since leaving harbour.

Browne said, 'Fine ship, sir.' He looked around at the bustling figures, the stamp of bare feet as the seamen hauled hard on the braces.

Bolitho walked along the weather gangway, oblivious to the darting glances from the seamen and Emes' shadow behind him.

He stopped suddenly and pointed below the opposite gangway. No wonder she had seemed changed. Instead of her original lines of twelve-pounders, each gunport was filled by a blunt-muzzled carronade. The carronade, or 'smasher' as it was respectfully termed by the sailors, was carried in almost every man-of-war. Normally mounted on either bow, it could throw an enormous ball which burst on impact and discharged a murderous hail of grape through an enemy's unprotected stern with horrifying effect. But as a ship's armament, never. It had been tried experimentally some years back in another frigate, the *Rainbow*, but had proved unsuccessful and not a little dangerous in close combat.

Emes said quickly, 'They were already mounted before I took charge of the refit, sir. I understand that they were taken into consideration when *Phalarope* was selected for this sector.' He waved his hand to the quarterdeck. 'I still have eight nine-pounders as well, sir.' He sounded defensive.

Bolitho looked at him. 'Admiral Sir George Beauchamp had been doing more planning than I realized.' When Emes did not even blink, he imagined he as yet knew nothing of his orders.

A midshipman called, '*Styx* is signalling, sir!'

Emes grunted, 'I shall come aft.' He sounded relieved. 'If you will excuse me, sir?'

Bolitho nodded and walked slowly along the gangway, his ears searching for lost voices, his eyes catching brief pictures of almost forgotten faces on the strangers around him.

A clean, smart ship, with a captain who would stand no nonsense. It seemed incredible that Pascoe should be the senior lieutenant. His nephew's dream had come true. Bolitho tried to find comfort there. He would have been the same, or was there still the other memory, the stain which had left a lasting mark in this ship?

Allday murmured, 'All these smashers, sir. She'll shake her innards on to the sea-bed if she's called to give battle.'

Bolitho paused on the forecastle, his palm resting on a worn handrail.

'You were *here* at the Saintes, Allday.'

Allday glanced around the pitching deck. 'Aye, sir. Me an' a few others.' His voice strengthened and he seemed to rise from his depression. 'God, the Frenchies were at us that day, an' that's no error! I saw the first lieutenant fall, an' the second. Mr Herrick, *young* Mr Herrick he was in them days, took their place, and more than once I thought my time had come.' He watched Bolitho's grave features. 'I saw your coxswain fall too, old Stockdale.' He shook his head affectionately. 'Protecting your back from the Frog marksmen, he was.'

Bolitho nodded. The memory was still painful. The fact he had not even seen Stockdale die in his defence had made it worse.

Allday grinned. But it made him look sad. 'I determined right then, that if you was alive at the end o' the day, I'd be your coxswain in his place. Mind you, sir, I've regretted more'n once since then, but still . . .'

Pascoe clattered up a ladder from the gundeck. 'Captain Emes has released me to act as your guide, sir.' He smiled awkwardly. 'I suspect she is little altered.'

Bolitho glanced aft and saw Emes outlined against the bright sky. Watching him, wondering if they were exchanging secrets he could not share. It was wrong and unfair, Bolitho thought. But he had to know.

'Did you see Mrs Laidlaw, Adam?'

'No, sir. I had gone before she returned.' He shrugged. 'I left her a letter, of course, Uncle.'

'Thank you.'

He was glad now that he had told Pascoe about his father. If he had not . . .

As if reading his thoughts, Pascoe said, 'When my father fought against us during the American Revolution he

attacked this ship. I've thought about it such a lot, and have
tried to see how it was for you *and* him.' He watched Bolitho
anxiously and then blurted out, 'Anyway, Uncle, I wanted to
join her. Even as the most junior lieutenant I'd have come.'

Bolitho gripped his arm. 'I'm glad.' He looked at the
tilting deck. 'For both of you.'

A midshipman ran forward and touched his hat. 'Captain's
respects, sir, and there is a signal for you.'

But on the quarterdeck once more Emes seemed unruffled
by the news.

'*Styx* has sighted a brig to the south'rd, sir.' He looked up
with sudden irritation as his own masthead called that he had
sighted a strange sail. 'Must be blind, that one!'

Bolitho turned to hide his face. He knew that Neale often
trusted a lookout or a midshipman aloft with a powerful
telescope when the visibility made it worth while.

Emes contained his anger. 'Would you care to come
below, sir? Some claret perhaps?'

Bolitho looked at him calmly. Emes was afraid of him. Ill
at ease.

'Thank you. Signal *Styx* to investigate, if you please, while
you and I share a glass.'

The cabin, like the rest of the ship, was neat and clean, but
with nothing lying about to show something of its owner's
character.

Emes busied himself with some goblets while Bolitho
stared aft through the salt-smeared windows and allowed his
mind to grapple with old memories.

'Young Mr Pascoe is performing well, sir.'

Bolitho eyed him across the claret. 'If he were not, I would
expect no favour, Captain.'

The directness of his reply threw Emes into confusion.

'I see, sir, yes, I understand. But I know what people say,
what they think.'

'And what am *I* thinking?'

Emes paced across the cabin and back again. 'The fleet is so
short of experienced officers, sir, and I, as a post-captain,

have been given command of this old ship.' He watched
Bolitho for a sign that he might have gone too far, but when
he remained silent added forcefully, 'She *was* a fine vessel, and
under your command one of great distinction.' He looked
around, deflated and trapped. 'Now she is old, her frames and
timbers weakened by years of harbour duty. But I am glad to
command her for all that.' He looked Bolitho straight in the
eyes. 'Grateful would be a better word.'

Bolitho put down the goblet very carefully. '*Now* I
remember.'

He had been so full of his own worries, so affected by the
return of his old command, he had barely thought of her
captain. Now it came like a fist in the darkness. Captain
Daniel Emes of the frigate *Abdiel*, who had faced a court
martial about a year ago. He *should* have remembered. Emes
had broken off an engagement with a larger enemy force not
many leagues from this very position, but by so doing had
allowed another British ship to be captured. It had been
rumoured that only Emes' early promotion to post-rank, and
his previously excellent record, had saved him from oblivion
and disgrace.

There was a tap at the door and Browne peered in at them,
his face suitably blank.

'My pardon, sir, but *Styx* has signalled that she is in
contact. The brig is from the southern squadron with
despatches.' He glanced swiftly at Emes' strained features.
'It would seem that the brig is eager to speak with us.'

'I shall return to *Styx* directly.' As Browne hurried away
Bolitho added slowly. '*Phalarope* was a newer ship when I
took command, but a far less happier one than she is today.
You may think she is too old for the kind of work we have to
do. You may also believe she is not good enough for an officer
of your skill and experience.' He picked up his hat and
walked to the door. 'I cannot speak for the former, but I shall
certainly form my own judgement on the latter. As far as I am
concerned, you are one of my captains.' He looked at him
levelly. 'The past is buried.'

Every inch of the surrounding cabin seemed to throw the last words back in his face. But he had to trust Emes, had to make him return that trust.

Emes said thickly, 'Thank you for that, sir.'

'Before we join the others, Captain Emes. If you were faced tomorrow with the same sort of situation as the one which led to a court martial, how would you act?'

Emes shrugged. 'I have asked myself a thousand times, sir. In truth, I am not sure.'

Bolitho touched his arm, sensing his rigidity and wariness outwardly protected by the bright epaulettes.

He smiled. 'Had you said otherwise, I think I would have requested a replacement for your command by the next brig!'

Later, as the two frigates tacked closer together, and the far off brig spread more sail to beat up to them, Bolitho stood by the quarterdeck rail and looked along the length of the upper deck.

So much had happened and had nearly ended here. He heard Emes rapping out orders in his same crisp tones. A difficult man with a difficult choice if ever he had to make it again.

Allday said suddenly, 'Well, sir, what d'you think?'

Bolitho smiled at him. 'I'm glad she's come back, Allday. There are too few veterans here today.'

Bolitho waited for the glasses to be refilled and tried to contain his new excitement. The *Styx*'s stern cabin looked snug and pleased with itself in the glow of the deckhead lanterns, and although the hull groaned and shuddered around them, Bolitho knew that the sea was calmer, that true to the sailing master's prediction the wind had backed to the north-west.

He looked around the small group, and although it was black beyond the stern windows he could picture the other two frigates following in line astern while their captains awaited his pleasure. Only *Rapid*'s young commander was absent, prowling somewhere to the north-east in readiness to dash down and alert his consorts if the French attempted a breakout under cover of darkness.

How would the parents and families feel if they could see their offspring on this night, he wondered? The bluff, red-faced Duncan of *Sparrowhawk*, relating with some relish, and to Neale's obvious amusement, a recent entanglement with a magistrate's wife in Bristol. Emes of the *Phalarope*, alert and very self-contained, watching and listening. Browne leaning over the fat shoulders of Smith, Neale's clerk, and murmuring about some item or other.

Aboard the three frigates of Bolitho's small force the first lieutenants would in turn be wondering at the outcome of this meeting. What would it mean to each of them personally? Promotion, death, even a command if their lord and master should fail.

The clerk straightened his shoulders and silently withdrew from the cabin.

Bolitho listened to the sluice of water around the rudder, the faint tap, tap, tap of halliards, and a restless step of a watchkeeper overhead. A ship. A living thing.

'Gentlemen. Your health.'

Bolitho sat down at the table and turned over a chart. The three ships were standing inshore towards the Loire Estuary, but that was nothing unusual. British ships, in company or alone, had done it a thousand times to keep the French fleet guessing and to sever their precious lines of supply and communication.

The brig which today had made contact with *Styx* was already well on her way to the north and England. Despatches from the vice-admiral commanding the southern squadron, another piece of intelligence which might eventually be used by the brains of Admiralty.

But, as was customary in local strategy, the brig's commander had been instructed to make contact with any senior officer he discovered on passage. A keen-eyed lookout had ensured that the officer concerned was Bolitho.

He said, 'You all know by now the bones of our orders, our true reason for being here.'

He glanced around their intent faces. Young and serious, each aware of the supposedly secret peace proposals, and conscious that with peace could come the sudden end of any hope for advancement. Bolitho understood very well. Between the wars he had been one of the very fortunate few who had been given a ship when the majority of officers had been thrown on the beach like paupers.

'A week ago, two of our patrols to the south'rd fell in with a Spanish trader and tried to take her as a prize. It was near dark and the Spaniard made a run for it. But with a few balls slammed into his hull, and a shifting cargo for good measure, he began to capsize. A boarding party was just in time to seize some papers, and discover that the vessel's holds were filled with building stone. With encouragement the Spanish master admitted he was bringing his cargo into *this* sector.' He touched the chart with his fingers. 'Fifteen leagues south of our present position, to the Ile d'Yeu.'

As he had expected, some of their earlier excitement had given way to disappointment. He decided not to play with them any longer.

'The Spanish master stated that he had visited the island several times, and on every occasion had landed a cargo of stone.' He picked up the brass dividers and moved them over the chart. 'He also said that the anchorage was filled with small vessels, newly built and fitted out. He did not know of their purpose until shown some drawings of French invasion craft of the kind being gathered in the Channel ports.' He nodded seeing their immediate interest. 'The very same. So while we watch Belle Ile and Lorient, the French admiral is moving his flotillas of gun-brigs and bombs whenever he is told it is safe to do so.'

Duncan opened his mouth and shut it again.

Bolitho asked, 'Captain Duncan, you have a question?'

'The stone, sir, I don't see the point of it. Och, even new craft don't need that much ballast while they are fitting out, and I'm sure there must be plenty closer to the building yards.'

'Perhaps by moving their craft close inshore they prefer to use the stone as ballast until they are ready for final commissioning at Lorient or Brest. The stone would then be off-loaded and used for fortifications and local batteries. It would make good sense, and draw far less attention than the movement of larger vessels in our area. All this time we have been watching the wrong sector, but now we *know*, gentlemen, and I intend to act upon this information.'

Neale and Duncan grinned at each other, as if they were being included in a mission already fought and won.

Emes said flatly, 'But without further reinforcements, sir, it will be a hard nut to crack. I know the Ile d'Yeu, and the narrow channel between it and the mainland. An easy anchorage to protect, a hazardous one to attack.' He withdrew behind his mask as the others stared at him as if he had uttered some terrible oath.

'Well said.' Bolitho spread his hands across the chart. 'We will create a diversion. The French will not expect a raid within such confined waters if they see us elsewhere, where they *expect* to see us.'

He turned to Browne who had been trying to catch his eye for several minutes.

'Yes?'

'Well, sir, if we wait until reinforcements arrive, as Sir George Beauchamp *desired* in his original plan, we could stand a better chance of success surely? Or if the brig which brought the news eventually returns with new orders countermanding our present commitment, then we shall be obliged to do nothing.'

Duncan exploded, 'Do *nothing*, man! What are you saying?'

Bolitho smiled. 'I take your point, Browne.'

Like Herrick and Allday, he was trying to shield him. If he attacked and failed, his head would be on the block. If he held back, nobody could blame him, but Beauchamp's trust would be dishonoured for ever.

He said quietly, 'If there is to be peace, it must be decided on fair and equal terms and not under the threat of invasion. If later there is to be war, we must ensure now that our people are not outmanoeuvred from the moment the treaty is torn in shreds. I don't see that I have any choice.'

Duncan and Neale nodded firmly in agreement, but Emes merely brushed a loose thread from his sleeve, his face expressionless.

In the silence, Bolitho was conscious of Smith's pen scraping on paper, and of his own heart against his ribs.

He added, 'I have seen too many ships lost, too many lives tossed away, to ignore something which may be important, even vital, to our future. I suggest you return to your duties, gentlemen, and I shall endeavour to do mine.'

As the three captains left the cabin, Bolitho said, 'Thank you for trying to protect me, Oliver. But there was never any choice. Even without this new information, I should have been forced to act. At least I know where. The *how* always takes a mite longer, eh?'

Browne smiled, touched at Bolitho's confidence in him, the familiar use of his name.

When Bolitho spoke again his voice was preoccupied, even distant.

'And something troubles me . . .' He thought of Emes, withdrawn and resentful, of his nephew, Adam, so pleased with the realization of a dream, and of the girl in Falmouth.

'When I have discovered what it is, I shall feel more confident perhaps.'

If I have not already left it too late.

4

The Stuff of Battle

Seven days after calling his captains together in conference, Bolitho was growing more and more restless for news. It was like being abandoned by the world beyond *Styx*'s hull, or being cast adrift because of some terrible plague.

He had deliberately sent the other two frigates to maintain close watch on Belle Ile and its approaches. This would ensure that the French would believe their enemy's blockade remained unchanged. Also, if the Spanish shipmaster's information proved false, it might allow time to call heavier vessels from the other squadrons if there was an attempt to break out.

So while *Styx* cruised slowly back and forth along a twenty-mile triangle to the south, Bolitho had ordered the little brig to maintain contact between them.

It was frustrating, almost maddening, to know nothing, and it was all he could do to restrain himself from going on deck whenever he heard a cry from the masthead or some unusual disturbance among the men on watch. The weather did nothing to help. The wind had fallen away to a leisurely breeze, with barely a whitecap to break the Bay's shark-blue emptiness. The ship's company, although much aware of the responsibility of carrying their admiral about his affairs, grew slack and casual. Here and there seamen would loll at their monotonous tasks of splicing and whipping, polishing and stitching, and, hidden from the quarterdeck, others would lie sprawled in the tops, fast asleep.

Bolitho had noticed that neither Neale nor Browne had

mentioned the lack of support from north or south. Beauchamp's wishes must have been translated into deeds by now, even the gun-brigs from Gibraltar should have arrived to give him the support he needed. The fact that Browne stayed silent suggested he and not his rear-admiral was closer to the truth. No support *would* arrive. The strategy so carefully planned by Beauchamp would be allowed to lie in some Admiralty strongbox until conveniently forgotten.

Allday entered the cabin and removed Bolitho's sword from its rack to give it a daily polish. He hesitated, his thick shadow swaying easily to the ship's gentle lift and plunge.

'That brig could have been delayed, sir. Wind was against her. Takes time to beat up channel. I remember when we was in—'

Bolitho shook his head. 'Not now. I know you mean well, but she must have made port with days to spare. Those craft are well used to their work.'

Allday sighed. 'No sense in blaming yourself, sir.' He paused as if expecting Bolitho to turn on him. 'These past days you've been like a falcon on a line, not able to do what he wants.'

Bolitho sat down on the bench beneath the stern windows. It was strange, but a fact, that it was easy to talk with his big coxswain, whereas he could never express even the hint of a doubt to Neale or any of his officers. That would imply weakness, uncertainty, what a man remembered when the iron began to fly, when he most needed to be inspired.

Allday was probably right. It was all too soon after the Baltic. Allday would realize that better than any of them. He had carried him in his arms when his wound had burst open and he almost died.

He asked, 'What does your falcon do, Allday?'

Allday drew the old sword and raised it level with his eye until the edge gleamed in the reflected sunlight like a silver thread.

'He bides his time, sir. If he's meant to be free, somehow he'll manage it.'

They both looked up, off guard, as the masthead's voice echoed through the skylight. 'Deck there! Sail on th' larboard quarter!'

Feet pounded across the planking and another voice snapped, 'Alert the captain, Mr Manning! Mr Kilburne, aloft with you, smartly now!'

Bolitho and Allday exchanged glances.

It was the part Bolitho hated most. Having to wait. Not able to rush up and join the others and make his own judgement. Neale was the captain.

Voices sighed back and forth across the quarterdeck, but more subdued now. They were conscious either of Neale's arrival on deck or of the fact that the cabin skylight was propped fully open.

Allday murmured, 'God damn them, they are taking an age!'

In spite of his own anxiety, Bolitho was forced to smile.

'Easy, Allday. I will assist you if things become too difficult!'

But when a breathless midshipman arrived and blurted out his captain's respects, and that a sail was closing to larboard, he found his admiral apparently at ease and untroubled on the stern bench and his coxswain engrossed in polishing a sword.

On the quarterdeck the sun was very hot, and made the shadows of rigging and shrouds criss-cross the pale planking like black bars.

Bolitho joined Neale by the hammock nettings. Like the other officers, he had discarded his heavy coat and was wearing shirt and breeches, with nothing to distinguish him from his subordinates. Anyone in *Styx*'s company of some two hundred and forty souls who did not recognize his admiral after twc weeks of cramped isolation was beyond help, Bolitho thought.

Neale said, 'Lookout thinks there are two vessels, sir.' He shifted under Bolitho's gaze. 'The heat haze is making it hard to determine.'

Bolitho nodded, unaware that in his eagerness he had been

almost glaring at him.

'Deck, sir! She's a brig!' A pause, and then the midshipman named Kilburne shouted, 'And – and one other, sir!'

The sailing master whispered to one of his mates, 'Gawd 'elp us!'

Neale cupped his hands. 'What the *hell* are you talking about, sir?'

The second lieutenant who was on watch said helpfully, 'I could get aloft, sir.'

'Remain here!' Neale turned to his first lieutenant. 'Mr Pickthorn, I must ask you to go as I am seemingly supported by blind men and cripples!'

Pickthorn concealed a grin and was swarming up the ratlines before Neale had recovered his composure.

The air shook to the far-off bang of a gun, and Bolitho had to move to the lee side to hide his own impatience.

'Deck! 'Tis *Rapid*, sir! In pursuit of a small vessel, possibly a yawl!'

Neale squinted at the masthead pendant and the listless rise and fall of his sails and exclaimed, 'Damn them! We'll stand no chance!'

Bolitho said sharply, 'What is the course to steer for Ile d'Yeu?'

Neale dragged his mind away from the thought of losing prize money, no matter how small.

The sailing master called, 'Due east, sir, as makes no difference.'

Bolitho strode across the deck, barely conscious of the curious stares, the sun which had already changed his shirt into a wet rag.

'Bring her about, Captain Neale, and beat to wind'rd! When you are within signalling distance, I wish you to order *Rapid* to stand away!'

Pickthorn arrived on deck with a thump. He said hoarsely, 'The yawl is making a run for it, sir! But *Rapid*'s overhauling her fast!' He sensed the tension. 'Sir?'

'Signal *Rapid* to disengage! Then call the hands and prepare to come about.' Neale glanced quickly at Bolitho. 'We are taking over the chase.'

Pickthorn stared. 'I see. Aye, at once, sir!'

Calls shrilled, and within minutes the men were straining at the braces, bringing the frigate heeling round until her canvas was almost aback. Sails banged and flapped in wild confusion, and had the wind been any stronger, she would have been in danger of losing a few spars.

The other midshipman on watch closed his telescope and said, '*Rapid* has acknowledged, sir.'

There was no need to add what everyone was thinking. It was unheard of for any ship, let alone the one wearing the flag of a rear-admiral, to snatch a prize from a consort. With *Styx* standing almost into the wind, it was even likely the elusive yawl would slip clean away from both of them. That would raise a few jeers in some French harbour tonight.

The master yelled, 'Nor'-nor'-west, sir! Full an' bye!'

Bolitho did not have to be told. The frigate was pitching unsteadily, the air filled with the din of canvas and blocks, of angry voices trying to hold the ship on course.

Bolitho shut the others from his mind as he levelled a telescope and concentrated everything on the distant patch of sails. She was big for a yawl, and had every piece of canvas set in her favour as she ran free with the wind. Courier, smuggler, it was of no account. She needed to get to safety, and the nearest land was the Ile d'Yeu.

Neale said bitterly, 'If I change tack to starboard and gain more wind I might still head her off. We have six hours before dusk.' He sounded disappointed and confused.

'Remain as you are, Captain Neale. I shall require you to luff directly. *Put her in stays.*'

'But, but . . .' Neale was at a loss for words. To snatch then lose a prize, deliberately at that, was more than he could accept.

Bolitho eyed him calmly. 'I want that yawl to *believe* we have been taken aback.'

Neale nodded jerkily. 'Aye, sir. Mr Pickthorn! We are

standing into the wind! Stand by tacks and sheets!' He added huskily, 'I believe it myself, sir!'

As the helm was put up still further, *Styx* lifted like a stag caught by a musket ball in mid-air. Under Pickthorn's guidance, and the curses and blows of the frantic petty officers and topmen, the ship plunged down into a deep trough, the sails flapping against the masts and forcing the hull over like a waterlogged cutter.

A seaman fell from the ratlines, the sea directly below his kicking feet before two of his companions hauled him gasping to safety. But not a spar cracked apart, nor did any sail split into ribbons, as the stricken frigate wallowed helplessly out of control.

Bolitho raised his glass again and watched for the yawl's tan-coloured sails. Well to starboard now, her hull partly hidden in the blue water.

'A moment more, Captain Neale.'

Bolitho handed the telescope to Allday. If Allday thought he had gone mad he certainly did not show it.

Then Bolitho said, 'Get her under way again and continue the chase. Do not set your t'gallants. I want a chase, but if you catch that yawl I'll make you *eat* your prize money!'

It was like seeing a cloud part across a clear sky as Neale stared at him with amazement and admiration.

'Follow the Frenchie all the way to the island, sir?'

Bolitho watched the disorganized bunches of seamen being rounded up and set to the braces and halliards once more.

'All the way.'

As Neale hurried to pass his orders to his lieutenants, Bolitho turned and looked at Allday. 'Well?'

Allday wiped his mouth with the back of his fist. 'I reckon the falcon is free, sir, an' that's no error!'

'Deck there! Land ahead! Fine on th' lee bow!'

Bolitho tried to conceal his rising excitement as officers

and master's mates jostled each other at the quarterdeck rail
to train their telescopes.

Neale commented worriedly, 'The wind is dropping, sir.'

Bolitho glanced up at the topsails, the almost painful way
they lifted to the wind and emptied just as swiftly.

The chase had been going on for two hours, with the yawl
running in direct line ahead of the frigate's jib boom. To lose
her now, with the land in sight, would be sheer stupidity.

'Set your t'gallants, stuns'ls too if you think fit.'

Bolitho turned away as Neale beckoned to his first lieutenant and walked aft to the wheel.

He nodded to the sailing master and asked, 'What is the
channel like beyond the Ile d'Yeu, Mr Bundy?'

The master was a small, shabby man with a face like
cracked leather. Old Ben Grubb, the sailing master of the
Benbow, would make four of him, Bolitho thought.

But there was nothing shabby about his mind or reply.

'A bad 'un, sir. 'Bout ten mile from the island to the
mainland, but a bad bottom, no more'n three fathom at the
most at low water.' He stared ahead of the flapping sails as if
he could already see the island. 'A place to anchor a flotilla of
small craft, I reckon.' He rubbed his chin thoughtfully. 'The
'ole island is no longer than five mile accordin' to my chart.'

'Thank you, Mr Bundy.'

Bolitho turned away to rejoin Neale and did not see the
relief and pleasure on Bundy's lean features. Bolitho had not
merely asked his opinion, but had made certain that his
mates and helmsmen had heard him do so.

'I can just make it out, sir.' Neale waited for Bolitho to pick
up a telescope. 'But the haze makes everything shapeless.'

Bolitho held his breath and waited for the deck to rise
again. There it was, a patch of darker blue against the sea.
The island where the Spanish ship had off-loaded her cargo of
building stone.

The yawl was heading for the northern tip of the island,
but once around the sheltered side would probably stand even
closer inshore and follow the coast further south to Nantes.

Her master would have the wind at his disposal should the pursuing frigate try to head him off at the last minute or be joined by another patrol from the south. Bolitho smiled wryly. It was unlikely there was another British man-of-war within two hundred miles south of this quarterdeck.

He lowered the glass and watched the seamen strung out along the upper yards as the topsails were set and sheeted home, their bellies filling listlessly to the warm breeze. Four hours of good daylight left. It would have to be enough. To stand off until daylight would be like blowing a warning trumpet to the nearest French garrison.

Many telescopes were probably laid on the speedy yawl and the menacing pyramid of sails in pursuit. A horseman would be despatched to the local commander. An artillery battery would be alerted to warn off the foolish English captain who was risking everything in order to catch such a small prize.

Neale asked casually, 'What do you intend, sir?'

Perhaps he took Bolitho's silence for uncertainty. 'We could alter course and make better use of the wind. Then head for the southern end of the island, maybe catch the Frogs as they break free of the channel?'

'Yes. But if the yawl decided not to head further south?'

Neale shrugged. 'We shall lose her.'

Bolitho raised the glass again and steadied it on the distant island.

'We have done that already, Captain Neale.'

Neale stared at him. 'Then you intend to work as close to the island as you can and estimate the defences?' He was completely lost.

Bolitho smiled at him. 'I intend we should do better than that. We shall enter the channel itself. With the wind under our coat tails, I think even the French will be surprised!'

Neale swallowed hard. 'Aye, sir. But Mr Bundy says—'

Bolitho nodded. 'I know. Three fathoms at low water. It will have to be done well.' He grinned and touched his arm, glad that he was able to mask his own anxiety from the young captain. 'I have every faith in you.'

He turned towards the companionway. 'Allday, fetch me something cool from the wine store.' He nodded to the watching lieutenants. 'I have to think.'

Allday followed him down the ladder and aft to the cabin, while overhead the decks shook to the immediate activity of hurrying seamen.

He grinned admiringly. 'By God, sir, that stirred them well enough!'

Bolitho walked to the stern windows and leaned out to stare at the rippling wake from the rudder. He heard the muffled shout of commands, the squeal of trucks as somewhere up forward the bow-chasers were prepared for the first shots of the engagement.

How he had wanted to remain on deck and take part. But he had to accept that Neale was an extension of himself. Without being told what to do he had already accepted Bolitho's strategy, and would execute it without question. In a matter of hours he might be lying dead or screaming on his surgeon's table. His beloved *Styx* could become a drifting dismasted hulk, or pushed hard aground because the chart was mistaken. And all because of his admiral's order.

Bolitho said, 'Fetch Mr Browne and ask him to join me for a glass.'

Bolitho relaxed very slowly as the door closed behind Allday. Browne was different from anyone he knew. At least he might keep his mind away from the very real possibility of failure.

When Bolitho returned to the quarterdeck the little island had grown considerably, so that it sprawled across the starboard bow like a blunt-headed monster.

Neale said, 'We are overhauling her, sir.' He waited to watch Bolitho's reactions. 'But the yawl is almost abreast of the headland.'

Bolitho studied the sloping island, the lively white crests around some reefs and a smaller islet like the monster's pup.

The yawl was keeping very near to the tip of the island, so that she appeared to be trying to climb bodily on to dry land.

Neale called sharply, 'Bring her up a point, Mr Bundy!'

'Aye, sir. East by north.'

Bolitho moved the glass very carefully, seeing the flapping jib-sail and two seamen standing on the forecastle, like giants as they were captured in the lens.

A few low buildings at the foot of the island, probably more on the landward side. He stiffened as he saw some grey walls near to the top of the headland. A battery perhaps? Even as he watched he saw a tiny pin-prick of colour caught in the sunlight like a butterfly. The mast was still invisible, but the butterfly was a tricolour.

He said, 'Clear for action, Captain Neale. And please tell your gunner to try a few shots on that yawl.'

As the marine drummers beat their sticks so rapidly that their hands were blurred, and the boatswain's mates yelled, 'Hands to quarters! Clear for action!', Bolitho could sense the wild excitement being unleashed about him like a tide-race.

The starboard bow-chaser crashed out violently and threw itself inboard on its tackles, and even as its crew darted around it to sponge out and reload, Bolitho saw the ball drop in direct line with the yawl's sails, flinging up a column of water like a spouting whale.

The other gun belched smoke and flames, and a second waterspout brought a chorus of cheers from the topmen and those who were able to see it.

Neale said, 'No chance of a hit unless we can close the range.'

The first lieutenant hurried aft and touched his hat. 'Cleared for action, sir.'

Neale deliberately tugged his watch from his breeches and studied it, his round face impassive as he said, 'Twelve minutes, Mr Pickthorn. Won't do. I want it done in ten or less.'

Bolitho had to turn away. It could have been himself speaking when he had commanded *Phalarope* and Neale had been the junior midshipman.

The bow-chasers continued to fire after the yawl, and although the balls were dropping short by a cable, the Frenchman obviously did not know how lucky he was, for he began to tack violently from side to side as if to avoid the next fall of shot.

Neale smiled. 'Interesting, sir. If he continues like that we may take him yet.'

Smoke drifted harmlessly from the grey wall on the headland, and after what seemed like an eternity some eight or nine spouts of water shot from the sea well away from the frigate's side.

Bolitho listened to the dying echo of the concealed battery. Just a token, a warning.

'Bring her up now, Captain Neale.'

Neale nodded, his mind grappling with the dozen or so problems which were most immediate to him.

'We will alter course four points to larboard, Mr Pickthorn, and steer nor'-east by north.'

'Hands to the braces there!'

As the big double wheel was turned steadily to leeward, *Styx* responded easily to the pressure of sail and rudder, the island appearing to slide away to starboard.

Bolitho raised his glass once more. Across the starboard bow was the beginning of the channel, and far beyond it, barely visible through the haze, was a deeper tone, the coast of France.

No more shots came from the battery, and while the yawl continued to move past the island's northern shoreline, *Styx* headed purposefully away, as if she intended to discontinue the chase.

Bolitho walked to the quarterdeck rail and looked along the upper deck. Beneath the gangway on either side he saw the gun crews crouching by each sealed port, the instruments of their trade within ready reach. Each gun-captain was a king, every breech a small demanding kingdom.

The decks had been well sanded, and high above the busy

seamen and marines chain-slings had been fixed to each yard and nets spread above their heads to further protect them from falling wreckage.

Neale watched him. 'Another fifteen minutes, sir.' He added hesitantly, 'I've put two of my best leadsmen in the chains. The tide is already on the ebb, I fear.'

Bolitho nodded. Neale had thought of everything. He saw some of the men at the nearest guns staring up at him. Trying perhaps to decide their own fates this day by what they saw in him.

Bolitho said, 'Fetch my coat, Allday.'

He heard Neale give a small sigh and added, 'Have no fear, there'll be no sharpshooters today, I think.'

Allday held out his coat and slipped it over his shoulders. The effect was instant, as if there had been something lacking.

Several seamen gave a cheer, and the marines in the main-top who were manning the swivels waved their hats as if something special had just happened.

Neale said quietly, 'That was good of you, sir. They like to see. To know.'

'And you? What about your feelings?'

Neale gave a great grin, as if, like the cheering, it had been held back for this small moment.

'Your flag flies in *my* ship, sir. It's a proud day for all of us, but especially for me.' His gaze shifted to the two bright epaulettes on Bolitho's shoulders. 'There's many who'd wish to be here with us today.' He did not have to mention their names.

Bolitho looked past him at the creaming water alongside. 'Then so be it.' He saw Browne hurrying to join him, all signs of sea-sickness gone. 'When you are ready, Captain Neale.'

Neale cupped his hands. 'Stand by to come about, Mr Pickthorn! We will steer south-east!'

With yards creaking round, and hull dipping to the pressure of increased sail, *Styx* turned her bows purposefully to starboard until she pointed towards the centre of the channel. Caught unaware, and showing her full length for the first time, the distant yawl appeared to be pinioned on the jib boom and incapable of movement.

'South-east, sir! Steady as she goes!'

'Get the royals on her, Mr Pickthorn! Then load and run out!'

Bolitho stood close against the rail, watching the island moving in again to starboard, some drifting smoke against the sky which might be anything from burning gorse to a furnace heating shot. *Styx* was moving very rapidly through the water, as with royals and topgallants at last responding to a following wind she headed into the channel.

A whistle shrilled and along either side the port lids were hauled open, and at another signal the *Styx*'s guns were run out, their black muzzles poking into the dying sunlight like teeth.

Bolitho shivered slightly in spite of his coat. If the French had had any doubts about their intentions, they would soon disappear now.

Without turning his head he knew Allday and Browne stood at his back, that Neale was nearby. What had Browne called the original squadron before Copenhagen? *We Happy Few*. As spray dashed over the tightly packed hammock nettings to sting his cheeks like ice, he knew exactly what he had meant.

He watched the frigate's two other lieutenants pacing slowly back and forth behind the guns, swords drawn and across their shoulders like walking-sticks as their ship sailed into action. These were the sailors who were never seen by the people they defended through each day of war. The powers of Admiralty could plan and scheme, and dissect every item of intelligence about the enemy's intentions and movements, but it was left to men and boys like these to do the job. The stuff of battle. Bolitho smiled quietly. One of his old captains had described his own men like that in another war.

Around him, some of the men saw the smile and knew it was because of them.

Because it was *their* day.

5

Single-Handed

'By th' mark seven!' The leadsman's voice seemed unnaturally loud to the intent figures on *Styx*'s quarterdeck.

Bolitho looked up quickly as the big mainsail and forecourse filled and hardened to the breeze. You could hardly call it a wind, but with her canvas drawing well *Styx* was making a favourable eight or nine knots through the water.

He watched the island as it grew larger above the starboard bow. The sun had moved across it in the last few minutes, or so it appeared, and the nearest rise of headland was already in shadow.

The bow-chasers continued to fire at regular intervals, while far ahead of the *Styx*'s beakhead the French yawl was wavering from side to side, her master apparently still convinced he was the prime target.

Neale lowered his telescope and said, 'Dusk early tonight, sir.' He added bitterly, 'It damn well would be!'

Bolitho said nothing but concentrated on the small island. As the ship stood deeper into the channel between it and the mainland, he was conscious of the tension around him, and wondered what the French were doing across that narrowing strip of water. There had been no more shots, and he felt the returning bite of anxiety, the feeling he might have miscalculated, that there was nothing important here after all.

Allday shifted his feet and muttered, 'Must be asleep, the lot o' 'em!'

Browne remarked, 'I can see smoke. There, low down, man!'

Neale hurried across the deck, thrusting a midshipman aside like an empty sack.

'Where?' He trained his glass again. 'God dammit, it's not smoke, it's *dust*!'

Bolitho picked up a telescope and followed the bearing carefully. Dust it was, and the reason became clear as a team of horses charged from behind some low scrub, a limber and cannon bouncing behind them as they headed for the other end of the island. Within minutes another limber and field-piece following it along the track, the dying sunlight glint-ing briefly on the outriders' uniforms and equipment.

Bolitho closed his glass and tried to control his excite-ment. He had not been mistaken. The French had been so sure of their safe anchorage that they had relied on field-artillery rather than a fixed shore battery. They probably intended to remove the guns altogether once the last of the new invasion craft had been delivered to their final destination.

No wonder *Styx* had not been fired on after the first warning shots. The fall of shot had been too precise, fired by soldiers used to the ways of a land battle. A naval gunner would have laid and fired each of his battery by hand. Just to be certain and to avoid wasting shot. The latter was always paramount in a sailor's mind when he was aboard ship and a long way from ready supplies, so why should he change his ways ashore?

'Deck there!'

Neale wiped his mouth with the back of his hand and growled, 'Well, come on, man, spit it out!'

But the masthead lookout was too well trained to be bothered by the impatient group far beneath his dangling legs.

Then he called, 'Ships at anchor round the point, sir!'

One of the leadsmen shouted from forward, 'By th' mark five!' But apart from Bundy, the master, nobody seemed to care. Some peered beyond the bows, others stared up at the masthead, eager for more news.

'A dozen or more at anchor, sir!' Even the distance from deck to topmast could not hide the man's disbelief as he added hoarsely, 'No, sir, far more'n that!'

Neale clapped his hands together. 'Got 'em, by God!'

Bundy said quickly, 'We're enterin' the shallows, sir.' He flinched under Neale's stare. 'Sorry, sir, but you had to know.'

'Deep *four*!' The leadsman's voice was like a sad chant.

The first lieutenant joined Bundy by his chart. 'Tide's still on the ebb.' He glanced meaningly at his captain and then at the upper yards.

Neale said, 'Get the royals on her. We'll run with the tide.' He looked at Bolitho and added, 'With your consent, sir?'

'I agree. We need haste above all.'

He forgot the cries of the seamen as they freed the sails from the upper yards, the bark of orders and squeal of halliards, for as the ship forged on a converging track towards the next headland he saw the first of the anchored vessels. No wonder the lookout was amazed. There were dozens of them, some moored in pairs, others, possibly gun-brigs or bombs, anchored separately, a veritable armada of small ships. It was not difficult to imagine them disgorging French dragoons and infantry on to the beaches of southern England.

'Deep four!' The leadsman hauled up his line so rapidly that his muscular arm appeared blurred in the red sunlight.

Neale shouted, 'Stand by, starboard battery!' He watched as every gun-captain raised his hand along the side, while behind them their lieutenants continued to prowl up and down like strangers to each other.

The island was much deeper in shadow, and against it the crowded hulls of the newly-built vessels looked like one vast, ungainly raft.

Bolitho stared at the glowing red ball of sunlight. Not long now. If only *Sparrowhawk*, even *Rapid*, were here. As it was, it would soon be too shallow to manoeuvre without running aground, and they could never sink or damage more than two or three.

He snapped, 'Where's the yawl?'

Neale called, 'Fine on the starboard bow, sir. I think she intends to anchor amongst that lot, if she can.'

Bolitho made up his mind. 'Tell your gun-captains to hit the yawl. A guinea for the first crew to cripple her!'

There were a few gasps of surprise at the choice of target, but after some quick adjustments with handspikes and tackles, the gun-captains shouted their readiness.

'As you bear!' Neale raised his curved hanger above his head. 'On the uproll!' Seconds became hours. *'Fire!'*

Down the frigate's side each gun muzzle belched fire and smoke and hurled itself inboard on its tackles. The forward guns were being sponged out and reloaded even as the after-most division added to the din.

The yawl, caught at the very moment she was trying to change tack towards the other vessels, seemed to collapse under the weight of iron as each double-shotted gun blasted across a range of less than two cables.

Around the stricken yawl the sea was patterned with splashes as falling shot, wreckage and splintered spars cascaded down on every side.

A tiny pin-prick of light winked from the battered hull and almost immediately blossomed into a great gout of fire. A powder cask touched by a spark, a dazed seaman caught off balance with a lantern between decks, it could have been anything.

Bundy exclaimed thickly, 'God, she's ablaze!'

Bolitho tried to contain the sick pity he felt for the men on that blazing vessel. One heavy ball would have been enough to sink her, a broadside had changed her into an inferno. A fire-ship.

He kept his voice level as he said, 'That should make the others up-anchor!'

Something punched through the maincourse and left a hole big enough for a man to climb through. One of those horse artillery gunners had reached his site.

The first lieutenant yelled, 'They's cutting their cables!'

Caught by wind and tide, the wide cluster of moored craft was already opening up as each master endeavoured to fight his way clear, to make sail and to hell with his consorts. Anything but stay and be destroyed by fire or the enemy frigate which was rushing headlong towards them with only a few feet beneath her keel.

'As you bear! Continue firing!'

Neale hurried to the quarterdeck rail as the nearest vessels loomed out of the deepening shadows, his cheeks glowing in the reflected flames.

'Larboard battery, *stand by*!'

The crews started to cheer as another vessel appeared on the opposite bow, some sails already set and her stem pointing towards France.

As the larboard battery joined in the fight, the escaping craft was deluged in falling waterspouts, while above her deck masts and canvas were flung about as if lashed by a great gale.

Neale said, 'She's done for.' He flinched as metal shrieked low above the hammock nettings and smashed down in the sea abeam.

Bolitho stared at the chaos which seemed in danger of colliding with and snaring the attacking frigate. Vessels which had cut their cables too soon were drifting down entangled with some of their consorts, and others were risking everything to escape into open water. They were as much in danger from their own artillery ashore as they were from Neale's guns. For it was almost dark now, apart from the flashing tongues of cannon fire, the flames of burning vessels having been quenched by the sea.

'Cease firing, Captain Neale.'

Bolitho tried to free his mind of the elation the taste of battle had created around him. Not one ball had hit *Styx*, and not a man had even been injured. The kind of sea-fight every sailor dreamed about.

'Sir?' Neale watched him eagerly.

'If you were the French commander here, what would you do? Recall the vessels and anchor them again while you set up a new battery to protect them, or send them packing to the north where they were intended?'

Neale grinned at two of his smoke-blackened seamen who were cheering and capering in a wild dance.

Then he became serious. 'I'd not send them back to their original harbours. It would seem like incompetence, cowardice even, with such urgency demanded for their delivery.' He nodded slowly. 'I'd send them on, sir, before we can summon heavier reinforcements.'

Bolitho smiled gravely. 'I agree with you. So tell the master to lay a course to clear this channel and then beat back to the rendezvous. As soon as we sight *Rapid* I'll send her to find the others. I'll wager *Rapid* is still close at hand and wondering what the devil we have been doing. Apart from stealing her prize, that is!' He gripped Neale's arm, unable to keep the excitement to himself. 'We shall have the wind in our favour, think of it, man! We know that no support is coming from Lorient or Brest for these craft, otherwise *Sparrowhawk* or *Phalarope* would have sighted it. We have just created panic, but panic will not last. We must act at once. *Phalarope*, with her armament of carronades, can reap a rich harvest amongst these flimsy vessels.'

He looked up sharply as the sails flapped noisily above the deck. They were drawing under the lee of the island, but once in deeper water they could soon fight their way back to their friends.

Neale said doubtfully, 'We shall be close inshore, sir.' He grinned. 'But you are right, we can do it.' He shouted, 'Mr Pickthorn! Hands to the braces! Stand by to come about!'

Bolitho made to leave and then said, 'I shall not forget your support, Captain Neale. You could have lost your keel back there.'

Neale watched him go and remarked, 'After *that*, I think I could sail this ship on a heavy dew!'

Bundy looked at his mates and grimaced. 'Not with *me*, 'e bloody won't!'

Bolitho opened his eyes and groaned. His body felt as if it had been kicked in several different places, and he realized he had fallen asleep in Neale's chair.

His senses returned instantly as he saw Allday bending over him.

'What is it?'

Allday placed a mug of coffee carefully on the table.

'Wind's freshening, sir, and it'll be first light in half an hour.' He stood back, his head bowed between the deckhead beams, and eyed Bolitho critically. 'Thought you'd want a shave before dawn.'

Bolitho stretched his legs and sipped the coffee. Allday never forgot anything.

Now, as the deck lifted and quivered beneath the chair, he found it hard to believe that in the hours since they had burst upon the anchorage they had made contact with the brig *Rapid*, which in turn had hurried away to complete the link in the chain of command with *Phalarope*.

The rest had been much easier than expected. Turning once more to take full advantage of the wind, the two frigates had steered south-east, while *Rapid* had continued her search for Duncan's *Sparrowhawk*.

It was not much of a flotilla, Bolitho conceded, but what it lacked in numbers it certainly made up for in agility and fire power. He had seen it in *Styx*, the wildness which was akin to some kind of insanity when the guns had roared out their challenge. If they could find and get amongst the enemy invasion craft just once again, the panic they had already created would spread like a forest fire.

Then he could make his report to the Admiralty, Beauchamp's wishes had been carried out.

There was a tap at the door, but this time it was Neale, his round face flushed from the wind and spray.

'*Phalarope*'s in sight astern, sir. Sky's brightening, but the wind's backed to north by west. I've sent the people to breakfast early. I have a feeling we shall be busy today. If the Frogs have sailed, that is.'

Bolitho nodded. 'If they have not, we shall repeat yesterday's tactics, only this time we shall have *Phalarope*'s carronades.'

He sensed Allday's sudden stiffness, the way the razor had stilled in mid air.

Neale cocked his head as voices echoed along the upper deck. He did not see Allday's apprehension as he hurried away to his duties.

Bolitho lay back in the chair and said quietly, 'The sea is *empty*, Allday. We shall destroy those craft today, come what may. After that . . .'

Allday continued to shave him without comment.

It was strange to realize that *Phalarope* was sailing somewhere astern, in sight as yet only to the keen-eyed masthead lookouts. The ship which had changed everything for him, for Allday, and others who were so near to him. It was also unnerving to accept he was probably more excited about seeing *Phalarope* under full sail and awaiting his wishes than he was at the prospect of destroying helpless craft which could not hit back. But their menace was real enough, as Beauchamp had seen for many months. He sighed and thought instead of Belinda. What would she be doing at this moment? Lying in her bed, listening to the first birds, the early farm carts on the move down the lanes? Thinking of him perhaps, or the future? After today things might be different. Again, he could find himself ordered to the other side of the world. Belinda's late husband had hated being a soldier and had resigned his commission to serve with the Honourable East India Company. Would she equally hate being married to a sailor?

Another tap at the door broke his thoughts and he was almost grateful. Almost.

It was Browne, all sickness gone, and as impeccable as if he was about to carry a despatch to Parliament itself.

'Is it time?'

Browne nodded. 'Dawn's coming up, sir.'

He glanced at Allday and saw him shrug. It was not like him to look so disconsolate.

Bolitho stood and felt the ship's eager thrusting movement. The wind had backed again, Neale had said. They would have to watch out they did not run on a lee shore. He smiled grimly. So would the French.

He slipped into his coat. 'I am ready.' He looked at Allday again. 'Another dawn.'

Allday made a great effort. 'Aye, sir. I hope when we greet the next one the taffrail will be pointing at France. I *hate* this bay, and all it means to a seaman.'

Bolitho let it lie there. When Allday was having a rare mood, it was best left well alone. There were other things at stake today.

After the sealed warmth of the cabin the quarterdeck felt almost icy. Bolitho returned Neale's greeting and nodded to the other officers on watch. The ship was cleared for action, or would be once the last screen between Neale's quarters and the gundeck had been removed, but there was little hint of it yet.

The gun crews lounged in the shadows beneath the gangways, and the men in the tops were hidden by the black rigging and lively canvas.

Bolitho walked aft to the taffrail, aware of the marines resting by the nettings on either side, their muskets propped against the packed hammocks. How pale their cross-belts looked in the weird light, while their uniforms appeared to be black.

He tensed as for the first time he saw the old frigate following astern.

Her topgallant yards and masthead pendant held the first light on them, while the rest of the sails and the hull itself were lost in darkness. A ghost ship indeed.

He shook himself out of his doldrums and thought instead about the rest of his command. *Rapid* may have found

Duncan by now. Other ships might be on their way to assist as Beauchamp had originally directed. Like Browne, he doubted it.

Neale joined him by the rail and together they watched the dawn spreading and spilling over from the land. A fiery red dawn. Bolitho smiled and remembered his mother. *Red sky at morning, shepherd's warning*: He felt a sudden chill at his spine and turned to look for Allday. Allday had been a shepherd when the press gang had seized him. Bolitho swung round again, furious with himself and with his fantasy.

He said, 'As soon as you can, make contact with *Phalarope*. Signal her to maintain station to windward.'

As Browne hurried away to prepare his signal, Bolitho said to Neale, 'When *Phalarope* has acknowledged, we shall stand closer inshore.'

Neale hesitated. 'We shall be seen at once, sir.'

Bolitho shrugged. 'By then it will be too late.'

He wished suddenly that Herrick was here with him. Like a rock. Part of himself. And ready to argue in his stubborn way. Neale would follow him to and through the gates of hell without a murmur, but not Herrick. If there was a flaw in the plan he would see it.

Bolitho looked up at the masthead pendant and then at his own flag. Stiff, like banners. The wind was still rising.

Unconsciously his fingers played with the worn pommel of his sword. He was being unfair. To Neale and to Allday, to Herrick, who was not even present.

It was his flag at the mizzen masthead, and the responsibility was his alone.

Surprisingly, he felt more at ease after that, and when he took his regular walk along the side of the quarterdeck there was nothing to betray the fear that he had almost lost his confidence.

Bolitho saw *Styx*'s first lieutenant cross to the compass and glance at it before studying each sail in turn.

Nothing was said, nor was there need. The professionals in the frigate's company knew their ship like they knew each other. Any comment from Pickthorn that the wind had backed another point would have been resented by the master, and judged by Neale to be a display of nerves.

Bolitho had seen it all before, and had endured it too. He walked aft again, watching the colour spreading across the sea and its endless parade of white-horses. Salt stung his mouth and cheeks but he barely noticed it. He stared towards *Phalarope* as she plunged obediently to windward, squarely on *Styx*'s starboard quarter. She looked splendid, with her closed gunports making a chequered line along her side. The gilded figurehead was bright in the early sunlight, and he could just make out a knot of blue figures on her quarterdeck. One of them would be Adam, he thought. Like Pickthorn, watching over his sails, ready to order men here or there to keep each piece of canvas filled and hard to the wind. *Phalarope* was heeling heavily towards him, pushed over by the press of sails and the occasional steep crest under her keel.

How this ship must look.

Bolitho turned and walked down to the quarterdeck rail again. The gun crews were still at their stations, the tension gone as daylight laid bare an empty sea. The second and third lieutenants were chatting together, swords sheathed, their attitudes of men at ease in a park.

Neale was moving his telescope across the larboard nettings, studying the undulating, slate-coloured slopes of the mainland. They were standing some five miles out, but many eyes would have seen them.

Neale tossed his glass to a midshipman and commented glumly, 'Not a damn thing.'

Browne joined Bolitho by the rail. 'She's really flying, sir.'

Bolitho looked at him and smiled. Browne was more stirred by the lively ship beneath him as she lifted and plunged through the white-horses than he was troubled by the inaction.

'Yes. My nephew will have his hands full but will enjoy

every second, no doubt.'

'I don't envy him *that*, sir!' Browne was careful never to mention *Phalarope*'s captain. 'A raw company, lieutenants no more than boys, I'll be content with my duties here!'

Bundy called, 'Mist ahead, sir!'

Neale grunted. He had seen it already, seeping low down like pale smoke. The fact the master had mentioned it implied he was troubled. In a moment or so the lookouts would see the southern headland of the Loire Estuary. After that, the next report would be sighting the Ile d'Yeu. Right back where they had started, except that they were much closer inshore.

He looked over at Bolitho, who stood with his hands behind his back, his legs apart to take the deck's uneven roll. *He will never turn back. Not in a thousand years.*

Neale felt strangely sorry for Bolitho at this moment. Disturbed that what had started as a daring piece of strategy had seemingly gone wrong.

'Deck there! Sails on the larboard bow!'

Neale climbed into the shrouds and beckoned urgently for his telescope.

Bolitho folded his arms across his chest, certain that if he did not everyone around him would see them shaking with anxiety.

The mist dipped and swirled as the wind found it and drove it inshore. And there they were, like a phalanx of Roman soldiers on the march, six lines of small vessels under sail. In the bright glare even the pendants and ensigns looked stiff, like lances.

Browne breathed out slowly. 'In daylight there look even more of them.'

Bolitho nodded, his lips suddenly like dust. The fleet of small vessels was making hard going of it, tacking back and forth in an effort to retain formation and to gain some progress against the wind.

Neale exclaimed, 'What will they do now? Scatter and run?'

Bolitho said, 'Make more sail, Captain Neale, every stitch you can carry, and let us not give the enemy a chance to decide!'

He turned and saw Browne smiling broadly while men dashed past him to obey the shrill pipe to loose more canvas. The great studding-sails would be run out on either beam like huge ears to carry them faster and still faster towards the mass of slow-moving hulls.

Across the starboard quarter Bolitho saw *Phalarope's* pyramid of pale canvas tilt more steeply as she followed suit, and he thought he could hear the scrape of a fiddle as her seamen were urged to greater efforts to keep station on the rear-admiral's flag.

Midshipman Kilburne, who had managed to keep his glass trained on the other frigate in spite of the bustle around him, called, 'From *Phalarope*, sir! *Sail to the nor'-west!*'

Neale barely turned. 'That'll be *Rapid*, most likely.'

Bolitho gripped the rail as the ship slid deeply beneath him. The decks were running with spray, as if it was pouring rain, and some of the bare-backed gun crews looked drenched as *Styx* plunged towards the widening array of vessels.

The bearing would be right for *Rapid*. She must have found *Sparrowhawk* and was coming to join the fight. He bit his lip. Slaughter, more likely.

'Load and run out, if you please. We will engage on either beam.'

Bolitho tugged out his watch and opened the guard. Exactly eight in the morning. Even as the thought touched him the bells chimed out from the forecastle. Even there, a ship's boy had managed to remember his part of the pattern which made a ship work.

'The enemy is dividing into two flotillas, sir.' Pickthorn shook his head. 'They'll not outrun us now, and there are only rocks or the beach beyond them!' Even he sounded dismayed at the enemy's helplessness.

Kilburne jammed the big signals telescope against his eye until the pain made it water. Bolitho was barely two feet from him and he did not want to disturb his thoughts by making a stupid mistake. He blinked hard and tried again, seeing *Phalarope*'s iron-hard canvas swoop across the lens, the bright hoist of flags at her yard.

He was not mistaken. Shakily he called, 'From *Phalarope*, sir. She's made *Rapid*'s number.'

Bolitho turned. It was common practice for one ship to repeat another's signal, but something in the midshipman's tone warned him of sudden danger.

'From *Rapid*, sir. *Enemy in sight to the nor'-west!*'

Browne murmured softly, 'Hell's teeth!'

'Any orders, sir?' Neale looked at Bolitho, his face and eyes calm. As if he already knew, and accepted it.

Bolitho shook his head. 'We will attack. Alter course to larboard and head off any of the leaders who try to break past us.'

He turned on his heel as once again the men dashed to the braces and halliards, most of them oblivious to the menace hidden below the horizon.

Allday pushed himself away from the nettings and strode deliberately to Bolitho's side.

Bolitho eyed him thoughtfully. 'Well, perhaps you were right after all, old friend. But there's no getting round it.'

Allday stared past him towards the converging array of sails and low hulls, hating what he saw, what it might cost.

But he said simply, 'We'll dish 'em up, sir. One way or the other.'

Some muskets and a few swivels crackled from the leading vessels, their puny challenge blanketed by the roar of *Styx*'s first broadside.

Neale cupped his hands. 'Mr Pickthorn! Shorten sail! Get the royals and t'gan's'ls off her!' He watched as the studding-sail booms were hauled bodily inboard to their yards, men calling to one another as guns crashed out and recoiled below them, and a few musket balls and enemy canister scythed wickedly between the shrouds.

Bolitho said, 'Mr Browne. Make to *Phalarope*. *Engage the enemy.*'

There was still time. With *Styx* riding astride the channel to part and scatter the enemy's neat columns, *Phalarope*'s massive armament of carronades would demolish the van and centre and give them room to beat clear and join *Rapid* to seaward. But *Phalarope* was already making another signal.

Midshipman Kilburne shouted in between the explosions from each battery, 'Repeated from *Rapid*, sir! *Estimate three enemy sail to the nor'-west.*' His lips moved painfully as the gun below the quarterdeck rail crashed inboard on its tackles, its crew already darting around it with fresh powder and shot. He continued, '*Estimate one ship of the line.*'

Allday's palm rasped over his jaw. 'Is that all?'

As if to add to the torment, the masthead lookout yelled, 'Deck there! Land on th' starboard bow!'

Bundy nodded, his eyes like stones. The Ile d'Yeu. Like the lower jaw of a great trap.

Pickthorn dropped his speaking trumpet as his topmen came swarming down the ratlines again. '*Phalarope*'s shortening sail, sir.'

Bolitho glanced up at *Styx*'s last hoist of flags. His order to Captain Emes to close with the enemy formation and engage them.

He heard Browne snap angrily, 'Has she not *seen* the signal, Mr Kilburne?'

Kilburne lowered his glass only to reply. 'She has acknowledged it, sir.'

Browne looked at Bolitho, his face white with disbelief. '*Acknowledged!*'

Canister screamed over the quarterdeck and punched the hammock nettings like invisible fists.

A marine dropped to his knees, blood pouring from his face, as two of his comrades dragged him to safety. Their first casualty.

A blazing lugger, ungainly and out of command, with flames darting from weapon ports like red tongues, passed dangerously down the larboard side, where the boatswain and his men waited with water buckets and axes to quench any outbreak of fire in the tarred rigging and vulnerable canvas.

Neale said flatly, '*Phalarope* is not responding, sir.'

'Signal *Phalarope* to *make more sail*.' Bolitho felt some of the men watching him, still unwilling or unable to believe what was happening.

'She's acknowledged, sir.'

It was almost impossible to think with guns firing and the decks filled with choking smoke.

Bolitho looked at Neale. If he broke off the action now and abandoned the enemy, they could come about and with luck fight clear. If not, *Styx* could not hope to destroy more than a handful of vessels, and only then at the cost of her own people.

He stared at the other frigate as she fell further and further astern, until his eyes and mind throbbed with pain and anger.

Browne had been right from the beginning. Now there was no chance left, and it was certainly not worth losing a whole ship and her company.

He cleared his throat and said, 'Discontinue the action, Captain Neale. Bring her about. It is finished.'

Neale stared at him, his face filled with dismay.

'But, sir, we can still hit them! Single-handed if we must!'

The masthead lookout's voice shattered the sudden silence even as the guns ceased firing.

'Deck there! Three sail in sight to the nor'-west.'

Bolitho felt as if the whole ship had been stricken. No one moved, and some hands on the forecastle who had cheered the last order, believing it to be the signal of their victory, now peered aft like old men.

Perhaps the lookouts, good though they were, had been distracted by the oncoming mass of small vessels, and then the menace of larger ships hull-up on the horizon, but whatever the reason, they did not see the real danger until it was already upon them.

It fell to one of Neale's leadsmen as he took up his station in the chains as *Styx* had headed towards the same shallow channel to scream, 'Wreck! Dead ahead!'

Bolitho gripped the rail and watched as the men near him broke from their trance and stampeded to obey the cry to shorten sail still further, while others strained at the braces to haul round the yards and change tack.

It was possibly one of the very craft they had sunk the previous day, drifting waterlogged with wind and tide until it found its destroyer. Or it might have been an older wreck, some stubborn survivor from the chain of reefs and sandbars which guarded the Loire's approaches like sentinels.

The shock when it came was not sudden. It seemed unending as the frigate drove on and over the hulk, her frames shaking, until with the crashing roar of an avalanche the main and fore masts thundered down across the forecastle and into the sea. Great coils of trailing shrouds and splintered spars followed, while men shrieked and cursed as they were smashed underneath or dragged bodily over the side by the tendrils of runaway rigging.

Only the mizzen remained standing, Bolitho's flag still flapping above the destruction and death as if to mark the place for all time. Then as the wreck tore free from *Styx*'s keel and giant air bubbles exploded obscenely on either beam, it too swayed and then plunged headlong to the gundeck.

Neale yelled, 'Mr Pickthorn!' Then he faltered, aware of the blood on his hand which had run down from his scalp, and of his loyal first lieutenant who had been cut in half by one of the broken shrouds as it had ripped over him with the whole weight of the topmast stretching it like a wire.

He saw Bolitho as Allday aided him to his feet and gasped, 'She's done for!'

Then he swayed and would have fallen but for Bundy and one of the midshipmen.

Bolitho said harshly, 'Clear the lower decks. Get as many wounded from the wreckage as you can.' He heard the growl of water surging through the hull, the squeal of trucks as a gun broke free and careered across the deck. 'Mr Kilburne, muster all available hands and launch what boats have survived. Mr Browne, stay with the captain.'

Men were lurching out of the piles of fallen debris, confused, frightened, and some half mad as they ran blindly to the gangways.

A few marines tried to restore order, and Bolitho saw the third lieutenant, probably the only surviving one, pushed aside, his arm broken and useless, as he attempted to restrain them.

The deck gave another shudder, and Bolitho saw water seeping through some gunports as the hull tilted still further, dragged down by the great burden of wreckage alongside.

Allday shouted, 'The quarter-boat is being warped round, sir.' He looked dangerously calm, and his cutlass was in his fist.

Bundy seized his chronometer and sextant, but found time to report, 'I've got some 'ands lashing a raft together, sir.'

Bolitho barely heard him. He was staring over the broad stretch of water with its freedom somehow symbolized by the white-capped waves which stretched towards the horizon and the oncoming pyramid of sails.

Then he saw *Phalarope*, stern on as she braced her yards hard round, her shadow leaning over the creaming water while she went about, her gilded bird pointing away from him, away from the enemy.

Allday said brokenly, '*God damn him! God damn his cowardly soul!*'

A boat appeared at the tilting gangway, and another was being pulled down the side, the boatswain and a burly gunner's mate hauling wounded and drowning men from the water and dropping them on the bottom boards like sodden bales.

Neale opened his eyes and asked huskily, 'Are they safe?' He seemed to see Bolitho through the blood on his face. 'The people?'

Bolitho nodded. 'As many as possible, so rest easy.'

He looked at the widening array of makeshift rafts, floating spars and casks to which the survivors clung and waited for a miracle. Many more floundered in the sea itself, but few sailors could swim, and soon many of them gave up the fight and drifted on the tide with the rest of the flotsam.

Bolitho waited for a few more dazed and bleeding men to be dragged into the quarter-boat, then he climbed in and stood beside Allday, with Neale slumped unconscious between them.

Midshipman Kilburne, who had changed from youth to manhood in the last few moments, called, 'Stand quietly, lads! Easy, all!'

Like the other boat, this one was so crammed with men it had barely ten inches of freeboard. Each had run out just two oars to keep them stem on to the waves, which such a short while before had been their allies, and now seemed determined to capsize and kill them.

'*She's going!*'

Several men cried out, shocked and horrified, as *Styx* rolled over and began to slide into the water. Some of the older hands watched her in silence, moved and too stunned to share their sense of loss. Like all ships, she meant much more to the seasoned hands. A home, old faces, familiar ways. Those too were gone for ever.

Browne whispered, 'I'll not forget this. Not ever.'

Styx dived, but the sea was so shallow that she struck the bottom and reappeared as if still fighting for life. Water streamed from her gunports and scuppers, and a few corpses, caught in the broken shrouds, swayed about as if waving to their old shipmates.

Then with a final lurch she dived and stayed hidden.

Allday said dully, 'Boats shoving from the shore, sir.'

He sensed Bolitho's complete despair and added firmly, 'We've bin prisoners afore, sir. We'll get through this time, an' that's no error.'

Bolitho was looking for the *Phalarope*. But, like Neale's ship, she had disappeared. It was over.

6

Ready for Sea

Thomas Herrick, acting-commodore, sat with his elbows on the polished table in *Benbow*'s great cabin and ran his eyes once more over his painstakingly worded report.

He should have been proud of what he had achieved, when even the most optimistic shipwrights and carpenters had prophesied that his ship would be another month at least undergoing repairs. Tomorrow was the first day of August, far ahead of anything he had dared to hope.

Those words he had waited impatiently to write in his report to their lordships – *Being in all respects ready for sea, etc, etc* – were right there, waiting for his signature, and yet he could summon little jubilation or enthusiasm.

It was not the news, but the lack of it. He suspected it had all started when the shot-torn frigate *Unrivalled*, one of Bolitho's new squadron in the Bay, had anchored in Plymouth, her pumps clanking to keep her afloat until help arrived. Even then it should not have upset Herrick more than any other such wartime event. He had seen too many ships go, too many dead and wounded being landed as were the *Unrivalled*'s casualties, to display his inner and private emotions.

But ever since Bolitho had shifted his flag to *Styx*, and had sailed away on what Herrick had considered to be a very doubtful mission, he had been troubled.

Phalarope's name in the signal book, and the bald announcement that she was being appointed to Bolitho's command, had done little to ease his apprehension. Dulcie, who was ever near and staying at the Golden Lion Inn in Plymouth, had done everything to comfort him. Herrick's mouth softened at the thought. It made him feel almost guilty to be so lucky. But Dulcie did not understand the ways of the sea or the Navy. If he had any say in it, nor would she, Herrick had firmly decided.

He heard footsteps in the adjoining cabin. Ozzard, Bolitho's servant, like a lost soul since his master had gone without him. There were several like him in *Benbow*'s fat hull. Yovell, Bolitho's clerk, who had written this report in his round hand. Round, like the man and his Devonshire accent.

The deck moved very slightly, and Herrick stood up to walk to the open stern windows. There were fewer ships being repaired now, less din of hammers and creaking tackles aboard the masting-craft.

He could see Keen's seventy-four, *Nicator*, swinging to her cable, her awnings and windsails spread to make life between decks as easy as possible in this sultry heat. And *Indomitable*, their other two-decker, whose new captain, Henry Veriker, had already made something of a reputation for himself in the small squadron. He was almost deaf, an injury inflicted at the Nile, common enough after hours of continuous firing. But his deafness came and went, so that you were never sure what he had heard or misinterpreted. It must be difficult for his lieutenants, Herrick thought. It had been bad enough on the one night they had dined together.

He leaned over the sill and saw the new frigate, the one he had seen shortly after her launching when he had rejoined his own ship. Lower in the water, a black muzzle at each open port, and all three masts and standing rigging set up. Not long now, my beauty. Who was her lucky captain to be, he wondered?

Seeing the new frigate reminded him yet again of Adam Pascoe. Young devil to take the appointment without a thought of what it could mean. *Phalarope*. Bolitho had *made* that ship, given her life. But Herrick still remembered her as she had been when he had stepped aboard as her junior lieutenant. Bitter and desperate, with a captain who had looked upon any sort of humanity as a sin.

He heard the sentry's muffled voice and turned to see the first lieutenant striding beneath the deckhead beams, bent right over to save his ginger head from a collision.

'Yes, Mr Wolfe?'

Wolfe's deepset eyes flitted briefly to the written report and back to his captain. He had worked harder than most, but had still found time to knock some sense into his youthful and barely trained lieutenants.

'Message from the officer of the guard, sir. You can expect the port admiral in half an hour.' He bared his uneven teeth. 'I've already passed the word, sir. Full side party an' guard of honour.'

Herrick considered the news. The port admiral, a rare visitor. But what he had seen he had liked. A portly, comfortable man, now better used to the ways of dockyards and chandlers than to a fleet at sea.

He replied, 'Very well. I don't think there's anything to fear. We've even beaten Captain Keen's *Nicator* to a state of readiness, eh?'

'Orders, d'you think, sir?'

Herrick felt uneasy at the prospect. He had not even had time to select himself a flag-captain for, no matter how temporarily his broad-pendant might fly above *Benbow*, select one he must. Maybe it was too final, he thought. Severing the last link with his rear-admiral and true friend when he still knew nothing of what was happening.

More feet clattered, and after the marine's announcement from the outer lobby, the fifth lieutenant stepped smartly inside, his cocked hat jammed beneath one arm.

Wolfe scowled at him and the youth flinched. Actually, the first lieutenant was quite pleased with the young officer, but it was far too early to show it. Wait until we get to sea, he usually said.

'A — a letter, sir. From the Falmouth coach.'

Herrick almost snatched it from him. 'Good. Carry on, Mr Nash.'

As the lieutenant fled, and Wolfe settled himself in another chair, Herrick slit open the envelope. He knew the handwriting, and although he had been hoping for a letter, he had been dreading what she might say.

Wolfe watched him curiously. He knew most of it, and had guessed the rest. But he had come to accept the captain's strange attachment for Richard Bolitho, even if he did not fully understand it. To Wolfe, a friend at sea was like a ship. You gave to each other, but once parted it was best to forget and never go back.

Herrick put down the letter carefully, imagining her chestnut hair falling over her forehead as she had written it.

He said abruptly, 'Mrs Belinda Laidlaw is coming to Plymouth. My wife will take good care of her during her visit.'

Wolfe was vaguely disappointed. 'Is that all, sir?'

Herrick stared at him. It was true. She had sent her warmest greetings to him and to Dulcie, but there it had ended. But it was a step in the right direction. Once here, amidst Bolitho's world, she would feel free to speak, to ask his advice if she ever needed it.

Voices echoed alongside and Wolfe snatched up his hat and exploded, 'The admiral! We forgot all about *him*!'

Breathing heavily, and grasping their swords to their sides to avoid being tripped, the stocky captain and his lanky first lieutenant ran for the quarterdeck.

Admiral Sir Cornelius Hoskyn, Knight of the Bath, hauled himself up to and through the entry port, and in spite of his portliness was not even breathless as he doffed his hat to the quarterdeck and waited patiently for the marine fifers to complete a rendering of *Heart of Oak* for his benefit.

He had a warm, fruity voice and a complexion as pink as a petticoat, Herrick thought. A man who always had time to listen to any visiting captain and do his best for him.

The admiral glanced up at the flapping broad-pendant and

remarked, 'I was glad to hear about *that*.' He nodded to the assembled lieutenants and added, 'Your ship does you credit. Ready to sail soon, what?'

Herrick was about to say that his readiness report only needed his signature but the admiral had already moved on towards the shade of the poop.

Behind him trooped his flag-lieutenant, secretary, and two servants with what appeared to be a case of wine.

In the great cabin the admiral arranged himself carefully in a chair, while his staff busied themselves, with Herrick's servant's guidance, laying out goblets and wine cooler.

'This the report?' The admiral dragged a minute pair of spectacles from his heavy dress coat and peered at it. 'Sign it now, if you please.' In the same breath he added, 'Good, I hope that glass is cool, man!' as he took some wine from one of his minions.

Herrick sat down as the lieutenant and secretary retreated from the cabin, the latter clutching Herrick's sealed report like a talisman.

'Now.' Sir Cornelius Hoskyn regarded Herrick searchingly over the top of his spectacles. 'You will receive your orders, possibly tonight. When I leave I shall expect you to call your other captains to conference, prepare them for sailing without further dalliance. Short-handed or not, leaking, I don't care, it is *their* problem. Some say peace will soon be upon us, pray God it is so, but until I am convinced otherwise, the state of war still exists.' He had not even raised his voice, and yet his words seemed to echo around the sunlit cabin like pistol shots.

'But with all respect, Sir Cornelius,' Herrick was out of his depth but persisted 'my ships are still under the command of Rear-Admiral Bolitho, and you will of course be aware that—'

The admiral eyed him gravely and then deliberately refilled their goblets.

'I have the greatest respect for you, Herrick, for that reason I came to do a task I hate more than any other.' His tone softened. 'Please, drink some more wine. It is from my own cellar.'

Herrick swallowed the wine without noticing it. It could have been pump water.

'Sir?'

'I have just received news by special courier. I must tell you that ten days ago, whilst apparently attempting to destroy enemy shipping south of the Loire Estuary, His Britannic Majesty's frigate *Styx* was wrecked and became a total loss. It happened quickly and in a rising wind.' He paused, watching Herrick's face. 'And due to the arrival of several enemy vessels, including a ship of the line, the attack was discontinued.'

Herrick asked quietly, 'Our other vessels *withdrew*, sir?'

'There was only one of any consequence, and her captain, as senior officer present, made the decision. I am terribly sorry to have to tell you. I have heard what your particular friendship meant.'

Herrick stood up as if he had been struck. '*Meant?* You mean . . .'

'There could not have been many survivors, but of course we can always hope.'

Herrick clenched his fists and strode blindly to the stern windows.

'He often said it would be like that.' He asked harshly, 'Who was the other captain, sir?' In his heart he already knew.

'Emes of the *Phalarope*.'

Herrick could not face him. Poor Adam must have seen it happen, while that bloody coward Emes took to his heels.

Another thought made him exclaim, 'My God, sir, she's coming here from Falmouth!' The words tumbled out of him. 'The girl he was to marry! What shall I tell her?'

The admiral rose to his feet. 'I think it best that you go about your duties and try to lose yourself in them. It has been common enough in this everlasting war. But you never get used to it, nor will I try to console you, when I know there *is* no consolation. If I hear more I shall let you know as soon as possible.'

Herrick followed him to the broad quarterdeck, only partly aware of what was happening.

When his mind eventually cleared, the admiral's barge had left the side, and Wolfe faced him to ask permission to dismiss the guard and side party.

'Will you tell me, sir?' His hard, flat voice was somehow steadying.

'Richard Bolitho, the *Styx*, all gone.'

Wolfe swung round, shielding him from the others.

'Right then, you laggards! Move your lazy carcasses or I'll have the bosun use his rattan on your rumps!'

Herrick returned to the cabin and slumped down in a chair. The ship, his broad-pendant, even his new-found happiness meant nothing.

Wolfe reappeared at the screen door. 'Orders, sir?'

'Aye, there are always those, Mr Wolfe. Make a signal to *Nicator* and *Indomitable*. *Captains repair on board*.' He shook his head helplessly. 'It can wait. Sit you down and have some of the admiral's wine. He says it is very good.'

Wolfe replied, 'Later I'll be glad to. But I have certain duties to deal with. I'll make that signal at eight bells, sir. Time enough then.'

Outside the cabin Wolfe almost fell over the tiny shape of Ozzard. God, the man had been weeping. Everyone must know already. Always the same in the Navy. No damn secrets.

Wolfe paused in the sunlight and took several deep breaths. He had no special duties, but it was more than he could do to sit and watch Herrick's anguish. The fact he could do nothing for a man he had come to respect so much troubled him deeply, and he could not recall ever feeling so useless.

In the cabin Herrick poured himself another goblet of wine, then another. It did not help, but it was something to do.

His hand paused in mid air as his glance settled on the sword rack and the presentation sword which Bolitho had left behind when he had gone over to *Styx*.

It was a beautiful piece of craftsmanship. But not much to show for the man who had earned it a hundred times over.

Herrick climbed out of the *Benbow*'s green-painted barge and waited for his coxswain to join him on the jetty.

He was later, much later, than he had intended in getting ashore. There was a dusky red glow over the Sound and anchorage, and the ships looked at peace on the flat water.

Herrick had sent a message to his wife, telling her as much as he could. She was a sensible woman and rarely lost her self-control. But Herrick had meant to be with her when the Falmouth coach rolled in.

'Return to the ship, Tuck. I'll get a wherry when I return. Mr Wolfe knows where I am.'

The coxswain touched his hat. He knew all about it but was thinking more of Allday than Bolitho. As coxswains they had come to know each other well, and got along together.

'Aye, aye, sir.'

'And, Tuck, if there is any rumour through the lower deck . . .'

Tuck nodded. 'Aye, sir, I *know*. I'll be across 'ere so fast the keel won't touch the water.'

Herrick strode along the jetty, his shoes clicking on the round, worn cobbles which had felt the tread of a legion of seafaring men as far back as Drake, and further still.

Herrick paused, unnerved, as he saw the Golden Lion, its windows glowing red in the sunset, as if the whole building were ablaze. In the yard a coach stood empty, abandoned by its team of horses, a servant or two loading boxes on its roof for the next leg to Exeter.

It was bad enough as it was, but for the coach to be on time, even early on this particular evening, made it worse.

He saw a one-legged man, balanced on a crude crutch,

playing a tin whistle to the amusement of some urchins and a few passers-by. His shabby red coat showed he had once been a marine, the darker patch on one sleeve where the chevrons had once been sewn told Herrick he had also been a sergeant.

Herrick fumbled for some coins in his pocket and thrust them at the crippled figure. He was ashamed and embarrassed, angry too that such a man could end like this. If peace did eventually come, there would be many more red coats begging in the streets.

But the man did not seem at all perturbed. He gave a broad grin and touched his forehead with mock smartness.

'Sar'nt Tolcher, sir. This is the life, eh, Cap'n?'

Herrick nodded sadly. 'What ship, Sergeant?'

'Last one, sir? The old *Culloden*, Cap'n Troubridge, a real gennelman 'e was, for a sea-officer, that's to say.'

Herrick needed to go, but something held him. This unknown marine had been at the Nile when he and Bolitho had been there. Another ship, but *there*.

'Good luck to you.' Herrick hurried away towards the entrance.

The marine pocketed the money, aware that his small audience had gone. But the stocky captain with the bright blue eyes had made up for a lot.

Down to the Volunteer now for a few pots of ale with the lads.

His crutch scraping over the cobbles, the crippled marine, one-time sergeant in the *Culloden*, was soon lost from sight.

Both women were facing the door as Herrick entered their room, as if they had been there for hours.

He said, 'I am sorry, Dulcie, I was detained. Fresh orders.'

He did not see the sudden anxiety in his wife's eyes for he was looking at the girl who was standing by an unlit fire.

God, she is beautiful. She was dressed in a dark green gown, her chestnut hair tied back to the nape of her neck by a matching ribbon. She looked pale, her brown eyes filling her face as she asked, 'Any news, Thomas?'

Herrick was moved both by her control and the easy use of his name.

He replied, 'Not yet.' He walked to a small table, picked up a glass and put it down again. 'But news travels slowly, *good* news that is.'

He walked across to her and took her hands in his. Against his hard seaman's hands they felt soft and gentle. Helpless.

She said quietly, 'Dulcie told me what you wrote in your note. And I heard something about the loss of the ship from some officers downstairs. Is there any hope?'

Her eyes lifted to his. They made her outward calm a lie. Her eyes were pleading with him.

Herrick said, 'We know very little at present. It's a foul bit of coast there, and as far as I can discover, *Styx* foundered after hitting something, possibly a wreck, and went down immediately.'

Herrick had gone over it a hundred times, even while he had been explaining his orders to the other captains. He knew well enough what it would have been like. Herrick had lost a command of his own. He could hear the din of falling spars, the screams, the pandemonium of a well-ordered ship falling apart. Men swimming and dying. Some going bravely, others cursing their mothers' names until the sea silenced them.

'But your Richard was in good company. Allday would be at his side, and young Neale was a first-rate captain.'

She looked quickly at the other woman. 'Who will tell his nephew?'

Herrick released her hands very gently. 'No need for that. He was there. Aboard the ship which—' He caught the words in time. 'In *Phalarope*. She was in company at the time.'

Dulcie Herrick touched her breast. 'Bless the boy.'

'Aye. He'll take it badly.'

Belinda Laidlaw sat down for the first time since she had left the coach.

'Captain Herrick.' She tried to smile. '*Thomas*, for you are his friend, and now mine too, I hope. What do *you* think happened?'

Herrick felt his wife place a glass in his hand and eyed her warmly.

Then he said, 'Richard has always been a frigate captain at heart. He would want to go for the enemy, waste no time. But as the rear-admiral in total command he had other responsibilities this day. To execute Admiral Beauchamp's plan to help rid England of a mounting threat of invasion. It was his task, his duty.' He looked at her imploringly. 'God, ma'am, if you knew how he cared, what it cost him to put to sea without seeing you, without explaining. The last time I saw him he was fretting about it, the unfairness to you.' He added firmly, 'But if you know Richard, really know him, you will understand that to him honour and love are as one.'

She nodded, her lips moist. 'That I do know. I will have it no other way. We met only last year, merely months ago, of which time I have been with him just a few days. How I envy you, Thomas, sharing things with him, looking back on memories I shall never know.' She shook her head, her hair tossing over one shoulder. 'I will never give him up, Thomas. Not now.'

Tears ran unheeded down her cheeks, but when Herrick and his wife moved towards her she said, 'No. I am all right! I do not intend to lose myself in self-pity now that Richard needs me.'

Herrick stared at her. 'That warms me deeply, ma'am. But do not destroy yourself for hoping too much, promise me.'

'Too much?' She walked to the open windows and stepped out on to the balcony, her slim figure framed against the sea and sky. 'Impossible. He is what I live for. There is nothing more I care about, dear friend.'

Herrick felt his wife's hand in his and squeezed it gently. Belinda was like a ship caught aback by a fierce squall. Only time would tell.

He looked at his wife as she whispered, 'You spoke of orders, Thomas?'

'Forgive me, dearest. With all this on my mind . . .' He looked at the window as the girl re-entered the room. 'I have been ordered to sail with a merchant convoy to Gibraltar. Several valuable cargoes, I understand, and a rich prize at any time.'

He recalled his dismay and fury at being sent on a convoy when he *needed* to be here. Admiral Hoskyn had spoken of his respect for him. But if he refused to accept this first duty as acting-commodore, not respect, love, even a knighthood would save him. The Navy had a long, long memory.

He added, 'It will be a safe if wearisome task, and I shall be back in Plymouth before you know it.' It was only half a lie, and came easier than he had expected.

Belinda touched his sleeve. 'Will the ships come here?'

'Aye. Two from Bristol and the others from the Downs.'

She nodded her head, her eyes very bright. 'I shall take passage in one of them. I have some friends in Gibraltar. With friends and money I might be able to discover some news of Richard.'

Herrick opened his mouth to protest but shut it as he saw Dulcie give a brief shake of the head. It was true that more information had been gleaned from Spain and Portugal about dead or missing officers than through accepted sources, but her sincerity, her incredible belief that Richard Bolitho was alive and safe would leave her vulnerable, and a long way from help if the worst happened.

'One is an Indiaman, the *Duchess of Cornwall*. I believe you had some contact with John Company in India. I am certain they will make you as comfortable as they can. I will send her master a letter.' He forced a grin. 'Being a commodore *must* have some uses!'

She smiled gravely. 'Thank you. You are good to me. I only wish I could sail with you instead.'

Herrick flushed. 'Lord, ma'am, with all the roughknots and gallows'-bait I have to carry as my company, I'd not rest easy in my cot!'

She tossed her hair from her shoulder. No wonder Bolitho was completely captivated, Herrick thought.

She said, 'At least I shall see your ship every day, Thomas.

I will not feel so alone.'

Dulcie took her hand in hers. 'You will never be *that*, my dear.'

Herrick heard a clock chime and cursed it silently.

'I have to leave.' He looked at the girl in the green gown. 'You will have to get used to this too.' He was deceiving her. Or was he gaining some of her courage, her belief?

Outside in the cooler evening air everything looked much as before. Herrick glanced at the street corner, half hoping to see the one-legged marine there.

At the jetty he saw the barge riding motionless in shadow, then the oars swinging into life as she headed towards him.

Herrick gripped his sword tightly and wished his eyes would stop stinging. Tuck would no more let him take a waterman's boat than spit on the flag.

Between them, Tuck and the beautiful girl with the chestnut hair had given him a new strength, although deep inside him he knew he would probably pay dearly for it. But that was tomorrow. This was now.

He tapped his scabbard on the worn cobbles and said half to himself, 'Hold on, Richard! We're not done yet!'

'You wish to see me, sir?' Lieutenant Adam Pascoe stood in the centre of the cabin, his eyes on a point above the captain's right epaulette.

Emes sat back in his chair, his fingertips pressed together. 'I do.'

Beyond the screen and the darkened stern windows it was quiet but for the muffled sounds of sea and wind, the regular creak of timbers.

Emes said, 'It is five days since *Styx* foundered. Tomorrow it will be six. I do not intend to go through another hour, let alone a day, with you saying nothing but the briefest words demanded of your duties. You are my first lieutenant, an honoured appointment for one so young. But perhaps you are *too* young after all?'

Pascoe looked at him squarely. 'I can't understand! How could you do it? How could you leave them to die like that?'

'Keep your voice down, Mr Pascoe, and address me as *sir* at all times.'

Tap . . . tap . . . tap . . . his fingers touched each other very gently and exactly.

'The attack on those French vessels was pointless, once the presence of larger men-of-war was realized. This is a very *old* frigate, Mr Pascoe, not a *liner*!'

Pascoe dropped his gaze, his hands shaking so that he had to press them against his thighs to control himself. He had thought about it, dreamt about it, and never lost it since that terrible moment. If his uncle had died, it would not be death he would have feared. But the sight of the *Phalarope*, the ship he had once loved, going about to leave him and his men to drown or to perish from their wounds, would have been the worst part for him.

Emes was saying in his usual controlled tones, 'If your uncle had not been aboard *Styx*, you might have felt differently. You are too involved, too close to accept the facts. *Styx* had no chance. My first responsibility was to this ship, and as senior officer to take control of the remainder of our strength. A brave but pointless gesture would get no thanks from the Admiralty, nor from the widows you would create if you had your way. I am satisfied with your duties up to a point. But if I have cause to admonish you again, I will see you stand before a court martial, do you understand?'

Pascoe blurted out hotly, 'Do you think I care about—'

'*Then you should!*' Both hands came down on the table with a bang. 'From what I have heard, your uncle's family has a proud name, am I right?'

Pascoe nodded jerkily. 'He has done everything for me. Everything.'

'Quite so.' Emes relaxed very slowly. 'You are of that family, the same blood.'

'Yes, sir.'

'Then remember this. You may be the last of the Bolitho

family.' He held up one hand as Pascoe made to protest. 'You *may* be. Just as I am the last in mine. When you return home, others will be looking to you. There is more at stake now than your despair. Hate me if you will, but do your duty well — that is all I ask, no, *demand*!'

'May I go, sir?'

Emes looked down at his hands and waited for the door to close behind the young lieutenant with the unruly black hair. Then he touched his forehead and looked at his palm. It was wet with sweat, and he felt dirty and sick.

It was not over, and he knew that it would take more than time to heal it. Pascoe would not let it lie there, and in his despair might destroy everything.

Emes picked up his pen and stared emptily at his log book. He had been right, he *knew* he had been right, and he must make the others recognize the fact.

Would the nightmare never end? The accusations and the contempt he had been shown by those who had never heard a shot fired or known the agony of a captain's worst decision.

Those same unknown inquisitors would condemn him outright. To be given a chance, and then allow his admiral to be lost without some personal sacrifice could have no defence in their eyes.

He glanced round the cabin, remembering Bolitho here, how he must have felt aboard his old command after all this time. If he needed further reminder of that meeting he only had to look at his first lieutenant, it was stark and clear in his eyes.

In his neat hand he began to write. *Today's patrol passed without further incident* . . .

7

The Secret

Singly and in groups, defiant, or dazed to the point of collapse, the survivors from Neale's command staggered up the shelving beach which in the time it had taken to reach it had been ringed by a cordon of armed soldiers.

Almost the worst part of it was the complete silence. The bewildered sailors lay or squatted on the wet sand and stared not at their captors but at the lively water where their ship had once been. Others walked dejectedly in the shallows, peering at the flotsam, searching for a swimmer amongst the drifting corpses while the gulls hovered eagerly overhead.

Further along the beach a few women were tending to some other survivors. A handful of seamen from one of the invasion craft which *Styx* had sunk before she too had foundered. They glared at the growing crowd of British sailors, showing a hatred which even the distance and the line of soldiers could not hide.

Bolitho watched the boats pulling off shore, fishermen mostly, hastily commandeered by the local military to search for the living, friend and foe alike.

Neale groaned and tried to get to his feet. 'How many?'

Allday replied, 'Hundred, maybe more. Can't be sure.'

Neale fell back and stared dazedly at the blue sky. 'Less than half, dear God!'

Browne, who had somehow managed to retain his hat during the pull to the beach, asked, 'What happens now? I am somewhat unused to this.'

Bolitho held his head back and allowed the sun to penetrate the ache in his eyes and brain. *Prisoners*. Somewhere on the enemy coast. Because of his own folly.

He said shortly, 'Go amongst the others. Call a muster.'

He saw *Styx*'s surgeon on his knees beside a spreadeagled seaman. Thank heaven *he* had survived. Some of the men looked in a bad way.

The three midshipmen had all lived through it, as had the youthful third lieutenant, although he was barely conscious, and delirious with his shattered arm. Bundy, the master, the boatswain too, and one or two marines, although most of the afterguard had been swept away when the mizzen had crashed amongst them. As Neale had said, less than half. In the twinkling of an eye.

Bolitho shaded his face and stared seaward again. The mist seemed thicker, and there was no sign even of the French men-of-war. But the flotillas of invasion craft were assembling into some kind of order and would soon be on their way again. This time they would know they had an escort nearby and also be more vigilant against another surprise attack.

Allday whispered, 'Here they come, sir.'

The cordon at the top of the beach had parted, and three French officers with a close escort of soldiers strode purposefully towards the scattered groups of sailors.

He recognized the uniform of the leading officer as that of a captain of artillery. Probably from one of the coastal batteries.

The captain reached the three midshipmen and eyed them coldly.

Bolitho said, 'Give them your weapons and the third lieutenant's sword.'

Allday drove his cutlass savagely into the sand and said vehemently, 'I wish this was in his belly!'

Browne unclipped his own sword and stooped down to remove Neale's from his belt.

For the first time since he had been carried into the boat Neale seemed to show some of his old zest and courage. He struggled to his feet, clawing his hanger from its scabbard, while around him the soldiers raised their pistols and muskets, taken off guard by Neale's apparent recovery.

Neale yelled in a cracked, barely recognizable voice, 'To me, lads! Face your front! Repel boarders!'

Bolitho saw the French captain's pistol swing up from his hip and stepped quickly between him and the delirious Neale.

'*Please*, Capitaine. He is ill!'

The Frenchman's eyes darted swiftly from Neale to Bolitho, from the terrible wound on the young captain's head to the epaulettes on Bolitho's shoulders.

The silence closed round again like a wall. Neale remained swaying on his feet, peering at his men, who in turn were watching him with pity and embarrassment.

It was a tense moment. To the French soldiers, more used to monotonous garrison duty than to seeing an enemy ship sink in minutes and disgorge her company on a hitherto untroubled beach, it was like a threat. One wrong act and every musket would be firing, and the sand red with blood.

Bolitho kept his back on the Frenchman's pistol, sweat trickling down his skin as he waited for the crack, the smashing impact in his spine.

Very gently he took Neale's hanger from his fingers. 'Easy now. I'm here, and Allday.'

Neale released his grip and let his arm fall. 'Sorry.'

He was giving in to the pain at last, and Bolitho saw the ship's surgeon hurrying up the beach towards him as Neale added brokenly, 'Loved that bloody ship.' Then he collapsed.

Bolitho turned and handed the hanger to the nearest soldier. He saw the officer's gaze on his own sword and unfastened it, pausing only to feel its worn smoothness slipping through his fingers. A dishonoured end, he thought bitterly. In a few months it would be a hundred years old.

The French captain glanced at the weapon curiously and then tucked it under his arm.

Allday muttered, 'I'll get it back somehow, you see!'

More soldiers and some waggons had arrived at the top of

the beach. Wounded and injured men were being bustled unceremoniously into them, and Bolitho saw the surgeon being ordered to take charge.

He wanted to speak to the files of exhausted men who were already losing personality and purpose as like sheep they followed the impatient gestures, the menacing jerks of bared bayonets.

Perhaps that was what had roused Neale from his torpor. What they were all trained for, those last few moments before a victory or a defeat.

Bolitho glanced at some of the civilians as he followed the French officers up to a narrow roadway. Women mostly, carrying bundles of bread or clean washing, caught in their domestic affairs by the sudden intrusion of war.

He saw a dark-haired girl, her apron twisted bar-taut in her hands, watching the seamen as they limped past. As he drew level her eyes became fixed on him, unwinking and without expression. Maybe she had lost somebody in the war and wanted to know what the enemy looked like.

Further along the roadway a man pushed through the crowd and tried to seize one of the seamen by the shoulder. A soldier gestured threateningly and the man vanished in the crowd. Who was he, Bolitho wondered? Another one unhinged by battle? Curiously, the seaman had not even noticed the attack and was plodding obediently after his messmates.

Browne whispered, 'They've got a carriage for us, sir.'

The final parting. A French naval lieutenant had now appeared and was busy writing details of the captives on a list, jerking his finger at the soldiers to separate and divide the prisoners into their proper stations.

The midshipmen were behaving like veterans, Bolitho thought. Young Kilburne even smiled at him and touched his hat, as with his two companions and a handful of junior warrant officers he was directed back along the road.

The artillery captain relaxed slightly. Whatever happened now, he could control it.

He pointed to the carriage, a faded vehicle with scarred paintwork, a relic of some dead aristocrat, Bolitho thought.

Allday scowled as a bayonet barred his path, but the naval lieutenant gave him a curt nod and allowed him to climb into the carriage.

The door was slammed shut, and Bolitho looked at his companions. Browne, tight-lipped and trying desperately to adjust to his change of circumstances. Neale, his head now wrapped in a crude bandage, and propped beside him, *Styx*'s remaining commissioned officer, the unconscious third lieutenant.

Allday said hoarsely, 'No wonder they let *me* on board, sir. Always need a poor jack to carry his betters!'

It was a wretched shadow of a joke, but it meant more than gold to Bolitho. He reached over and gripped Allday's thick wrist.

Allday shook his head. 'No need to say nothing, sir. You're like me just now. All bottled up inside.' He glared through the dirty window as the coach gave a lurch and began to move. 'When it bursts out, them buggers will have to watch for themselves, an' that's no error!'

Browne lay back against the cracked leather and closed his eyes. Neale was looking terrible, and the lieutenant, blood already seeping through his bandages, was even worse. He felt a touch of panic, something new to him. Suppose he got separated from Bolitho and Allday, what then? A strange country, probably already reported dead . . . he shook himself and opened his eyes again.

He heard himself say, 'I was thinking, sir.'

Bolitho glanced at him, worried that another of his companions was about to give in.

'What?'

'It was as if we were expected, sir.' He watched Bolitho's level stare. 'As if they knew from the beginning what we were doing.'

Bolitho looked past him at the humble dwellings and

scurrying chickens beside the road.

The missing flaw, and it had taken Browne to uncover it.

The journey in the jolting, swaying coach was a torment. The road was deeply rutted, and with each savage jerk either Neale or Algar, the third lieutenant, would cry out with agony, while Bolitho and the others tried to shield them from further harm.

It was useless to try and halt the coach or even ask the escort to slow down. Whenever he tried to attract the coachman's attention, a mounted dragoon would gallop alongside and make threatening passes with his sabre to wave him away from the window.

Only when the coach stopped for a change of horses was there any respite. Lieutenant Algar's arm was bleeding badly, in spite of the bandages, but Neale had mercifully fainted into painless oblivion.

Then with a crack of the whip the coach took to the road again. Bolitho caught a glimpse of a small inn, some curious farm workers standing outside to stare at the coach and its impressive troop of dragoons.

Bolitho tried to think, to discover substance or disproof in Browne's idea that the French had known all about their movements. His head throbbed from the jolting motion, and the ache of despair which grew rather than lessened with each spin of the wheels. They were heading away from the sea, north-easterly, as far as he could judge. He could smell the rich aromas of the countryside, the earth and the animals, much the same as in Cornwall, he thought.

Bolitho felt trapped, unable to see a course to take. He had destroyed Beauchamp's hopes, and had lost Belinda. Men had died because of his tactics, because of their trust. He looked through the window, his eyes smarting. He had even lost the family sword.

Browne broke into his thoughts. 'I saw a roadside stone, sir. I am almost certain we're heading for Nantes.'

Bolitho nodded. It made sense, and the bearing was about right.

The pace slowed a little after that and Bolitho said, 'They must have orders to reach there before dusk.'

'*Alive*, I hope!' Allday wiped the lieutenant's face with a wet rag. 'What wouldn't I give for a good tot right now!'

Browne asked hesitantly, 'What will become of us, sir?'

Bolitho lowered his voice. 'Captain Neale will doubtless be exchanged for a French prisoner of equal rank when he is well enough to be moved.'

They both looked at Lieutenant Algar, and Bolitho added, 'I fear he may not live long enough to be exchanged.' He turned his gaze to Neale again, his face normally so pink from wind or sun was like a sheet. Even with good care he might never be the same again. He said, 'I want you to agree to any French proposals on exchange, Oliver.'

Browne exclaimed, 'No, sir. I cannot leave you . . . what are you saying?'

Bolitho looked away. 'Your loyalty warms me, but I shall insist. It is pointless for you to remain if offered the chance.'

Allday asked gruffly, 'D'you think they will keep you then, sir?'

Bolitho shrugged. 'I don't know. Not many flag-officers get taken prisoner.' He could not hide the bitterness. 'But we shall see.'

Allday folded his massive arms. 'I'm staying with you, sir. An' there's an end to it.'

Once again the coach shook itself to a halt, and as two mounted dragoons took station on either side, the rest of the escort dismounted.

A face appeared at Bolitho's door. It was the French naval lieutenant, his blue coat covered in dust from the hard ride across country.

He touched his hat and said in careful English, 'Not much longer, m'sieu.' He glanced at the two bandaged figures. 'A surgeon will be waiting.'

'Nantes?'

Bolitho expected the lieutenant to turn away, but instead he gave an amused smile.

'You know France, m'sieu.' He thrust two bottles of wine through the window. 'The best I can manage.' He touched his hat again and sauntered towards the other officers.

Bolitho turned, but said nothing as he saw the intent expression on Browne's face.

'Look, sir!'

There were a few trees beside the road and some tiny dwellings nearby. But rising above all else was a newly built tower, and there were some masons still working around its base and chipping away at the gold-coloured stone.

But Bolitho stared at its summit and an ungainly set of mechanical arms which were clearly framed against the sky.

He said, 'A semaphore tower!'

It was so obvious he was stunned by the discovery. Even the stone which had gone into the rough walls must be some of that brought from Spain. It was certainly not from hereabouts.

The Admiralty too had ordered the construction of semaphore towers, south from London to link their offices with the main ports and fleets, and the French had been using their own signalling system for even longer. But both countries had concentrated on the Channel, and nothing at all had been reported about the wider usage of this new chain of towers. No wonder their movements had been so swiftly reported up and down the Biscay coast, and French men-of-war had been ready to move into planned positions before any possible raid on their harbours and shipping.

Allday said, 'I think I saw one just as we were leaving the coast, sir. But not like that. The semaphore was mounted on the top of a church.'

Bolitho clenched his fists. Even at Portsmouth the semaphore was set on the cathedral tower to command the anchorage at Spithead.

'Here, open those bottles!' Bolitho pushed them into Allday's hands. 'Don't look at the tower. That lieutenant will see us.'

He dragged his eyes away as the semaphore arms began to swing and dance like a puppet on a gibbet. Ten, maybe twenty miles away a telescope would be recording each movement before passing it on to the next station. He recalled reading of the new chain of towers which linked London to Deal. In a record-breaking test they had sent a signal all seventy-two miles there and back in eight minutes!

How the local admiral must have gloated when *Styx*'s first penetration of the channel beyond the Ile d'Yeu had been reported. After that it had been simple. He must have despatched three ships to seaward during the night, and when *Styx*, accompanied by *Phalarope*, had attempted to engage the invasion craft, his own vessels had pounced. No time wasted, no vessels squandered or wrongly deployed. *Like a poacher's sack*. Bolitho felt the anger rising to match his despair.

The coach began to roll forward again, and when Bolitho glanced through the window he saw that the semaphore arms were still, as if the whole tower, and not its hidden inmates, was resting.

A new thought probed his mind like a needle. Herrick might be ordered to mount an attack with heavier ships of the squadron. The result would be a disaster. The enemy would gather an overwhelming force of vessels, and with the advanced knowledge arriving hourly on their new semaphore system, almost every move Herrick would make could be countered.

He looked at the sky. It was already darker, and soon the signal stations would be rendered dumb and blind until daylight.

The horses and the iron-shod wheels clattered over a made-up road, and Bolitho saw larger buildings and ware-houses, and a few windows already lit and cheerful.

There still had to be some faint hope. Twenty-five miles down the Loire from Nantes was the sea. He felt the chill of excitement on his skin in spite of his efforts to contain it. One step at a time. No more hope without a constructive thought to sustain it. He opened the window slightly and imagined he could smell the river, and pictured it wending its way towards the open sea, where ships of the blockading squadron maintained their endless vigilance.

Allday watched him and recognized the mood.

He said quietly, 'Remember what you asked afore, sir? About the falcon on a line?'

Bolitho nodded. 'Don't hope for too much. Not yet.'

Voices challenged and equipment jingled as the carriage and escort clattered beneath an archway and into a walled square.

As the coach responded to its brake, Browne said, 'We have arrived, sir.'

Bayonets moved across the windows like pale rushes, and Bolitho saw an officer carrying a large satchel watching from a doorway. As promised, a doctor was waiting. Even that order must have been passed directly here by semaphore. Yet it was all of forty miles from the beach where they had struggled ashore.

The door was wrenched open and several orderlies lifted the moaning lieutenant and carried him towards the nearest building. Then it was Neale's turn. Still unconscious and unaware of what was happening, he too was carried bodily after his lieutenant.

Bolitho looked at the others. It was time.

The French lieutenant made a polite blow. 'If you will please follow me?' It was courteously asked, but the armed soldiers left no room for argument.

They entered another, heavily-studded door on the other side of the square, and then into a bare, stone-flagged room with a solitary window, barred, and too high to reach. Apart from a wooden bench, a foul-smelling bucket and some straw, the room was empty.

Bolitho had expected some sort of formal investigation to begin at once, but instead the heavy door slammed shut, the sound echoing along the corridor like something from a tomb.

Browne looked round in dismay, and even Allday seemed at a loss.

Bolitho sat down on the bench and stared at the stone floor between his feet. *Prisoners of war*.

The French naval lieutenant stood with arms folded as Bolitho, assisted by Allday, slipped into his coat and tugged his neckcloth into place.

They had been awakened early by the usual commotion of the military. The main building and smaller outlying ones had obviously been commandeered by the local garrison, but still bore the mark of grandeur and privilege. A great house and home farm before the revolution, Bolitho thought. He had seen a small part of it when he had been escorted to another room where Allday, watched the whole time by a keen-eyed guard, had been allowed to shave him.

Bolitho knew it was useless to ask Allday to leave him now. They would make the best of it, as they had been forced to do before. But to all outward appearances Allday must be seen as his personal servant. If he was recognized as a professional seaman he would soon be sent to join the rest of *Styx*'s company, wherever they were.

The lieutenant nodded approvingly. '*Bon*.' He ignored Allday's warning scowl and brushed some dust from Bolitho's shoulder. 'Are you ready, m'sieu?'

Bolitho, followed by Browne and Allday, walked out into the corridor and began to climb a grand staircase to the next floor. Much of the stairway had been damaged, and Bolitho saw several holes in the plaster where musket balls had cut down some of the previous occupants.

Some orderlies had given them food, minutes after the first trumpet call. The food had been coarse but plentiful, with some rough wine to wash it down. Bolitho had forced it down rather than worry his two companions.

The French lieutenant was saying, 'You will now meet my superior officer, Contre-Amiral Jean Remond. He 'as travelled much of the night to be 'ere.' He gave a brief smile. 'So please do not rouse 'is temper!'

Before Bolitho could make a sharp retort, he added almost apologetically, 'For *my* sake, m'sieu!'

Leaving them with an escort he strode on ahead to a pair of high doors.

Browne whispered, 'He must be the French admiral's flag-lieutenant, sir.' For a few seconds it seemed to amuse him.

Bolitho looked towards a window and beyond. The country-side was lush and green in the morning sunlight. Between some houses he saw the glint of water, the masts of a moored vessel. The river.

The lieutenant reappeared and beckoned to Bolitho. To Browne and Allday he said shortly, 'Remain 'ere.' His casual attitude was gone. He was on duty again.

Bolitho entered the big room and heard the door close quietly behind him. After the abused lower floor and staircase this room was sumptuous. Thick carpets, and a towering painting of a battle which seemed to involve many hundreds of horses, gave the room a kind of arrogant elegance.

He walked towards an ornate table at the opposite end of the room. The distance seemed endless, and he was very aware of his dishevelled appearance when compared with the figure behind the desk.

Contre-Amiral Remond was dark-skinned, even swarthy, but incredibly neat. His hair, as black as Bolitho's, was brushed forward across a broad forehead, beneath which his eyes glittered in the filtered sunlight like stones.

He stood up only briefly and waved Bolitho to a gilded chair. That too, like the carefully measured distance from the door, was placed just so.

Bolitho sat down, again conscious of his own salt-stained clothes, the throbbing ache of his wounded thigh, all of which added to his feeling of defeat. The fact he guessed that was the intention of his captor did nothing to help.

In spite of his guard he felt his eyes drawn to his sword

which lay across the table as if for a court martial.

The French admiral said curtly, 'Is there anything you wish to tell me?'

Bolitho met his unwinking stare. 'The officers and men of the frigate *Styx*. I am responsible for them. Their captain is too ill to plead for them.'

The French officer shrugged as if it was of no importance. 'My officers will deal with the matter. It is you who interest me.'

Bolitho fought for time. 'You speak very good English.'

'Naturally. I was a prisoner of your people for some months before I was released.' He seemed to grow irritated at revealing something personal and snapped, 'We of course knew of your new command, of the misguided attempt to interfere with French ships. In fact, we know a great deal about you and your family. Of a noble tradition, would you say?' He hurried on without waiting. 'Whereas I had to work my way up from nothing, without privilege.'

'So did I!' It came out sharper than he had intended.

Remond gave a slow smile. He had very small teeth, like a terrier's. 'No matter. For you the war is over. As your equal in rank it was my duty to meet you, nothing more.' He picked up the old sword and casually turned it over in his hands.

Bolitho had the strange feeling that Remond was less sure of himself. He was testing him, trying to find out something. He dropped his eyes, praying that the swarthy-faced admiral would not see his sudden determination. The new semaphore system. Remond needed to know if he had discovered it.

Perhaps the French had a Beauchamp all of their own who had created a plan to destroy the would-be destroyers?

Remond remarked, 'A fine old blade.' He replaced it carefully on the table, nearer to Bolitho. 'You will be given suitable quarters, naturally, and allowed to keep your servant with you. And if you give your word of honour not to try and escape, you will also be afforded certain liberty as decided by your guards.' He looked at the sword. 'And you will be permitted to keep your sword also. When peace is signed you will be sent home without a stain on your character.' He sat back and eyed Bolitho bleakly. 'So?'

Bolitho stood up slowly, his eyes on the man across the table.

'Peace is only a rumour, Contre-Amiral Remond. War is still a reality. I am a King's officer and find no comfort in waiting for others to fight for me.'

His answer seemed to take Remond aback.

'That is absurd! You reject captivity with all the rights of your rank? You have hopes for escape, perhaps? That too is ridiculous!'

Bolitho shrugged. 'I cannot give my word.'

'If you intend to persist with this attitude, all hope of rescue or escape are gone. Once I leave here, the military will be in charge of you!'

Bolitho said nothing. How could he stay in comparative comfort after losing a ship and so many lives? If he ever returned home it would be with honour, or not at all.

Remond nodded. 'Very well. Then your companions shall stay with you. If the injured captain dies because of his captivity, you will be to blame.'

'Must the lieutenant stay too?' Strangely, Bolitho felt calmer with the threats, now that the promises had been pushed aside.

'Did I forget to mention him?' The French admiral picked a piece of thread from his breeches. 'The surgeon had to remove his arm during the night, I believe. But he died nevertheless.'

Remond lowered his voice and continued, 'Try to see reason. Many of the garrisons are manned by fools, peasants in uniform. They have no love for the British navy, the blockade, the attempt to starve them into submission. In Lorient now, you would be with your fellow officers and protected by the sailors of France.'

Bolitho lifted his chin and replied coldly, 'My answer is unchanged.'

'Then you are a fool, Bolitho. Soon there will be peace.

'What use is a dead hero then, eh?'

He shook a little bell on his desk and Bolitho sensed the doors open behind him.

Remond walked round the desk and eyed him curiously. 'I think we shall not meet again.' Then he strode from the room.

The lieutenant joined Bolitho by the table and looked at the sword. He gave a deep sigh and said sadly, 'I am sorry, m'sieu.' He beckoned to the escort and added, 'It is arranged. You will be taken to another prison today. After that . . .' He spread his hands. 'But I wish you luck, m'sieu.'

Bolitho watched him hurry to the stairway. No doubt Remond had somebody superior to him waiting at Lorient. The chain of command.

The soldiers fell in step with him, and moments later he was back in the cell, and alone.

8

The Ceres

It was a whole week before Bolitho was taken from his isolation and put into a shuttered carriage for the journey to his new prison. It had taken every ounce of his self-control and determination to endure the seven days, and he had thanked his hard upbringing in a King's ship more than once as time seemed to stretch to an eternity.

His guards must have been hand-picked for their coarseness and brutality, and their ill-fitting uniforms only added to their air of menace.

Bolitho was made to strip naked while several of the guards searched him and removed every personal possession from his clothing. Not content with that, they had removed his rear-admiral's epaulettes and gilt buttons, presumably to be shared round as souvenirs. And all the while they had subjected him to every humiliation and insult. But Bolitho knew men as well as he understood ships, and had no illusions about his guards. They were seeking an excuse to kill him, and showed their disappointment when he remained silent and apparently calm.

Only once had his will almost cracked. One of the soldiers had dragged the locket from about his neck and had peered curiously at it for several moments. Bolitho had tried to appear unconcerned, even though he wanted to hurl himself at the man's throat and throttle him before the others cut him down.

The guard had prised open the locket with his bayonet, and had blinked with astonishment as a lock of hair had blown across the floor and then out of the open door.

But the locket was gold, and he had seemed satisfied. He would never know what it had meant to Bolitho, the lock of Cheney's hair which she had given him before he had left her for the last time.

Without a watch, or anyone to speak with, it was hard to mark the passing of time, even the pattern of events beyond the walls.

As he was led from the cell into the courtyard and saw the waiting carriage, he was grateful. If the new prison was worse, or he was about to face a firing-party instead of captivity, he was glad of an end to waiting.

Inside the darkened coach he found the others waiting for him. It was unexpected and moving for each one of them. As the carriage began to move and the mounted escort took station behind it, they clasped hands, barely able to speak as they examined each other's faces in the chinks of sunlight through the shutters.

Bolitho said, 'Your being here is my fault. Had I given my word you would have been sent home, soon perhaps. Now,' he shrugged, 'you are as much a prisoner as I am.'

Allday seemed openly pleased, or was he relieved to find him still alive?

'By God, I'm fair glad to be rid of those scum, sir!' He held up his two fists like clubs. 'Another few days o' these *mounseers* an' I'd have swung for 'em!'

Neale, propped between Browne and Allday, reached out and touched Bolitho's hands. His head was heavily bandaged, and in the fleeting stabs of sunshine his face looked as pale as death.

He whispered, 'Together. Now we'll show them.'

Allday said gently, 'He's doing his best, sir.' He looked at Bolitho and gave a quick shake of the head. 'Not changed a mite since he was a young gentleman, eh, sir?'

Browne said, 'I was interrogated by two of the French officers, sir. They asked a lot about you. I heard them discussing you later, and I suspect they are worried.'

Bolitho nodded. 'You did not let them know you speak and understand French?'

He saw Browne smile. He had almost forgotten about his flag-lieutenant's other assets. A small thing, but in their favour.

Browne clung to a strap as the carriage gathered speed. 'I heard some talk about more invasion craft being sent up to Lorient and Brest. Two types, I think. One is called a *chaloupe de cannonière*, and the other is a smaller type, a *péniche*. They have been building them by the hundred, or so it sounds.'

Bolitho found he was able to relate this sparse information to his own predicament without despair. Perhaps the testing he had endured, alone in the cell, had given him the hatred he needed to think clearly, to plan how best to hit back.

He looked at Neale as he lolled against Allday's protective arm. His shirt was open to the waist, and Bolitho could see the scratches on his skin where someone's fingers had torn off the locket Neale always wore. It had contained a portrait of his mother, but they had seized it nonetheless. Poor, broken Neale. What was his mind grappling with now, he wondered, as the wheels clattered and bounced along the open road. Of his beloved *Styx*, of his home, or of his first lieutenant, the taciturn Mr Pickthorn, who had been an extension of his own command?

But for me, he would be safe in hospital.

Dozing, and reawakening as if fearful that their reunification might be just one more taunt and part of the nightmare, they sustained each other, and endured the heat of the shuttered coach without knowing where they were or where they were bound.

Several times the coach halted, horses were watered or changed, some bread and wine were thrust into the carriage without more than a swift glance from one of the escorts, and they were off again.

'If we are separated again we must try to keep contact somehow.' Bolitho heard a carriage clatter past in the opposite direction. A wide road then, not some winding lane. 'I intend to escape, but we shall go together.' He felt them looking at him, could even sense their awakened hope. 'If one of us falls or gets taken, the others must go on. Get the news to England *somehow*, tell them the truth of the French preparations and their new signals system.'

Allday grunted. 'Together, sir. That's what you said. If I have to carry all of you, begging yer pardon, sir, we'll stay together, an' England will have to wait a mite longer.'

Browne chuckled, a welcome sound when they might all be shot dead before another day had passed.

He said, 'Keep your place, Allday. You're an admiral's servant, not his cox'n, remember?'

Allday grinned. 'I'll never live it down.'

Bolitho put his finger to his lips. 'Quiet!'

He tried to loosen one of the shutters but only managed to move it very slightly. Watched by the others, he knelt down on the floor, ignoring the pain in his wounded thigh, and pressed his face to the shutter.

He said softly, 'The sea. I can smell it.' He looked at them, as if he had just revealed some great miracle. To sailors it was just that. *The sea*.

They would be taken out of the carriage and shut away once more in some stinking prison. But it would not be the same, no matter what privation or suffering they had to face. How many men must have seen the sea as an enemy, a final barrier to freedom. But any sailor nursed it in his heart like a prayer. *Just get me to the sea, and somehow I'll reach home*.

The carriage stopped, and a soldier opened the shutters to let in some air.

Bolitho sat very still, but his eyes were everywhere. There was no sign of water, but beyond a series of low, rounded hills he knew it was there.

On the other side of the road was a great stretch of bare, barren looking land, across which, in rolling clouds of thick dust, troops of mounted horsemen wheeled and reformed, the spectacle like part of that huge picture in the commandant's room.

Browne said softly, 'Like the escort, sir. French dragoons.'

Bolitho heard the blare of a trumpet and saw the sun gleam across black-plumed helmets and breast-plates as the horses changed formation and cantered into another wall of dust. Open country. Very suitable for training cavalry, perhaps for invasion. Also, they represented a real threat to anyone trying to escape from captivity. As a boy, Bolitho had often watched the local dragoons parading and exercising at Truro, near his home in Falmouth. Had seen them too hunting some smugglers who had broken away from the revenue men, their sabres glittering as they had galloped in pursuit across the moor.

The shutters were replaced and the coach jerked forward. Bolitho knew the act had been a warning, not an act of compassion. No words could have made it clearer. Those proud dragoons shouted it from the skies.

It was dusk by the time they finally alighted from the carriage, stiff and tired after the journey. The young officer in charge of the escort handed some papers to a blue-coated official, and with a curt nod to the prisoners turned on his heel, obviously glad to be rid of his charges.

Bolitho looked past the official, who was still examining the papers as if he was barely able to read, and looked at the squat building which was to be their new prison.

A high stone wall, windowless, with a central tower which was just visible through the shadows of the gates.

An old fort, a coastguard station, added to and altered over the years, it might have been anything.

The man in the blue coat looked at him and pointed to the gates. Some soldiers who had been watching the new arrivals fell in line, and like men under sentence of death Bolitho and the others followed the official through the gates.

Another delay, and then an elderly militia captain entered the room where they had been left standing against a wall and said, 'I am Capitaine Michel Cloux, commandant here.'

He had a narrow, foxy face, but his eyes were not hostile, and if anything he looked troubled with his command.

'You will remain as prisoners of France, and will obey whatever instruction I give without question, you understand? Any attempt to escape will be punished by death. Any attempt to overthrow authority will be punished by death. But behave yourselves and all will be well.' His small eyes rested on Allday. 'Your servant will be shown what to do, where to go for your requirements.'

Neale gave a groan and staggered against Browne for support.

The commandant glanced at his papers, apparently unnerved. In a gentler tone he added, 'I will request aid from the military surgeon for er, Capitaine Neale, yes?'

'Thank you, I would be grateful.' Bolitho kept his voice low. Any sign that he was trying to assert his rank might destroy everything. Neale's distress had made a small bridge. The commandant obviously had distinct instructions about the care and isolation of the prisoners. But he was probably an old campaigner who had lost comrades of his own. Neale's condition had made more sense to him than some coldly worded orders.

The commandant eyed him warily, as if suspecting a trap.

Then he said, 'You will attend your quarters now. Then you will be fed.'

He replaced his cocked hat with a shabby flourish.

'Go with my men.'

As they followed two of the guards up a winding stone stairway, supporting Neale in case he should slip and fall, Allday murmured, 'They can't steal anything from me here. I've naught left!'

Bolitho touched his throat and thought of the locket, her face as he had last seen her. And he thought too of Belinda the day he and Allday had found her in the overturned coach on the road from Portsmouth. Allday was probably right. The locket had been a link with something lost. Hope was all he had now, and he was determined not to lose it.

*

For Bolitho and his companions each day was much like the one which had preceded it. The food was poor and coarse, but so too was it for their prison guards, and the daily routine equally monotonous. They soon discovered they had the little prison to themselves, although when Bolitho and Browne were allowed to walk outside the gates with an armed escort, they saw a heavily pitted wall and some rough graves to show that previous occupants had met a violent end here before a firing-squad.

The commandant visited them every day, and he had kept his word about sending for a military surgeon to attend Neale.

Bolitho watched the surgeon with great interest. He was the same one he had seen at Nantes who had removed the young lieutenant's arm. Later Browne told him that he had heard him saying he must get back to his barracks, a good three hours ride.

To men kept deliberately out of contact with the rest of the world, these small items of news were precious. They calculated that Nantes was to the east of their prison, twenty or thirty miles inland. That would fix the prison's position no more than twenty miles or so north of where they had stumbled ashore from the wreck.

It made sense, Bolitho thought. They had been taken inland, then brought back to the coast again, but nearer to the Loire Estuary. In his mind's eye Bolitho could see the chart, the treacherous reefs and sand-bars, the start and end of many a voyage.

He had noticed that the commandant only allowed two of them to take a walk or exercise outside the walls at any given time. The others remained as surety and hostages. Maybe the graves marked where others had tried to outwit the little commandant and had paid the price.

On one hot August morning Bolitho and Browne left the gates, but instead of heading for the road, Bolitho gestured westwards towards the low hills. The three guards, all mounted and well armed, nodded agreement, and with the horses trotting contentedly over the grass they strode away from the prison. Bolitho had expected the guards to break their usual silence and order them back, but perhaps they were bored with their duties and glad of a change.

Bolitho tried not to quicken his pace as they topped the first rise.

Browne exclaimed, 'God, sir, it looks *beautiful*!'

The sea, a deeper blue than before, spread away on every side, and through the dazzling glare and drifting heat haze Bolitho could see the swirl of currents around some tiny islets, while to the north he could just discern another layer of land. The far side of the estuary, it had to be. He glanced quickly at the guards but they were not even watching. Two had dismounted, the other still sat astride his horse, a bell-mouthed blunderbuss resting across his saddle, ready for instant use.

Bolitho said, 'There should be a church, if I'm right.'

Browne made to point, but Bolitho snapped, '*Tell* me!'

'To our left, sir. On the blind side of the prison.'

Bolitho shaded his eyes. A square-towered church, partly hidden by the hillside, and nestling into the ground as if it had been there since time had begun.

'We'll go back now.' Bolitho turned reluctantly away from the sea. 'Someone might be watching.'

Browne fell in step, completely mystified.

Bolitho waited until he heard the jingle of harness behind him and then said, 'I know exactly where we are, Oliver. And if I'm not mistaken, that church tower is occupied by French sailors rather than priests!' He glanced at the lieutenant, the urgency making his voice desperate. 'I would lay odds that it is the last semaphore link this side of the estuary.' He strode towards the prison, his hands clasped behind him. 'If only we could break out long enough to destroy it.'

Browne stared at him. 'But they will build another, surely, sir, and we . . .'

'I know. Executed. But there has to be a way. If our ships attack, and I believe they will, if only to prove Beauchamp's plan too hazardous, they will be completely destroyed. And as to time, my friend, I think there may be little enough of it left. England will know of *Styx*'s loss, and efforts begun to obtain exchanges at least for the surviving officers.'

Browne bit his lip. 'Captain Neale will be reported missing, some of *Styx*'s people are bound to speak out and say what happened to him and ourselves.'

Bolitho smiled gravely. 'Aye. Neutral sources will soon be selling that information to the right ears. My guess is that the French intend to delay matters over releasing any of *Styx*'s people until they are ready and their new invasion fleets are in position. Admiral Beauchamp was *right*.'

'He chose wisely for his commander,' said Browne.

Bolitho sighed. 'I would like to think so, Oliver. The longer I remain in captivity and useless, the more I think about that attack. I should have seen the flaw in the plan, ought to have allowed for it, no matter what intelligence the Admiralty was able to offer.' He stopped and looked Browne squarely in the eyes. 'When I saw *Phalarope* stand away, I nearly cursed her captain's soul to damnation. Now I am not so convinced. He may have acted wisely and with some courage, Oliver. I have always said a captain should act on his initiative if his set orders tell him nothing.'

'With respect, I must disagree.' Browne waited for a rebuke then hurried on. 'Captain Emes should have risked a hopeless battle against odds rather than leave *Styx* unaided. It is what you would have done, sir.'

Bolitho smiled. 'As a captain perhaps. But when my flag fell, Emes took over command. He really had no choice at all.'

Bolitho could feel Browne's disagreement more strongly than a shouted argument.

Allday was waiting in the upper part of the tower, and as the two officers, sweating from their walk in the sunlight, climbed the curving stairway, he said, 'The surgeon's been back, sir. Cap'n Neale is pretty bad.'

Bolitho brushed past him and hurried into the larger of the

two rooms. Neale lay on his back, his eyes wide open and staring at the ceiling, while his chest heaved and fell as if it would burst. One of the guards was removing a bucket which contained some bloodstained dressings, and Bolitho saw the little commandant standing by the barred window, his face grave.

'Ah, Contre-Amiral Bolitho, you are here. Capitaine Neale is worsening, I fear.'

Bolitho sat carefully on the rough cot and clasped Neale's hand. It was like ice, in spite of the room's warmth. 'What's this, John? Come on, my lad, speak to me.' He squeezed his hand very gently but there was no response. *Not you too. God in heaven, not you.*

The commandant's voice seemed to come from far away. 'I have orders to transfer you to Lorient. There, Captain Neale will be in safer hands.'

Bolitho looked at him, his mind grappling with his words, what they meant. It was for nothing. Neale was going to die, and they were being sent to Lorient where there would be no chance to escape and wreck one of the towers.

He protested, 'M'sieu, Captain Neale cannot survive another coach journey!'

The commandant turned his back and stared towards the sea. 'I am *ordered* to send you to Lorient. The surgeon knows of the risks, but assures me that only by remaining with you does the young capitaine hold on to life at all.' His tone softened as it had at their very first meeting. 'But you will travel by sea. It is little enough, m'sieu amiral, but my influence is equally small.'

Bolitho nodded slowly. '*Thank* you. I shall not forget. None of us shall.'

The commandant squared his narrow shoulders, embarrassed perhaps at their sudden contact.

'You will be put aboard ship tonight. After that . . .' He shrugged. 'It is out of my hands.'

He left the room, and Bolitho bent over Neale again. 'Did you hear that, John? We're taking you somewhere where you'll get proper care. And we shall all keep together, eh?'

Neale's eyes moved towards him, as if even that effort was too much.

'No . . . use. They've . . . done . . . for . . . me . . . this . . . time.'

Bolitho felt Neale trying to grip his hand. To see him try to smile almost broke his heart.

Neale whispered, 'Mr Bundy will want to speak about his charts again.' He was rambling, his gaze blurred with pain. 'Later . . .'

Bolitho released his hand and stood up. 'Let him rest.' To Browne he added, 'Make sure we leave nothing behind.' He was speaking to give himself time. They had nothing to leave behind, as Allday had already pointed out.

Allday said quietly, 'I'll take care of Captain Neale, sir.'

'Yes. Thank you.'

Bolitho crossed to the window and pressed his forehead against the sun-warmed bars. Somewhere to his left was the church tower, although he could not see it. It would take days to get the attacking ships into position, but mere minutes to send a signal by semaphore to summon reinforcements to destroy them.

Nobody knew. Perhaps nobody would ever know. And Neale with so many of his men would have died for nothing.

He pressed his face still harder until the rough iron steadied him. Neale was *not* dead, and the enemy had *not* won.

Browne watched him anxiously, wanting to help, and knowing there was nothing he could do.

Allday sat down and peered at Neale. His eyes were closed and his breathing seemed easier.

Allday thought of the French ship which would take them to Lorient, wherever in hell *that* was. He despised the 'mounseers' as he called them, but any ship was better than a carriage and a lot of damn soldiers.

Anyway, he did know that Lorient was to the north, and *that* was nearer to England.

*

The little commandant waited by the doorway and looked at Bolitho curiously.

'It is time, m'sieu.'

Bolitho glanced round the room, their prison for such a short time. Neale, strapped unconscious to a stretcher, and with Allday close by his side, had been carried out earlier that afternoon. Without him and his desperate efforts to cling to life, the room already seemed dead.

Browne said, 'Listen to the wind.'

That too was like an evil omen. Within an hour of Neale being carried away the wind had started to rise. The weather's moods were always very noticeable in the prison's central tower, but now as they stood by the door it sounded wild and menacing. It sighed around the prison and moaned through the small windows like a living force, eager to find and destroy them.

Bolitho said, 'I hope Neale is safely aboard.'

The commandant led the way down the curving stairway, his boots fitting into the worn stones without conscious effort.

Over his shoulder he remarked, 'It must be tonight. The ship will not wait.'

Bolitho listened to the rising gale. Especially now, he thought.

Outside the prison gates the contrast to that morning when he and Browne had walked to the hillside was even more impressive. Low scudding clouds, with occasional shafts of silver light from the moon to make the picture stark and savage. Lanterns bobbed around him, and at a shouted command they moved towards the rear of the prison. Ahead of them the commandant strode unerringly with neither moonlight nor lantern to guide him. They were taking almost the same path they had discovered that morning, although in the darkness and buffeted by the wind it might have been anywhere.

He could feel the guards watching him, and recalled the commandant's last warning. 'You will leave my care like officers not thieves. Therefore I will not put the irons on your hands and feet. But if you try to escape . . .'

The closeness of the guards and long bayonets required no further explanation.

Browne said, 'We're descending now.'

The path curved to the right and dipped steeply. As it did so the hiss and moan of the wind faded slightly, cut off by a wall of cliff.

Bolitho stumbled and heard a metallic click behind him. They were that watchful. Ready to shoot him down if he ran for it. Then he heard the sea, rebellious against the beach, and with only an occasional necklace of foam to betray its direction. He found he was counting the seconds and minutes, as if it was vital to know the exact place where he would leave the land and head for another destination.

Another group of lanterns swayed up the beach and boots squeaked on wet sand.

Bolitho heard a boat's keel grating in the shallows and wondered where the ship lay at anchor. The shelter afforded by the headland told him that the wind had not only risen but had also shifted considerably. From the east? It seemed likely. You never really knew in Biscay.

The commandant's face floated out of the darkness in a beam of lantern light.

'Farewell, m'sieu. I am told your Capitaine Neale is safely on board the *Ceres*.' He stood back and touched his hat. 'Good luck.'

The light vanished and with it the commandant.

A new voice shouted harshly, *'Dans la chaloupe*, vite!'

Led, pushed and dragged, they found themselves in the sternsheets of a longboat, and even as they were squeezed between two invisible seamen the hull was pushed into deep water, the oars already thrashing wildly to regain control.

Once clear of the land it was like riding on the back of a porpoise. Up and plunge, the oarsmen working in desperate rhythm, urged on occasionally by the coxswain at the tiller.

It was a rough night, and would get worse. Bolitho

thought of Neale and hoped he would find peace in more familiar surroundings, French or not. He could sense the difference around him. The smell of tar and brandy, the sweat of the oarsmen as they fought against their constant enemy.

Ceres. He had heard her name before somewhere. A frigate, one of those used to pierce the British blockade and carry despatches between the various fleets. If the French continued to extend their semaphore system, the frigate's life would be an easier one.

Browne touched his arm, and he saw the French ship loom out of the darkness, the sea boiling around her stem and anchor cable as if she had just risen from the depths.

After three attempts the boat hooked on to the chains, and Bolitho, followed by Browne, jumped for his life as the boat fell away into another surging trough.

Even so, they arrived on the frigate's deck soaked to the skin, their coats, stripped of buttons and insignia, hanging around them like rags from a scarecrow.

Bolitho sensed the urgency and the need to get under way; equally he was impressed that the vessel's captain, pre-warned of his passenger's rank, took time from his duties to meet him at the entry port.

Then it was done, and Bolitho found himself being led down ladders and beneath low-beamed deckheads to the world he knew so well.

The motion between decks was violent, and he could feel the ship jerking at her cable, eager to get away from the surrounding rocks and seek open water.

As they descended another ladder to the orlop deck, Bolitho heard the clink of a capstan, orders carried away by the wind as the seamen prepared to make sail.

Stooping figures passed through the shadows, and Bolitho saw dark stains on the deck which could only be blood. Not all that recent, but too deep to be scrubbed away. Like any other orlop, he thought grimly. Where the surgeons managed as best they could while the guns thundered overhead and their screaming victims were pinioned to a table for the saw or knife.

He saw Neale in a cot by one of the great frames, and Allday rising to meet him as if their reunion was all that mattered in the world.

Allday said quickly, 'She's the *Ceres*, thirty-two, sir.' He led the way to some old sea chests which he had covered with canvas and fashioned into seating for them. He added, 'She was in a fight with one of our patrols a while back. The cook told me.' He grinned. 'He's Irish. Anyways, sir, she's on passage to Lorient.' He cocked his head as the wind roared against the side. 'Short-handed they are too. Hope they runs aground, damn them!'

'How's Captain Neale?'

Allday became serious again. 'Sometimes he thinks he's back in *Styx*. Keeps giving orders. Other times he's quiet, no trouble.'

More far-off cries and then the deck tilted violently. Bolitho sat on a chest, his back pressed against the timbers, as the anchor broke from the ground and the *Ceres* began her fight to beat clear. He noticed that Allday had piled some old canvas in a corner, but enough to hide the manacles and leg irons which in turn were attached to chains and ring-bolts. One more reminder that they were prisoners and would be treated harshly if there was any sort of trouble.

Allday looked at the deckhead, his eyes and ears working like a cat in the dark.

'They're aweigh, sir. Close-hauled by now, I reckon.' As an afterthought he said, 'They have plenty to drink, sir. But no real ale.' He wrinkled his nose with disgust. 'Still, what can you expect?'

Bolitho looked at Neale and then at Browne. Both were asleep, each trapped in his own thoughts and so momentarily secure.

Around them the ship groaned and plunged, every timber straining, while the wind endeavoured to break the hold of helm and seamanship. Again and again Bolitho heard the sea thunder against the side, and could imagine it leaping over

the gangways and sweeping unwary and tired men in its path
like leaves.

He thought of Belinda, of the house beneath Pendennis
Castle, of Adam, and his friend Thomas Herrick. He was still
trying to determine their faces when he too fell into an
exhausted sleep.

When next he opened his eyes he was instantly aware that
things had changed. As his mind grappled with his surroundings, he realized he must have been asleep for hours, for he
could see creeping fingers of grey light playing down one of
the companion ladders.

Allday was sitting bolt upright on his canvas, and Browne
too was rubbing his eyes and yawning, as if he thought he was
still dreaming.

Bolitho leaned forward and felt the ship moving unsteadily
beneath his feet. What had awakened him?

He said, 'Go to that ladder, Oliver. Tell me if you can hear
anything.'

Allday asked uneasily, 'Can't be there already, can we?'

'No. Off shore gale, and in these waters, it will double the
passage.'

He saw Browne cling to the ladder as a voice echoed from
the deck above.

'*En haut les gabiers! En haut pour ferler les huniers!*'

Browne hurried over, his body steeply angled to the deck
like a man on a hillside.

'They're reefing topsails, sir.'

Bolitho heard the stumbling feet overhead as the watch off
duty ran to obey the last order. It made no sense. Short-
handed, Allday had said, so why wear out men further by
reefing now? If only he could see what was happening.

A lantern cast a yellow glow down the ladder, and Bolitho
saw a lieutenant and two armed petty officers hurrying
towards him.

The lieutenant was young and looked worried. The two
old hands wasted no time in snapping the manacles over
Bolitho's wrists and ankles, and then did the same to

Browne. As they moved towards Allday, the lieutenant shook his head and gestured towards Neale. Allday, it seemed, was being kept free to continue looking after the injured captain.

Bolitho looked at the iron manacles and said, 'I do not understand.'

The ship leaned further to one side, whilst overhead voices yelled back and forth and blocks squealed like pigs at a slaughter. The captain was trying to change tack, but from the violent motion, Bolitho doubted if he had succeeded. Without topsails he . . . Bolitho sat bolt upright until restrained by the chain.

The French captain had wanted to remain unseen, and had taken in his upper sails to help conceal his ship against the tossing backcloth of waves.

Like an echo to his own thoughts he heard a voice shout, '*Tout le monde à son poste! Branle-bas de combat!*'

Browne stared at him wide-eyed. 'They're clearing for action, sir!'

Bolitho listened to the increasing jumble of sounds as the frigate's company began to remove screens and hammocks, and the rumble of gun trucks being manoeuvred in readiness for the order to load.

They looked at one another as if unable to believe what was happening.

Then Allday said fervently, 'It's one of ours, sir! By God, it must be!'

Shadowy figures bustled past, heads bowed beneath the beams. Lanterns were lit and hung in a spiralling circle, and more chests were dragged to the centre of the deck and quickly secured with lashings. Light gleamed briefly on long aprons and across the glittering array of instruments as the surgeon's mates laid out the tools of their trade.

Nobody paid any attention to the three men in the shadows or the swaying cot beside them.

Bolitho tugged at the manacles again. So it was not over after all. It would be a cruel ending to go to the bottom in these manacles after being in battle with a King's ship.

The deck steadied slightly, and one of the surgeon's mates laughed. But the sound was without humour. Even he would know that the steadier motion meant that their captain had set more sail, that the ruse to conceal his ship had failed. He was going to fight, and soon these same men would be too busy to care for mere prisoners.

Neale opened his eyes and called in a surprisingly clear voice, 'Sentry! Fetch the master-at-arms!' But nobody turned to stare or wonder.

Bolitho leaned back and tried to adjust his mind. 'Allday!'

'Sir?'

'Be ready.'

Allday looked at the lighted door of the sickbay, the absence of any sort of axe or weapon.

But he said hoarsely, 'I'll be ready, sir. Don't you fret on it.'

The waiting got worse, and some of the surgeon's assistants prowled inside the circle of swinging lanterns as if performing some strange ritual.

'Chargez toutes les pièces!'

It was the order to load, and as if he was responding to a pre-arranged signal, the surgeon left his sickbay and walked slowly towards the lights.

Bolitho licked his lips and wished he had something to drink.

Once again others had decided what the next hours would bring.

9

Price of Freedom

Herrick clung to *Benbow*'s quarterdeck rail, his teeth bared as he peered into the stinging force of wind and spray. In spite of her bulk, the seventy-four was shipping water over the forecastle and weather gangway as if she was already on her way to the bottom. Even Herrick, with all his years of hard won experience, had lost count of time and the orders he had shouted above the gale's onslaught.

He heard Wolfe staggering across the slippery planking, cursing horribly until he joined his captain by the rail.

'Should be damn soon, sir!' His harsh voice seemed puny against the din of wind and waves.

Herrick wiped his streaming face with his hand. His skin felt numb and raw, and he sensed an unusual anger rising to match the weather. Ever since he had left Plymouth with his small but valuable convoy he had been plagued with misfortune. The other seventy-four, *Nicator*, had lost two men overboard within a day of sailing, and despite his liking and respect for her captain, Valentine Keen, Herrick had nursed a few hard thoughts as he had endeavoured to keep his ships together. Five merchantmen, with two seventy-fours and a solitary frigate to protect them. Herrick knew that when light eventually cut across the horizon it was very likely there would be no more than two of the ships in sight. The gale had roared out of the eastern horizon like a hurricane, shutting out sea and sky in a crazed world of spray and spindrift, which had left the hands battered and dazed, until with reluctance Herrick had ordered the ships to lie to and ride it out as best they could.

He felt *Benbow* sway over again, her close-reefed mainsail cracking and booming in protest while she fought her own battle, served by men who whenever they were ordered aloft were convinced they would never return alive.

He wondered if Wolfe was critical of him for not appointing a flag-captain before weighing anchor. The captain in question had been delayed on the road by his carriage losing a wheel. A fast rider had carried the news on ahead to Plymouth, but Herrick had decided to sail without further delay. But why? Was it really because of the need to reach Gibraltar and rid himself of the convoy, or was it because he could not still accept his temporary appointment to commodore, or wished to delay its confirmation for some reason he still did not understand?

Herrick shouted, 'According to the master we are some twenty-five miles off the French coast!' He ducked into the wind. 'God knows how old Ben Grubb can be so damn sure!'

Wolfe gasped as a solid sheet of spray burst through the nettings and drenched the already sodden watchkeepers and lookouts.

'Don't worry, sir! We'll round up the others when the wind eases!'

Herrick pulled himself along the rail. *If* it eases. He had been given just one frigate, the *Ganymede*. It was all the admiral could spare. Herrick swore quietly. Same old story. A small twenty-six-gun vessel at that, and she had made a fine beginning by losing her main topgallant mast within minutes of the gale raking the convoy like a giant's broadside.

Herrick had signalled her to stand closer inshore. With the gale rising at the time she might find more shelter and be able to rig a jury-mast and avoid further storm damage.

Soon afterwards Herrick had been unable to make any more signals, the wind and then an early darkness had made certain of that.

Wolfe struggled along the rail to join him again.

'The master insists that the wind will back by the forenoon, sir!' He peered at Herrick's sturdy outline, sensing his stubbornness. '*Ganymede* will have to beat clear if it backs further still!'

Herrick swung on him. 'God damn it, Mr Wolfe, I *know* that!' He relented just as quickly. 'The convoy's scattered, but John Company's *Duchess of Cornwall* is well able to fend for herself, she's probably better manned than *Benbow*, and certainly as well armed.'

He thought of Belinda Laidlaw who was aboard the big Indiaman, as safe as anyone could be in a summer storm in the Bay with the enemy's coast abeam.

Dulcie had made certain she had a good maid to take passage with her. She would be all right. But it troubled Herrick nonetheless. Women did not belong at sea, even as passengers.

He said, 'If only I *knew* . . .' He broke off, despising himself for baring his uppermost worry. Richard Bolitho might still be alive and somewhere out there in the darkness in a filthy Frog prison. Or lying helpless and dying in some fisherman's cottage.

In his heart Herrick knew that was one of his reasons for leaving Plymouth without waiting for his new flag-captain. To reach Gibraltar and return with a minimum of delay. There had been no news of *Styx*'s loss, not even a rumour about her people. Maybe they were all dead after all.

Water thundered along the upper deck, cascading over each tethered eighteen-pounder as if breaking across a line of reefs.

Herrick pictured Bolitho, saw him clearly as if he and not Wolfe was his companion.

He said shortly, 'I'm going aft, Mr Wolfe. Call me the instant you need me.'

Wolfe said, 'Aye, sir.'

He watched Herrick lurch to the companion way and then shook his head. If that was what friendship did to a man, you could keep it, he thought.

He saw the officer of the watch reeling below the poop, floundering in receding spray like a drowning man, and yelled, 'Mr Nash, sir! I'll trouble you to attend your duties! God damn your eyes, sir! You are like a whore at a wedding, all aback!'

The wretched lieutenant disappeared beneath the poop to join the helmsmen and master's mates by the big double wheel, more afraid of Wolfe than all the perils of sea-sickness and discomfort.

In the great cabin the sounds of wind and sea were muffled by the ship's massive timbers. Herrick sank into a chair, a puddle spreading across the chequered canvas from his watchcoat and boots.

He heard his servant come to life in the pantry, and was suddenly reminded of his thirst and hunger. He had taken nothing since noon yesterday. Had wanted nothing.

But it was little Ozzard who brought the food and drink to Herrick's table. He placed the tray carefully by his elbow, crouching like a small animal as he waited for the deck to fall and then steady itself again.

Herrick eyed him sadly. What was the point of trying to reassure Ozzard when he felt his own sense of loss like a wound?

Ozzard said timidly, 'I shall be close by if you want anything more, sir.'

Herrick sipped a goblet of brandy and waited for its heat to drive out the damp and the rawness of salt spray.

The marine sentry interrupted his thoughts. 'Midshipman o' th' watch, sir!'

Herrick turned wearily as the youth entered the cabin.

'Well, Mr Stirling?'

The midshipman was fourteen years old, and after the first few weeks of being appointed to *Benbow*, his first ship, was enjoying every minute. Protected by youth, and by the ability to thrive even on the ship's stale and unimaginative food, he was untouched by the sheer drama in which he was now involved.

'First lieutenant's respects, sir, and the horizon is lightening.'

His eyes moved quickly around the spacious cabin, a palace after the midshipman's berth on the orlop. Something to write to his parents about, to tell his fellow 'young gentlemen' during the watch below.

Herrick felt his head droop with fatigue and snapped, 'The wind?'

The youth swallowed hard under the captain's blue stare.

'Steady from the east'rd, sir. The master thinks it may be dropping.'

'Does he?' Herrick yawned and stretched. 'He's usually right.'

He realized that the midshipman was staring at the glittering presentation sword on the bulkhead.

He thought suddenly of Neale when he had been one of *Phalarope*'s midshipmen, of Adam Pascoe, who craved for a command of his own but was doubtless mourning the loss of his beloved uncle. Of all the other dozens, hundreds of midshipmen he had seen down the years. Some were captains, others had quit the sea to seek their fortunes elsewhere. And there were many who had not even reached young Stirling's tender years before death or injury had cut them down.

Herrick said quietly, 'Take it down if you like, Mr Stirling.'

The midshipman, his blue coat smeared with salt and tar stains, crossed to the rack, watched by Herrick and the small, stooped Ozzard. He took down the sword and held it beneath a deckhead lantern, turning it slowly to catch the engraving, the arms and decorations.

He said in a hushed voice, 'I never thought, sir, I — mean . . .' He turned, his eyes very bright. 'He must have been a fine officer, sir.'

Herrick jerked upright in the chair. '*Must* have been!' He saw the youth recoil and added hastily, 'Yes, Mr Stirling, he was. But better than that, boy, he was a man. The best.'

The midshipman replaced the sword very carefully and said, 'I'm very sorry, sir. I meant no hurt.'

Herrick shook his head. 'None taken, Mr Stirling. Because others hoped and believed, so too did I. I forgot that Lady Luck can only do so much, miracles are harder to come by.'

'I – I see, sir.'

Stirling backed to the door, his mind grappling with Herrick's words, not wanting to forget a single second of what had occurred.

Herrick watched him leave. *You don't see at all*. But one day, if you are one of the lucky ones, you *will* understand.

Minutes afterwards the goblet dropped from his fingers and broke in pieces on the deck.

Ozzard stared at the sleeping captain, his hands opening and shutting at his sides. He stooped to gather up the broken glass but then stood away again, his pinched features suddenly hostile.

The captain's own servant could do it. Ozzard glanced at the pantry door and tried to shut Herrick's words from his mind. He was wrong. They all were, damn them.

Ozzard went to the pantry and sat down in one corner while the ship shivered and groaned around him.

He was Rear-Admiral Bolitho's servant, and would be here when he returned, and that was an end to it!

Herrick hurried across the quarterdeck, half blinded by spray as he looked for Wolfe's tall shape by the nettings.

Wolfe shouted, 'There, sir! Hear it?'

Herrick licked his lips and ignored the shadowy figures and staring faces. There it was again. No doubt about it.

He said hoarsely, 'Gunfire.'

Wolfe nodded. 'Light artillery, sir. Probably *Ganymede* and another craft of the same ilk.'

Herrick strode up the tilting deck, his eyes straining into the feeble grey light and the panorama of tossing wave crests.

'Well, Mr Grubb?'

The master pouted and then nodded his ruined face. 'Right bearing, sir. Not likely to be any other King's ship thereabouts.'

Herrick glared at the tossing sea like a trapped animal. 'Any of our vessels in sight yet?'

Wolfe replied, 'I've already warned the masthead lookouts, sir. But nothing reported so far.'

Herrick heard it again, rolling down wind like staccato thunder. Two ships right enough. Fighting in the gale. Probably stumbled on one another by accident.

Wolfe asked, 'Orders, sir?'

'Until we sight *Nicator* we shall continue to hove to, Mr Wolfe.' He looked away. 'Unless . . .'

Wolfe grimaced. 'That's a powerful big word, sir.'

Herrick squinted, as if by doing so he would see the lay of the French coast as he had so many times on Grubb's charts. It would take an eternity to beat inshore against this easterly wind, but *Ganymede* might already be in desperate need of support. When full daylight broke, just the sight of *Benbow*'s canvas on the horizon would give them heart and throw uncertainty amongst her attackers.

Captain Keen would know what to do. As soon as he realized that the convoy was scattered he would set-to with his *Nicator* and chase them into formation again.

But suppose Keen could not collect all the ships and some arrived at Gibraltar unescorted? Herrick had no illusions as to what might happen. His time as commodore would be short-lived, and any sort of promotion would remain as one of Dulcie's dreams.

And if peace was to be signed between the old enemies, for no matter how short a respite, Herrick knew that when the drums beat to quarters once again his services would be shunned. It had happened to far better men with the background and influence he had never known.

He glanced at Wolfe, at Grubb's great lump of a figure in his shabby watchcoat, at the youthful Midshipman Stirling who had unknowingly touched his heart with his admiration for Bolitho, a man he had never met. His eyes moved on past them, unblinking despite the heavy droplets of spray, as he looked at his command, the *Benbow* and all her tightly-sealed world of people and memories. *His ship*. He would certainly lose her too.

Wolfe watched him, knowing it was important to all of them without understanding why.

Grubb, the sailing master who had played the old *Lysander* into battle with his tin whistle while all hell had exploded around him, *did* understand.

He said gruffly, 'If we brings 'er about now, sir, and lays 'er on th' larboard tack . . .'

Herrick turned and faced him. Once the decision was made, the rest was simple.

'I agree.' He looked at his gangling first lieutenant. 'Call all hands, Mr Wolfe. We shall make sail at once. Hands aloft, if you please, and loose tops'ls.' He stared abeam as more gunfire followed the wind. 'We will go and see what *Ganymede* has uncovered, eh?'

Herrick walked aft to the poop as calls shrilled and seamen and marines bustled to obey the pipe.

He paused by the wheel as Grubb gestured with a great fist to his master's mates to be ready to alter course. Young Midshipman Stirling was scribbling on a slate beside the chart table and waiting for a ship's boy to swing the half-hour glass. He looked up from his writing as Herrick drew near, and could not restrain a smile.

Herrick eyed him with a calmness he did not feel. 'What amuses you, Mr Stirling? May I share it?'

Stirling's smile faded as Grubb glared at him threateningly for disturbing the captain.

Then he said, 'You spoke of Lady Luck, sir. Perhaps she is still with us after all?'

Herrick shrugged. 'We shall see. In the meantime, take yourself to the foremast cross-trees and carry a glass with you. Let us see if your eyes are as sharp as your wits!'

Grubb watched the midshipman run for the weather

gangway, a telescope bobbing across his shoulder like a quiver.

'Gawd, sir, I really don't know! These young varmints 'ave got no respect, no understandin' of facts an' responsibilities.'

They faced each other gravely, and Herrick said softly, 'Not like us, eh, Mr Grubb? Not like us at all.'

Grubb grinned broadly as Herrick moved away. Then he saw the nearest helmsman watching him and roared, 'Stand by, you idle bugger! Or I'll be about yew with a pike, so 'elp me Gawd!'

Moments later, with her yards braced almost fore and aft, her lee gunports awash as she tilted heavily to the wind, *Benbow* came slowly about.

Herrick smiled with quiet satisfaction as topmen dashed about the upper yards, whilst on the deck below others ran to assist, to throw their weight on braces and halliards to make their ship turn deliberately towards the land.

It would be a slow and wearing process, with miles of tacking this way and that to gain a cable's advance.

But as Herrick watched his men, and studied the set of each sail, the strain of each piece of standing rigging, he was glad he had acted against his saner judgement.

'Full an' bye, sir!' A master's mate shouted excitedly, as if he too was sharing Herrick's mood. 'South by east!'

Herrick looked across at Wolfe who was directing his men through his long speaking trumpet. With his wings of bright red hair poking beneath his salt-stained hat he looked more like a Viking warrior than a King's officer, Herrick thought.

Perhaps it would be too late, or all a waste of time. But if they could capture a French ship, or even seize a few of her people, they might learn something of *Styx*'s survivors. Just a hint, the tiniest shred of information, would make it all worth while.

Wolfe lowered his speaking trumpet and called, 'We'll shake out another reef if the wind allows, sir.'

Herrick nodded. Wolfe understood now. 'Aye. And to hell with the consequences.'

Wolfe raised his eyes to the men working high above him and glanced at the scarlet broad-pendant which streamed from the masthead.

The captain had spoken of consequences. And there was the biggest one of all.

Bolitho pressed his shoulders against the frigate's timbers and winced as the ship yawed and plunged deeply into another trough. It was as if the hull would never rise again, and when the keel struck the side of the trough Bolitho felt the blow run through his body as if the vessel had driven hard aground.

He tried again and again to picture what was happening on deck and across the water where another ship was preparing to fight. The *Ceres* would have the wind-gage, but with such a deep swell running that could hinder as much as help. He heard distant shouts, the occasional rasp of spray-swollen rigging through blocks as the *Ceres'* captain worked his ship with every skill he knew to discover some advantage.

Allday made his way to a water cask and took his time filling a mug for Neale. He darted a glance up the nearest ladder and tried to understand what the Frenchmen were saying. The preparations for battle he understood of old, the quick, stooping shadows of powder-monkeys, the squeak of gun tackles, and above all the drumming force of wind into the reefed canvas.

He waited for the deck to settle and then hurried towards the side again. As he clung to the cot and held the mug to Neale's lips he said, 'Still a big sea running, sir. I can hear the water swilling about the gundeck.' He forced a grin. 'Give the Frogs somethin' to sweat on!'

Browne drew his knees up to his chin and examined his manacles with disgust.

'If only we could get away somehow.'

Bolitho lifted his eyes to the deckhead as more thuds and the clatter of handspikes told of the gun crews' difficulties.

The wind was driving them away from safety, and they would have to fight whether they wanted to or not.

He looked at the surgeon and his assistants. They were standing or squatting around their makeshift table like patient ghouls. It was a sight which never failed to unnerve him.

'Listen!'

They strained forward on their chains as a metallic voice penetrated the sounds of sea and wind like a trumpet.

'Rassemblez-vous à la batterie de tribord!'

Browne nodded jerkily. 'They're engaging to starboard first, sir!'

Allday gritted his teeth. 'Here we go. Up she rises!'

The broadside was violent and unexpected in spite of the warning. Bolitho felt the hull buck like a wild thing, saw the deck planking shiver as the guns crashed out in unison, the yells of their crews lost in the squeal of trucks, the urgent commands from aft.

Again. The *Ceres* seemed to fall steeply to one side as the guns roared out, the sound magnified and compressed into the orlop until Bolitho thought his ears would burst. Dust spurted from the planking, and he saw smoke drifting down the companion ladders like a moorland fog.

Some of the surgeon's men were flinching and staring at the smoke, others busied themselves with their instruments and buckets.

Browne said huskily, 'Two broadsides, sir. Nothing in return.'

Bolitho shook his head, not wishing to comment in case he missed something. He recognized all the sounds as well as Allday, the rammers and sponges, the scampering feet of shot-carriers, disjointed yells from individual gun-captains as they laid on their target.

What sort of ship was she? Large or small?

Once more the broadside flung them about, the guns riding inboard on their tackles like maddened beasts as their crews fought to control them and reload. Firing to leeward would make it difficult in these seas, Bolitho thought. The ports would be almost awash, and it would be hard to obtain full elevation if the other ship kept her wits about her.

There was some haphazard cheering, and then a slower broadside, pairs of guns firing from bow to stern with seconds between each shot.

Allday muttered bitterly, 'Our lads must be standing off, sir. Either that or the Frenchies have dismasted 'em.'

Bolitho watched the circle of lanterns around the table swing towards the deckhead and remain there as if held by invisible hands as the ship tilted over and then came slowly upright again. The captain had changed tack and was running more smoothly now with the wind under his coat tails, Bolitho decided. He had found his confidence, and was using the full force of the gale to quit the shelter of the land and go for the enemy. Bolitho tried to hide his disappointment. That meant the other ship was crippled or that her captain had found himself outmanoeuvred and probably outgunned.

The crash and thunder of iron against the hull was like an avalanche.

Bolitho gasped with pain as he was flung to the full extent of his manacles and chains, his head swimming as the orlop exploded in smoke and noise.

He felt the deck shiver as rigging and spars fell from aloft, and a deeper thunder as if a gun had been overturned. Men were shouting in the din, and other voices screamed pitifully as a second broadside smashed into the hull within minutes of the first.

Partly hidden by smoke, figures slithered and groped down the ladders, and others were dragged bodily into the lanterns' glow as the surgeon's mates came to life, roused by the sight and smell of blood.

The deck was swaying over again, and the French crews were returning fire. Balls slammed into the lower hull, and Bolitho heard the clank of a pump as the other ship's iron smashed home.

Above the table the surgeon's shadow rose and fell, the

lanterns glinting on a knife and then on a saw as he struck at the writhing, naked shape which his men were struggling to hold still.

Another man darted forward, and Bolitho saw the wounded sailor's arm tossed aside like so much meat.

More sobbing, protesting men were dragged and carried down to the orlop. Time had lost all meaning, and even the early daylight was blanketed now by swirling smoke and the fog of battle.

The surgeon seemed to dominate the place with his merciless energy. Bodies came and went, the more fortunate already unconscious as he went to work while his assistants stripped the next victim for his butcher's hands.

The gunfire was less controlled now, but louder, and Bolitho guessed that the other ship was very near, the roar of cannon trapped between the two antagonists, the pace so hot that the end must surely be soon.

Browne watched the surgeon, his eyes wide with fascinated horror. He was not a young man, but he moved with the speed of light. Fleshing, sawing, stitching and discarding each of the wounded without even pausing as more shots slammed into the hull and the sea alongside. His hands and apron were bright red. It was a scene from hell.

Browne said thickly, 'If I die, please God let it be on deck, and spare me this murder!'

There were warning cries, a brief chilling silence and then a prolonged thunder as a mast carried away and plunged down to the deck. The hull shook as if trying to free herself from the great mesh of fallen rigging and wildly flapping canvas, and even as the ring of axes echoed through the smoke, Bolitho heard the sharper bangs of swivel guns and muskets and said quickly, 'They're almost up to us!'

Shouts and screams filtered through the sounds of battle, and more wreckage fell across the upper deck, the dragging clatter of broken shrouds reminding Bolitho of *Styx*'s last moments when she had been dismasted.

Neale struggled up in the cot, his eyes wild as he shouted,

'To me, lads! *Stand fast!*' He tried to strike out at Allday but the blow was that of a child.

Allday said harshly, 'I'm going to get you out, Cap'n Neale! So you behave yourself!'

He ducked into some shadows where two wounded seamen lay apparently overlooked by the surgeon's mates. Allday rolled one of them on to his back. The Frenchman had a wood splinter the size of a dirk in his throat and was staring at Allday in agonized terror. Unable to speak, and barely capable of breathing, he watched Allday as he dragged a cutlass from his belt and thrust it through his own.

The second man was already dead and unarmed, so Allday made to move away. But something held him in spite of his anger and his hatred.

The eyes were staring at him, filling the man's face, as all the while his life ebbed away. He seemed to be pleading, asking the unknown man with the cutlass to spare him the terrible agony of his wound.

Allday bent down, and after a further hesitation drove the guard of his cutlass into the Frenchman's jaw.

'Die in peace, *mounseer*!'

He rejoined Bolitho and started to prise with the cutlass at the ring-bolt which secured his chain.

'I saw that.' Bolitho watched him, moved by Allday's rough compassion in spite of the nearness of death for all of them.

Allday said between his teeth, 'Might have been me, sir.'

Voices, confused and frightened, announced more arrivals on the orlop, but this time it was different. Bolitho saw an outflung arm, the spreading red stain on the man's side where a heavy ball had smashed through his ribs, but more than that, he saw the captain's gold epaulettes.

Two soldiers also came down the companion ladder, and Bolitho recognized their uniforms as those of a maritime regiment.

They stood apart from all the rest, their hands gripping their bayoneted muskets as they looked at the shackled prisoners, their intentions obvious.

The surgeon cut open the French captain's shirt and then gestured to his men.

'*Il est mort.*'

Stricken wounded men peered through the smoke, unable to accept what had happened.

Overhead there was less firing, as if everyone who had survived was still shocked by the loss of their commander.

Then came the slithering impact of the other ship grinding alongside.

The deck swayed steeply, and Bolitho guessed that the other captain had allowed the crippled *Ceres* to drift down to him, and now with rigging and spars entangled they were held firmly in a last embrace.

'*Huzza! Huzza!*' The shouts sounded wild and inhuman. 'To me, Ganymedes!'

Then the awful clash of steel, the occasional bang of musket and pistol before feet trampled over them as they tried to reload.

To the soldiers it was like a signal. Bolitho saw the nearest one, a corporal, raise his musket, the bayonet glinting in the lanterns as he aimed it straight at Neale's chest.

'Too late, matey!' Allday bounded up from the side, the big cutlass swinging and hacking the soldier across the mouth like an axe in a log. As the man fell writhing in his own blood, Allday turned towards the second one. The man had also raised his musket but was stricken like a rabbit confronted by a fox after seeing his companion fall.

Allday yelled, 'Not so brave now, eh?'

Browne swallowed hard as the cutlass slashed the man's cross-belt apart. The force of the blow made the soldier double over, his cries silenced as the cutlass hacked him across his exposed neck.

Above and seemingly all around the air was rent with shouts, curses and screams. Steel on steel, while feet staggered and slipped in blood, and bodies thrust and ducked to gain and hold an advantage.

Allday clung to the swaying cot with one hand and threatened any circling figure who came near. A musket ball slammed into the side within inches of Bolitho's shoulder, and he heard Allday's blade hiss over his head like a protective scythe.

A corpse fell headlong down the companion ladder, and someone gave a terrible cry before a blade silenced him instantly, as if a great door had been slammed shut.

Hatless, his white breeches smeared with blood, and his eyes blazing like fuses, a British marine stood on the ladder, his levelled bayonet shaking on the end of his musket.

He saw Allday with his bared cutlass and yelled, 'Here, lads! There are more o' the bastards!' Then he lunged.

Allday had fought alongside the marines in many a boarding party or skirmishes ashore, but never before had he seen the madness of battle from the other side.

The man was crazed with fighting, a kind of lust which had left him a survivor in the fierce struggle from ship to ship.

Allday knew it was pointless to fight the man off until he could explain. More figures were stumbling down the ladder, marines and seamen alike. He would be dead in seconds unless he acted.

'*Stand still, you stupid bullock!*' Allday's bellow brought the marine skidding to a halt. 'Cut these officers free or I'll cleave your skull in!'

The marine gaped at him and then began to laugh. There was no sound, but his whole body shook uncontrollably, as if it would never stop.

Then a lieutenant appeared, a bloodied hanger in his hand as he peered around the orlop, sniffing for danger.

He pushed past the marine and stared at Neale and then at the others.

'In God's name. Get these men on deck. Lively, the captain's ordered our recall.'

A seaman brought a spike and levered the ring-bolt out of the timber, then hoisted Bolitho and Browne to their feet.

The lieutenant said sharply, 'Come along now! No time to dawdle!'

Bolitho loosened the manacles on his wrist, and as two seamen prepared to lift Neale from his cot said quietly, 'That is Captain John Neale of the frigate *Styx*.' He waited for the lieutenant to turn. 'I'm afraid I did not catch *your* name Mr, er . . . ?'

The first madness of battle was already passing, and several of the boarding party even managed to grin at their lieutenant's discomfort.

The lieutenant snapped, 'Nor I yours, *sir*!'

Browne took a first careful step towards the waiting seamen. How he managed it he did not know, although Allday later swore he never even blinked.

Browne said coldly, '*This* is Rear-Admiral Richard Bolitho. Does that satisfy you, sir? Or is this the day for hurling insults at all your betters?'

The lieutenant sheathed his hanger and flushed. 'I – I am indeed sorry, sir.'

Bolitho nodded and walked slowly to the foot of the companion ladder. High above him he could see the hatch which opened on to the gundeck. It was unnaturally bright, and he guessed the ship had been completely dismasted.

He gripped the ladder hard to control his shaking hands.

To the lieutenant he said, 'You did well. I heard you shout *Ganymede*.'

The lieutenant wiped his mouth with his sleeve. He was beginning to shiver. Now it was over, later would come the pain of what he had seen and done.

Discipline helped, and he was able to forget his humiliation when he had all but dragged Bolitho to his feet in his eagerness to get back to the ship.

He replied, 'Aye, sir. We are part of an escort. Under the broad-pendant of Commodore Herrick.'

Bolitho looked at him for several seconds. It was impossible. He was as mad as the marine.

'Perhaps you know him, sir.' The lieutenant winced under Bolitho's gaze.

'Very well.'

Bolitho climbed on deck, each step on the ladder standing out with unusual clarity, every sound distinct and extra loud.

He passed through stained and panting boarders, resting on their weapons, grinning and nodding to him as he passed.

Bolitho saw the other ship grappled alongside, a midshipman hurrying aft to inform the captain whom they had discovered in the *Ceres* before Bolitho arrived.

The captain strode to meet him, his pleasure clear in his voice as he exclaimed, 'You are most welcome, sir, and I am grateful that my ship was of service.' He gestured ruefully to the damage to his rigging and decks. 'I was outgunned, so I tempted him into a chase. After that . . .' He shrugged. 'It was all a question of experience. The French have some fine ships. Fortunately, they do not have our Jacks to man them.'

Bolitho stood on the *Ganymede*'s deck and took a deep breath. In a moment he would awake in the carriage or the prison, and then . . .

The captain was saying, 'We have sighted two enemy sail, but they are staying their distance. But I fear we must abandon our prize. The wind is shifting.'

'Deck there! Sail on th' lee bow!'

The captain said sharply, 'Recall the boarding party and cast that hulk adrift. She'll not fight again.'

The masthead lookout yelled again, 'Ship o' th' line, sir! Tis the *Benbow*!'

Bolitho walked across the deck and knelt beside Neale who had been laid there to await the surgeon's attention.

Neale stared up at the sky and whispered, 'We did it, sir. Together.'

His hand lifted from his side and clasped Bolitho's as firmly as he could.

'*It was all I wanted, sir.*'

Allday crouched on his other side to shield his eyes from the early sunlight.

'Easy, Cap'n Neale. You're going *home* now, you see.'

But Bolitho felt the hand go limp in his, and after a moment he bent over to close Neale's eyes.

'He's there, Allday. He's gone home.'

10

For the Admiral's Lady

'I *still* can't believe it, sir.'

Herrick shook his head again, unable to accept what his decision had brought. From the moment he had made signalling contact with the frigate *Ganymede* he had paced up and down the quarterdeck, cursing the time it took for both ships to draw together, the further, seemingly endless delay as his own coxswain, Tuck, had taken the barge to collect Bolitho.

He had listened enthralled as Bolitho had sat by the stern windows in his torn clothing and had allowed Ozzard to fuss over him like a nursery maid.

And now, with the frigate following in *Benbow*'s wake, they were standing away from the French coast, the wind no longer an enemy.

Bolitho explained, '*Ganymede* was at a disadvantage. Her captain tried an old ruse and tempted the *Ceres* to follow him. He even took some severe damage to give the enemy over-confidence.' He shrugged heavily. It no longer seemed to matter. 'Then he luffed, and put two broadsides into her before she knew what was happening. It still could have gone against him, but the last raking cut down *Ceres*' captain, and the rest you know, Thomas.'

He had already told Herrick about the new chain of semaphore stations, but even that seemed unimportant set against Neale's death.

Herrick saw the pain in his eyes and said, 'The French ships which were sighted as *Benbow* showed herself must have been directed to aid *Ceres* by that same semaphore.' He rubbed his chin. 'Well, we know about it now, damn them.'

Bolitho stared past him at the empty sword rack. 'And they will know we know. The danger is there just the same.'

He thought of the two soldiers who had fallen to Allday's cutlass. They must have had specific orders to kill the prisoners if the ship was in danger of being seized. It had been that close.

But the arrival of the French ships had made *Ceres'* capture impossible. It would not be long before the French high command knew that their prisoners had escaped, that the secret would be out.

Lieutenant Wolfe entered the cabin and tried not to stare at Bolitho as he was stripped of his shirt and torn breeches by Loveys, the ship's surgeon, while he lay against the seat and consumed his fifth cup of scalding coffee.

Wolfe said, 'With respect, sir. Convoy in sight to the sou'-east. All accounted for.'

Herrick smiled. 'Thank you. I'll come up presently.'

As the door closed Bolitho said, 'You took a wild risk, Thomas. Your head would have been on the block if the convoy had been in danger. The fact *you* thought it safe would have carried as much water as a shrimping net at your court martial.'

Herrick grinned. 'I felt certain I'd discover something if only I could help *Ganymede* to take the enemy.' He eyed Bolitho warmly. 'I never dreamed . . . .'

'Neither did I.'

Bolitho looked up as Ozzard, followed by Allday, entered the cabin with clean clothing and his other dress coat.

He said wearily, 'Fetch the old sea-going one, Ozzard. I don't feel like celebrating.'

Allday stared at Herrick with disbelief. 'You've not told him, sir?'

'Told me what?' He needed to be alone. To sift his feelings, decide what to do, discover where he had gone wrong.

Herrick looked almost as astonished as Allday. 'Damn my eyes, in all the excitement I forgot to explain!'

Bolitho listened without a word, as if by inserting a

question, or by trying to smooth out the ridges in Herrick's tale, he might destroy it completely.

As Herrick lapsed into silence he said, 'And she is in the convoy, Thomas? *Right here*, amongst us?'

Herrick stammered, 'Aye, sir. I was that worried, you see—'

Bolitho stood up and took Herrick's hard hands in his. 'Bless you, old friend. This morning I believed I had taken enough, more than I could safely hold. But now . . .' He shook his head slowly. 'You have told me something which is stronger than any balm.'

He turned away, as if he expected to see the other ships through the stern windows. Belinda had taken passage to Gibraltar. Danger and discomfort had meant nothing, his likely fate had not shaken her confidence for an instant. And now she was here in the Bay.

Herrick moved towards the door, content and troubled at the same time.

'I'll leave you. It will be a while before we exchange signals.' He hesitated, unwilling to cast a shadow on the moment. 'About Captain Neale . . .'

'We'll bury him at dusk. His friends and family in England will have their memories of him. As he once was. But I think he'd wish to stay with his men.'

The door closed silently, and Bolitho lay back again and allowed the sun to warm him through the thick glass.

Neale had known from the beginning he was going to die. Only his occasional bouts of delirium had deceived the rest of them. One thought, one force had kept him going, and that had been freedom. To gain it in company of his friends so that he could die in peace had been paramount. *It was all I wanted*, he had said. His last words on earth.

Bolitho found he was on his feet without noticing he had moved. He did not even see Browne enter the cabin, or Allday's sudden concern.

John Neale was gone. He would not die unavenged.

*

Barely making a ripple above her own black and buff reflection, *Benbow* moved slowly past other anchored vessels, all of which were dwarfed by the towering natural fortress of Gibraltar.

It was morning, with the Rock and surrounding landscape partly hidden in mist, a foretaste of the heat to come.

Bolitho stood apart from the other officers and left Herrick free to manoeuvre his command the last cable or so to the anchorage. With all canvas but topsails and jib clewed up, *Benbow* would make a fine sight as she altered course very slightly away from her convoy, the largest vessel of which was already making signals to the shore.

It had taken nearly nine days to reach Gibraltar, and Grubb had described it as a fair and speedy passage. To Bolitho it had been the longest he could recall, and even the daily sight of Belinda on the Indiaman's poop had failed to calm his sense of urgency and need.

From the beginning, when Herrick had made a signal to the *Duchess of Cornwall*, their daily rendezvous, separated by the sea and one other ship, had been without any sort of arrangement. It was as if she knew he would be there, as if she had to see him to ensure it was not a dream but a twist of fate which had brought them together. Bolitho had watched her through a telescope, oblivious to the glances of his officers and other watchkeepers. She always waved, her long hair held down by a large straw hat which in turn was tied beneath her chin by a ribbon.

Now the waiting was almost over and Bolitho felt strangely nervous.

Herrick's voice interrupted his thoughts.

'Hands wear ship!'

Wolfe's long legs emerged from the mizzen mast's shadow. 'Man the braces, there! Tops'l sheets!'

Bolitho shaded his eyes and looked towards an anchored man-of-war. She had already been identified by the signals midshipman. She was the *Dorsetshire* – 80, flagship of Vice-Admiral Sir John Studdart. He could see the admiral's flag drooping almost lifelessly from the *Dorsetshire*'s foremast, and wondered what the officer of the watch would make of his own flag at *Benbow*'s mizzen instead of Herrick's broad-pendant.

'Tops'l clew lines! *Wake up*, that man!'

Grubb called, 'Ready, sir!'

'Helm a-lee!'

With tired dignity *Benbow* turned very slowly into the breeze, the way going off her as the remaining sails flapped in confusion before they were fisted to the yards by the waiting topmen.

'*Let go!*'

Spray flew above the forecastle as the big anchor splashed down into the clear water and more feet stampeded to the boat tier in readiness for lowering the barge alongside with a minimum delay.

Glasses would have been trained on the *Benbow*'s performance from the moment she had begun her final approach, her fifteen-gun salute to the vice-admiral's flag booming and reverberating around the bay like a bombardment. Gun for gun the flagship had replied, the smoke drifting upwards on the warm air to mingle with haze which encircled the Rock like cloud.

'Away, barge crew!' That was Allday, his face showing nothing of the strain he must have endured as a prisoner, his natural sense of responsibility for Bolitho making it that much worse for him.

Herrick joined Bolitho by the nettings and touched his hat.

'Will you go across to the flagship now, sir?'

'Aye, Thomas. No sense in delaying. Someone else might get to Sir John's ear before me otherwise.' His eyes moved to the distant Indiaman. 'I have much to do.'

Herrick saw the quick glance. It was not lost on him, any more than all the other times when he had seen Bolitho on deck, looking for the slim figure in the shady straw hat.

'Barge alongside, sir.' Wolfe watched him curiously, ever

ready to learn something from the bond which linked Bolitho to Herrick.

Major Clinton's marines were at the entry port, the boatswain's mates ready with their silver calls and moistening them on their lips.

Bolitho pressed his sword against his hip, sensing its unfamiliarity, the feeling of loss for his old family blade. He gritted his teeth and walked towards the port. He tried not to limp or to show his sadness for what had gone before. Little pictures flitted through his mind. The old sword on the French commandant's table, the swarthy rear-admiral, Jean Remond, who had been unable to accept that Bolitho would not swear to make no escape attempt. Above and through it all he saw Neale. Brave, despairing, and in the last seconds of life, strangely content.

The marines presented arms, the calls shrilled, and Bolitho climbed swiftly down to the barge where Allday, splendid in his blue coat and nankeen breeches, and hat in hand, stood to receive him.

Browne was already in the sternsheets, expressionless as he studied Bolitho's face.

They all watch me, Bolitho thought. Did they expect to see more than a man?

'Bear off forrard! Give way, all!' Allday thrust the tiller bar over, his eyes slitted against the reflected glare.

Bolitho asked softly, 'You feel glad to be back, Allday?'

The big coxswain nodded, but did not take his eyes from the nearby guard-boat.

'I've damned the fleet an' all it stands for a few times, sir, an' I'd be a Tom Pepper if I said different.' He glanced briefly at the guard-boat, her oars tossed, a lieutenant standing to remove his hat as the rear-admiral's barge sped past him. 'But it's my world for now. Home.'

Browne said, 'I can understand that too, sir.'

Bolitho settled down on the thwart, his hat tugged firmly across his forehead.

'We all but lost it, Oliver.'

'Toss your oars! Stand by, bowman!' Allday ignored the faces above the *Dorsetshire*'s gangway, the glint of sunlight on bayonets, the scarlets and blues, the difference of one ship from another.

Bolitho climbed up to the entry port and the clatter and shrill of salutes began all over again.

He saw the vice-admiral by the poop as he waited for his flag-captain to complete the formal welcome before he strolled across the quaterdeck to make his own.

Bolitho had known Studdart as a fellow captain during the American revolution. But he had not seen him for several years and was surprised he had aged so much. He had grown portly, and his round, untroubled face looked as if he enjoyed good living to the full.

He shook him warmly by the hand and exclaimed, 'Damn me eyes, Bolitho, you are a sight indeed! Last thing I heard was that the Frogs had stuck your head on a pike!' He laughed loudly. 'Come aft and tell me all. I'd like to be on the same tack as the news bulletins.' He gestured vaguely towards the side. 'No doubt the Dons in Algeciras saw your arrival just now. They'll pass the word to Boney, of that I'm certain.'

In the great cabin it was comparatively cool, and after dismissing his servants and sending Browne on an errand, Vice-Admiral Sir John Studdart settled down in silence to listen to Bolitho's story. He did not interrupt once, and as Bolitho outlined his ideas on the enemy's chain of semaphore stations he found time to admire Studdart's relaxed self-control. No wonder he had been promoted ahead of his time. He had taught himself not to worry, or at least not to show it.

Bolitho touched only lightly on Neale's death, and it was then that the vice-admiral felt moved to speak.

'*Styx*'s loss was an accident of war. The death of her captain no less distressing.' He reached out to refill their wine goblets. 'However, I would not expect you to blame yourself for his death. Your flag flies above *Benbow*, as mine does here. It is why we were given the honour to lead, and why Admiral Beauchamp selected *you* for the task in Biscay. You did all you could. No one can blame you now. The very fact you discovered the presence of an efficient French semaphore system, when none of our so called agents has seen fit to inform us, is an additional bounty. Your value to England and the Navy is your life. By escaping with honour, you have fulfilled the faith which Admiral Beauchamp bestowed on you.' He leaned back and studied him cheerfully. 'Am I right?'

Bolitho said, 'I've still not achieved what I was sent to do. The destruction of the enemy's invasion craft before they are moved to the Channel took priority in my orders. As for our knowing about the semaphore stations along the Biscay coast, it can make no difference. The French can still direct their ships where they are most needed while ours are floundering off shore for all to see. And the newly built invasion craft are all the safer now that our captains are aware of their additional protection.'

Studdart smiled wryly. 'You've not changed, I'll say that. Dashing about the countryside like a junior lieutenant, risking life and limb when you should be ordering others to take a few chances.' He shook his head, suddenly grave. 'It won't do. You have your written orders, and only their lordships can alter them. Once they know you are safe. Maybe news will arrive in the next vessel from England, who knows? But you are in a position to postpone all further action. Beauchamp's strategy is already out-of-date because of what you discovered when you were taken prisoner. Let it lie, Bolitho. You have a record which anyone, even Nelson, would envy. Don't create enemies in high places. Peace or war, your future is assured. But stir up trouble in Admiralty or Parliament and you are done for.'

Bolitho rubbed his palm along the arm of his chair. He felt trapped, resentful, even though he knew Studdart's advice was sound.

Who would care next year what had happened in Biscay? Perhaps it was all rumour anyway and the French were as desperate for peace as anyone, and with no thought of forcing an invasion when their old enemy was off guard.

Studdart was watching him. 'At least *think* about it,
Bolitho.' He waved one hand towards the stern windows.
'You could remain here a while, and perhaps request new
orders. You might be sent into the Mediterranean to join
Saumarez on his campaign, anything would be preferable to
the damned Bay of Biscay.'

'Yes, sir. I shall think about it.' He put down his goblet
very carefully. 'In the meantime, I have to complete some
despatches for England.'

The vice-admiral tugged out his watch and examined it.
'God's teeth, I am expected ashore by the general in one
hour.' He got to his feet and regarded Bolitho calmly. 'Do
more than think about it. You are a flag-officer, and must not
involve yourself with the affairs of subordinates. You command, they obey, it is the old order of things, as well you
know.'

Bolitho stood up and smiled. 'Yes, sir.'

The vice-admiral waited until his visitor had reached the
door and then said, 'Give the lady my warmest regards. She
might care to sup with me before she leaves the Rock, eh?'

As the door closed Studdart walked slowly to the stern
windows and stared at the anchored ships of his squadron.

Bolitho would not take heed of his advice, and they both
knew it.

The second time he might not be so lucky. Either way.
Death or ignominy would be the outcome if he failed again.

Yet in spite of that realization Studdart was surprised to
find he envied him.

The Honourable East India Company's ship *Duchess of
Cornwall* presented a scene of orderly confusion which left
little room for the courtesies of greeting a King's officer, even
a rear-admiral.

Leaving Allday scowling up from the barge, and followed
closely by Browne, Bolitho allowed himself to be led aft by a

harassed lieutenant.

She was a fine ship, he thought grudgingly. No wonder sailors preferred the pay and comfort of an Indiaman to the harsh life in a man-of-war.

Tackles swayed and bobbed from lighters alongside, and as cargo was unloaded with skilled ease, more boxes and well-packed nets were lowered through the hatches for the next leg of the voyage.

The most unfamiliar setting to Bolitho was the chattering crowd of passengers who had either come aboard or were waiting to be ferried across to the garrison.

Wives of senior officers and officials, Bolitho supposed, part of that unseen army of which the people at home knew very little. Storemen and chandlers, sailmakers and farriers, ships' agents and soldiers of fortune, they must surely outnumber the rest by two to one.

'The captain is here, sir.'

Bolitho scarcely heard him. She was standing by the rail, one hand holding her hat to shield her face from the sun. Its ribbon was pale blue like her gown, and when she laughed at something the captain had said to her, Bolitho felt his heart almost stop beating.

An instinct made her turn towards him, her brown eyes very steady as she held his gaze with hers.

The Indiaman's captain was thickset and competent. Another Herrick perhaps.

He said, 'Welcome aboard, sir. I've just been telling Mrs Laidlaw that I'd willingly sacrifice every penny I make on this voyage just to keep her as my passenger.'

She joined with his laughter, but her eyes told Bolitho to ignore it. Other people's words had no value here.

Bolitho took her hand and kissed it. The touch of her skin, the smell of its freshness, almost broke his reserve. Maybe he had not recovered and would make a fool of himself when all he wanted to do was . . .

She said softly, 'I prayed for this moment, dearest. For this and all the others to come.' Her lip quivered but she tossed her head with something like defiance. 'I never doubted you would come. Never.'

The ship's captain backed away to join the other passengers, murmuring something which neither of them heard.

She looked at Browne and smiled. 'I am glad you are safe, Lieutenant. And free again.'

Then she put her hand through Bolitho's arm and turned him towards the side, shutting out everyone but themselves.

'Thomas Herrick sent word over to the ship, Richard.' She squeezed his arm tightly. 'He told me something of what you endured, about your friend Neale. Don't hide the hurt from me, dearest. There's no need any more.'

Bolitho said, 'I wanted him to live so much, but perhaps it was to reassure myself because of what I had brought him to. I – I thought I understood, but I had learned nothing. Perhaps I care too much, but I cannot change now, nor can I toss lives away merely because my orders are unquestioned.' He turned and looked down at her face, fixing it in his mind like a perfect portrait. 'But my love for you is real. Nothing can ever change that. I did think—'

She reached up and closed his lips with her fingers. 'No. I am here because I wanted to try and help. It must have been decided we should meet here.' She tossed back her hair and laughed. 'I am happy now. And I shall make you so!'

Bolitho touched her hair and remembered how it had hidden her face in the overturned carriage. That too had been 'decided'. Prearranged. So there was a fate, just as there was hope.

A master's mate hovered beside them and touched his hat nervously. He did not look at Bolitho, who guessed the man had probably run from the Navy originally to find security in the East India Company.

'Beggin' yer pardon, ma'am, but the boat's waitin', with your maid already aboard with your boxes.'

'Thank you.' She squeezed Bolitho's hand's until her nails bit into his skin. She whispered, 'I'm so sorry, my dearest, but I am close to tears. My joy is almost too much.' She smiled and pushed the hair from her eyes. 'I must say farewell to the ship's captain. He has been most attentive. But I think he was somewhat in awe when he saw you in the *Benbow*!'

Bolitho smiled. 'I never thought I'd want to be a grocery captain like him. But with you for a passenger, I'm not so sure.'

Browne watched fascinated as the lines softened around Bolitho's mouth and eyes. A few minutes together and she had done that for him. One day he would meet a girl like Belinda Laidlaw, such as the one in his dreams, galloping to meet him on a splendid mount.

A thought crossed his mind, and when Bolitho walked to the entry port he saw *Benbow*'s barge directly below him, the maid and a pile of boxes filling the sternsheets where Allday stood beaming up at him.

Browne explained awkwardly, 'Well, sir, I thought, for the admiral's lady it should be an admiral's barge.'

Bolitho looked at him gravely and then touched his arm. 'That was well said, Oliver. I'll not forget.'

Browne flushed. 'And here she comes, sir.'

She joined them by the port and stared down at the green-painted barge for several seconds.

Then she looked at Bolitho, her eyes misty. 'For me, Richard?'

Bolitho nodded. 'I'd give you the world if I could.'

With great care she was assisted into the barge, the seamen in their checkered shirts and tarred hats peering round their tossed oars as if a creature from another world had suddenly come amongst them.

Allday held out his hand to guide her to a cushion on the thwart, but she took it in hers and said quietly, 'I am *pleased* to see you again, John Allday.'

Allday swallowed hard and waited for Bolitho to sit down. She had come to them. She had even remembered his name.

He glanced at the maid and winked.

'Bear off forrard!'

Allday thought of the lordly Indiaman and the easy discipline of her people. Then he looked at his barge crew, men hardened by the sea and by war. Originally from the jails and the gutters, but he knew he would not change one of them for John Company's hands.

'Give way, all!'

'What will you do now, Belinda?' It was even hard to speak her name aloud after nursing it in his mind for so long.

'Take passage for England.' She turned to look at *Benbow* as the barge swept abeam. 'I would that I could sail with her!'

Bolitho smiled. 'In a King's ship? Poor Thomas would never rest at nights with you in his care!'

She dropped her eyes. 'I must be alone with you. I am ashamed of the way I feel, but I am helpless.'

Bolitho saw the eyes of the stroke oarsman fix on a point somewhere above the girl's shoulder. If he had heard her words the stroke would have been thrown into chaos.

'I am the same. Once I have seen you received ashore I shall see what must be done for your safe passage to England.' He wanted to touch her, to hold her.

She asked, 'When will *you* be going home?'

Bolitho heard the note of anxiety in her voice. 'Soon.' He tried not to think about his despatches which he would send in the next fast packet. Orders which would bring *Indomitable* and *Odin* to make up the full strength of his small squadron. In her heart Belinda must already know how it would be. He said, 'Then we shall be together.'

At the jetty there were two civilians, a man and a woman, waiting to meet them.

The man, a ruddy, genial giant, said, 'We'll take good care of her, Admiral! Visit whenever you will, though from all the rumour flying round the Rock, my guess is that you'll up-anchor again soon!' He grinned, not realizing what he was causing. 'Give those Frogs a bloody nose or two, eh, sir!'

Bolitho removed his hat and murmured something appropriate.

Once more they held hands and looked at one another without caring, without hiding their feelings.

'I shall come, Belinda. No matter what.'

He kissed her hand, and as he did so he saw her other hand move as if to touch his face. He released her fingers and stood back.

At the jetty he found Browne prowling up and down above the barge. He saw Bolitho and touched his hat.

'I have just seen a packet drop anchor, sir. She hoisted a signal to the Flag, despatches on board for the admiral.'

Bolitho looked past him. The big Indiaman and another of the ships from the convoy were already shortening their cables and shaking out their canvas ready to sail. Far out to sea, her upper yards hidden in mist, a frigate lay hove to, an escort to shepherd them clear of any potential danger.

Life went on. It had to. It was what Studdart had tried to explain, just as he had warned him of the consequences of failure.

The packet had probably brought new orders for Herrick, as nobody in England would yet have heard of *Ceres'* destruction and their escape.

What then? Should he take Studdart's advice and await a further ruling from the Admiralty?

Again he thought of the *Styx*, the bleeding and dazed survivors on the beach. The Frenchman who had attacked one of the sailors, the girl who had stared at him from the crowd.

There was no easy way, nor had there ever been.

He looked down into the waiting barge. *For the admiral's lady*.

If he turned back now he would dishonour himself. Worse, she might despise him too when time sharpened the memory of his decision.

Allday recognized the mood better than words.

Here we go again, John. He thought he knew how Bolitho felt, and later on he might even share it with him.

He grinned unsympathetically at his bargemen. The rest? They would follow the flag and do their duty, for that was the lot of poor Jack.

11

So Little Time

'Make six copies and bring them to me for signature.' Bolitho looked over Yovell's shoulder and marvelled that so large a man could write with such a neat, round hand.

Herrick sat by the stern windows and watched the smoke from his long pipe as it curled out and over the placid water of the bay. It was still only afternoon, and it had been bustle, bustle, bustle from the moment the anchor had hit the bottom.

He said, 'When the Admiralty receive your despatches they'll *know* you're alive and well, sir.' He chuckled softly. 'Your intended action against the Frogs will make a few sore heads in Whitehall, I'll wager.'

Bolitho moved restlessly about the cabin and tried to discover if he had forgotten anything. Captain Inch would have already sailed his repaired *Odin* around from the Nore to join Veriker's *Indomitable* at Plymouth, and Keen's ship lay at anchor here, less than a cable distant. *We happy few*. They were getting fewer.

The fast packet which had anchored during the forenoon with despatches for Sir John Studdart had also carried further orders for Herrick, as he had suspected. He was to return to Plymouth with *Nicator* and the frigate *Ganymede* in company, where he would take overall charge of the squadron until further instructions.

Fast packets, like the hard-worked courier-brigs, had little time to themselves. This one, the *Thrush*, would sail in the morning, and his despatches had to be on board.

Their lordships would get a shock when they found that not only was he alive, but had been rescued by his own flagship.

He watched the clerk gather up his papers and stride heavily from the cabin. He had no need to ask him to hurry. Yovell would have everything ready to sign with time to spare.

Bolitho thought of the one sour note in Herrick's orders. He was to make contact with the blockading force off Belle Ile and notify Captain Emes that he would stand before a court martial once *Phalarope* was relieved from her station.

He thought it wrong and unfair, even though the instigators of the orders had no idea that the squadron's rear-admiral was alive and free from captivity.

Herrick, on the other hand, had been adamant in his contempt for Emes' actions.

'Of course he was wrong, sir. Leave *Styx* to fend for herself and disobey your orders to close with the enemy? If I'd been there I'd have run him up to *Benbow*'s main-yard and save the expense of a court martial!'

A boat pulled slowly below the stern, some seamen singing and skylarking as they made their way back to their ship. Bolitho watched them. To the *Thrush*. He had already discovered that no other such vessel was leaving for England for a week.

Belinda would have to be put aboard for, although he had learned that the people with whom she was staying were friends she had known in India, Gibraltar was no place for her to remain. The squadron would put to sea without delay. If fate turned against him after raising his hopes so high, she would need to be in England, in Falmouth where she would be cared for and loved.

He gestured to Ozzard to fetch some wine from his cooler and said, 'Now, Thomas, there is a matter I wish to discuss.'

Herrick emptied his pipe and proceeded to refill it with slow, deliberate stabs of his finger.

He did not look up but said, 'You have already done so, sir, and my answer is the same. I was appointed acting-commodore because the squadron was divided. You still command the full force as described in the orders.' He looked up, his blue eyes hidden in shadow. 'Do you want me to be like Emes and run when I'm needed?'

Bolitho took two goblets from Ozzard and carried them to his friend.

'You know that is rubbish, Thomas. It is not the risk of battle which worries me, but the threat to your future. I can send you with another force to watch over Lorient. That would keep your broad-pendant where it belongs, at the masthead. Damn it, man, you deserve it and much more beside! If you had obeyed the rules and left *Ganymede* to cut and run from the French, I would still be a prisoner. D'you imagine I'm not grateful for that? But if the price for my safety is your loss of promotion, then I'm not so sure of the bargain.'

Herrick did not flinch. 'I didn't wait for the arrival of my new flag-captain when I quit Plymouth. I never expected to command a ship-of-the-line such as *Benbow*. So a captain I'll probably remain until they kick me on to the beach for good.' He grinned. 'I know one dear lady who would not be too worried by that.'

Bolitho dropped on to the bench and studied him gravely. 'And if I order you, Thomas?'

Herrick held a taper to his pipe and puffed placidly for several seconds.

'Ah, well, sir. We'd have to see. But, of course, if you send me out of the main squadron before you commit it to an attack, which in all probability will be cancelled anyway, their lordships will see your act as a lack of confidence.' He eyed him stubbornly. 'So if I am to face ruin either way, I'd rather remain here as your second-in-command.'

Bolitho smiled. 'God, man, you're like Allday!'

'Good.' Herrick reached for his goblet. 'He is the only man I know who makes you listen to sense.' He grinned. 'No disrespect, sir.'

Bolitho laughed. 'None taken.'

He stood up and walked to the sword rack. 'I wonder what has happened to the old sword, Thomas?' He shook himself as if to drive away the past. 'In truth, I have nothing left. They took my watch, everything.'

Herrick nodded. 'A new start. Perhaps that too was intended.'

'Maybe.'

Herrick added, 'Anyway, let's get to sea and finish this damnable waiting.' When Bolitho remained silent he said, 'For once you are not so keen to leave, sir. And I'm sure I don't blame you.'

Bolitho took down the bright presentation sword and examined it while he tortured himself with his doubts.

Herrick said, 'A lot of good folk put their faith into that sword, sir. Because they trusted you, because you are one of their own sons. So don't you fret on it now. Whatever happens they'll stand by you.' He stood up abruptly and added, 'And so will I.' He lurched unsteadily against the seat and grinned. 'Ship's a bit lively, sir.'

Bolitho watched him, moved as always by his sincerity.

'It's like a mill-pond, Thomas. Too much wine, that's your trouble.'

Herrick gathered up his dignity and walked towards the door. 'And why not, sir? I'm celebrating.'

Bolitho watched him leave and murmured, 'And God bless you for that, Thomas.'

Browne must have been waiting in the lobby, and as he entered Bolitho said, 'Visit the *Thrush*'s master, Oliver, and arrange passage for—' he turned and faced him '—your admiral's lady. Make certain she is well cared for. You, better than anybody I know, can manage that.'

Browne watched him impassively. 'They sail tomorrow, sir. Early.'

'I know.'

All this way she had come to find him, directed by some uncanny faith in his survival. Now he was putting her aboard another ship. And yet somehow he knew he was right, that she would understand.

He said suddenly, 'I'm going ashore. Have them pipe for my barge crew.' He was speaking quickly in case he should discover an argument against his own actions. 'If anything happens, I shall be . . .' He hesitated.

Browne handed him his hat and the regulation pattern sword which Herrick had given him.

'I understand, sir. Leave everything to me.'

Bolitho clapped him on the shoulder. 'How did I ever manage without you?'

Browne followed him on deck, and while the calls shrilled to muster the barge crew he said, 'It is mutual, sir.'

As the barge pulled rapidly clear of *Benbow*'s shadow, Bolitho looked up at her maze of spars and rigging and at the haughty figurehead of Admiral Sir John Benbow. He had died of wounds after being betrayed by certain of his captains.

Bolitho thought of Herrick and Keen, Inch and Neale who had perished for his loyalty.

If Admiral Benbow had been as lucky as he was, it would have been a very different story.

Allday looked down at Bolitho's squared shoulders, the black queue above the gold-laced collar. Admiral or Jack, it made no difference, he thought. Not when it came to a woman.

The room was small but comfortably furnished, with only the thickness of the outer wall giving any hint that it was part of Gibraltar's fortifications. There were a few portraits and ornaments to mark the comings and goings of various company agents who had lodged briefly amongst the garrison and the naval presence.

Bolitho said quietly, 'I thought they would never leave us.'

He had known the Barclays for only a few moments but already thought of them as a single entity rather than individuals.

She smiled and held out her hands to grasp his. 'They are

kindly people, Richard. But for them . . .'

He slipped his arm around her waist and together they walked to the window. The sun had already moved over the Rock, and against the deep blue water the precisely anchored men-of-war looked like models. Only the occasional tail of white spray marked the movements of oared boats, the fleet's busy messengers.

She leaned her head against his shoulder and murmured, 'The *Thrush* seems so tiny from up here.' She looked at the *Benbow* anchored at the head of the other vessels. 'To think that you command all those men and ships. You are like two people.'

Bolitho moved behind her and allowed her hair to touch his mouth. They were alone. On this overcrowded, unnatural outpost they had found a place to be together. It was like looking down on another world, upon himself at a distance.

She was right. Down there he was a commander, a man who could save or destroy life by a single hoist of flags. Here he was just himself.

She leant against him and said, 'But if you are leaving here, then so am I. It is all arranged. I believe that even Polly, my new maid, is eager to go, for I think she hopes to see Allday again. She is much taken with him.'

'I have so much to tell you, Belinda. I have seen you for so short a while, and now . . .'

'Soon we are to be separated again. I *know*. But I am trying not to think about that. Not for a few more hours.'

Bolitho felt her tense as she asked, 'Is it so very dangerous? It's all right, you can tell me. I think you know that now.'

Bolitho looked over her head at the ships swinging to their cables.

'There will be a fight.' It was a strange feeling. He had never discussed it like this before. 'You wait and you wait, you try to see things through the eyes of the enemy, and when it eventually happens it is all suddenly different. Many people at home believe their sailors fight for King and country, to protect their loved ones, and so they do. But when the guns begin to thunder, and the enemy is right there alongside rising above the smoke like the devil's fury, it is John who calls for Bill, one messmate seeking another, as the bonds of sailormen are stronger than symbols beyond their ship.'

He felt her sob or catch her breath and said quickly, 'I am sorry, that was unforgivable!'

Her hair moved against his mouth as she shook her head in protest.

'No. I am proud to share your thoughts, your hopes. I feel a part of you.'

He moved his hands up from her waist and felt her stiffen as he touched her breasts.

'I want you to love me, Belinda. I have been so long in the ways of ships and sailors I am frightened of turning you away.'

For a moment she did not speak, but he could feel her heart beating to match his own as he clasped her body to his.

When she spoke he had to bend his head to hear.

'I told you before. I should be ashamed of the way I feel.' She twisted round in his arms and looked up at him. 'But I am not ashamed.'

Bolitho kissed her neck and her throat, knowing he must stop, but unable to contain his emotions.

She stroked his hair and moaned softly as his mouth brushed against her breast.

'I *want* you, Richard. After today neither of us knows what may happen.' When he made to protest she said calmly, 'Do you think I want to remember only the embraces of my dead husband, when it is you I want? We have both loved and been loved, but that is in the past.'

He said, 'It *is* past.'

She nodded very slowly. 'There is so little time, my dearest.'

She held out her hand, her eyes averted as if she were suddenly aware of his nearness. Then with the toss of her head which Bolitho had come to love, she walked to the

curtained-off compartment at the end of the room, tugging
at his hand like a wanton child.

Bolitho pulled back the curtain from around the bed and
watched her as she unfastened her gown, her hands almost
tearing at it until with a gasp she stood and faced him, her
hair hanging over her naked shoulders in a last attempt at
modesty.

Bolitho put his hands around her throat and thrust her hair
back and over her spine. Then with infinite care he laid her on
the bed, almost afraid to blink in case he missed a second of
her beauty and his need for her.

Moments later he lay beside her, their bodies touching,
their eyes searching each other for some new discovery.

Bolitho's shadow moved over her and he saw her eyes
following him, while at her sides her fists were clenched as if
it was the only way she could withstand the torture of
waiting.

Across the floor the blue gown and pale undergarments
lay entangled amongst the dress coat with the bright
epaulettes, like the ships below the window, discarded and
forgotten.

They lost all sense of time and were conscious only of each
other. They discovered a love which was both tender and
demanding, passionate and gentle.

Darkness fell over the anchorage, but Gibraltar could have
been split in halves and they would not have known.

In the first uncertain glow of dawn Bolitho moved carefully from the bed and walked to the window.

A few lights bobbed around the ships, and his returning
instinct told him that life had restarted there. The hands had
been called, the decks would be holystoned as the yawning
watchkeepers waited for the bells to chime, the half-hour
glasses to be turned to greet another day.

He heard her move and turned back to the bed where she
lay like a fallen statue, one arm outstretched towards him.

He sat down beside her and touched her skin, feeling his
resolve crumble, the desire returning to match hers.

Somewhere, a million miles away, a trumpet blared raucously and soldiers blinked away their sleep.

He said softly, 'I have to go, Belinda. Your friends will be coming soon to prepare you for the passage to England.'

She nodded. 'The Barclays.'

She was trying to smile, but when he touched her body she seized his hand and squeezed it hard around her breast.

'I am not so strong as I believed. The sooner you leave, the quicker will be our reunion, I *know* that!'

Bolitho looked down at her. 'I am so lucky.' He turned away. 'If—'

She gripped his hand more tightly. 'No, my darling, not if, *when*!'

He smiled and slowly released himself from her grip.

'When.' He looked at the crumpled uniform on the floor. 'It has a good ring to it.'

Then he pulled on his clothes, not daring to look at her until he had clipped on the sword and was ready to leave.

Then he sat down again, and in an instant she threw her arms around his neck, her naked body pressed against his coat as she kissed him with something like desperation while she breathed words into his skin.

He felt the salt tears against his lips, his or hers, he did not know.

She made no attempt to follow him, but sat on the bed, her knees drawn up to her chin, as she watched him move towards the door.

Then she said huskily, 'Now you are the admiral again, and you belong down there with your world. But last night you belonged to me, dear Richard.'

He hesitated, his hand on the door. 'I shall always belong to you.'

The next instant he was outside in the passageway, as if it were all a broken dream.

Two servants were in a yard below the walls chopping sticks for a fire, and a garrison cat strolled along the rough stones as if undecided how to begin the day.

Bolitho strode down the slope towards the landing-stage, looking neither right nor left until he reached the jetty.

Then, and only then, did he look back, but the Rock's shadow had swallowed the house completely.

The guard-boat was idling past the jetty, a lieutenant dozing in the sternsheets while his men continued their monotonous sweep around the squadron. The lieutenant was soon wide awake when he saw Bolitho's epaulettes in the first sunlight.

As he directed his boat to steer for the squadron's flagship, the lieutenant's mind was awhirl with speculation. The admiral had been to a secret meeting with the military governor. He had received instructions on a move to parley with the enemy on a new peace mission.

Bolitho was unaware of the lieutenant's interest and of everything else but the night which had gone by in minutes, or so it seemed now.

And he had thought of himself as a man of honour! He waited for the shame and the dismay to come, but instead he felt only happiness, as if a great weight had been lifted from him.

'*Boat ahoy!*'

Bolitho looked up, startled to see *Benbow* towering high above the boat. He could see the marine sentry with his fixed bayonet moving above the beakhead on his little platform where he watched for unlawful visitors and would-be deserters alike.

The boat's coxswain cupped his hands and bellowed, 'Flag! *Benbow*!'

Bolitho straightened his shoulders and gave a rueful smile. Now they would all know. Their rear-admiral was back in command.

But he could not let go so easily. *Belinda*.

'Sir?' The lieutenant stooped attentively by his side.

Bolitho shook his head. 'Nothing.' He must have spoken her name aloud.

What had Sir John Studdart said of him? *Like a junior lieutenant.*

He certainly felt like one.

Herrick walked from beneath the poop and nodded to the master and his men by the wheel before he continued on to the quarterdeck. Without even being aware of it his eyes recorded that everything was as it should be on what promised to be another scorching day.

The ratlines and yards were alive with scurrying figures, and he heard the petty officers' hoarse cries as they urged the topmen to greater haste.

Herrick paused by the rail and glanced along his command. The barge was hoisted inboard, as were the other boats. There was the usual air of excitement and expectancy which even discipline and routine could not completely disguise.

Wolfe strode across the deck, his arms and great feet moving like pistons.

He touched his hat and reported, 'Ship ready to sail, sir.' He glanced across at their consort and added, 'I think we have an edge on *Nicator* this time.'

Herrick grunted. 'I should hope so, dammit.'

Below on the gundeck more men surged about in response to the shouted commands, raising fists as names were checked against a watch-bill or duty list.

Benbow was preparing to weigh. At any other time it was rare indeed to see so many of her people disgorged on to the upper decks. Seamen and marines, idlers and ships' boys, the highest to the most junior. The ship was leaving harbour again. Where bound and to what purpose was not their concern.

Wolfe, like every first lieutenant worth his salt, was going through his own list for the day. At sea or in port, the work had to continue, and his captain must be kept informed.

'Two hands for punishment this forenoon, sir. Page, two

dozen lashes for drunkenness and quarrelling.' He paused and glanced from his list to Herrick's features. 'Belcher, twelve lashes for insolence.' He folded his list, satisfied. 'All hands aboard, none deserted.'

'Very well. Man the capstan. Get the ship under way.'

Herrick beckoned to a midshipman for his telescope and then trained it on the eighty-gun *Dorsetshire*. No last minute argument from Sir John Studdart. He was probably keeping well out of it. Bolitho had the bit between his teeth, and anyone seen to agree with him or encourage further action against the enemy's invasion fleet might be painted with the same brush. He smiled grimly. As if anyone could or would stop Bolitho now. He glanced up at the flag at the mizzen masthead. Lifting quite well in a rising breeze. It would have to do. He tried not to think of what Dulcie would say when he lost his broad-pendant.

Wolfe said, 'I was about early this morning, sir. I saw the rear-admiral come off shore.'

The blue eyes regarded him mildly. 'And?'

Wolfe shrugged. 'Nothing, sir.' He swallowed hard. 'Capstan's manned. That damn fiddler is scraping like a blind man's spoon. I'd best go forrard.'

Herrick hid a smile. He knew about Bolitho's return at first light. The whole ship probably knew or guessed the reason. It was always like that. Good or bad, you shared it.

Clank . . . clank . . . clank . . . The capstan was turning slowly, the men straining over the bars, sweating and breathing hard, while the fiddler kept them going to a well-known shanty.

The great forecourse, loosely brailed, stirred at its yard, and far above the decks the fleet-footed topmen raced each other in readiness to set the upper sails in obedience to Wolfe's speaking trumpet.

Across the glittering water Herrick could see similar activity aboard *Nicator*. It would be good to draw the squadron together again. For the last time? Even to think of peace after all the years of fighting was a mockery, he decided.

He heard feet on deck and saw Bolitho, with Browne marching in his shadow, crossing the quarterdeck to join him.

They greeted each other formally as Herrick said, 'No instructions from the flagship, sir. The anchor's hove short, and it looks like being a fine day.' As an afterthought he added, '*Ganymede* sailed at eight bells as you instructed, sir. She will keep company with the packet *Thrush* until they are clear of these waters.' He watched Bolitho, waiting for a sign.

Bolitho nodded. 'Good. I saw them go. *Ganymede* will contact the rest of our ships long before we reach the rendezvous.'

Herrick said, 'I'd give a lot to see young Pascoe's face when he learns that you are alive, sir. I know how *I* felt!'

Bolitho turned and looked at the other seventy-four. As he had said, he had watched the little *Thrush* clearing the approaches and setting her tan-coloured sails within minutes of catting her anchor. Belinda had probably been watching *Benbow* from her temporary quarters. Like him, unable to share the moment under the eyes of the squadron.

The signals midshipman called, '*Nicator*'s cable is hove short, sir!'

'Very well, Mr Stirling. Acknowledge.'

Browne took a sudden interest in a seaman who was busily flaking down a line beside him.

He heard Herrick ask politely, 'Was everything satisfactory, sir?'

Bolitho eyed him impassively. 'It was, Captain Herrick.'

Then like conspirators they both smiled broadly at each other and Herrick said, 'I wish you both every happiness, sir. My God, when—'

'Ready, sir!'

Wolfe's harsh voice made Herrick hurry to the rail.

'Loose heads'ls!' He gestured above his head. 'Loose tops'ls!'

'*Anchor's aweigh*, sir!'

With her canvas rippling and banging in disorder *Benbow*

paid off to the wind, her fat hull brushing the water as she dipped to the pressure.

'Braces there! *Heave, lads!*'

Round and still further round, with the foreshore and the misty hills pivoting beyond the hurrying seamen and flapping topsails, until the master took control with his helm and compass.

Nicator was already setting more sail as she tilted to the freshening breeze, her scarlet ensign and masthead pendant streaming almost abeam as she took station her flagship.

'The Dons saw us arrive. Now they'll know we are at sea again.' Bolitho looked at the land but saw only that quiet room, her pale arms open to receive him.

He walked up to the weather side and listened to the shouted orders, the squeak of tackles and blocks as miles of running rigging took the strain.

Up forward, the anchor had been secured to the cathead, and he heard Drodge, the gunner, bellowing instructions to his mates as they checked the lashings on every weapon.

A boatswain's mate was supervising the rigging of a grating at the gangway in readiness for awarding punishment. One of the sailmaker's crew sorted through some scraps of canvas with the same lack of emotion. Routine and discipline. It held the ship together no less securely than copper and tar.

He saw Allday carrying his new cutlass towards an open hatch. To sharpen it himself exactly as he wanted it. Who now owned Allday's old cutlass, Bolitho wondered? The one he had driven into the French beach with such disgust when they had been taken prisoner.

Allday seemed to feel his gaze and turned to peer up at the quarterdeck. He touched his forehead and gave a small smile which only Bolitho or Herrick would recognize.

Some midshipmen were lined up for instruction at one of the upper battery's eighteen-pounders, and a youthful lieutenant was pointing out the various positions where its crew could change round if a man fell wounded in battle, so that the speed of loading and firing would not be lost.

He spoke with crisp authority, very aware of Bolitho's tall figure just above him. Bolitho smiled. The lieutenant was about a year older than some of his pupils.

From the galley he saw a puff of smoke as the cook made the most of whatever fresh food he had been able to snatch during their brief stay at Gibraltar, and as he watched the market-place activity of the crowded upper deck he recalled the vice-admiral's advice to stay aloof and not to involve himself in the affairs of subordinates.

A boatswain's mate hurried along the deck, his call twittering above the sounds of canvas and spray.

'All hands! Hands lay aft to witness punishment!'

Herrick stood by the rail, his chin sunk in his neckcloth, the Articles of War tucked beneath one arm, as seamen and marines surged aft in a human tide.

Bolitho turned towards the poop. *I am involved. It is how I am made.*

Into the shadows and past the stiff sentry beneath the spiralling lantern.

Browne followed him into the great cabin and shut the door.

'Can I do anything, sir?'

Bolitho handed his coat to Ozzard and loosened his shirt and neckcloth.

'Yes, Oliver. Close the skylight.'

It might be necessary, but he still hated the sound of the cat across a man's naked back. He sat on the stern bench and stared out at *Nicator*'s tall shape following obediently on a new tack.

Browne said warily, 'Your clerk is here, sir, with some more papers which seem to require your signature.' He faltered. 'Shall I tell him to go away, sir?'

Bolitho sighed. 'No, ask Yovell to come in. I think I *need* to lose myself.'

Overhead in the bright sunlight the lash rose and fell on the first man to be seized up for punishment. Most of the assembled company watched with empty eyes, and only the victim's close friends looked away, ashamed for him and perhaps themselves.

The grating was unrigged and the hands piped to the midday meal, with a pint of Black Strap to wash it down.

The two men who had been flogged were taken below to the sickbay to have their backs attended to and their confidence restored by a liberal dose of rum from the surgeon's special cask.

Alone at last in the cabin, Bolitho sat at his table, a sheet of paper before him. She would probably never read the letter, it might not even be sent. But it would help to keep her with him as the breadth of ocean tried to force them apart.

He touched his cheek where she had kissed him, and then without hesitation began to write.

My dearest Belinda, It is only a few hours since I left you . . .

On deck, as dusk closed in once more and painted the horizon with dull copper, Herrick discussed the reefing arangements and emergency signals for the night watches. The land had already vanished in shadows, here any strange sail might be an enemy.

And *Benbow* was a King's ship, with no time to spare for the frailties of the men who served her.

12

The Flag Commands

Lieutenant the Honourable Oliver Browne, with his hat clamped tightly beneath one arm, stepped into the stern cabin and waited for Bolitho to look up from his charts and scribbled notes.

'Yes?'

Browne kept his urbane features expressionless. 'Sail in sight to the nor'-east, sir.' He had learned from experience that Bolitho had already heard the cry from the masthead, just as he would know that Browne knew it.

'Thank you.'

Bolitho rubbed his eyes. It had taken over a week to reach the rendezvous area. Two days of good sailing, with a favourable wind across the quarter when neither reefing nor changing tack was required. Then other days, with frustrating hours of retrimming yards and canvas, tired men scrambling aloft to shorten sail in a sudden squall, only to be piped up the ratlines immediately to loose them again.

Westward into the Atlantic and then up along the coast of Portugal. They had sighted a few vessels, but the distance and the slowness of the two seventy-fours made any kind of investigation impossible.

Bolitho had kept much to himself during the passage. Going over Beauchamp's original plans but coming up allstanding whenever he had set them against an actual attack.

He threw his brass dividers on to the charts and stood up. 'What ship, I wonder?'

And what would he find in his little squadron? *Ganymede*

should have contacted each ship, and every man would know their rear-admiral's flag would soon be joining them.

Browne said, 'They *say* she's a frigate, sir.'

Their eyes met. Then it would be *Phalarope*, unless it was a Frenchman who had slipped through the blockade undetected.

Browne added, 'May I ask what you intend, sir?'

'I shall see Emes.'

He seemed to hear Herrick inside his mind. *Let me deal with him, sir. I'll settle his future for him!* Loyal, but biased. How would Adam see it, he wondered? He had twice nearly lost his young life trying to defend his uncle's name. *No.* Emes did not strike him as a man who would ruin Adam's career to save his own. But before a court martial anything could happen.

He heard Herrick's shoes in the lobby, and as Ozzard hurried to open the screen door Bolitho said, 'Leave us, Oliver.'

Herrick bustled into the cabin and barely noticed the flag-lieutenant as he passed.

Bolitho said, 'Sit down, Thomas, and *be calm*.'

Herrick peered around the cabin, his eyes still half-blinded from the glare on the quarterdeck.

'Calm, sir? It is a lot to ask!' He grimaced. 'She's *Phalarope* right enough.' He raised his eyebrows. 'I can see that you are not surprised, sir?'

'No. Captain Emes has been in command here during our absence. He is a post-captain of experience. But for his previous trouble, his actions at the Ile d'Yeu might have roused little criticism, even from you.'

Herrick shifted in his chair, unconvinced. 'I doubt that.'

Bolitho moved to the stern windows and looked at some gulls which were swooping and screaming below the counter. The cook had probably hurled some scraps outboard.

'I *need* every competent officer, Thomas. If one is at fault, the blame must lie with his captain. If it is a captain who shows weakness, then the responsibility must lie with his admiral.' He smiled wryly. 'In this particular case, me.' He hurried on. 'No, hear me out, Thomas. Many of the squadron's officers are raw replacements, and the worst wrath they have faced so far is that of a sailing master or first lieutenant, am I right?'

'Well, I suppose so, sir.'

Bolitho smiled fondly. 'That's hardly an agreement, but it is a start. If, as I intend, we are to attack and destroy those French vessels, I shall draw heavily upon my captains. It is obvious that we are getting no more support, and Sir John Studdart knew nothing of any extra craft from his own command.' He did not conceal the bitterness. 'Not even one solitary gun-brig!'

Beyond the cabin they heard Wolfe's voice through his speaking trumpet, the responding clatter of blocks and halliards as men ran to obey him.

Herrick stood up. 'We are about to change tack, sir.'

'Go to them, Thomas. When you are ready, you may heave to and request that Captain Emes comes aboard. He'll be expecting it.'

'I still think . . .' Herrick grinned ruefully and said instead, 'Aye, aye, sir.'

Browne re-entered the cabin. 'They're signalling *Phalarope* now, sir.' He sounded puzzled. '*Captain repair on board flagship*. I thought you might ask for your nephew to come across too, sir?'

'I am longing to see him.' Bolitho looked up at the deckhead beams as bare feet slapped across the dried planking. 'I am not proud of the fact I am using him.'

'Using him, sir?'

'Emes commands *Phalarope*, and he can decide if he shall bring his first lieutenant as a courtesy to me. If he does not choose to do so, he will have the stage to himself, unchallenged, as he is the first captain to meet us on this station. But if he decides to bring him, he must risk whatever my nephew may say.'

Browne's face cleared. 'That is very shrewd, sir.'

'I am learning, Oliver. Very slowly, but I am learning.'

The cabin tilted heavily to one side and Bolitho heard the creak of yards as *Benbow* swung slowly into the wind. He saw *Nicator* standing at a distance under shortened sail as she watched over her consorts.

Browne said, 'I'll go on deck, sir.'

'Yes. Let me know what is happening.'

Browne picked up his hat and asked hesitantly, 'If Captain Emes fails to satisfy you, sir . . .'

'I shall send him packing by the next available vessel. I need good officers, and I have said as much to Captain Herrick. But I'd rather send *Phalarope* amongst the enemy with a midshipman in command than risk more lives to satisfy my vanity!'

Browne nodded and hurried away, another lesson learned.

Herrick saw him emerge into the sunlight and asked irritably, 'What have you been doing, Mr Browne?'

'Our admiral, sir. The way he sees things. Like an artist painting a picture.'

'Humph.' Herrick turned to watch the frigate heading into the wind, her sails aback as she prepared to lower a boat. He said grimly, 'Just so long as somebody doesn't break the frame before the picture is finished!' He saw the surprise on Browne's face and added, 'Oh yes, Mr Browne with an *e*, a few of us do have minds of our own, you know!'

Browne hid a smile and walked to the lee side as Major Clinton, his sun-reddened face almost matching his tunic, marched to Herrick and barked, 'Guard of honour, sir?'

'Yes. Man the side, Major. He is a captain.' He moved away and added under his breath, 'At the moment.'

The midshipman of the watch called, 'Boat's put off, sir!'

Browne hurried to the poop. He found Bolitho standing by the windows as if he had not moved.

'*Phalarope*'s gig is heading for us, sir.' He saw the way Bolitho's hands gripped one another behind his back. Tense. Like a spring.

Browne said quietly, 'Captain Emes has your nephew with

him, sir.' He expected some instant response, a show of relief.

Instead Bolitho said, 'I used to believe that all flag-officers were like gods. They created situations and formed decisions while we lesser beings merely obeyed. Now I know differently. Perhaps Vice-Admiral Studdart was right after all.'

'Sir?'

'Nothing. Tell Ozzard to bring my coat. If my emotions are at war with each other, I am certain Emes will have fared far worse. So let's be about it, eh?'

He heard the twitter of calls, the muffled stamp of booted feet by the entry port.

As Ozzard held his coat up to his shoulders, Bolitho thought suddenly of his first command. Small, crowded, intimate.

He had believed then, as he did now, that to be given a ship was the most coveted gift which could be bestowed on any living creature.

Now others commanded, while he was forced to lead and decide their destinies. But no matter what, he would never forget what that first command had meant to him.

Browne announced, 'Captain Emes of the *Phalarope*, sir.'

Bolitho stood behind the table and said, 'You may withdraw.'

Had he met Captain Emes ashore or in any other surroundings he doubted if he would have recognized him. He still held himself very erect as he stood opposite the table, hat beneath his arm, his sword gripped firmly, too firmly, in the other hand. In spite of his employment on the Belle Ile station and the favourable weather which had given most of the ships' companies a healthy tan, Emes looked deathly pale, and in the reflected sunlight from the stern windows his skin had the pallor of wax. He was twenty-nine, but looked ten years older.

Bolitho said, 'You may sit, Captain Emes. This is an informal meeting for, as I must tell you, it seems likely you will be required to face at best a court of enquiry, at worst . . .'

He shrugged. 'In the latter case, I would be called more as a witness than as a member of the court or as your flag-officer.'

Emes sat down carefully on the edge of the chair. 'Yes, sir. I understand.'

'I doubt that. But before further action is taken I need to know your own explanation for your conduct on the morning of the 21st July when *Styx* became a total loss.'

Emes began slowly and deliberately, as if he had rehearsed for this very moment. 'I was in the favourable position of being able to see the French to seaward, and the other force which you were intending to engage. With the wind in the enemy's favour, I concluded there was no chance of our destroying the invasion craft with time available to beat clear. I held my ship in position to wind'rd as ordered, in case . . .'

Bolitho watched him impassively. It would be easy to dismiss him as a coward. It was equally possible to feel pity for him.

He said, 'When *Styx* struck the wreck, what then?'

Emes stared round the cabin like a trapped animal. '*Styx* had no chance. I saw her take the full force of the collision, her masts fall, her helm abandoned. She was a hulk from that moment. I – I wanted to drop my boats and attempt a rescue. It is never easy to stand off and watch men die.'

'But you did just that.' Bolitho was surprised at his own voice. Flat, devoid of hope or sympathy.

Emes' eyes settled on him only briefly before continuing their tortured search around the cabin.

He said tightly, 'I was the senior captain present, sir. With just *Rapid* to support me, and she only a brig of fourteen guns, I saw no reasonable chance of a rescue. *Phalarope* would have been caught by the enemy ships which were moving down wind under all sail. A ship of the line and two frigates. What possible chance would an old vessel like mine have stood, but for making a useless and bloody gesture? *Rapid* would have been destroyed also.'

Bolitho watched the emotions on Emes' pale features as he

relived the battle of conscience versus logic.

'And as senior officer I had responsibilities to Captain Duncan in *Sparrowhawk*. He was in ignorance of what was happening. Alone and unsupported, he would have been the next to go. The whole force would have been destroyed, and the enemy's back door left unguarded from that moment.' He looked down at his hat and pressed it on to his knees as if to find the strength to go on. 'I decided to discontinue the action, and ordered *Rapid* to follow my directions. I have continued with the patrols and the blockading of harbours as instructed. With *Ganymede*'s arrival I was able to fill the gap left by Captain Neale's ship.' He looked up, his eyes wretched. 'I was shocked to learn of his death.' His head dropped again. 'That is all I have to say, sir.'

Bolitho leaned back in his chair and watched him thoughtfully. Emes had not pleaded or attempted to excuse his actions.

'And now, Captain Emes, do you regret your decisions?'

Emes gave a shrug which seemed to shake his whole body. 'In all truth, sir, I do not know. I knew that by abandoning *Styx* and her survivors I was also leaving my flag-officer to his fate. In view of my record, I think perhaps I should have cast common sense to the wind and gone down fighting. Officers I have since met make no bones on their sentiments. I could feel the hostility when I stepped aboard *Benbow*, and there are some who will be eager to damn me in your eyes. A court martial?' He lifted his head again with something like defiance. 'It was inevitable, I suppose.'

'But you think their lordships would be wrong to proceed with it nevertheless?'

Emes struggled with his conscience as if it was alien to him. 'It would be easy to throw myself on your mercy, sir. After all, you could have been killed by a stray ball within minutes of starting the action, and then I would have been the senior captain anyway. I would then have ordered Neale to discontinue the engagement. Had he disobeyed me, sir, he and not I would be facing a court martial.'

Bolitho stood up and moved to the stern windows. He saw *Phalarope* lying hove to some two cables away, her ginger-bread glittering cheerfully in the sunlight. What did she think of her latest captain? He saw Emes' reflection in the thick glass, the way he sat rigidly yet without life. A man counting the odds yet unwilling to give in.

Bolitho said, 'I knew John Neale very well. He was once a young midshipman under my command. As was Captain Keen of *Nicator*, while Captain Inch, who will shortly be joining us in *Odin*, was once my lieutenant. And there are many more I have known for years, have watched grow to the Navy's demands or have died because of them.'

He heard Emes murmur huskily, 'You are fortunate, sir. I envy you those friends and their methods.'

Bolitho turned and regarded him searchingly. 'And there is my own nephew, of course. Midshipman, and now first lieutenant under your charge.'

Emes nodded. 'I have no doubts at all of his scorn for me, sir.'

Bolitho sat down and glanced at the litter of charts and notes which would still be there after he had dismissed Emes. It would be simple to remove him without even waiting for a suitable replacement. A senior lieutenant, someone like Wolfe, could easily assume command until told otherwise. Why take unnecessary chances when so much was at stake?

And yet . . . The two words stuck in his skin like thorns.

'They are all a comfort to me, Emes, whereas to you they are an additional hurdle. Because of me, they may despise you. Even my good friend, Commodore Herrick, a man of great integrity and no little courage, was quick to speak his anger. He, after all, risked his position, maybe even this ship, on a whim, on a simple belief he might be able to find me. So you see, your decision, though logical, might be seen differently by others who were not even present on that damnable morning.'

Emes waited and then said dully, 'Then there is no hope, sir.'

How quiet the ship seemed to be, Bolitho thought. As if she were holding her breath, like all the men who worked within her deep hull. He had known many such moments. Like the bad days of the mutinies at Spithead and the Nore. The boom of a signal gun, the breaking of a court martial jack which had finished many a good officer just as surely as a halter at the mainyard or a merciless flogging round the fleet had ended the lives of their men.

'There is always hope, Captain Emes.' Bolitho stood up and saw Emes lurch to his feet as if to receive a sentence. He continued, 'For my part, I think you acted correctly, and I *was* there.'

'*Sir?*' Emes swayed and held his head on one side as if he had suddenly lost his hearing.

'I know now that the French ships were there by arrangement. But none of us did at the time. Had I been in your position I ought to have behaved in exactly the same way. I shall write as much to their lordships.'

Emes regarded him for several seconds. 'Thank you, sir. I don't know what to say. I wanted to do the honourable thing, but everything I believed stood in my way. I am more than merely grateful. You will never know how much it means. I can bear what others say and think of me, they are unimportant. But you,' he shrugged, at a loss, 'I hope I would act with such humanity if our roles were reversed.'

'Very well. Send me a full report of what your patrols have discovered during my, er, absence, and when you sight *Rapid*, ask her to make contact with me immediately.'

Emes licked his lips. 'Yes, sir.' He turned to leave and still hesitated.

'Well, Captain Emes, spit it out. Very soon we shall all be too busy for recriminations.'

'Just one thing, sir. You said just now, *I ought to have behaved in exactly the same way*.'

Bolitho frowned. 'Did I?'

'Yes, sir. It was good of you to say so, but now that I understand how your people feel for you, even though I have never been fortunate to serve you and learn about it for myself, I know that the word *ought* is the true key.'

Bolitho said, 'Well, you serve me *now*, Captain Emes, so let that be an end to it.'

Browne entered the cabin silently as Emes departed, his eyes brimming with curiosity.

Bolitho said heavily, 'He should be the admiral, Oliver, not me.'

He shook himself and tried to disperse the truth. Emes had been correct. Perhaps the word *ought* had been used intentionally. For in his heart he knew he would have gone to *Styx*'s aid, no matter what. But Emes was in the right, that was equally certain.

Browne coughed politely. 'I can see that you are going to have some explaining to do, sir.'

He held open the door and Bolitho saw Pascoe half-running across the other cabin in his eagerness to reach him.

They stood for several long moments, and then Pascoe exclaimed, 'I cannot tell you what the news did for me, Uncle. I thought . . . when there was no word . . . we all thought . . .'

Bolitho put his arm around the youthful lieutenant's shoulder and together they walked to the stern windows. The ship was all behind them. Here was only the sea, empty now that *Phalarope* had fallen down wind and had laid bare the horizon.

The lieutenant's uniform had done little to change the youth who had joined his old *Hyperion* as a young midshipman. His black hair, cut in the new short length, was as unruly as ever, and his body felt as if it needed six months of Cornish cooking to put more flesh on it.

He said, 'Adam, you must know I had some concern about your joining *Phalarope*, even though the opportunity of being first lieutenant at twenty-one is enough to tempt a saint, which you are certainly not! Captain Emes has not made any report on your progress, but I have no doubt—' He felt Pascoe tense as he turned to face him incredulously.

'But, *Uncle*! You've not allowed him to remain?'

Bolitho shook his finger. 'You may be a nephew, and when I am in despair I sometimes admit that I am quite fond of you—'

It was not working this time. Pascoe stood with his hands clenched at his sides, his dark eyes flashing as he said, 'He left you to die! I couldn't believe it! I pleaded with him! I very nearly flew at him!' He shook his head violently. 'He's not fit to have *Phalarope*, or any other ship!'

'How did *Phalarope*'s people behave when Captain Emes ordered them to change tack away from the enemy?'

Pascoe blinked, disconcerted by the question. 'They obeyed, naturally. In any case, they do not *know* you as I do, Uncle.'

Bolitho gripped the youth's shoulders and shook him gently but firmly.

'I love you for that, Adam, but it must surely prove my point? The same one I just made to your captain.'

'But, but . . .'

Bolitho released him and smiled ruefully. 'Now I am not speaking as uncle to nephew, but as rear-admiral command-ing this squadron to one of his officers, a damned cheeky one at that. Emes acted in the best way he knew. Even after considering what people would say and read into his interpret-ation at the time. We cannot always know the man who leads, just as I am no longer privileged to recognize the face of every sailor and marine who obeys.'

'I think I can see that.'

Bolitho nodded. 'Good. I have enough problems without you starting a war of your own.'

Pascoe smiled. 'Everything will be all right now, Uncle, you see.'

Bolitho said, 'I am being serious. Emes commands, and you owe it to him to give everything you know for the ship's benefit. If you were to fall in battle, there must be no gulf between captain and company. The bridge made by any first lieutenant between poop and fo'c's'le *has* to survive. And if

Emes were to die, the people have got to look to you as their leader, and not remember the petty bickering which went before. I am *right*, Adam.'

'I suppose so, Uncle. All the same—'

'God, you're getting like Herrick. Now be off with you. To *your* ship, and heaven help you if I see any slackness, for I shall know where to lay the blame!'

This time Pascoe grinned and could not control it.

'Very well, Uncle.'

They walked out to the quarterdeck where Herrick waited in unsmiling silence beside Captain Emes.

Herrick said, 'Wind's freshening, sir. May I suggest that I have *Phalarope*'s gig piped to the chains?' He glanced meaningly at Emes. 'Her captain will want to get back on board, I shouldn't wonder.'

Pascoe darted a quick glance between them and then stepped smartly up to his captain.

'Thank you for allowing me to accompany you, sir.'

Emes eyed him warily. 'A pleasure, Mr Pascoe.'

For a moment longer Bolitho held on to the relationship he shared with his nephew.

'I met Belinda Laidlaw at Gibraltar. She is now on passage to England.' He could feel his cheeks flushing under the youth's stare.

Pascoe smiled. 'I see, Unc – sir. I did not know. It must have been a very happy reunion.'

He glanced from Bolitho to Herrick and smiled. 'I'm sure it was, in every way.'

They touched their hats, and then Emes followed Pascoe down into the tossing gig alongside.

Herrick whispered fiercely, 'Impudent young bugger!'

Bolitho faced him gravely. 'About what, Thomas? Did I miss something?'

'Well, er, I mean to say, sir—' Herrick lapsed into confused silence.

Wolfe's great shadow loomed over them.

'Permission to get the ship under way, sir?'

Bolitho nodded curtly. 'Granted. I fear the commodore is choking on words.'

Bolitho walked up to the weather side as the hands ran to the braces and halliards once again.

There was some cloud about, and the sea was lively with sharp-backed wavelets. They might be in for a blow.

He watched the *Phalarope*'s gig manoeuvring alongside her parent ship, and recalled Pascoe's words. *It must have been a very happy reunion*. Had he really guessed, or had he merely touched upon his uncle's sense of guilt?

But one thing was certain. Pascoe was pleased for them both, and that would help the weeks to pass better than he would ever know.

The first excitement of rejoining his small force of ships became more difficult for Bolitho to sustain as days dragged into weeks with nothing achieved. The blockade had not changed merely because he wanted it to. The boredom and drudgery of beating up and down the enemy coast in all weathers had produced its inevitable aftermath of slackness and subsequent punishment at the gangway.

It was not difficult to imagine the French admiral watching their sails from a safe vantage point on the shore, while he took his time to prepare his growing fleet of invasion craft for the next and possibly last move into the English Channel.

Ganymede had gone close inshore to spy out the whereabouts of anchored shipping, and had been forced to run from two enemy frigates which had pounced on her in the middle of a rain squall. The close-knit system of semaphore stations was working as well as ever.

But *Ganymede*'s captain had discovered an increase in local fishing craft before he had been chased into open water.

At the end of the third week the lookouts sighted *Indomitable* and *Odin* running down to join their flagship. Bolitho felt a sense of relief. He had been expecting a firm recall from the Admiralty, or a request for him to return home and to leave Herrick in overall command. It would mean the end of Beauchamp's plans, and also that *Styx*'s sacrifice had been in vain.

As the three ships of the line manoeuvred ponderously under *Benbow*'s lee, the unemployed hands lined the gangways and stared at their consorts, as sailors always did and always would. Familiar faces, news from home, anything which might make the dreary routine of blockade bearable until they were eventually relieved.

Bolitho was on deck with Herrick to watch the exchange of signals, to feel the sense of pride at the sight of these familiar ships. Bolitho had not seen *Odin* since her savage battering at Copenhagen, but without effort he could visualize Francis Inch, her horse-faced captain, the way he would bob with genuine pleasure when they next met. But that would have to wait a while longer. There was news to be exchanged, despatches to read and answer. And anyway, Bolitho thought with sudden disappointment, he had nothing to call his captains together for.

Bolitho took his usual stroll on the quarterdeck and was left alone to his thoughts. Up and down, up and down, his feet avoiding gun tackles and flaked cordage without effort.

The ships shortened sail, and a boat was sent across to *Benbow* with an impressive bag of letters and Admiralty instructions.

By the time he had completed his walk and had returned to his quarters, Bolitho felt vaguely depressed. Perhaps it was the absence of news and the hint of a chill in these September days. Biscay could be a terrible station in really bad weather. It would take more than gun and sail drills to keep the ships' companies alert and ready to fight.

It had to be soon. Otherwise the French would be prevented from moving the bulk of their new invasion craft by worsening weather, just as their enemies would be driven away from the dangerous coastline for the same reason. *Soon*.

Browne was opening envelopes and piling official documents to one side while he placed personal letters on Bolitho's table.

The flag-lieutenant said, 'No new orders, sir.'

He sounded so cheerful that Bolitho had to bite back a rebuke. It was not Browne's fault. Perhaps it had never been intended that their presence here was to be anything but a gesture.

His eyes fell on the letter which lay uppermost on the table.

'Thank you, Oliver.'

He sat down and read it slowly, afraid he might miss something, or worse that she had written of some regret for what had happened at Gibraltar.

Her words were like a warm breeze. In minutes he felt strangely relaxed, and even the pain in his wounded thigh left him in peace.

She was waiting.

Bolitho stood up quickly. 'Make a signal to *Phalarope*, Oliver, repeated to *Rapid*.' He walked across the cabin, the letter clutched in his hand.

Browne was still staring up at him from the table, fascinated by the swift change.

Bolitho snapped, 'Wake up, Oliver! You wanted orders, well, here they are. Tell *Rapid, investigate possibility of capturing a fishing boat and report when ready*.'

He tapped his mouth with Belinda's letter and then held it to his nose. Her perfume. She must have done it deliberately.

Browne wrote frantically on his book and asked, 'May I ask why, sir?'

Bolitho smiled at him. 'If they won't come out to us, we'll have to go inshore amongst them!'

Browne got to his feet. 'I'll signal *Phalarope*, sir.'

There would be more than a little risk in seizing one of the local boats sighted by *Ganymede*. But it would involve only a handful of men. Determined and well-led, they might be the means to provide the picklock to Contre-Amiral Remond's back door!

Browne returned a few moments later, his blue coat bright with droplets of spray.

He said, 'Wind's still getting up, sir.'

'Good.'

Bolitho rubbed his hands. He could picture his signal being passed from ship to ship with no less efficiency and speed than the enemy's semaphore. *Rapid*'s young commander, Jeremy Lapish, had only just been promoted from lieutenant. He was said to be keen and competent, two sound qualities for a man who was after recognition and further advancement. Bolitho could also imagine his nephew when he heard of the signal when it was passed on from his own ship. He would see himself in charge of the raid, with all its risks and the wild cut and thrust of close action.

Browne sat down and continued to study the despatches tied in their pink Admiralty tape.

'Looking back, sir.' He watched Bolitho gravely. 'When we were prisoners, in some ways it was Captain Neale who held us together. I believe we were too worried for *his* safety to care for our own predicament. I often think about him.'

Bolitho nodded. 'He'll be thinking of us, I shouldn't wonder, when next we beat to quarters.' He smiled. 'I hope we do something he'd be proud of.'

The wind rose and veered, the sea changed its face from blue to grey, and as dusk closed down the sight of land the squadron took station for the night.

Deep down on *Benbow*'s orlop deck, as the ship swayed and groaned around them, Allday and Tuck, the captain's coxswain, sat in companionable silence and shared a bottle of rum. The smell of the rum and the swinging lantern was making both of them drowsy, but the two coxswains were content.

Tuck asked suddenly, 'D'you reckon your admiral's goin' to fight, John?'

Allday held his glass against the guttering candle and examined the level of its contents.

'Course he will, Frank.'

Tuck grimaced. 'If I 'ad a woman like the one 'e's got 'is grapnels on, I'd stay well clear o' the Frenchie's iron.' He grinned admiringly. 'An' *you* lives at 'is 'ouse when you're ashore, right?'

Allday's head lolled. He could see the stone walls and the hedgerows as if he were there. The two inns he liked best in Falmouth, the girl at the *George* who had done him a favour or two. Then there was Mrs Laidlaw's new maid Polly, she was a neat parcel and no mistake.

He said, 'That's right, Frank. One of the family, that's me.'

But Tuck was fast asleep.

Allday leant his back against a massive frame and wondered why he was changing. He always tried to keep his life afloat separate from the one which Bolitho had given him at Falmouth.

He thought of the coming battle. Tuck must be mad if he believed Bolitho would give way to the Frogs. Not now, not after all they had seen and done together.

Fight they would, and Allday was troubled that it affected him so deeply.

Aloud he said to the ship, 'I'm getting bloody old, that's what.'

Tuck groaned and muttered, 'Wassat?'

'Shut up, you stupid bugger.' Allday lurched to his feet. 'Come on then, I'll help sling your hammock for you.'

Some eight miles from Allday's flickering lantern another scene was being enacted in the *Rapid*'s small cabin as Lapish, her commander, explained what was required.

The brig was pitching violently in a steep offshore swell, but neither Lapish not his equally youthful first lieutenant even noticed it.

Lapish was saying, 'You've seen the signal from the Flag, Peter, and you know what to look for. I'll drop the boat as close as I can and stand off until you return, with or without a fisherman.' He grinned at the lieutenant. 'Does it frighten you?'

'It's one way to promotion, sir.'

They both bent over the chart to complete their calculations.

The lieutenant had never spoken to his rear-admiral, and had only seen him a few times at a distance. But what did it matter? Tomorrow there might be a new admiral in command. The lieutenant laid his hanger on a bench beside his favourite pistols. *Or I might be dead.*

In the long chain of command the next few hours were all that mattered.

'Ready, Peter?'

'Aye, sir.'

They listened to the dash of spray over the deck. A foul night for boatwork, but a perfect one for what they had in mind.

And anyway, they had their orders from the Flag.

13

No Fighting Sailor

Lieutenant Wolfe ducked his head beneath the deckhead beams and clumped noisily into the cabin. He waited while Bolitho and Herrick completed some calculations on a chart and then said, 'Signal from *Rapid*, repeated by *Phalarope*. *French boat captured. No alarm given.*'

Bolitho glanced at Herrick. 'That was good work. The brig is aptly named.' To Wolfe he said, 'Signal *Rapid* to send her prize to the flagship. The fewer prying eyes to see her the better. And tell Commander Lapish, well done.'

Herrick rubbed his chin doubtfully. 'No alarm roused, eh? Lapish must have taken full advantage of the foul weather yesterday, lucky young devil.'

'I expect so.' Bolitho kept his voice non-committal as he stooped over the chart once more.

There was no point in telling Herrick how he had lain awake worrying about his orders to *Rapid*. Even one man lost to no purpose was too many. He had felt this way ever since *Styx* had gone and Neale had died with so many of his company. He looked at Herrick's homely face. No, there was no point in disturbing him also.

Instead he ran his finger along the great triangle on the chart. It stretched south-east from Belle Ile to the Ile d'Yeu, then seaward to a point some forty miles to the west. Then north once more to Belle Ile. His three frigates patrolled along the invisible thread nearest to the coast, while the ships of the line were made to endure the uncertainties of unsheltered waters where they could be directed to attack if the

French attempted to break out.

Amongst and between Bolitho's ships the little *Rapid* acted as messenger and spy. Lapish must have enjoyed his successful cutting-out raid, no matter how brief it had been. Action soon drove away the cobwebs, and his men would have the laugh on the companies of their heaviest consorts.

He said, 'The French must be getting ready to move. We have to know what is happening closer inshore.' He looked up as Browne entered the cabin. 'The captured fishing boat will be joining us directly. I want you to board her and make a full investigation.'

Herrick said, 'I can send Mr Wolfe.'

Bolitho smiled. 'I need something different from seamanship, Thomas. I think Mr Browne may see what others might miss.'

'Humph.' Herrick stared at the chart. 'I wonder. Still, I suppose it may be worth a try.'

Browne said calmly, 'May I suggest something, sir?'

'Of course.'

Browne walked to the table. He had completely recovered from sea-sickness, and even the squall which had battered at the squadron throughout the night had left him untouched.

'I've heard that the fishermen have been gathering for weeks. It is customary so that they can work under the protection of the French guard-boats. If *Rapid*'s commander is certain that nobody saw his men seize one of the boats, a picked prize crew could surely work inshore again and see what is happening?'

Herrick sighed deeply. 'Well, naturally, man! It was what we intended! And I thought you had something new to offer!'

Browne gave a gentle smile. 'With respect, sir, I meant that the boat could be sailed right amongst the others, for a time anyway.'

Herrick shook his head. 'Mad. Quite mad. They would be seen for what they were within an hour.'

Browne persisted. 'If someone aboard spoke fluent French . . .'

Herrick looked despairingly at Bolitho. 'And how many French scholars do we have aboard, sir?'

Browne coughed. 'Me, sir, for one, and I have discovered that Mr Midshipman Stirling and Mr Midshipman Gaisford are passable.'

Herrick stared at him. 'Well, I'll be double damned!'

Bolitho said slowly, 'Is there any alternative?'

Browne shrugged. 'None, sir.'

Bolitho studied the chart, although in his mind he could see every sounding, shoal and distance.

It might work. The unlikely so often did. If it failed, Browne and his men would be taken. If they were wearing disguise when they were captured it would mean certain death. He thought of the little graves by the prison wall, the scars of musket balls where the victims had been shot down.

Browne was watching his uncertainty. He said, 'I should like to try, sir. It would help in some way. For Captain Neale.'

From that other world beyond the cabin the marine sentry shouted, 'Midshipman o' th' watch, sah!'

Midshipman Haines tiptoed nervously towards his betters and said in a whisper, 'The first lieutenant's respects, sir, and the French prize is in sight to the north-east'rd.'

Herrick glared at him. 'Is that all, Mr Haines?'

'N-no, sir. Mr Wolfe said to tell you that there are three French soldiers on board.'

Unwittingly the boy had left the most vital part until the end.

Bolitho said, 'Thank you, Mr Haines. My compliments to the first lieutenant, and ask him to keep me informed as she draws closer.'

It was all suddenly startlingly clear. He recalled the French soldiers aboard those other fishing boats on that terrible morning when *Styx* had foundered. Perhaps the local garrison always kept a few available for such duties. It was not unknown for fishermen and smugglers from either side to meet offshore and exchange news and contraband. Contre-

Amiral Remond would not wish his squadron to be betrayed by some careless scrap of gossip.

Three enemy soldiers. In his mind's eye he could already see Browne in one of the uniforms, and when he looked at the lieutenant he could tell he was thinking exactly that.

'Very well. Search the boat and report to me. After that . . .' His gaze fell on the chart. 'I shall decide.'

Herrick asked, 'You know the risks?'

Browne nodded. 'Yes, sir.'

'And you still want to go?'

'Yes, sir.'

Herrick spread his hands. 'As I thought, quite mad.'

Bolitho glanced from one to the other. Both so different, yet each so important to him.

He stood up. 'I shall take a walk on deck, Thomas. I need to think.'

Herrick understood. 'I shall see that you are not disturbed, sir.'

Later, as Bolitho paced back and forth on the quarterdeck, he tried to put himself in Remond's place. He had met him for just that short while, and yet it made such a difference. Now the enemy had a face, a personality. Maybe it was better if the foe remained anonymous, he thought.

It was nearly dusk by the time the little fishing boat had manoeuvred under *Benbow*'s lee and Browne had gone across to examine her.

While the ratlines and gangways were crammed with curious seamen, Bolitho stood aloof and watched the newcomer with no less interest. A dirty, hard-worked vessel with patched sails and a littered deck, she was not much bigger than *Benbow*'s barge. Her appearance was less than heroic and would turn the average naval boatswain grey with disgust.

Browne in his blue and white uniform made a stark contrast against the vessel's squalor.

The jolly-boat returned with a young lieutenant whom Bolitho guessed to be the leader of the cutting-out party. As he climbed up *Benbow*'s tumblehome and touched his hat to the side party, Bolitho saw he was a mere youth, nineteen at the most.

Wolfe was about to take him aft to the captain's quarters when Bolitho called impetuously, 'Come here!'

Young and in awe of the flagship's surroundings he might be, but the lieutenant had that certain panache as he hurried aft to the quarterdeck. The mark of a victor.

He touched his hat. 'Lieutenant Peter Searle, sir, of the brig *Rapid*.'

'You took the prize, I believe, Mr Searle?'

The lieutenant turned and glanced across at the grubby fishing boat. He seemed to see her for the first time for what she really was.

He replied, 'She was anchored apart from the others, sir. I put two men outboard, good swimmers, and sent them to cut the cable so that she could drift down on my own boat. There was half a gale blowing by that time and my boat was leaking badly.' He smiled as he remembered what it had been like, the lines of strain falling from his face. 'I knew we had to take her right then or swim in search of *Rapid*!'

'Was there a fight?'

'There were four soldiers aboard, sir, I'd been told nothing about them. They killed poor Miller and stunned Thompson before we could get to grips. It was quickly done.'

Bolitho said, 'I'm proud of you.' It was strange how the unfortunate man named Miller had suddenly become so real even though he had never met him.

'And nobody raised the alarm?'

'No, sir. I'm certain of it.' As an afterthought Searle said, 'I dropped the corpses over the side in the darkness, there were only three, including Miller. But I had them hurried down with some ballast around them. They'll not be afloat anywhere to tell the tale.'

'Thank you, Mr Searle.'

The lieutenant added hesitantly, 'I am told you intend to

use the boat against the enemy, sir? If so, I'd like to volunteer my services.'

'Who told you that?'

The lieutenant flushed under Bolitho's gaze. 'I – I forget, sir.'

Bolitho smiled. 'No matter, I think I can guess. I shall be glad to appoint you in charge of the prize. You are obviously a man of resourcefulness. With that and my flag-lieutenant's uncanny habit of being right, you should be a great asset.'

They both turned as Herrick appeared on deck, and Bolitho said, 'We will begin tonight. Tell Major Clinton I require four of his top marksmen to accompany the prize crew, and they'll need a good master's mate as well. And see he is the best Mr Grubb can offer, not the one least likely to be missed.'

Herrick looked as if he was going to protest but changed his mind.

Bolitho turned to the lieutenant again. 'I shall give you your orders, but you must know that if you are captured there is little hope for you.'

'I understand, sir.' He smiled cheerfully. 'All my party are volunteers.'

Bolitho looked at the fishing boat. Now he understood. He had been worried about risking lives, but this young lieutenant was actually grateful to him. For the chance, the rare, precious opportunity which every young officer prayed might come his way. *To think that I was exactly like him.*

He said, 'Bring the prisoners over, and put some of our people aboard to aid Mr Browne.' He glanced at the gathering dusk, the last daylight which still clung to *Nicator*'s upper yards. 'My God, Thomas, I am sick and tired of waiting for the enemy to shift himself. It is time we stirred them a little!'

He saw Allday on the larboard gangway. He too was staring over at the fishing boat, his thick body stiff and tense. At least Allday would be spared from this piece of reckless endeavour, Bolitho thought.

He waited on deck until the handful of prisoners were ferried across, the first being three French soldiers. They were followed by one of Clinton's marines who carried a bloodied uniform across his arm, his features screwed up with distaste. The uniform's previous owner would have no further use of it.

Eventually, when it was almost dark and the ships were reefing down for the night, Browne returned on board.

'That boat stinks like a sewer, sir! As do those who man her!'

'Did you discover anything?'

Browne nodded. 'She hails from Brest and is no local craft. We are in luck. I managed to convince her master that he would be freed later on if he told us the truth. Equally he would swing from the mainyard if he did not. He assured me that there is a large French squadron, which he believes to be under local control, for the sole purpose of guarding the invasion fleet. It certainly sounded as if Contre-Amiral Remond is in immediate command.' He saw the flicker of hurt in Bolitho's eyes. 'I knew we should meet him again, sir.'

'Yes. Are you still intent on this mission, Oliver? We are alone now, so speak as you will. You know me better than to blame you if you change your mind.'

'I *want* to go, sir. Now more than ever, for some reason. Perhaps because of Remond, of *Styx*, and for being able to help you, properly, instead of handing you despatches and writing signals.'

Bolitho touched his arm. 'Thank you for that, Oliver. Now go and prepare yourself.'

Herrick walked across to rejoin him as Browne hurried away.

'He's no fighting sailor, sir.'

Bolitho looked at his friend, both surprised and moved that Herrick could show such concern which until now he had done everything to hide.

'Perhaps, Thomas. But he has real courage, which he needs to use.'

Herrick frowned as Wolfe strode across the deck with a new list of names gripped in his hand.

'More questions to be answered, dammit!'

Bolitho smiled and walked aft to the poop. Almost too casually he said, 'I have a signal to be sent to *Phalarope*. I will write it now so that it can be hoisted at first light.'

Wolfe waited, imperturbable as ever. 'Trouble, sir?'

'I'm not sure.' Herrick could not conceal his uncertainty. 'Give me the broadside and the din of war any time, Mr Wolfe! This cat and mouse game is not my plaything!'

Wolfe grinned. 'Now about this list of promotions, sir . . .'

With her patched sails hard-bellied to the wind the fishing boat punched through the steep waves, her lee gunwale awash.

Lieutenant Searle who, like most of his prize crew, was dressed in fisherman's smock and heavy boots, called sharply, 'Hold her close to the wind!'

Beside him near the tiller Browne tried to stay on his feet as the boat plunged and reeled beneath him. In his soldier's coat and white cross-belt it was all he could do to retain his dignity and keep his mind on the approaching danger.

It was almost dawn, but another cloudy one, and the sea appeared much wilder and more dangerous than from *Benbow*'s lofty quarterdeck.

They had worked through the night to make the boat as comfortable as possible, and had jettisoned much of the spare fishing gear. But the stench remained, and Browne found some comfort that he was at least on deck and not crammed in the hold with the rest of the party.

The master's mate, who had taken the tiller himself, said, 'Enemy coast ahead, sir.'

Browne swallowed hard. 'Thank you, Mr Hoblin.'

He must take his word, for as Grubb, the master, had

assured him before they had set sail, 'Mr Hoblin's got a nose for it, sir!'

Searle bared his teeth as cold spray dashed over the gunwale and soaked his head and shoulders.

He gasped, 'I doubt if the French will have a guard-boat running this early. They're not eager to get a wetting!'

Midshipman Stirling, piratical in his smock and a large red woollen hat, asked, 'How close shall we go, sir?'

Browne glanced down at him. There was no fear in the boy's voice. If anything, he sounded impatient for something to happen.

'As near as we dare.'

Searle said, 'The wind's steady enough. Nor'-east. If we can just slip amongst the others we should be safe enough. When they see you they'll be in no mood for talk.' He grinned. 'Fishermen the world over have no love for uniforms. Customs officers, the navy, even the honest trooper is an enemy to them.'

A seaman who lay prone in the bows called hoarsely, 'Two boats, fine to starboard!'

Hoblin said, 'Fishermen. Under way too.'

The seamen rushed to the halliards but slowed as Browne called, 'Easy! This is a fisherman, not a King's ship, so *take your time*!'

They grinned and nudged each other as if it was all a huge joke.

Searle said, 'Bring her about. But hold to wind'rd of those two.' He twisted round as the sails shook noisily and then filled again. 'Belle Ile must be to the north of us now.'

The master's mate nodded and squinted at his boat's compass. 'No more'n two mile, I'd say, sir.' Nobody questioned his judgement and he was vaguely pleased. He was after all the oldest man in the boat by some ten years.

'Damn, here comes the rain.'

Browne nodded miserably and tried to draw his coarse uniform about his throat. The smell of stale sweat left by its owner was almost worse than the fish.

Great heavy drops of rain, sporadic at first and then hissing across the water like metal bars to hammer the boat and occupants without mercy.

Browne groaned. 'I'll *never* complain about fish again! The men who catch it earn every penny!'

Slowly and reluctantly the feeble daylight pushed through the clouds and heavy rain. More boats took shape and personality, and as one sighted another they fanned out into casual formations in readiness to begin their work.

Searle ordered, 'Steer due east. Steady as you go.' To Browne he added, 'That will give us the wind-gage. It will also take us nearer to the mainland.' He was staring at Browne through the rain. 'Not far from where *Ganymede* found you.'

'Yes.'

Browne blinked the rain from his eyes. He still could not bring himself to talk about it, except to Bolitho. It was something terrible, and yet very special, between them.

He squinted up at the mainmast with its frayed rigging which looked as old as time itself.

'Feel like a climb, Mr Stirling?'

The midshipman tightened his belt. 'Aye, sir. What am I to do?'

Searle leaned over and tapped Browne's shoulder. 'Good idea. Get aloft, my lad, and pretend to be doing some running repairs. Take a palm and needle with you, though I doubt if any of the Frenchies carries a telescope.'

Stirling swarmed up the quivering rigging like a monkey and was soon outwardly engrossed in his work.

Corporal Coote, one of the four marines who was enduring the stench and violent motion of the hold, raised his head above the coaming and surveyed the two lieutenants hopefully.

Browne asked, 'Well, Corporal?'

'We just found some wine in an old box down 'ere, sir.' His face was a picture of innocence. 'When we'm on these jobs our own officers usually let us take a wet when there's some lying handy.'

Browne nodded. 'I suppose that would be all right.'

The master's mate voice exploded between them like a charge of canister. 'How does it feel to be a damn liar, Coote? I see rightly enough how it looks!'

The corporal sank slowly from view as Hoblin muttered, 'Bloody bullocks, beggin' your pardon, gentlemen, but they'd take the wooden leg off a cripple to kindle a fire!'

Browne looked at Searle and grinned. 'I could manage a drink myself!'

Searle turned aside. Browne was his superior, but obviously had not been trained in the ways of the lower deck, or the barracks either for that matter. He loosened his hanger at his side. It would certainly be a sharp end to their mission if they arrived amongst the enemy with half of the crew dead-drunk.

He said, 'Bring her up another point.' He mopped his streaming face with his sleeve. 'Sharp lookout, everyone!'

There were about thirty fishing vessels, as far as Browne could see. By skilful use of helm and wind, the master's mate held the boat clear of the others, while on the cluttered deck the sailors dragged tackle and floats about as if they had been fishermen all their lives.

'Don't see any soldiers. Not on deck anyway.' Searle banged his hands together. 'If only I dared to use a glass on them!'

Above the deck, swinging from his shaking perch, Midshipman Stirling peered at the other vessels and allowed his legs to dangle in the rain. Like most fourteen-year-old midshipmen, Stirling was untroubled by heights. The fishing boat's mainmast was like a pike after *Benbow*'s dizzy topgallant yards. What a story he would have to tell the others when he returned to *Benbow*. Like the moment when the commodore had allowed him to take down and hold Bolitho's sword. Even if his fellow midshipmen had not altogether believed a word of it, it was still one of the greatest things which had happened in his young life.

He watched the rain passing away from the hull and across

the nearest boat which was sailing a cable's length to starboard. He continued with the pretence of stitching although he had lost the sailmaker's needle within minutes of climbing from the deck.

Below him the boat yawed unsteadily in a trough, and Stirling heard the squeak of a block as he was swung against the mast like a bread sack.

And there they were, shining in the grey light, their rigging and crossed yards glistening from the downpour.

He called, 'Larboard bow, sir! Five, no *six* sail of the line!' He was almost incoherent with excitement. 'All at anchor!'

On deck the lieutenants and Hoblin exchanged questioning glances. The master's mate said, 'They wasn't there two days back, sir! Must have slipped out of Lorient. They'd have been seen else.'

Browne looked up at the dangling figure. 'Any more?'

'Can't tell, sir. I think it's raining again over there! But there are some small ships at anchor, I – I'm certain of it!'

Browne looked at Searle and exclaimed, 'Remond's flying squadron, it must be.' He clapped his new friend on the arm. 'It's strange. We came to discover something, but now that we've found it, the shock is almost greater.'

'What now?'

Browne stared across the spray. Stirling had good eyes, he thought. As far as he could see there was just the cruising ranks of white crests with a blurred image of land far beyond.

'We must rejoin the squadron. The French are out, and Rear-Admiral Bolitho will need to know it.'

'Steady, sir!'

A seaman jabbed a tarred thumb towards the other boats. One which they had not previously noticed was on a converging tack, and as the rain moved clear Browne saw two uniforms, and worse, a swivel gun mounted above the stem.

Searle called hoarsely, 'Pass the word! Take no notice!'

Browne saw the immediate change. Even Stirling had wrapped one arm around the mast as if to protect himself.

'Let her fall off two points.'

Hoblin murmured, 'No use. The bugger's seen us.'

'*Damn!*' Searle looked at Browne. 'What do you want me to do?'

Hoblin said, 'They can head us off. We've no chance.'

Browne stared at the other vessel. Two more uniforms had appeared. There had after all been four soldiers originally in this boat.

'No chance to run, but we can fight.'

Searle nodded. 'If we board her and put her out of action before they range that swivel on us, we might be able to run for it.' He shivered. 'Anyway, I'm not being taken prisoner like this!'

Hoblin grimaced as a beam of pale sunlight touched the sails as if to betray them to the enemy.

'When we need the sun we get rain! Now it's t'other way round, blast it!'

Searle licked his lips. 'They'll be in hailing distance soon.' Without looking up he said, 'Mr Stirling! When I give the word get down from there on the double! Corporal Coote! Marksmen ready!'

Boots scraped in the hold, and Browne heard the clatter of equipment as the marines prepared themselves. It was what they knew best, no matter what the odds might be.

Browne called, 'You can have all the wine you can drink after this, Corporal!'

Somebody actually managed a laugh.

'They're shortening sail, sir.'

Browne saw the men on the other boat taking in the sails, and one of the soldiers making his way forward to the gun. The soldier appeared quite relaxed, and one of his companions was smoking a pipe while he watched the fishermen fisting the rough canvas into submission.

'They're calling us alongside!' Hoblin sounded as if he was speaking through his teeth. 'Ready, sir?'

Searle glanced at Browne and then barked, 'Stand by, lads!'

He watched the other boat's shadow writhing across the crested water, the sudden uncertainty as they drew nearer and nearer, an arrowhead of water trapped between them like something solid.

'Now! *Helm a-lee!*'

The boat swayed over to the unexpected thrust, and even as the seamen ran to shorten sail the hulls collided, surged away and then struck again.

Midshipman Stirling slithered to the deck and almost pitched between the two boats as Hoblin swung the tiller bar and nursed the bows into the other vessel's bulwark.

Corporal Coote yelled, 'Ready! Take aim!' The four muskets poked over the hold's coaming like lances. '*Fire!*'

On the opposite deck four men, including two soldiers, dropped where they stood. The swivel exploded with a deafening bang, but the man who held the firing lanyard was also dead, while the full charge of canister scythed harmlessly into the air.

Grapnels held the boats together, and yelling like madmen a handful of boarders leapt on to the Frenchman's deck, boarding axes and cutlasses painting the scattered rigging and tackle with daubs of scarlet.

Searle shouted wildly, 'Cut her adrift! Get back on board, lively, you mad bastards!'

He had seen Hoblin's frantic signals, and now as the others turned away from the dead soldiers and cowering fishermen they saw the stiff pyramid of sails cleaving from the rain like some terrible dorsal fin.

'Cast off! *Make sail!*'

Searle dragged a seaman headlong over the gunwale as the two hulls drifted apart.

Browne watched the desperate preparations, the previous excitement changing into something like panic. But for the unexpected meeting with the other boat and its soldiers they would have escaped undetected.

He turned and stared across the quarter as the boat plunged over the crests and pointed her bows seaward once more. It had all taken a few minutes. It would not take much longer to end it.

The pursuing ship was changing tack with neat precision, her yards swinging together as she headed towards her quarry.

Hoblin remarked, 'French corvette. Seen plenty round here.' He spoke with nothing more than professional interest, as if he realized the hopelessness of it.

The other fishing boats had scattered in disorder, like spectators stampeding away from a mad bull.

Browne unfastened his borrowed coat and then threw it over the side. It would make no difference, but he felt better for it. He heard Stirling talking to himself, in prayer, or to hold up his pretence of courage, he did not know.

'How long?'

Searle looked at him calmly. 'Thirty minutes. Her captain will try to work round astern of us. There are some shallows near his larboard side, and he'll want all the sea-room he can get to perform his execution!' Even he spoke without anger or bitterness.

The French man-of-war was small and agile, and from the deck of the fishing boat looked as big as a frigate. She was carrying so much sail it made Browne feel that their own boat was unmoving, and as the distance fell away he thought of Bolitho, waiting for the news he could no longer give him.

He blinked and realized that a tongue of flame had flashed from the Frenchman's forecastle. Then came the bang and a foreshortened whistle as a ball slapped down to starboard and ricocheted across the waves like a mad thing.

'Ranging shot, sir.'

Searle said sharply, 'Alter course two points to starboard.'

The fishing boat responded slowly, and when the next ball sliced through the water it hurled a cascade of spray halfway across the deck.

Corporal Coote lay full length on the deck and tried to aim his musket at the pursuing ship.

Then disgustedly he said, 'Can't do it. I'll wait a bit longer. Might take a couple with me.'

Midshipman Stirling jammed his knuckles in his mouth

and bit on them as another ball punched through the mainsail and threw up a tall waterspout a full cable away.

Searle said, 'Trying to dismast us. Wants us taken alive.' He drew his hanger. 'Not me.'

The game could not be prolonged for ever. As the land and all the other boats dropped back astern the corvette's commander must have realized it was taking too long.

He altered course several points to larboard to present three of his forward gunports. Before he resumed his original course each gun fired a carefully laid shot, one of which smashed through the fishing boat's counter with the force of a reef.

Hoblin lurched back on his feet and gasped, 'Helm's still answering, sir!'

Browne heard water gurgling and sluicing through the hold. It was madness, pathetic and proud at the same time.

Searle nodded sharply, 'Steady as you go then!'

Crash. The corvette's bow-chaser struck home with devastating effect. A marine who had been hurrying to help the seamen with the foresail spun round like a top, one leg severed by the ball before it ploughed on to kill two of the sailors and smash them into a broken, bloody shambles. Wood splinters flew everywhere, and the hull was so deep in the water it was a wonder they were making headway.

Browne stared at the dying marine with dismay. They were all being killed like dumb animals. What was the point? What did it prove?

Another waterspout shot above the bulwark, and Midshipman Stirling spun round, his hand clutching his arm where a feather of jagged wood stood out like a quill.

He gasped, 'I'm all right, sir!' Then he stared at the blood which ran through his fingers and fainted.

Browne looked at Searle. 'I can't let them die like this!'

Corporal Coote lurched aft to join them and pointed through the smoke from the last shot.

'Mebbee they won't 'ave to, sir!'

Browne turned and stared, unable to accept it, or that the

corvette was going about, still wreathed in her own guns-
moke.

'It's *Phalarope*!'

Nobody spoke, and even the dying marine lay silent as he
stared up at the sky and waited for the pain to end.

With her gilded figurehead shining in the weak sunlight,
the old frigate was shortening sail, her topmen spread along
her yards like birds on perches as they stood inshore towards
the sinking hulk.

Then Hoblin exclaimed, 'Gawd, she's taking a chance! If
the Frogs come out now . . .'

'Never mind.' Browne stooped down and lifted the midshipman to his feet. 'Get ready to abandon. Help the
wounded.' It could not be happening.

A voice echoed across the water. 'We're coming alongside!'

Browne watched the frigate's yards swinging again, the
way her deck lifted to the pressure of canvas as she was steered
further and further into the wind.

There would not be much time.

Corporal Coote picked up a fallen musket and looked at the
marine who had lost his leg.

'You won't need this any more, mate.' He turned away
from the dead marine, his eyes blank. 'Be ready, lads!'

Phalarope towered above them, and faces bobbed on the
gangways to reappear on the chains or at the gunports,
anywhere a man could be hauled to safety.

The next moments were like the climax of the same
nightmare. Startled cries, the splintering of wood and the
clatter of falling spars as the frigate drove unerringly against
the listing boat.

Browne felt Searle thrust him towards some waiting seamen, and to his astonishment saw that he was half laughing,
half sobbing as he shouted, 'I'm last off! Only command I've
ever had, y'see?'

Then Browne felt himself being dragged over hard and
unyielding objects before being laid face upwards on the
deck.

A shadow covered his eyes and he saw Pascoe looking down at him.

Browne managed to gasp, 'How did you manage to get here?'

Pascoe smiled sadly. 'My uncle arranged it, Oliver.'

Browne let his head fall back to the deck and closed his eyes. 'Madness.'

'Didn't you know?' Pascoe beckoned to some seamen. 'It runs in the family.'

14

The Toast is Victory!

Bolitho stood with arms folded and watched his flag-lieutenant swallow a second glass of brandy.

Herrick grinned and said, 'I think he needed that, sir.'

Browne placed the glass on the table and waited as Ozzard moved in like a dancer to refill it. Then he looked at his hands as if he was surprised they were not visibly shaking and said, 'There were some moments when I thought I had misjudged my abilities, sir.'

'You did well.'

Bolitho recalled his feelings when he had received the signal from *Phalarope*. The fishing boat had sunk, but all except three of the prize crew were safe.

He walked to the chart and spread his hands around the vital triangle. Remond's squadron had left harbour, knowing that sooner or later their presence would be discovered. The French were obviously expecting to move their fleet of invasion craft before the weather worsened and place them across the Channel from England. Added to the ever-present rumour of intended attack, their arrival would give plenty of weight to the enemy's bargaining power.

Browne said wearily, 'Mr Searle of *Rapid* did all the hard work, sir. But for him . . .'

'I shall see that his part is mentioned in my despatches.' Bolitho smiled. 'But you were the real surprise.' He grinned wryly at Herrick. 'To some more than others.'

Herrick shrugged. 'Well, sir, now that we know the enemy is out of port, what shall we do? Attack or blockade?'

Bolitho paced across the cabin and back again. The ship felt calmer and steadier, and although it was now late evening he could see a bronze sunset reflecting against the salt-caked windows. *Soon, soon*, the words seemed to hammer at his brain.

'Captains' conference tomorrow forenoon, Thomas. I can't wait any longer.'

He frowned as voices murmured in the outer cabin, and then Yovell poked his head around the screen door. It was impossible to avoid interruptions in a flagship.

His clerk said apologetically, 'Sorry to trouble you, sir. Officer o' the watch sends his respects and reports the sighting of a courier-brig. *Indomitable* has just hoisted the signal.'

Bolitho looked at the chart. The brig would not be able to communicate before daylight tomorrow. It was as if more decisions were being made for him.

'Thank you, Yovell.' He turned to Herrick. 'The French squadron will stay in readiness at its anchorage, that's my opinion. Once the invasion craft begin to move from Lorient and their other local harbours, Remond will be kept informed of our intentions by semaphore. There will be no need for him to deploy the main part of his force until he knows what I attempt.'

Herrick said bitterly, 'The defender always has the edge over any attacker.'

Bolitho watched him thoughtfully. Herrick would follow him to the death if so ordered. But it was obvious he was against the plan of attack. The French admiral had all the advantage of swift communications right along the vital stretch of coast. Once the British squadron chose to attack, Remond would summon aid from Lorient, Brest and any-where else nearby while he closed with *Benbow* and her consorts.

In his heart Bolitho was equally certain that the unex-pected arrival of a courier-brig meant fresh orders. To cancel the attack before it had begun. To save face rather than endure the humiliation of a defeat while secret negotiations were being conducted.

Without realizing it he said aloud, 'They don't have to fight wars! It might knock some sense into their heads if they did!'

Herrick had obviously been thinking about the brig's arrival.

'A cancellation, a recall even, would save a lot of bother, sir.' He hurried on stubbornly, 'I understand what is right and honourable, sir. I suspect their lordships only know what is expedient.'

Bolitho looked past him at the stern windows. The glow of sunset had vanished.

'We'll have the conference as planned. Then,' he looked calmly at Herrick, 'I intend to shift my flag to *Odin*.' He saw Herrick jerk upright in his chair, his expression one of total disbelief. 'Easy, Thomas. Think before you protest. *Odin* is the smallest liner in the squadron, a little sixty-four. Remember, it was Nelson who shifted his command flag from the *St George* to the *Elephant* at Copenhagen because she was smaller and drew less water for inshore tactics. I intend to follow our Nel's example for this attack.'

Herrick had struggled to his feet, while Browne sat limply in his chair, his eyes heavy with fatigue and too much brandy, as he watched them both.

Herrick exploded, 'That's got nothing to do with it! With respect, sir, I know you of old, and I can see right through this plan as if it were full of holes! You want my broad-pendant above *Benbow* when we clear for action, so that in any defeat I shall be absolved! Just as you signalled *Phalarope* to stand inshore this morning to allow for any trouble over the fishing boat.'

'Well, Thomas, it turned out to be necessary.'

Herrick would not yield. 'But that was not the reason, sir! You did it to give Emes another chance!'

Bolitho eyed him impassively. '*Odin* is the more suitable ship, and there's an end to it. Now sit down and finish your drink, man. Besides which, I need the squadron to be split in two. It is our only chance of dividing the enemy.' He waited, hating what he was doing to Herrick, knowing there was no other way.

Browne muttered thickly, 'The prison.'

They both looked at him, and Bolitho asked, 'What about it?'

Browne made to rise but sank down again. 'You remember, sir. Our walk from the prison. The French had a semaphore station on that church.'

Herrick said angrily, 'Do you wish to go and pray there?'

Browne did not seem to hear him. 'We decided it was the last semaphore station on the southern side of the Loire.' He made to slap his hand on the table but missed. 'Destroy it and the link in the chain is broken.'

Bolitho said quietly, 'I know. It is what I intended we should try to do. But that was then, not now.' He watched him fondly. 'Why not turn in, Oliver? You must ' be exhausted.'

Browne shook his head violently. 'S'not what I meant, sir. Admiral Remond will *depend* on information. He'll know full well we'd never attempt a night attack. Any ship of the line would be aground before she's moved more than a mile in those waters.'

Bolitho said, 'If you're suggesting what I think you are, then put it right out of your mind.'

Browne got to his feet and dragged the chart across the table. 'But think of it, sir! A break in the chain. No signals for twenty miles or more! It would give you the time you must have!' The strength left his legs and he slumped down again.

Herrick exclaimed, 'I must be getting old or something.'

'There is a small beach, Thomas.' Bolitho spoke quietly as he relived the moment. The little commandant and his watchful guards. The wind dying as they had felt their way down the path to the shore. The only suitable place for *Ceres'* captain to send his boat to collect them. 'From it to the semaphore station is hardly any distance, once you are there. It would be folly.'

Browne said, 'I could find the place. I'm not likely to forget it.'

'But even if you *could* . . .' Herrick scanned the chart and then looked at Bolitho.

'Am I becoming too involved again, Thomas, is that it?' Bolitho watched him despairingly. 'Neale could have found the place, so too could I. But Oliver is my flag-lieutenant, and I've allowed him to risk his life enough already without this madcap scheme!'

Herrick replied harshly, 'John Neale's dead, sir, and for once *you* can't go yourself. The cutting-out of the fishing boat was your idea, and it proved to be well worth while, although I suspect you were more worried than you showed for the safety of your flag-lieutenant. I know I was.' He waited, judging the moment like an experienced gun-captain gauging the exact fall of shot. 'A marine and two good seamen died this morning because of that encounter. I knew them, sir, but did you?'

Bolitho shook his head. 'No. Are you saying I did not care because of it?'

Herrick watched him gravely. 'I am telling you you *must* not care, sir. The three men died, but they helped to give us a small advance knowledge which we may use against the enemy. At the conference tomorrow they would all answer the same. A few lives to save the many is any captain's rule.' His mouth softened and he added, 'Ask for volunteers and you would get more lieutenants than you could shake a stick at. But none of them would know that beach or the path to the semaphore. It is a terrible risk, but only Mr Browne knows where to go.' He looked sadly at the flag-lieutenant. 'If it gives us another advantage and a chance to reduce casualties, then it is a risk we must offer.'

Browne nodded vaguely. 'That's what I said, sir.'

'I know, Oliver.' Bolitho ran his fingers along the glittering sword on its rack. 'But have you weighed up the danger against the chances of success?'

'He's asleep, sir.' Herrick looked at him for several

seconds. 'Anyway, it's the only decision. It's all we have.'

Bolitho looked at the sleeping lieutenant, his legs out-thrust like a man resting by the roadside. Herrick was right of course.

He said, 'You do not spare your words, Thomas, when you know something should or must be done.'

Herrick picked up his hat and smiled grimly. 'I had a very good teacher, sir.' He glanced at Browne. 'Lady Luck may be fair to him again.'

As the door closed behind him Bolitho said quietly, 'He'll need more than luck this time, old friend.'

As one captain after another arrived on board *Benbow* at the arranged time, the stern cabin took on an air of cheerful informality. The captains, senior and junior alike, were among their own kind, and no longer required the screen of authority to conceal their private anxieties or hopes.

At the entry port the marine guard and side party received each one, and each would pause with hat removed while the calls trilled and muskets slapped to the present to pay respect to the gold epaulettes and the men who wore them.

In the cabin, Allday and Tuck, assisted by Ozzard, arranged chairs, poured wine and made their temporary guests as comfortable as possible. To Allday some of the arrivals were old friends. Francis Inch of the *Odin*, with his long horseface and genial bobbing enthusiasm. Valentine Keen of the *Nicator*, fair and elegant, who had served Bolitho previously as both midshipman and junior lieutenant. He had a special greeting for Allday, and the others watched as he grasped the burly coxswain's fist and shook it warmly. Some understood this rare relationship, others remained mystified. Keen could never forget how he had been hurled to the deck in battle, a great splinter driven into his groin like some terrible missile. The ship's surgeon had been too drunk to help him, and it had been Allday who had held him down and had personally cut out the wood splinter and saved his life.

Duncan of the *Sparrowhawk*, even redder in the face as he shouted into Captain Veriker's deaf ear, and the latest appointment to the squadron, George Lockhart of the frigate *Ganymede*. Some arrived in their own boats, others from the furthest extremes of the patrol areas were collected and brought to the flagship by the ubiquitous *Rapid* which now lay hove to nearby, ready to return the various lords and masters to their rightful commands.

But whether they flaunted the two epaulettes of captain in a lofty seventy-four, or the single adornment of a junior commander like Lapish, to their companies each was a king in his own right, and when out of contact with higher authority could act with almost absolute power, right or wrong.

Herrick stood like a rock amongst them, knowing everything about some, enough about the others.

Only Captain Daniel Emes of the *Phalarope* stood apart from the rest, his face stiff and devoid of expression as he gripped a full goblet in one hand while his other tapped out a slow tattoo on his sword-hilt.

It had taken most of the morning watch and half of the forenoon to gather them together, and during that time the courier-brig had sent over her despatches and then made off in search of the next squadron to the south.

Only Herrick amongst those present knew what the weighted bag had contained, and he was keeping it to himself. He knew what Bolitho intended. There was no point in discussing it further.

The door opened and Bolitho entered, followed by his flag-lieutenant. Browne had always been regarded as a necessary shadow by most of the others, but his recent escapades as an escaped prisoner of war, the partner in a daring probe amongst the enemy's shipping had raised him to a far different light.

Bolitho shook hands with each of his captains. Inch so obviously glad to be with him again, and Keen who had shared so much in the past, not least the death of the girl

Bolitho had once loved.

He saw Emes standing on his own and walked over to him. 'That was a well executed operation, Captain Emes. You saved my flag-lieutenant, but now it seems I am to lose him again.'

There was a ripple of laughter which helped to soften their dislike for Emes.

Only Herrick remained grim-faced.

They seated themselves again and Bolitho outlined as briefly as he could the French movements, the arrival of Remond's flying squadron, as it was now known, and the need of an early attack to forestall any attempt to convoy the invasion craft into more heavily protected waters.

There was need for additional warnings about this treacherous coast and the dangers from unpredictable winds. The conditions, like the war, were impartial, as the loss of *Styx* and the French *Ceres* had recently driven home.

Each captain present was experienced and under no illusions about an attack in daylight, and in many ways there was an air of expectancy rather than doubt, as if, like Bolitho, they wanted to get it over and done with.

Like players in a village drama, others came and went to the captains' conference. Old Ben Grubb, the sailing master, forthright and unimpressed by the presence of so many captains and his own rear-admiral, rumbled through the state of tides and currents, the hazards of wrecks, which would be carefully noted and copied by the industrious Yovell.

Wolfe, the first lieutenant, who in peaceful times had once served in these same waters for a while in the merchant service, had some local knowledge to add.

Bolitho said, 'When we mount our attack there will be no second chance.' He looked around their faces, seeing each one weighing up his own separate part of the whole. 'The chain of semaphore stations is as great an enemy as any French squadron, and to break it, for even a short while, demands the highest in courage and resolve. Fortunately for us, we have such a man who will lead a raid on the station which adjoins the prison we shared so recently.'

Bolitho could sense the instant change in the cabin as all eyes moved to Browne.

He continued, 'The raid will be carried out tomorrow night under cover of darkness and making full use of the tide and the fact there will be no moon.' He glanced at Lapish's intent face. 'Mr Browne has requested that your first lieutenant, Mr Searle, again be appointed to work with him. I suggest a maximum of six hand-picked men, with at least two who are experts in fuses and placing explosives.'

Lapish nodded. 'I have such hands, sir. One was a miner and well used to placing charges.'

'Good. I will leave that to you, Commander Lapish. You will stand inshore tomorrow night, land the raiding party and then withdraw. *Rapid* will rejoin the squadron and report by prearranged night signal.' He had gone over and over it again in his mind so that it was almost like repeating someone else's words. 'Commodore Herrick will take station off Belle Ile, with *Nicator* and *Indomitable* in company, and *Sparrowhawk* for close observation inshore.' He looked directly at Inch. 'I shall shift my flag directly to your ship, and with *Phalarope*'s carronades for good measure, we shall make the first attack on the invasion craft at their moorings.'

Inch bobbed and beamed, as if he had just been offered a knighthood. 'A *great* day, sir!'

'Perhaps.' Bolitho looked around the cabin. '*Ganymede* will be my scouting vessel, and *Rapid* will link our two forces together.' He let the murmur of voices die and then said, 'The squadron will attack at dawn the day after tomorrow. That is all, gentlemen, except to say that God be with you.'

The captains rose to their feet and gathered round Browne to slap him on the back and congratulate him for his bravery, even though each one of them probably knew he was saying goodbye to a man already as good as dead. If Browne was thinking the same, he certainly did not show it. He seemed to have matured over the past weeks, so that in some ways he appeared senior to the captains around him.

Herrick whispered fiercely, 'You did not tell them about the new orders, sir!'

'Recall? Discontinue the plan of attack?' Bolitho watched Browne sadly. 'They would still support me, and by knowing of their lordships' change of heart they would be considered accomplices at any court of enquiry later on. Yovell will have written it all down for anyone who cares to read it.'

Herrick persisted, 'That piece in the orders, sir, about using your discretion . . .'

Bolitho nodded. 'I know. Whatever happens I must accept the responsibility.' He smiled suddenly. 'Nothing changes, does it?'

One by one the captains departed, each eager to return to his own command and prepare his people for battle.

Bolitho waited until Browne arrived at the entry port, ready to be taken across to the waiting brig.

Browne said, 'I am worried about your not having a suitable aide, sir. Perhaps Commodore Herrick could select a replacement?'

Bolitho shook his head. 'The midshipman who was injured, I'll take him. He is good with signals, you said, and his French is passable, you said that too.' It was impossible to keep it casual and matter of fact.

'Stirling.' Browne smiled. 'Young but eager. Hardly suitable for your aide, sir.'

Bolitho looked at the *Benbow*'s barge being swayed outboard in readiness to carry him to Inch's ship.

'He will be only temporary, I trust, Oliver?' Their eyes met and then Bolitho grasped his hand. 'I am not happy about this. Take good care. I've got used to your ways now.'

Browne returned the handclasp but did not smile. 'Don't worry, sir, you'll get the time you need.' He stood back and touched his hat, the contact broken.

Herrick watched the brig's jolly-boat pulling away and said, 'Brave fellow.' Then he turned on his heel and strode away to attend to his ship.

Allday came aft and waited for Bolitho to see him.

'Ozzard's sent your gear across to *Odin*, sir. He's gone with it. Wouldn't stay in *Benbow* a second time, he said. Beggin' your pardon, sir, nor would I.'

Bolitho smiled. 'It seems we are always making this journey, Allday.'

He glanced at the midshipmen at the flag halliards preparing to strike his flag and hoist Herrick's broad-pendant as he departed. At least it would protect Herrick from any criticism if the worst happened.

He turned and shaded his eyes to watch for *Rapid*'s boat but it had already merged alongside and was lost from view.

Lieutenant the Honourable Oliver Browne had not even hesitated. It would make those in safe occupations ashore think again if they could have seen his sacrifice.

Herrick joined him and said, 'Your *acting* flag-lieutenant is here, sir.'

They all looked down at Midshipman Stirling, who with bag in one hand and signals book under his arm was staring at Bolitho.

Bolitho saw that the midshipman had one hand resting in a sling, and said, 'Take his things, Allday.'

Allday almost winked, but not quite. 'Aye, aye, sir. This way, young sir, I'll see you get no lip from them Odins.'

'Well, Thomas.'

Herrick rubbed his chin. 'Aye, sir, it's time.'

'Remember, Thomas, a victory now will put heart into the ordinary people at home. They've had much to bear over the years. It's not only sailors who suffer in a war, you know.'

Herrick forced a grin. 'Don't fret, sir, I'll be there with the squadron. No matter what.' He was making a great effort. 'Besides, I've got to be at the wedding, haven't I?'

They shook hands.

'I'd not forgive you otherwise, Thomas.'

Herrick straightened his back. 'Carry on, Major Clinton.'

Clinton's sword glittered in the pale sunlight. 'Marines! Present *arms*!'

The drums rolled and the fifers broke into *Heart of Oak*, and with a last glance at his friend Bolitho climbed down to the waiting barge.

'Bear off forrard! Out oars!' Allday's shadow rose over the rear-admiral and diminutive midshipman like a cloak. 'Give way, *all*!'

The green-painted barge turned swiftly away from *Benbow*'s side, and as it pushed out of her protective lee, Bolitho was startled by a sudden burst of wild cheering. He turned and looked back as *Benbow*'s seamen lined the gangway and swarmed into the shrouds to cheer him on his way.

Allday murmured softly, 'Good ship, sir.'

Bolitho nodded, unable to find words for the unexpected demonstration.

Benbow, which had been his flagship in some of the worst fighting he had known, was wishing him well.

He was glad of the cold spray which danced over the gunwale and touched his face as if to steady and reassure him. He saw Midshipman Stirling staring enthralled at the *Odin* where the ceremony would begin all over again.

Allday stared at the small two-decker with the fierce Norseman's figurehead and winged helmet waiting to receive them.

'Proper pot o' paint *she* looks!' he muttered disdainfully.

'What do you think of all this, er, Mr Stirling?'

The boy looked gravely at his rear-admiral and took a few seconds to answer. He had just been writing a letter in his mind to his mother, describing this very moment.

'It is the happiest day of my life, sir.'

He said it so seriously that Bolitho momentarily forgot his anxieties.

'Then we must try and keep it so, eh?'

The barge hooked on to *Odin*'s main chains, and Bolitho saw Inch peering down at him, not wishing to miss a minute of it as his ship hoisted the flag.

In his excitement Stirling made for the side of the barge, but was forestalled by Allday's great fist on his shoulder.

'Belay that, *sir*! This is the admiral's barge, not some midshipmite's bumboat!'

Bolitho nodded to them and then climbed swiftly up *Odin*'s tumblehome.

'Welcome aboard, sir!' Inch had to shout above the din of fifes and barked commands.

Bolitho glanced aloft as his flag broke from the mizzen truck. There it was, and there it would remain until it was finished. One way or the other.

'You may get the ship under way, Captain Inch.'

Inch was staring uncertainly at Midshipman Stirling.

Bolitho added calmly, 'Oh, Mr Stirling, signal, if you please. From *Flag* to *Rapid*. Make, *We Happy Few*.'

Stirling scribbled furiously on his book and then ran to muster the signalling party.

Bolitho shaded his eyes to watch the little brig as she turned stern on to the rest of the squadron. Stirling would not understand the signal, neither probably would *Rapid*'s signals midshipman.

But Browne would know. Bolitho turned towards the poop. And that mattered.

'*Rapid*'s acknowledged, sir.'

Bolitho entered his new quarters and saw Allday carefully placing the bright presentation sword on a rack.

Allday said defensively, 'Makes it more like home, sir.'

Bolitho sat down and watched Ozzard bustling around the cabin as if he had served in *Odin* for years.

Stirling entered and stood awkwardly, shifting from one foot to the other.

'Well, Mr Stirling, what do you suggest I do now?'

The boy regarded him warily and then said, 'I think you should invite some of the ship's officers to dinner, sir.'

Allday's face split into a grin. 'A proper flag-lieutenant already, sir, an' that's no error!'

Bolitho smiled. Perhaps by being with Browne, Stirling had also learned something.

'That is an excellent idea. Would you ask the first lieutenant to see me.'

The door closed and Allday said, 'I'll find you a good sword for later on.'

By later on, Allday meant the forthcoming battle with the French.

But now the rear-admiral would show his other face to *Odin*'s officers, the one which displayed confidence and a certainty of victory. For on the day after tomorrow they would be looking to him again and, right or wrong, they had to trust him.

Inch entered the cabin and peered round as if to assure himself that the quarters were suitable for his unexpected arrival.

He remarked, '*Phalarope*'s taken station to wind'rd as ordered, sir.' He tossed his hat to his own servant. 'If you'll pardon my saying so, sir, I would that your nephew was aboard *Odin* instead of that ship.'

'You never alter, Inch.' Bolitho lay back on the bench and listened to the sea surging around the rudder. 'But in this case I think you are wrong.'

He did not see the perplexed look on Inch's long face. When action was joined it was somehow right that his brother's son should be in that same old frigate. Like a joining of hands, after all the bitterness which had driven them apart.

Allday left the cabin, wondering what sort of companion Inch's coxswain would make. He saw Stirling hovering in the lobby and asked, 'All too much, is it?'

The boy turned on him as if to hit back but then smiled. 'It's a big step, Mr Allday.'

Allday grinned and squatted on the breech of a nine-pounder. 'Not *Mister*, just Allday, it suits well enough.'

The boy relaxed and studied him curiously. 'But you speak with the admiral like one of his equals.'

Allday looked down at his fists. 'Friend, more like. It's what he needs.'

He stood up suddenly and leaned over the midshipman's slight figure.

'If you go aft to him and act normal, he'll treat you the same.' He spoke with such force that Stirling was impressed into silence. 'Cause he's just a *man*, see? Not God Almighty! Right now he needs all his friends, not his bloody lieutenants, so just you remember that, *sir*!' He punched the midshipman gently on his uninjured arm. 'But you tell him what I said, or give him any of your lip, an' I'll take you apart, *sir*!'

Stirling grinned. 'Got you, Allday! And thanks.'

Allday watched him re-enter the cabin and sighed. Seems a nice lad, he thought. Of course, when he was made lieutenant he might well change. He looked round the shadowy between-decks at the tethered gun at every sealed port, brooding and waiting, like all the others in the squadron. Stirling was fourteen. What the hell was he doing here when they were about to sail into battle? What the hell were any of them doing here?

Allday shivered. It got worse, not better. Stirling was full of high spirits, in spite of his injury, or perhaps because of it. But he did not know what it would be like when those guns were surrounded with yelling, smoke-blackened madmen, and the order was to fire, reload and keep firing, no matter what.

He thought of the battle-crazed marine who had almost driven his bayonet through him on the *Ceres'* orlop deck.

Maybe peace was really coming, and this might be the last sea-fight for any of them.

Allday thought too of the *Phalarope* standing to windward of them. It made him feel uneasy, just to know she was there.

A sergeant of marines clumped out of the shadows and peered at him.

'Feel like a wet, matey?'

Allday grinned. 'From a bullock?'

The sergeant took his arm and led him towards the companion ladder.

'Why not?'

They climbed down through the familiar shipboard smells and the headier aroma of Jamaican rum.

Maybe *Odin* wasn't such a bad ship after all.

The marine sergeants and corporals shared a small, screened off portion of the lower gundeck. They greeted Allday with cheerful grins, and soon had him comfortably seated with a pot of rum by his elbow.

The colour-sergeant said, 'Now, matey, as the rear-admiral's personal cox'n, so to speak, you'll know wot we're goin' to do, right?'

Allday leant against the side and expanded. 'Well, usually me an' the admiral . . .'

By the evening of that day, *Odin*, with *Phalarope* keeping well to windward, were out of sight of the remainder of the squadron.

In the great cabin, resplendent with the table fully extended and the best glasses and silver laid before the chattering officers, Captain Francis Inch was bursting with pleasure and pride. Nothing could ever be quite so perfect again.

Bolitho sat at the head of the table and allowed the conversation and wit to flow around him, while glasses were refilled and toasts drunk with barely a break in between.

Bolitho glanced at the ship's lieutenants. Mostly they were so young, and like Allday, although he had no way of knowing it, he was thinking of this same carefree place as it would soon become when the ship was called to quarters.

He studied the officers in turn and tried to remember each by name. Sons, and lovers, but not many husbands amongst them. Yet. A normal enough wardroom in any ship of the line.

They would fight, and they must win.

One young lieutenant was saying, 'Yes, I'm really going to get married when we get home again.' He held up his hand to silence the derisive laughter. 'No, this time I mean it!'

Then he turned and looked at Bolitho, emboldened by claret or touched perhaps by the thought of the battle yet to come, he asked, 'May I ask, sir, are you married?'

Bolitho smiled. 'Like you, Mr Travers, I am getting married when we anchor again in Plymouth Sound.'

'Thank you for that, sir.' The lieutenant studied him anxiously. 'I thought, just for a moment—'

'I know what you were thinking.' He was suddenly glad he had remembered the lieutenant's name. 'The idea of marriage has given you something to stay alive for, am I right?'

Travers lowered his eyes. 'I am not afraid, sir.'

'I know that too.' He looked away. *How can I not become involved?*

Bolitho said, 'But it also gives you something to fight for, remember that and you'll not fail.'

As the most junior guest present, Midshipman George Stirling, whose home was in Winchester, sat enthralled and watched everything.

In his mind he was composing another long letter to his mother.

> *My dearest Mother . . . This evening we are standing towards the French coast. I am dining with Rear-Admiral Bolitho.*

He gave a secret smile. She might not believe it. He was not sure that he did either.

He tried again.

> *He is such a fine man, and I nearly cried when the people lined the ship to give their huzzas when he left for* Odin.

He realized that Bolitho was watching him down the length of the table.

Bolitho asked, 'Are you ready, Mr Stirling?'

The midshipman swallowed hard and lifted his goblet which suddenly seemed too heavy to hold.

Bolitho glanced at the others, their faces flushed and cheerful. Wars were not made by young men, he thought, but they had to fight them. It seemed right that Stirling should give the final toast. And it would be just that for some of these same young men.

Stirling tried not to lick his lips as every eye turned in his direction. Then he recalled what Allday had told him about

Bolitho. *He's just a man*.

'Gentlemen, the toast is Victory! Death to the French!'

The rest was lost in a roar of approval, as if the ship herself was eager to fight.

15

An Impudent Gesture

'Cap'n's comin' up, sir.'

Pascoe lowered his telescope and nodded to the master's mate.

'Thank you.'

He had been watching the *Odin* going through her sail and gun drills, the ports opening and closing as if controlled by a giant's touch, sails filling and then reefing with equal precision.

He heard Emes' step on the damp planking and turned towards him. He never knew what sort of mood might lie behind Emes' impassive features, what he might really be thinking and planning in the privacy of his cabin.

Pascoe touched his hat. 'Sou'-east by south, sir. Wind's veered a trifle, north by east.'

Emes strode to the quarterdeck rail and gripped it hard as he stared first along his command, the comings and goings of the watch, and the boatswain's party who were as usual splicing and repairing. An endless task. Then he shifted his gaze to *Odin* as she rode comfortably some four cables to starboard.

'Hmm. Visibility's poor.' Emes' lower lip jutted forward. It was the only sign he ever gave that he was worried about something. 'It'll be an early dusk, I shouldn't wonder.' He tugged a watch from his breeches and flicked open the guard. 'Your uncle appears to be giving Captain Inch some extra drill.' He smiled, but only briefly. 'Flagship indeed.'

Emes walked aft to the compass and peered at it, then at

the slate which hung nearby.

Pascoe watched the helmsmen and master's mate of the watch, the way they tensed when Emes was near, as if they expected him to abuse them.

Pascoe could not understand it. They were actually afraid of the captain. And yet Emes had done little or nothing to warrant such fear. He was unbending over matters of discipline, but never awarded excessive punishment like some captains. He was often impatient with subordinates, but rarely used his rank to insult them in front of their men. What was it about him, Pascoe wondered? A cold, withdrawn man who had not backed down to his rear-admiral even under the cloud of a possible court martial.

Emes walked across the deck and stared at the sea and damp mist. It was more like drizzle, which made the shrouds and canvas drip and shine in the strange light.

'Has Mr Kincade inspected all the carronades today, Mr Pascoe?'

Kincade was *Phalarope*'s gunner, a sour, taciturn man who appeared to love his ugly charges more than mankind itself.

'Aye, sir. They'll give a good account of themselves.'

'Really.' Emes eyed him bleakly. 'Eager for it, are you?'

Pascoe flushed. 'It's better than waiting, sir.'

The midshipman of the watch called hesitantly, '*Rapid*'s in sight to wind'rd, sir.'

Emes snapped, 'I'm going to my quarters. Call me before you shorten sail, and keep good station on the Flag.' He strode to the companion way without even a glance at *Rapid*'s murky silhouette.

Pascoe relaxed. Was that too part of an act, he wondered? To walk away without seemingly caring about *Rapid* as she headed towards the enemy shore. Like the way he deliberately refused to exercise the carronade crews, even though the flagship had been drilling for most of the day.

The sailing master, a gaunt, mournful-faced man who had obviously been keeping out of Emes' way, climbed on to the quarterdeck and glanced at the traverse board.

Pascoe said, 'What of the weather, Mr Bellis?'

Bellis grimaced. 'It'll get worse, sir. Can feel it in me bones.' He cocked his head. 'Listen to that lot!'

Pascoe thrust his hands behind him and gripped them together. He had heard the pumps going. They went during each watch now. Perhaps they were right about the old ship. The Bay was certainly playing hell with her seams.

The master warmed to his theme. 'Too long in port, sir, that's what. Should've left her be. I'll lay odds she's as ripe as a pear round the keel, no matter what the dockyard said!'

Pascoe turned away. 'Thank you for your confidence, Mr Bellis.'

The master grinned. 'My pleasure, sir.'

Pascoe raised his telescope and stared at the little brig. Almost lost now in another flurry of grey, wet mist.

He had read the fighting instructions, and pictured Browne now as he prepared himself for what lay ahead. Pascoe shivered. *Tonight*.

He wished more than anything he was going with him. Even the thought made him angry. He was getting disloyal like Bellis and some of the other old hands.

Phalarope had been a fine ship. He clutched the hammock nettings as the deck tilted steeply to the wind. His uncle had once stood just here. A chill seemed to touch his spine, as if he were standing naked in the wet breeze.

He must have stood and watched the other frigate, *Andiron*, approaching, her British colours hiding her new identity of a privateer.

Commanded by my father.

Pascoe looked along the gundeck and nodded slowly. Herrick, Allday and poor Neale had walked that deck, even Bolitho's steward Ferguson, who had lost an arm up there on the forecastle.

I've come to you now. Pascoe smiled self-consciously. But he felt better for it.

*

Lieutenant Browne had been hanging on to the jolly-boat's gunwale for so long his hand felt numb and useless. Ever since they had thrust away from the brig's protective side he had been beset by a procession of doubts and heart-stopping moments of sheer terror.

The heavily muffled oars had continued in their unbroken stroke, while a master's mate had crouched beside the coxswain, a lighted compass hidden beneath a tarpaulin screen.

Lieutenant Searle said, 'According to my calculations we should be close now. But as far as I can tell we might be in China!'

Browne peered from bow to bow, his eyes raw with salt spray. He felt the boat sidle and veer away on a sudden current, and heard the master's mate mutter new instructions to the coxswain.

Had to be soon. Must be. He saw a wedge of black rock rise up to starboard and slide away again, betrayed only by the uneasy surf.

He peered at the sky. Black as a highwayman's boot.

Searle stiffened at his side, and for one terrible moment Browne thought he had seen a French guard-boat.

Searle exclaimed, 'Look! Larboard bow!' He clapped his arm excitedly. 'Well done, Oliver!'

Browne tried to swallow but the roof of his mouth was like leather. He peered harder into the darkness until he thought his eyes would burst from their sockets.

It was there. A crescent of beach, a long frothing necklace of surf.

He tried to stay calm and unmoved. He could still be wrong. The rock he had remembered so vividly might look quite different from this bearing.

'Easy, all! Boat yer oars!'

The boat surged forward and ground on to the beach with an indescribable clatter and roar. Browne almost fell as seamen leapt into the shallows to steady the hull, while Searle watched their small party of six men until they were all clear and wading ashore.

Searle rasped, 'See to the powder, man! Nicholl, scout ahead, lively!'

There were a few quick whispers. 'Good luck, sir.' Another unknown voice called, 'I'll keep a wet for you, Harry!' Then the boat had gone, oars backing furiously as freed of her load she turned eagerly towards the open water.

Browne stood quite still and listened to the wind, the gurgle of water among rocks and across the tight sand.

Searle strode back to him, his hanger already drawn.

'Ready, Oliver?' His teeth shone white in the darkness. 'You know the way.'

Then Browne saw the rock standing above him. Like a squatting camel. As he remembered it from when he had stood there with Bolitho.

Searle had selected his men himself. Apart from two competent gunner's mates, there were four of the toughest, most villainous looking hands Browne had ever laid eyes on. Searle had described them as fugitives from more than one gibbet. Browne could well believe it.

They paused by a waving clump of salt-encrusted grass and Browne said quietly, 'The path begins here.'

He was surprised he was so calm now that the moment had arrived. He had been half afraid that his resolve might vanish once he had left the ship and the familiar faces and routine.

I am all right.

Searle whispered, 'Moubray, get up there and stay with Nicholl, Garner take rear-guard.'

The remaining seaman and the two gunner's mates lurched up the path, their bodies loaded with powder and weapons like so many pit ponies.

The path was steeper than Browne remembered, and at the top they all laid down in the wet grass to regain their breath and find their bearings.

Browne said softly, 'See that pale thing? That's the prison wall. If there are no new prisoners there, the guard will be pretty slack. Our target is to the right. Hundred paces and then round a low hill.'

The gunner's mate named Jones hissed, 'Wot's that, then?'

They all lay prone and Browne said, 'Horses. A night picket of the dragoons I told you about. They'll keep to the road.'

Mercifully, the slow, drumming hoofbeats were soon lost to the other night noises.

Searle rose to his feet. 'Advance.' He pointed with his hanger. 'Don't stumble, and the first man to loose off a weapon gets my blade on his neck!'

Browne found he was able to smile. Searle was only twenty, but he had the sturdy assurance of an old campaigner.

It took longer than expected, and Browne had the feeling they had wandered too far to the right.

He felt a great sense of relief when Nicholl, the seaman who was scouting ahead, called in a fierce whisper, 'There t'is, sir! Dead ahead!'

They all dropped flat while Browne and Searle examined the faint outline of the church.

'The door's on the far side, facing the road.'

Browne made himself think about the next minutes. They might be all there were left for him. What had he expected? It was necessary, but for him and the others it was almost certain death. He smiled to himself. At least his father might see some good in him after this.

He looked from side to side. 'Ready?'

They all nodded, and some bared their teeth like hounds on a leash.

Then, keeping close against the wall of the church, they edged their way around it towards the opposite side. It was if everyone else had died or been stricken by some terrible plague. Only the grass shivered in the sea-breeze, and the squeak of their shoes made the only other sound.

One man gasped aloud as a bird shot from cover almost between his feet and vanished croaking into the darkness.

Searle exclaimed hoarsely, 'Bloody hell!'

'*Still!*' Browne pressed his back against the rough stones and waited for a challenge or a shot.

Then he moved deliberately away from the wall and peered up at the square Norman tower which he could just determine against the sky. There was a faint glow from a narrow, slitted window. He tried to control his racing thoughts and remember what he had learned about semaphore stations. In England they were usually manned by an officer, one other of warrant rank, and two or three seamen. With the prison so close, it was likely some of them lodged there during the night. If so . . .

Browne joined Searle and whispered, 'Test the door.'

The gunner's mate called Jones grasped the heavy ring which formed the handle and turned it carefully. It squeaked but did not budge.

'Locked, sir.'

Searle beckoned to another of his men. 'Moubray, ready with the grapnel!'

Browne held his breath as the grapnel flew through the air and bounced off the wall to fall back amongst them.

But the second time it held firm, and Browne saw the next man swarm up the line and disappear, as if the old church had swallowed him alive.

Searle said between his teeth, 'Good man. Used to be a felon in Lime House 'til the press picked him up.'

The door handle squeaked again and this time it swung inwards to reveal the small seaman standing there with a grin splitting his face.

'Come inside! Bit warmer 'ere!'

'Hold your noise, damn you!' Searle peered into the shadows.

'S'all right, sir. No bother.' The seaman opened the shutter of a lantern and held it across some spiralling stone stairs. A body in uniform lay spreadeagled where he had fallen, his eyes like pebbles in the light.

Browne swallowed hard. The man's throat had been cut and there was blood everywhere.

The seaman said calmly, 'Only one 'ere, sir, 'e was. Easy as robbin' a blind baby, sir.'

Searle sheathed his hanger. 'You would know, Cooper.'

He walked to the stairs. 'Harding and Jones, prepare your fuses.' He looked at Browne and smiled tightly. 'Let us go and secure our prize, eh?'

Bolitho awoke with a start, his fingers gripping the arms of one of Inch's comfortable bergères in which he had been dozing on and off since nightfall.

He could tell immediately that the ship's movements were more lively and forceful, and he heard the sluice of water beneath the counter as *Odin* heeled over to the wind.

Apart from a solitary shuttered lantern, the stern cabin was in darkness, so that through the heavily streaked window the waves looked angry and near.

A door opened and he saw Allday's shadow against the screen.

'What's happening?' So he had been unable to sleep too.

'Wind's veered, sir.'

'More than before?'

'Aye. Nor'-east, or as makes no difference.' He sounded glum.

Bolitho grappled with the news. He had anticipated that the wind might shift. But as far round as the north-east was unthinkable. With only a few hours of darkness left to hide their stealthy approach, they would be slowed down to a mere crawl. It might mean an attack in broad daylight, with every enemy ship for miles around roused and ready to hit back.

'Fetch my clothes.' Bolitho stood up and felt the deck sway over as if to mock him and his plans.

Allday said, 'I've already told Ozzard. I heard you tossing and turning, sir. That chair's no place for a good sleep.'

Bolitho waited for Allday to open the lantern shutters very slightly. The whole ship was in darkness, the galley fire doused. It would put the final touch of disaster if the rear-admiral allowed lights to show from the cabin.

He smelt coffee and saw Ozzard's small shape moving towards him.

Ozzard murmured, 'Took the liberty of making this before they put out the fires, sir. Kept it wrapped in a blanket.'

Bolitho sipped the coffee gratefully, his mind still busy with alternatives. There could be no turning back, even if he wanted to. Browne would be there by now, or lying dead with his party of volunteers.

He knew he would not break off the attack whatever happened, even though his open-worded instructions to use his discretion left him room to manoeuvre up to the last minute. Perhaps his move to *Odin* had just been an excuse after all. To protect Herrick, but also to prevent his arguments from changing his mind.

Bolitho slipped his arms into his coat and strode to the door. He could not wait a moment longer.

On deck the air was alive with the chorus of canvas and clattering blocks. Figures loomed and faded in the shadows, while around the double wheel, like survivors on a tiny reef, the master and his mates, helmsmen and midshipman of the watch stood in a tight, shapeless group.

Inch's lanky figure bustled to meet him.

'Good morning, sir.' Inch was no actor and could not conceal his surprise. 'Is something wrong?'

Bolitho took his arm and together they moved to the rail. He said, 'It's the wind.'

Inch stared at him. 'The master thinks it will veer still more, sir.'

'I see.' *Thinks*. Old Ben Grubb would have *known*, as if God were on his side.

Streamers of spindrift twisted through the drumming shrouds, and almost lost abeam, but still on station, Bolitho saw *Phalarope*. A ghost ship indeed.

Bolitho bit his lip, then said shortly, 'Chartroom.' Followed by Inch and the sailing master, Bolitho strode into the shuttered space beneath the poop and stared hard at the chart.

He could almost feel Inch waiting for a decision, just as he could sense the urgency. Like sand running through a glass. Nothing to slow or stop it.

He said, 'We'll not delay any longer. Call all hands and clear for action right away.' He waited for Inch to relay his order to a boatswain's mate outside the chartroom door. 'You estimate that we are some ten miles to the south-west of the headland?'

He saw the sailing master nod soundlessly and got a brief impression of an anxious but competent face. He suddenly remembered. The man had been the senior master's mate at Copenhagen when the old master had been cut down. New and, until now, untried.

Inch craned forward to watch Bolitho move the brass dividers over the chart.

'The French squadron is anchored off the point, just north of the Loire Estuary.' Bolitho was thinking aloud. 'It would take hours for us to beat against the wind along the original course. We must pass the French squadron before full daylight and head into the bay where the invasion fleet is anchored.' He looked at the master. 'Well?'

Inch said encouragingly, 'Come along, Mr M'Ewan.'

The master moistened his lips then said firmly, 'We can claw inshore now, sir, then come about and steer nor'-west, close-hauled, into the bay. Provided the wind don't back on us, for if that happens we'll be in irons an' no mistake, sir.'

Inch opened his mouth as if to protest but closed it when he saw Bolitho nod his head.

'I agree. It will cut the approach by an hour, and with any luck we will slip past the French men-of-war with a mile to spare.' He looked at Inch. 'You were going to add something?'

'The wind is not only hard for *us*, sir.' Inch shrugged helplessly. 'The rest of the squadron will be delayed accordingly.'

'I know.'

He heard the muffled pounding of feet, the bang and

squeak of screens being removed and obstacles being lowered hastily to the orlop. A ship-of-war. Open from bow to stern, deck above deck, gun above gun, where men lived, hoped, slept and trained. Now was the testing time for them all.

The first lieutenant yelled, 'Cleared for action, sir!'

Inch examined his watch and bobbed. 'Nine minutes, Mr Graham, that is a good time.'

Bolitho turned away to hide his sudden sadness. Neale had done the same.

He said, 'If we delay, we could be destroyed piecemeal. Whether Commodore Herrick arrives in time to support us or not, we must be able to get amongst those invasion craft.' He looked Inch squarely in the eyes. 'It is all that matters.'

Surprisingly, Inch beamed. 'I know, sir. And *Odin* is the ship for the task.'

Bolitho smiled. Safe, trusting Inch would never question anything he said.

The chartroom door opened and Midshipman Stirling squeezed inside. Even in the poor lantern light he looked red-eyed and weary.

He said, 'I – I apologize for being late, sir.'

Bolitho glanced at Inch. 'I have forgotten how to sleep that soundly!'

Inch made to leave. 'I'll make the night signal to *Phalarope*, sir. I hope she's still there at daybreak!'

Bolitho leaned on the chart and stared at the neat figures and bearings. It was a risk. But then it had never been otherwise.

Even now it could all go against them before they had a chance to stand inshore. A solitary fisherman might be risking the weather and the wrath of French guard-boats to put out and earn his keep. He might just see the shielded flare which was now being shown to *Phalarope*.

He said, 'Damnation on doubt. It kills more good sailors than any round shot!'

Stirling glanced round quickly. Inch and the master had gone. Bolitho was speaking to *him*.

He asked unsurely, 'Could the French prevent our entering the bay, sir?'

Bolitho looked down at him, unaware he had voiced his anxiety aloud.

'They can try, Mr Stirling, they can *try*.' He clapped the boy on the shoulder. 'Come and walk with me. I need to have the feel of this ship.'

Stirling glowed with pride. Even the fact that Bolitho had unwittingly gripped his injured arm did not tarnish the moment.

Allday, a new cutlass jutting from his belt, watched them pass, and found he could smile in spite of his troubled thoughts.

The boy and his hero. And why not? They would need all their heroes this day.

'Wind's holding steady, sir!'

Bolitho joined Inch at the quarterdeck rail and peered along the ship's pale outline. Beyond the forecastle, reeling now as the yards were hauled further round until they were almost fore and aft, he could see nothing. He had purposefully stayed on deck so that his eyes would be accustomed to any change in the light, be ready to detect the first join between sea and sky. And the land.

The deck plunged ponderously in the offshore currents, and Bolitho heard the marines on the poop packing the hammocks even more tightly in the nettings for their protection, and to rest their muskets while they sought out their targets.

Figures moved occasionally below the gangways where every gun stood loaded and ready. Others clambered aloft to make last adjustments to chain-slings and nets, to hoist one more sack of canister to the swivels in the tops, or to splice another fraying line.

Bolitho watched and heard it all. What he did not see he could picture in his mind. Like all those other times, the remorseless grip on the stomach like steel fingers, the last-moment fear that he had overlooked something.

The ship was answering well, he thought. Inch had proved to be an excellent captain, and it was hard to believe that Bolitho had once thought it unlikely he would even rise above lieutenant.

Bolitho tried to shut his mind to it. The young lieutenant named Travers, now somewhere on the lower gundeck, waiting with all the other men for the ports to open on their red-painted hell and the guns to begin to roar. He was hoping to get married. And Inch, who was striding about the quarterdeck, his coat tails flapping, his cocked hat at a jaunty angle, as he chatted to his first lieutenant and sailing master. He had a wife named Hannah and two children who lived in Weymouth. What of them if Inch were to fall today? And why should he show such pride and pleasure at being ordered to a battle which could end in total defeat?

And Belinda. He moved restlessly to the nettings, unaware that Stirling was keeping near him like a shadow. He must not think of her now.

He heard a man say quietly, 'There's th' old *Phalarope*, Jim. Rather any other bugger than that un for company!' He seemed to sense Bolitho's nearness and fell silent.

Bolitho stared at the ghostlike outline as *Phalarope* lifted and plunged abeam. Like *Odin*, she had her sails close-hauled to make a pale pyramid while the hull still lay in darkness.

Two ships and some eight hundred officers, seamen and marines whom he alone would commit to battle.

He looked down at the midshipman. 'How would you like to serve in a frigate?'

Stirling puckered his mouth and considered it. 'More than anything, sir.'

'You should speak with my nephew, he—' Bolitho broke off as Stirling's eyes lit up momentarily like small coals.

Then, what seemed like an eternity later, came the dull boom of an explosion. Like the short-lived glow in the sky, that too was soon lost to the ceaseless murmur of sea and wind.

'What the hell was that?' Inch strode across the deck as if he expected to discover an answer.

Bolitho said quietly, 'The charges have been blown, Captain Inch.'

'But, but . . .' Inch stared at him through the darkness. 'They are surely too early?'

Bolitho turned away. Too early or too late, Browne must have had his reasons.

He felt Allday move up beside him and raised an arm to allow him to clip a sword to his belt.

'It's the best I could do, sir. Bit heavier than you're used to.' He gestured into the darkness. 'Mr Browne?'

'Aye. He said he could do it. I wish to God there had been another way.'

Allday sighed. 'He knows what he's about, sir.' He nodded firmly. 'Like the time you an' he rode off to fight that duel, remember?'

'I remember.'

Midshipman Stirling said, 'It looks brighter, sir.'

Bolitho smiled. 'So it does.' He turned his back on the midshipman and said softly, 'Allday, there is something I must say.' He saw the coxswain recoil as if he already knew. 'If, and I say *if*, I should fall today—'

'Look here, sir.' Allday spread his hands to emphasize each word. 'Anything I've said or done since we came to this place don't matter now. We'll be all right, sir, just like always, you see.'

Bolitho said, 'But *if*. You must promise me you'll never return to the sea. You'll be needed at Falmouth. To take care of things.' He tried to ease Allday's despair. 'I'd like to have your word on it.'

Allday nodded dumbly.

Bolitho drew the sword from its scabbard and cut through the air above Stirling's head.

Several seamen and marines standing nearby nudged each

other, and one shouted, 'We'll teach they buggers, sir!'

Bolitho dropped his arm and said, 'Now I'm ready, Allday.'

Captain Inch cupped his hands. 'Lay her on the starboard tack, Mr Graham!'

'After-guard, man the mizzen braces!'

Bolitho stood amidst and yet apart from the busy activity as *Odin* laid herself over to the wind again.

Inch said brightly, 'No sign of the French, sir!'

Bolitho glanced up at the braced yards and the hard-bellied canvas, already much paler against the sky.

'They'll be out soon enough.' He saw his flag streaming from the mizzen truck, as yet without colour. 'Have another flag ready to bend on, Mr Stirling.' He found he could actually smile at Inch. 'When they come, I want Remond to know who he is fighting, so even if it is shot away we'll hoist another directly!'

Allday watched Bolitho's face, the way he seemed to rouse the men around him merely with a glance.

He was suddenly afraid for him, for what this impudent gesture might cost.

A pale gold thread touched the rim of the land and Inch exclaimed, 'We've passed the French squadron, sir!'

Bolitho looked at Allday and smiled. He at least understood.

He said, 'Very well, Captain Inch. When you are ready, run out your guns.'

16

Flotsam of a Dream

Lieutenant Searle stood at the top of a straight ladder and peered at the complicated array of tackles and blocks which hung from the roof. They were obviously connected to the semaphore structure on the tower.

He said, 'No wonder they need sailors for this work, Oliver. No landsman would ever be able to untangle it.' He touched the damp stone wall and grimaced. 'We'll need a big charge to blow down the whole tower.'

Browne stared up at him. 'The *whole* tower?'

Searle was already beckoning to one of his gunner's mates. 'Up here, Jones! Move yourself, man!' To Browne he added, 'This place is built like a fortress. How long do you imagine it would take the Frenchies to mount another semaphore on the top of the tower, eh?'

Searle turned to the gunner's mate. 'Pack the charges tight beneath the stairway under the outer wall. That should do it.' When the man remained silent he snapped, 'Well, man?'

Jones rubbed his jaw and looked up the ladder to the square trap-door at the top.

'I reckon, sir.'

He clambered down again and could be heard talking with his companion.

'Bloody fools!' Searle pushed upwards at the trap-door. 'All of a quiver because it's a church! You'd think they were a bunch of saints!'

As Searle vanished through the trap-door, Browne followed him, chilled instantly by the breeze across the headland.

Searle was still fuming. 'More sins have been committed by the church than any seaman, I shouldn't wonder!'

'You're very cynical for one so young.'

Browne walked to the parapet and stared towards the sea. As yet it was still too dark to see it. But for the tang of salt, and the liberal coating of gull droppings on the tower, they could have been anywhere.

Searle chuckled. 'My father is a clergyman. I should know.'

Browne heard the thump of a body being hauled from the stairs and recalled that the French seaman had not even bothered to carry a weapon when Cooper, the cut-throat from Lime House, had killed him. He remembered the curious stares of the French people who had seen them marched along the road as prisoners. Why *should* they be on their guard? It was unlikely anyone in the north or west of England would anticipate being confronted by a Frenchman.

'Sir!'

'Not so loud!' Searle threw himself down on to the ladder. 'What is it now?'

'Someone comin'!'

Browne hurried to the other parapet and peered down to where the entrance should be. There was a path of sorts, made of small pale stones from a nearby beach. As he watched he saw a shadow move over it, and seconds later heard a metallic clang at the door.

'Hell's teeth!' Searle struggled down to the stairs. 'Earlier than I thought!'

Browne followed and heard Searle say, 'Shuffle your feet, Moubray! You, be ready to open the door!'

Browne clung to the ladder, barely able to breathe. After the total darkness of the roof, the little drama below seemed suddenly clear and stark. Searle, his breeches very white against the old stone wall, the seaman Moubray, shifting his feet as he pretended to walk towards the door. The key squeaked noisily and the door swung inwards, the man outside calling something as he hurried out of the chill air.

It all happened in a second, and yet to Browne it seemed as if the moment was frozen for a much longer time. The newcomer, another French sailor, standing mouth agape as he saw the half circle of crouching figures. Searle, his hanger drawn, while Jones, the gunner's mate, held a musket above his head like a club.

The picture broke up in short, frantic scenes. The Frenchman yelled and turned back towards the entrance, while Jones struck at him with the musket. But in the sudden tension they had all forgotten about the pool of blood which had run down the stairs when the first man had died. Jones gave a cry of alarm as his foot slipped from under him, the musket flew from his hands and exploded, the sound deafening in the confined space.

Browne heard the ball crack against the stone wall, but not before it had hit Jones in the face.

Searle yelled, 'Get that man, you fool!'

Cooper, small and deadly, threw himself down the steps, and seconds later they heard a terrible scream which was choked off instantly.

Cooper came back, breathing fast, his dirk bloody in his fist.

He gasped, 'More o' the buggers comin', sir!'

Jones was rolling on the floor, his blood mingling with that of the French sailor.

Browne said sharply, 'Take care of him!' To Searle he added tightly, 'We shall have to shift ourselves now!'

Searle had recovered his outward calm. 'Harding, carry on with the fuses.'

The second gunner's mate darted a look at his friend and said harshly, 'Not right, sir. In a church an' all.'

Searle plunged a hand into his coat and pulled out one of his pistols, and said coldly, 'Don't you talk to me like that, you superstitious oaf! I'll see you receive a checkered shirt at the gangway when we rejoin the ship, you've my word on that!'

Fists and boots hammered at the door, and Browne said,

'Keep away, lads.' He winced as a shot cracked into the stout door and more voices echoed around the building as if the dead had risen from their graves to seek revenge.

Cooper said, 'There's another door at the far end, sir. Very small. I think it's for fuel.'

Searle snapped, 'I'll look at it. Cooper, come with me.' He glanced meaningly at Browne. 'Watch 'em, Oliver. They'll cut and run if they think they're done for.'

He strode off beween the worn pillars of a doorway, his feet clicking on the flagstones as if he were on parade.

Outside the church it was very quiet and still, whereas Browne was conscious of Harding's irregular breathing as he cut his fuses, the occasional shuffle of feet on the ladder above the stairs as another seaman rammed home some of the charges.

Harding whispered, 'What you reckon they'm doin', sir?' He did not look up, and his thick, scarred fingers were as gentle as a child's as he worked to complete what his friend had begun.

Browne guessed that some of the French seamen or prison guards had hurried away to tell the dragoons. It would not take long for them to reach here. He thought of the black horsehair plumes and long sabres, the air of menace which even at a distance the dragoons had roused.

But he replied, 'Waiting to see what we intend. They don't know where we're from or who we are, remember that.'

Jones gave an agonized moan and Browne knelt over him. The musket ball had taken out one eye and a splinter of bone as large as a man's thumb. The seaman named Nicholl held a piece of rag over the terrible wound, and even in the feeble lantern light Browne could see the gunner's mate's life ebbing away.

Jones whispered, 'Done for, look you. Stupid thing to do, isn't it?'

'Rest easy, Jones. You'll be all right soon.'

Jones gave a terrible cry and gasped, 'Oh God, *help me!*'

Cooper returned and stared at him savagely. 'If it worn't

for you droppin' th' musket, this wouldn't 'ave 'appened, you Welsh bastard!'

Searle appeared at that moment, his knees and chest covered in dirt.

'There is a way out. Very small and not used for months, I'd say. Not since the navy commandeered this church, by the look of it.' He glanced at Harding. 'How long?'

'I've given it half an hour, sir.'

Searle turned to Browne and sighed. 'You see? Hopeless.' In a sharper tone he added, 'Make it ten minutes, no more.'

Then he looked thoughtfully at Browne. 'After that, I'm not sure, Oliver.'

Browne examined his pistols to give himself time. Searle was right in setting a short fuse. They had come to destroy the semaphore, to break the chain, and he guessed that most of them had not even expected to reach this far. But he wondered if he could have given the order with such cool authority.

'We'll leave.' As two of the men bent to pick up the groaning Jones, he added, 'He'll not get far.'

Searle said, 'A good gunner's mate, but put him ashore . . .' He did not finish it.

Carrying and dragging the luckless Jones they groped their way to the tiny door. When it was forced open Browne expected a fusilade of shots, and as Cooper thrust his thin body through it he had to clench his teeth as he waited for a blade to take him across the neck.

But nothing happened, and Searle muttered, 'The Frenchies are no better than Jones, it seems.'

'Wait here.' Browne looked back at the curved doorway where Harding waited beside his fuses. 'I'll do it. Then we'll make for the beach. You never know.'

As Searle wriggled through the tiny door Browne felt suddenly alone and ill at ease.

His shoes sounded like drumbeats as he joined Harding and asked, 'Are you ready?'

'Aye, sir.' Harding opened the lantern's shutter and lit a

slow-match which he had carried in his jacket. 'You can't trust 'em, sir. Not this short.' He stared into the shadows and added bitterly, 'But some'll not be told.'

Browne watched fascinated as the gunner's mate swung the slow-match around until the end shone like a glow-worm.

Then he said, 'Now.'

The fuses began to hiss loudly, and the sparks seemed to be moving at a terrible speed.

Harding grasped his sleeve. 'Come *on*, sir! No time to dally!'

They ran through the empty church, heedless of the noise or their dignity. Hands dragged them out into the cold air, and Browne found time to notice that there were a few pale stars right overhead.

Searle said, 'We heard horses!'

Browne stood up, it was too late for stealth. 'Follow me, lads!' Then they were stooping and running, with Jones dangling between them like a corpse.

Browne stared ahead and saw the prison wall. He veered away from it, and heard the others stumbling and cursing behind him. They were making a lot of noise, but it was just as well, he thought, as it helped to drown the sounds of pounding hoofs which were drawing rapidly closer.

He managed to gasp, 'They'll make for the church first!'

Searle replied jerkily, 'I hope it blows them to hell!'

Browne almost fell on wet grass as he ran towards the lip of the hill. The beach would be empty, but at least it was the sea.

He heard the louder clatter of horses and guessed they had at last reached the road.

Someone called, 'Got to stop, sir! Poor Jones is dyin'!'

They paused, gasping and wheezing like old men.

Browne said, 'We must keep on the move, it's our only chance!'

The gunner's mate Harding shook his head. 'S'no use. I'm stayin' with me mate. They'll catch us anyway.'

Browne stared wildly at him. 'They'll cut you down! Don't you see that?'

Harding stood firm. 'I wear the King's coat, sir. I've done nowt but obey orders.'

Browne tried to clear his mind, to remember how long they had been running since they had fired the fuses.

He turned away. 'Come along, the rest of you.'

They reached the top of the path and heard the familiar hiss and gurgle of surf.

As they plunged down the narrow path Browne thought he heard a shout, but it was lost immediately in a thunder of hoofs, and he knew the dragoons had found Harding and his dying friend.

Seconds later came the explosion, deafening and terrible, like Harding's revenge on his murderers. The whole hillside seemed to shake, and small stones rattled down the slope like musket balls.

Searle said, 'Get on ahead, Cooper.' He clutched at Browne for support. 'No quarter if we're taken. I hope it was worth it.'

Above them the light died as suddenly as it had exploded, and Browne caught the stench of burned powder drifting with the wind.

Cooper came back within minutes. 'I found a boat, sir. No more'n a skiff, but better than nothin'.'

Searle smiled in the darkness. 'I'd swim rather than die here.'

Cooper and Nicholl vanished into the gloom to find the boat, and Browne said, 'I think some of the dragoons are still up there.'

The explosion would have killed anybody within twenty yards of the church, he thought. But at dawn there would be soldiers by the hundred searching every cove and patch of cover.

He wondered if any of the squadron were near enough to hear the explosion.

Searle said, 'I've got my breath, Oliver. Lead on.'

They tramped past the camel-shaped rock and down towards the rocks where someone had beached a small boat. Smuggler or fisherman, Browne did not care. It was unlikely they would ever reach safety, but anything was better than waiting to be slaughtered.

'Halte-là!'

The voice craked out of the darkness like a shot.

Browne dragged Searle down beside him and pointed. 'Up to the left!'

It came again. 'Qui va là?' But this time there was also a click of metal.

Searle let out a sob of despair and anger. 'Damn their bloody eyes!'

Feet slipped and thudded over the rocks, and Browne heard one of the seamen yell, 'Take that, you bugger!'

He saw Nicholl shine suddenly in the blast of a musket fired at point-blank range, saw him drop his cutlass and fall dead.

But in the flash Browne had seen three, perhaps four, French soldiers.

'Ready?' He barely recognized his own voice. 'Them or us!'

Searle nodded violently, and together the two lieutenants rose to their feet, and with pistols drawn and cocked ran the last few yards along the beach.

There were more shouts, which changed to screams as the pistols flashed across wet sand and brought two of the soldiers kicking amongst the rocks.

Cooper's wiry shape darted forward, and a choking cry announced another victim to his dirk.

The remaining soldier threw down his musket and yelled at the top of his voice. That too was cut short with the suddenness of deafness, and the seaman named Moubray joined his lieutenants and cleaned his cutlass in the sand.

'That were for Bill 'Arding, sir.'

Browne tried to reload his pistols, but his hands were shaking so badly he had to give up.

'Launch the boat, lads.'

He saw Cooper stooping over a sprawled body, doubtless stealing something, he thought wearily.

Then he grasped Cooper's shoulder and pushed him roughly aside. 'Help the others. It'll be light very soon.'

He dropped on one knee and peered at the corpse. It was the little commandant who had bade them farewell on this same beach. Well, they had met once again after all.

Searle called, 'What is it?'

Browne stood up shakily. 'Nothing.'

Searle completed reloading his pistols without any difficulty.

'You really are a marvel, Oliver.'

Am I? Is that what you think?

Browne followed him down to the small boat, but paused long enough to stare back at the dark shape which was already being lapped by the tide.

For a moment longer Browne felt cheated and unclean. It was like leaving a friend, not an enemy.

Then he said, 'Pull hard, lads. We've a whole ocean to choose from.'

'North-west by north, sir! Full and bye!'

Bolitho glanced up as the main-topsail shook violently in protest. *Odin* was sailing closer to the wind than he had imagined possible. A heavier ship like *Benbow* would have been in real difficulties by now, he thought.

Inch said, 'I've put my best lookouts aloft, sir.'

Bolitho watched the water creaming away from the lee side as the sixty-four heeled over to the strengthening breeze. He could see the white patterns reaching out across the surface, when only a short while ago there had been darkness. Faces stood out too, and the uniforms of the marines looked scarlet and not black as they had appeared in the night.

'Deep nine!' The leadsman's chant floated aft.

Bolitho glanced briefly at M'Ewan, the master. He appeared calm enough, although nine fathoms was no great depth beneath *Odin*'s keel.

He saw the land for the first time, a ragged shadow to starboard which marked the entrance of the bay.

Inch observed, 'Wind's steady, sir.' He was thinking of his ship's safety this close inshore.

Bolitho watched Stirling and the ship's signal midshipman with their assistants, surrounded by flags to suit every demand.

Without turning his head, Bolitho knew Allday was standing just a few paces away, arms folded as he stared fixedly ahead beyond the gilded figurehead and bowsprit as the ship thrust towards the top of the bay.

'By the mark seven!'

Inch stirred uneasily. 'Mr Graham! We will alter course two points. Steer nor'-west by west!'

Graham raised his speaking trumpet. There was no need for silence any more. Either the invasion craft were here or they were not.

'Hands to the braces, Mr Finucane!'

Inch walked aft and consulted the binnacle as the ship paid off and then steadied on her new course. It was a small alteration but would keep the keel out of danger. Above the decks the sails hardened and filled as they too responded to the change.

'By the mark ten!'

The midshipman of the watch coughed into his hand to hide his relief, and several of the marine marksmen glanced at each other and grinned.

'Deck there! Anchor lights fine on th' weather bow!'

Bolitho followed Inch and his first lieutenant to the starboard side.

Dawn was minutes away. If they had kept to their original plan of attack they would be miles away, with every French ship and coastguard on full alert.

He tried not to think of Browne and what must have happened, but concentrated everything on the paler shadows and winking lights which must be the anchorage.

A distant boom echoed and re-echoed around the bay, and Bolitho knew the sound was being thrown back by the land. A signal gun, a warning which was already too late, and had been from the moment they had slipped past Remond's sleeping ships.

With the wind thrusting almost directly at the starboard side, and the ship tilting over to a steep angle, the guns would have all the help they required for the first broadsides.

Already the gun-captains were waving their fists and their crews were working feverishly with tackles and handspikes.

Inch called, 'On the uproll, Mr Graham, when I give the word!'

'Take in the mains'l!'

As the great sail was brought up to its yard Bolitho was reminded of a curtain being raised. There was sunlight too, probing out from the land where night mist and wood smoke drifted above the water like low cloud.

And there lay the anchored vessels of the invasion fleet.

For a moment Bolitho imagined the frail light was playing tricks, or that his eyes were deceiving him. He had expected a hundred such craft, but there must have been three times that number, anchored in twos and threes and filling the elbow of the bay like a floating town.

There was a medium sized man-of-war anchored nearby, a cut-down ship of the line, Bolitho thought, as he peered through his telescope until his eye throbbed.

The crowded vessels looked at peace through the silent lens, but he could picture the pandemonium and panic there must be as *Odin* sailed purposefully towards them. It was impossible, but an enemy ship was right amongst them, or soon would be.

Inch said, '*Phalarope*'s on station, sir.'

Bolitho trained his glass towards the frigate and saw her exposed carronades, blunt-muzzled and ugly, run out in a long black line. He thought he could see Pascoe too, but was not certain.

'Signal *Phalarope*. *Take station astern of the* Flag.'

He ignored the bright flags darting up to the yards and turned his attention back to the enemy.

He heard a trumpet, far-off and mournful, and moments later saw the guardship running out her guns, although as yet she had not made any attempt to up-anchor or set sail.

In his excitement Inch took Bolitho's arm and pointed towards the shore.

'Look, sir! *The tower!*'

Bolitho trained his telescope and saw a tower above the headland like a sentinal. At the top a set of jerking semaphore arms told their story better than shouted words.

But if Browne had destroyed the semaphore station on the church, there would be no one to see and relay the message to Remond's squadron. And even if the same message was passed in the other direction, all the way to Lorient, it was too late to save this packed assembly.

Odin's jib boom had passed the end of the anchored vessels now, which presented an unbroken barrier some half a mile away.

Smoke swirled above the guardship, and the rolling cash of gunfire showed that the French were now wide awake.

A few balls hurled spray into the air close abeam and brought cries of derision from *Odin*'s gun crews.

Graham watched as Inch slowly raised his sword above his head.

'On the uproll! *Steady*, my lads!'

A stronger gust of wind sighed into *Odin*'s topsails so that she heeled over and showed her copper in the pale sunlight. It was all Inch needed. The sword slashed down.

A midshipman who had been clinging to an open hatchway above the lower gundeck yelled, '*Fire!*'

But his shrill voice was lost in the devastating roar of the upper battery's eighteen-pounders.

Bolitho watched the waterspouts lifting amongst and beyond the anchored craft. The spray was still falling as the lower battery's thirty-two-pounders added their weight of iron to the destruction. Bolitho saw fractured planking and whole areas of decking flung into the air, and when the smoke cleared he realized that several of the smaller craft were already heeling over. In the telescope's lens he could see a few boats pulling clear, but in some cases the crews on the landward side of the anchorage had at last cut their cables and were trying to work clear.

'*Run out!*'

Again the trucks creaked and squealed up the slanting deck and the muzzles thrust through their ports.

'Stand by! As you bear!'

The sword came down again. '*Fire!*'

Slower this time, as each gun-captain waited and took more careful aim before jerking at his trigger line.

The French guardship was loosening her topsails, but had fouled two of the drifting invasion craft. She fired nevertheless, and two balls hit *Odin* just above the waterline.

Bolitho saw smoke around the guardship, and realized one of the other craft had caught fire. It might even have been caused by a blazing wad from one of the guardship's own guns. He could see the running figures, tiny and futile in distance, as they hurled water from the beakhead and tried to free their ship from the flames. But the entanglement of rigging and the persistent strength of the offshore wind were too much for them, and Bolitho saw flames leaping from hull to hull and eventually setting light to the guardship's jib-sails.

On their converging approach they were now within a cable of the nearest craft, and from the bows *Odin*'s leadsman yelled, 'Deep *six!*'

Inch looked anxiously at Bolitho. 'Far enough, sir?'

Bolitho nodded. 'Bring her about.'

'Stand by to come about!'

All available hands sprang to braces and halliards, some still gasping and rubbing their streaming eyes from the gun smoke.

'Ready ho!'

'Put the wheel down!'

The spokes glittered in the sunshine as the helm was put hard over, and then M'Ewan shouted, 'Helm's a-lee, sir!'

Bolitho watched the panorama of drifting and shattered vessels as they began to swing slowly across *Odin*'s bows until it appeared as if the jib boom was right above them. The sails flapped and thundered, while petty officers added their own weight to the braces to haul the yards round and lay the ship on the opposite tack.

Inch shouted, 'Stand by on the larboard battery! On the uproll, Mr Graham!'

'Steady as you go!'

M'Ewan waited until the last sail was brought under control, hard-bellied in the wind.

'Sou'-east by east, sir!'

'*Fire!*'

The larboard guns hurled themselves inboard for the first time, the smoke funnelling back through the ports as the whole broadside crashed and blasted amongst the invasion craft with terrible effect.

Bolitho watched *Phalarope*'s shape lengthening, her sails in confusion as she followed the flagship's example and tacked across the wind. She was even closer to the enemy, and Bolitho could imagine the terror those carronades would create.

The guardship was no longer under control and from her mainmast to forecastle was ablaze, the flames leaping up the sails and changing them to ashes in seconds.

Bolitho saw her shake and a topgallant mast fall like a lance into the smoke. She must have run aground, and several figures were floundering in the water, while others were swimming towards some rocks.

'*Cease firing!*'

A silence fell over the ship, and even the men who were still sponging out the guns from the last broadside stood up to the gangways to watch *Phalarope*'s slow and graceful approach.

Allday said thickly, 'Look at her. Moving closer. I could

almost feel sorry for the mounseers.'

Emes was taking no chances, either with his aim or with the effect on his ship's timbers. From bow to stern the carronades fired one by one. Not the echoing crash of a long gun, but each shot was hard and flat, like a great hammer on an anvil.

The carronades were hidden from view, but Bolitho saw the shots slamming home amongst the remaining invasion craft like a great gale of wind. Except that this wind was tightly packed grape contained in one huge ball which burst on contact.

If one ball from a 'smasher' exploded in the confines of a gundeck, it could turn it into a slaughterhouse. The effect on the smaller, thinly-planked invasion craft would be horrific.

Emes took his time, reefing all but his topsails to give his carronade crews an opportuntiy to reload and fire one last broadside.

When the echoes faded, and the smoke eventually eddied clear, there were barely a dozen craft still afloat, and it seemed unlikely that they had escaped some casualties and damage.

Bolitho shut the telescope and handed it to a midshipman. He saw Inch slapping his first lieutenant on the shoulder and beaming all over his long face.

Poor Inch. He looked up as the masthead lookout yelled, 'Deck there!'

'Sail on the lee bow!'

A dozen telescopes rose together, and something like a sigh transmitted itself along the upper deck.

Allday stood at Bolitho's shoulder and whispered, 'He's too bloody late, sir!' But there was no pleasure in his voice.

Bolitho moved his glass very carefully across the glittering wave crests. Three ships of the line, bunched together by the distance, their pendants and ensigns making bright patches of colour against the sky. Another vessel, probably a frigate, was just showing herself around the headland.

He heard the marines shuffling their boots and standing up to the hammock nettings again as they realized their work had not even begun.

Allday had understood from the beginning. Inch too in all probability, but he had been so engrossed in his ship's behaviour that he had put it from his mind.

He saw Midshipman Stirling shading his eyes to peer ahead towards the pale array of sails. He turned and saw Bolitho watching him, his eyes no longer confident but those of a confused boy.

'Come here, Mr Stirling.' Bolitho pointed to the distant ships. 'Remond's flying squadron. We'll have given him a rude awakening this morning.'

Stirling asked, 'Will we stand and fight, sir?'

Bolitho looked down at him and smiled gravely. 'You are a King's officer, Mr Stirling, no less than Captain Inch or myself. What would you have me do?'

Stirling tried to see how he would describe all this to his mother. But nothing formed in his mind, and he was suddenly afraid.

'Fight, sir!'

'Attend the signals party, Mr Stirling.' To Allday he added softly, 'If he can say that when he is terrified, there is hope for us all.'

Allday eyed him curiously. 'If you say so, sir.'

'Deck there! Two more sail of the line roundin' the point!'

Bolitho clasped his hands behind him. *Five to one.* He looked at Inch's despair.

There was no point in fighting and dying for nothing. A brutal human sacrifice. They had done what many had thought impossible. Neale, Browne and all the others would not have died in vain.

But to order Inch to strike his colours would be almost as hard as dying.

'Deck there!'

Bolitho stared up at the lookout in the mizzen cross-trees. He must have been so dazed by the sight of the oncoming squadron he had failed to watch his own sector.

'*Glass!*'

Bolitho almost snatched it from the midshipman's hand, and ignoring the startled glances ran to the shrouds and climbed swiftly until he was well clear of the deck.

'Three sail of the line on the lee quarter!'

Bolitho watched the newcomers and felt a lump rise in his throat. Somehow or other, adverse winds or not, Herrick had managed it. He wiped his eye with his sleeve and steadied the glass for another look.

Benbow in the lead. He would know her fat hull and thrusting figurehead anywhere. He saw Herrick's broad-pendant writhing uncomfortably as ship by ship the remainder of the squadron tacked for what must be the hundredth time as they struggled to beat upwind and join their admiral.

He lowered himself to the quarterdeck and saw the others watching him like strangers.

Then Inch asked quietly, 'Orders, sir?'

Bolitho glanced at Stirling and his colourful litter of flags.

'General signal, if you please, Mr Stirling. *Form line of battle*.'

Allday looked up as the flags broke stiffly to the wind. 'I'll lay odds mounseer never expected *that*!'

Bolitho smiled. They were still outnumbered, but he had known worse odds. So had Herrick.

He looked at Stirling. 'You see, I took your advice!'

Allday shook his head. How did he do it? In an hour, maybe less, they would be fighting for their very breath.

Bolitho glanced up at the masthead pendant and formed a picture of the battle in his mind. If the wind held they might fight ship to ship. That would offer Remond the advantage. Better to allow his captains to act individually after they had broken the enemy's line.

He looked along the deck, at the bare-backed gun crews and the boatswain's party who were preparing to hoist out the boats and drop them astern. A tier of boats only added to the splinter wounds, and these were not low-hulled invasion craft they were preparing to fight.

He saw some of the new hands murmuring to one another,

their first taste of victory soured by the arrival of the powerful French squadron.

'Captain Inch! Have your marine fifers play us into battle. It will help to ease their minds.'

Inch followed his glance, and then bobbed and said, 'Sometimes I forget, sir, the war has gone on for so long I think everyone must have fought in a real sea battle!'

And so the little sixty-four with the rear-admiral's flag at her mizzen sailed to meet the enemy in the bright sunlight, while her marine fifers and drummers marched and counter-marched on a space no bigger than a carpet.

Many of the seamen who had been staring at the enemy ships turned inboard to watch and to tap their feet to the lively jig, *The Post Captain*.

Astern of *Odin* and her attendant frigate, the bay was filled with drifting smoke and the scattered flotsam of a dream.

17

Blade to Blade

Bolitho was in *Odin*'s chartroom when Inch reported that the masthead had sighted the brig *Rapid* closing slowly from the south-west.

Bolitho threw the dividers on the chart and walked out into the sunlight. Commander Lapish obviously hoped to add his small ship to the squadron, odds or no odds.

He said, 'Signal *Rapid* as soon as you can. Tell her to find *Ganymede* and *harass the enemy's rear*.' It might prevent the only French frigate at present in sight from outmanoeuvring the heavier ships, at least until Duncan's *Sparrowhawk* joined them from the northern sector.

Inch watched the flags darting aloft and asked, 'Shall we wait for the commodore to join us, sir?'

Bolitho shook his head. The French squadron had formed into an untidy but formidable line, the second ship wearing the flag of a rear-admiral. Remond. It had to be.

'I think not. Given more time I would not hesitate. But time will also aid the enemy to stand into the bay and take the wind-gage while the rest of our squadron is floundering into the face of it.'

He raised his glass again and studied the leading ship. A two-decker, with her guns already run out, although she was still three miles distant. A powerful ship, probably of eighty guns. On the face of it she should be more than a match for the smaller *Odin*.

But this was where the months and years of relentless blockade and patrols in all weathers added their weight to the odds. The French, on the other hand, spent more time bottled up in harbour than exercising at sea. It was most likely why Remond had placed another ship than his own to point the attack, to watch and prepare his squadron in good time.

He said suddenly, 'See how the French flagship stands a little to windward of the leader.'

Inch nodded, his face totally blank. 'Sir?'

'If we attack without waiting for our other ships to join us, I think the French admiral intends to separate, then engage us on either beam.'

Inch licked his lips. 'While the last three in his line stand off and wait.'

Stirling called, 'Rapid's acknowledged, sir.'

Allday climbed on to the poop ladder and peered astern. How far away Benbow now seemed. Quite rightly Herrick was clawing his way into the bay so that he could eventually come about and hold the wind in his favour. But it took time, a lot of it.

There was a dull bang, and a ball skipped across the sea a good mile away. The leading French captain was exercising his bow chasers, probably to break the tension of waiting as much as possible.

It would not help him to have his admiral treading on his coat tails, Allday thought, and watching every move he made.

He turned and looked along Odin's crowded deck. There would not be many left standing if she got trapped between two of the Frenchmen without support. Was that what Bolitho meant to do? To damage the enemy so much that the remainder would be left to fight Herrick on equal terms?

He spoke aloud. 'Gawd Almighty!'

The marine colour-sergeant who was standing on the right of the nearest line of marksmen grinned at him.

'Nervous, matey?'

Allday grimaced. 'Hell, not likely. I'm just looking for a place to take a nap!'

He stiffened as he heard Inch say to the master, 'Mr M'Ewan, the rear-admiral intends to luff when we are within half a cable. We shall then wear and attack the second ship in the French line.'

Allday saw the sailing master's head nodding jerkily as if it was only held to his shoulders by a cord.

The colour-sergeant hissed, 'Wot's that then?'

Allday folded his arms and allowed his mind to settle. *Odin* would luff, and by the time she had turned into the wind would be all but under the other ship's bowsprit. Then she would wear and turn round to thrust between the leading vessels. If she was allowed. It was hazardous, and could render *Odin* a bloody shambles in a few minutes. But anything was better than being raked from either beam at the same time.

He replied calmly, 'It *means*, my scarlet friend, that you an' your lot are going to be very busy!'

Bolitho watched the oncoming formation, looking for a sign, some quick hoist of flags which might betray Remond's suspicion. He would be expecting something surely? One small sixty-four against five ships of the line.

He recalled Remond's swarthy features, his dark, intelligent eyes.

He said, 'Captain Inch, tell your lower battery to load with double-shot. The eighteen-pounders of the upper battery will load with langridge, if you please.' He held Inch's gaze. 'I want that leading ship dismasted when we luff.'

Bolitho looked up at the masthead pendant. Wind still holding as strong as ever. He almost looked astern but stopped himself in time. The officers and men nearby would see it as uncertainty, their admiral looking for support. It was best to forget about Herrick. He was doing all he could.

Graham, the first lieutenant, touched his hat to Inch. 'Permission to fall out the drummers and fifers, sir?'

Bolitho looked quickly at the minute figures in scarlet. He had been so wrapped in his thoughts he had barely heard a note.

Gratefully, the panting fifers hurried below to a chorus of ironic cheers.

Bolitho touched the unfamiliar hilt of his sword. They could still cheer.

Another bang from the leader, and the ball ploughed up a furrow of spray some three cables abeam. The French captain must be on edge. He's probably watching me now. Bolitho walked away from the mizzen bitts so that the sunshine would play on his bright epaulettes. At least he would know his enemy, he thought grimly.

He turned to watch a cluster of screaming gulls below the quarterdeck rail. They were unimpressed and quite used to a daily fight for survival.

Inch said, 'The French admiral's reset his t'gan's'ls, sir.'

Bolitho watched the weather bow of the enemy flagship show itself around the leader's quarter. He had guessed Remond's intention. Now it all depended on the men around him.

'Captain Inch, this needs to be carefully done.' He touched his arm and smiled. 'Though I need not tell you how to handle her, eh?'

Inch beamed with obvious pleasure. 'Thank you *kindly*, sir!' He turned away, the captain again. 'Mr Graham! Pipe the hands to the braces!' His arm shot out and pointed at a lieutenant on the gundeck. 'Mr Synge! Have both batteries been reloaded as ordered?'

The lieutenant squinted up at the quarterdeck rail and replied nervously, 'Aye, sir! I – I forgot to report it.'

Inch glared at the luckless lieutenant. 'I am glad to hear it, Mr Synge, for an instant I imagined you thought I was a mind-reader!'

Several of the gun crews chuckled and lapsed into silence as the flushed-faced lieutenant turned towards them.

Bolitho watched the French ships and found he could do it without emotion. He was committed. Right or wrong, there was no chance to break off the action, even if he wanted to.

'Ready ho!'

The men at the braces and halliards crouched and flexed their muscles as if they were about to enter a contest.

M'Ewan watched the shake of the topsails, the angle of the masthead pendant. Nearby his helmsmen gripped the spokes and waited like crude statuary.

'Helm a-lee!'

'Let go and haul!'

The ship seemed to stagger at the rough handling, then after what felt like an eternity she began to swing readily into the wind.

Graham's voice was everywhere at once. 'Haul over the boom! Let go the t'gallant bowlines!'

At each port the gun-captains watched the empty sea and ignored the commotion of thrashing canvas, the squeal of running rigging and the slap of bare feet on the planking.

Bolitho concentrated on the leading Frenchman, feeling a cold satisfaction as she continued on the same tack, although her officers must have wondered what Inch was doing. They might have expected his nerve to break, for him to tack to leeward with the wind from aft. Then the leading enemy ships would have raked *Odin*'s stern before grappling and smashing down her resistance at point-blank range.

But now *Odin* was answering, and heading into the wind with her sails billowing in disorder as her yards were hauled round. To any landsmen she would appear to be all aback and unable to proceed, but as she continued to flounder into the wind she slowly and surely presented her starboard side to the oncoming ship's bows.

Graham yelled through his trumpet, *'As you bear!'*

Inch's sword hissed down, and deck by deck *Odin*'s guns crashed out, the upper battery with its screaming langridge matched by the lower one's double-charged guns.

Bolitho held his breath as the forward guns found their targets. The French ship seemed to quiver, as if, like the guardship, she had run aground. The bombardment continued, with the lieutenants striding behind each gun as its trigger line was jerked taut. On the deck below the picture would be the same but more terrible as the naked bodies toiled around the guns as each one thundered back on its tackles to be instantly sponged out and reloaded.

The langridge or chain-shot was easier to determine, and Bolitho saw all the enemy's headsails and rigging hacked aside in a tangle, while most of the fore-topmast plunged over the side in a great welter of spray. As it crashed down the weight took immediate effect like an immense sea-anchor, so that even as he watched Bolitho could see the enemy's beak-head begin to swing awkwardly into the wind.

'As you bear, lads! *Fire!*'

The double-shotted charges smashed into the disabled ship to upend guns and rip through the lower deck with murderous impact. Overhead, rigging was scythed away, and as more and more sail area was exposed it too was punched through with holes and long streaming remnants.

Inch shouted, 'Stand by on the fo'c's'le!'

The starboard carronade belched fire and smoke, but the aim was too high and the great ball exploded on the enemy's gangway. It hit nothing vital, but the outward effect was horrific. Some twenty men had been working to cut free the dragging weight of spars and cordage, and when the ball exploded near them it painted the ship's tumblehome scarlet from deck to waterline.

It was as if the ship herself was mortally wounded and bleeding to death.

'Stand by to alter course to starboard!'

'Brace up your head yards!'

A few shots pattered against the hull and brought an instant retort from *Odin*'s marines who were yelling and cheering as they fired through the thickening smoke.

Bolitho felt the wind on his cheek and heard the sails filling untidily as *Odin* turned her stern towards the wind. She was no frigate, but Inch handled her like one.

A strong down-gust carried the smoke away, and he saw the French flagship riding on the starboard cathead as if she were caught there. In fact she was a good cable clear, but close enough to see her tricolour and command flag, the frantic activity as her captain changed tack to avoid colliding with the stricken leader.

Bolitho took a glass and steadied it while he waited for the guns to fire another broadside into the helpless Frenchman. He felt the planks buck beneath his shoes, saw the wildness in the eyes of the nearest crew as they hurled themselves on the tackles to restrain the smoking eighteen-pounder.

When he looked again he saw the flagship's tall stern and gilded quarter-gallery, and on her counter her name, *La Sultane*, as if he could reach out and touch it.

He moved the glass upwards slightly and saw some of her officers, one gesticulating up at the yards, another mopping his face as if he had been in a tropical downpour.

Just for a brief moment before the guns crashed out again he saw the rear-admiral's cocked hat, then as he walked briskly to the poop, the man's face.

Bolitho lowered the glass and allowed the small pictures to fall away with it. No mistake. Contre-Amiral Jean Remond, he would never forget him.

Allday saw the expression on Bolitho's face and understood.

Many senior officers would have taken the Frenchman's offer of a safe, comfortable house with servants and the best of everything, with nothing to do but wait for an exchange. It showed Remond did not, nor would he ever, understand a man like Bolitho who had waited only for the chance to hit back.

It was all part of the madness, of course, Allday decided philosophically, yet despite that he felt less afraid of what might happen.

Unaware of Allday's scrutiny, Bolitho kept his eyes on the disabled French ship. She was badly mauled by the constant battering, and thin red lines ran from her scuppers and down her smashed side to show how her people had died for their over-confidence.

But there was still time for Remond to stand off and fight

his way back to the Loire Estuary and the safety of the coastal batteries. He might think that *Odin*'s impudence was backed up by a knowledge that more support was on the way.

Bolitho looked towards *Phalarope*. Herrick would be remembering that other time when she had been made to take her place in the line of battle, to fight and face the broadsides of the giants. That had been at the Saintes, and she had been paying for that cruel damage ever since.

Inch said, 'They're reforming, sir.'

Bolitho nodded as he saw the flags break out above *La Sultane*. Four to one. It was nothing to feel pleased about.

Inch exclaimed, 'Converging tack, but we'll still hold the wind-gage!'

Bolitho watched narrowly as the French flagship's side shone in the smoky sunlight. Eighty guns, larger even than *Benbow*. He saw all her artillery run out and poking blindly towards the shore, her yards alive with seamen as they prepared to close with their enemy.

Bolitho asked softly, 'Where is our squadron, Mr Stirling?'

The boy leapt into the shrouds, then hurried back and said, 'They are fast overhauling us, sir!' He too had lost his fear, and his eyes were dancing with feverish excitement.

'Stay by me, Mr Stirling.' He glanced meaningly at Allday. The midshipman had lost his fear at the wrong moment. It could have been his only protection.

'Let her fall off a point, Captain Inch.'

'Steer sou'-east!'

He heard the rasp of steel as Allday drew the cutlass from his belt, saw the way the men on the starboard side were standing to their guns again.

At least we shall give Remond something to remember after this day.

Bolitho drew his sword and tossed the scabbard to the foot of the mizzen mast.

One thing was certain, *Odin*'s challenge would slow the

French down, and Herrick would be amongst them like a lion.

Bolitho smiled gravely. *A Kentish lion*.

Inch and the first lieutenant saw him smile then looked at each other for what might be the last time.

'Marines! Face your front!' *Odin's* marine captain walked stiffly behind his men, his eyes everywhere but on the enemy.

Allday brushed against the midshipman and felt him flinch. And no wonder.

Allday watched the towering criss-cross of shrouds and rigging, braced yards and canvas as it rose higher and higher above *Odin's* starboard bow until there was no sky left. He tugged at his neckerchief to loosen it. No air either.

Stirling pulled out his midshipman's dirk and then thrust it back again.

Against that awesome panorama of sails and flags it was like taking a belaying pin to fight an army.

He heard Allday say between his teeth, 'Keep with me.' The cutlass hovered in the air. 'It'll be hot work, I shouldn't wonder.'

'Alter course two points to wind'rd!'

Odin steered slowly away from the enemy, so that *La Sultane* seemed to loom even larger than before.

'As you bear!'

Inch peered across the narrowing arrowhead of water between his ship and the big two-decker. Just for a moment they had moved away to present their guns.

'Fire!'

Even as the ship jerked to the irregular crash of cannon fire Inch yelled, 'Bring her back on course, Mr M'Ewan!'

Bolitho saw the seamen on the forecastle crouching down as the French flagship's tapering jib boom, with some dangling rigging trailing from their brief encounter, probed past and above them.

Musket balls whined through the air, and several slapped into the packed hammocks or clanged against the guns.

Inch said fiercely, 'Here we go!' He straightened his hat

and yelled, 'At 'em, my Odins!'

Then the whole world seemed to explode in one great shuddering upheaval.

It was impossible to determine the number of times *Odin* had fired her broadside into the enemy or to measure the damage wrought by the French guns in return. The world was lost in choking smoke, lit from within by terrible orange tongues as the gun crews fired and reloaded like men driven from their reason.

Bolitho thought he heard the sharper notes of smaller cannon in the far distance whenever there was a brief pause in the bombardment, and guessed that *Ganymede* and *Rapid* were waging their own war against Remond's frigate.

The smoke was dense and rose so high between the two ships that all else was hidden. The other French ships, Herrick and the squadron could have been alongside or a mile away, shut from the tumult by the roar of gunfire.

Overhead the nets bounced to falling rigging and blocks, and then together, as if holding hands, three marines were hurled from the maintop by a blast of canister, their screams lost in the din.

A ball smashed through the quarterdeck rail and ploughed across to the opposite side. Bolitho saw the deck, and even the foot of the driver boom, splashed in blood as the ball cut amongst some marines like a giant's cleaver.

Inch was yelling, 'Bring her up a point, Mr M'Ewan!'

But the master lay dead with two of his men, the planking around them dappled scarlet where they had fallen.

A master's mate, his face as white as death, took charge of the wheel, and slowly the ship responded.

More marines were climbing the ratlines to the fighting tops, and soon their muskets were joining in the battle as they tried to mark down the enemy's officers.

Bolitho gritted his teeth as two seamen were flung from their gun below the quarterdeck, one headless, the other shrieking in terror as he tried to drag wood splinters from his face and neck.

'*Fire!*'

Small pictures of courage and suffering stood out through gaps in the swirling smoke. Powder-monkeys, mere boys, running with backs bent under the weight of their charges while they hurried from gun to gun. A seaman working with a handspike to move his eighteen-pounder while his captain yelled instructions at him over the smoke-hazed breech. A midshipman, younger than Stirling, knuckling his eyes to hold back the tears in front of his division as his friend, another midshipman, was dragged away, his body shot through by canister.

'And again, lads! *Fire!*'

Allday crowded against Bolitho as musket fire hissed and whined past. Men were falling and dying, others were screaming their hatred into the smoke as they fired, reloaded and fired again.

'Look up, sir!'

Bolitho raised his eyes and saw something coming through the smoke high overhead, like some strange battering-ram.

La Sultane may have intended to sail past on the opposite tack and smash *Odin* into surrender by sheer weight of artillery. Maybe her captain had changed his mind or, like M'Ewan who lay dead with his men, had been shot down before he could execute a manoeuvre.

But the oncoming tusk was *La Sultane*'s jib boom, and as more trapped smoke lifted and surged beneath the hulls, Bolitho saw the hazy outline of the Frenchman's figurehead, like some terrible phantom with staring eyes and a bright crimson mouth.

The jib boom crashed through *Odin*'s mizzen shrouds, and there was a loud, lingering clatter as the other ship's dolphin-striker tore adrift and trailing rigging flew in the wind like creeper.

'*Repel boarders!*'

Bolitho felt the hull jerk and knew it had been badly hit by the last broadside. He could not see through the burning smoke but heard warning shouts and then cries as the foremast thundered down. The sound seemed to deaden even the guns, and Bolitho almost fell as the ship rocked to the great weight of mast and rigging.

The master's mate yelled, 'She don't answer th' helm, sir!'

Bright stabbing flashes spat through the smoke from overhead, and Bolitho saw scrambling figures climbing along the enemy's bowsprit and spritsail yard as they tried to reach *Odin*'s deck.

But they were delayed by the spread nets, and, as a wild-eyed marine corporal threw himself to one of the poop swivels and jerked its lanyard, the determined group of boarders were flung aside like butchers' rags.

Inch strode through the smoke, his hat gone, one arm hanging at his side.

He said through clenched teeth, 'Must free ourselves, sir!'

Bolitho saw the first lieutenant waving his sword and urging more men aft to fight off the next wave of boarders. How the gun crews could keep firing with half of their number already smashed into silence was a miracle. On the deck below it would be far worse.

Bolitho stared round at the scene of destruction and carnage. The two ships were killing each other, all thought of victory lost in the madness and hatred of battle.

He saw Allday watching him, Stirling close at his side, his face pinched against the sights and sounds around him.

He saw the smoke quiver as new cannon fire rumbled across the water like a volcano. Herrick was here and at grips with the rest of the French squadron.

It was then that it hit Bolitho like a fist or a sharp cry in his ear. It was no longer a matter of pride or the need to destroy *Odin*'s flag.

'*Remond wants me.*' He realized he had spoken aloud, saw the understanding on Inch's face, the sudden tightening of Allday's jaw.

They would never fight free of *La Sultane* in time. Either

Odin would be totally swamped by her heavier artillery or both ships would be fought to a senseless slaughter.

Bolitho tried to contain the sudden madness, but could do nothing.

He leapt on to the starboard gangway and shouted above the crash and thunder of firing, 'Boarders away, lads! To *me*, Odins!' He blinked as muskets flashed from unseen marksmen. It is what Neale would have said.

Seamen cut away the boarding nets, and as others snatched up axes and cutlasses Bolitho's wildness seemed to inflame the upper deck like a terrible weapon.

Graham, the first lieutenant, jumped out and down, his sword shining dully in the smoke. From somewhere a boarding pike stabbed outboard like a cruel tongue, and without even a cry Graham fell between the two hulls. Bolitho glanced down at him only briefly, saw his eyes staring up before the two great hulls were thrust together yet again and he was ground between them.

Then he was slipping and stumbling from handhold to handhold, until he found himself on the enemy's forecastle. He was almost knocked aside as more of *Odin*'s boarders charged past him, yelling like fiends as they hacked aside all opposition until they had reached the starboard gangway.

Startled faces peered up from the guns which were still firing into *Odin*, even though the muzzles were almost overlapping above the slit of trapped water as *La Sultane* swung heavily alongside.

A French midshipman darted from the shrouds and was hit between the shoulder-blades by a boarding axe as he ran.

Gun by gun the enemy's broadside fell silent as men took up their pikes and cutlasses to defend their ship against this unexpected attack.

Bolitho found himself being carried along the narrow gangway, his sword-arm trapped at his side by the yelling, cheering seamen and marines.

Shots banged and whimpered from every angle and men were falling and dying, unable to find safety as they were forced along in the crush.

A lieutenant stood astride the gangway and saw Bolitho as he broke free from the men around him. Some of the boarders had dropped to the gundeck below, and small tight groups of men hacked and slashed at each other, gasping for breath, while they sought to kill their enemies.

Bolitho held his sword level with his belt and watched the lieutenant's uncertainty.

The blades circled and hissed together, and Bolitho saw the other man's first surprise give way to concentrated determination. But Bolitho held fast to a stanchion and wedged his hilt hard against his adversary's. The lieutenant lost his balance, and for an instant their faces almost touched. There was fear now, but Bolitho saw his enemy only as a hindrance for what he must do.

A twist and a thrust to push the man off balance. The blade was unfamiliar but straight, and Bolitho felt it grate on bone before it slid beneath the lieutenant's armpit.

He jerked it free and ran on towards the quarterdeck. Vaguely through the smoke he saw *Odin*'s misty outline, festooned with tattered canvas and severed rigging. Upended guns and motionless figures which told the story of every sea-fight.

Bolitho's sudden anger seemed to carry him faster towards the battling figures which surged back and forth across the quarterdeck while the air rang with steel and the occasional crack of a pistol.

A seaman swung at a French quartermaster and cut his arm, and yelling with fear the man ran the wrong way and was quickly impaled on a marine's bayonet.

Two of Inch's seamen, one badly wounded, were hurling fire buckets from the quarterdeck on to the heads of the Frenchmen below. Filled with sand, each bucket was like a rock.

A figure lunged through the smoke, but his blade glanced off Bolitho's left epaulette. But for it, the blade might have sliced into his shoulder like a wire through cheese.

Bolitho staggered aside as the French officer tried to

recover his guard.

'Not now, *mounseer*!'

Allday's big cutlass made a blur across Bolitho's vision and sounded as if it was hitting solid wood.

Where was Remond? Bolitho peered round, his sword-arm aching as he tried to gauge the progress of the battle. There were more marines aboard now, and he saw Allday's new friend, the colour-sergeant, striding between a line of his men, his handpike taking a terrible toll as they stabbed and hacked their way aft.

By the larboard poop ladder, protected by some of his lieutenants, stood Remond. He saw Bolitho at the same moment, and for what seemed like minutes they stared at each other.

Remond shouted, 'Strike! Without your flag, your ships will soon be gone!'

His voice brought a baying response from the British sailors and marines who had managed to fight their way the full length of the ship.

But Bolitho held out his sword and snapped, 'I am waiting, Contre-Amiral!'

He could feel his heart thumping wildly, knowing that he was exposing his back to any marksman who might still have the will to take aim.

Remond threw his hat aside and answered, 'I am ready enough, m'sieu!'

Allday said fiercely, 'Jesus, sir, he's got the *sword*!'

'I know.'

Bolitho stepped away from his men, sensing their wildness giving way to something like savage curiosity.

Just to see the old sword in Remond's hand was all the spur he required.

They met on a small, shot-scarred place below the poop, hemmed in by seamen and marines who for just a few moments were spectators.

The blades touched and veered away again. Bolitho trod carefully, feeling the stab of pain in his thigh which might betray him to the enemy.

The sword blades darted closer, and Bolitho felt the power of the man, the strength of his broad, muscular body.

Despite the danger and the closeness of death, Bolitho was very aware of Allday nearby. Held back because of his need to face Remond alone, but not for long, any more than this fight would end a battle. Even now La Sultane's lower gundeck would have realized what was happening, and officers would be mustering their hands to repel the boarders.

Clang, clang, the swords shivered together, and Bolitho recalled with sudden clarity his father using that same old blade to teach him how to defend himself.

He could feel Remond's nearness, even smell him as they pressed together and locked hilts before fighting clear again.

He heard someone sobbing uncontrollably and knew it was Stirling. He must have climbed after the boarders in spite of his orders and the risk of being hacked down.

They think I am going to be killed.

Like the sight of the old sword in his enemy's grasp, the thought made a chill of fury run through him. As their blades clashed and parried, and each man circled round to find an advantage, Bolitho could feel the strength going from his arm.

In one corner of his eye something moved very slowly, and for an instant he imagined that another of the French ships was going to take Odin from the other beam as first intended.

His breath seemed to stop. She was no ship of the line. She could only be Phalarope. As Odin had lain against her powerful adversary, and Herrick's ships had closed with their French counterparts, Phalarope had fought her way through the line to support him.

He gasped as Remond drove the knuckle-bow into his shoulder and punched him away. Perhaps for that second's hesitation Remond had seen Bolitho's surprise as defeat.

Bolitho fell back against the hammock nettings, his sword clattering across the deck. He saw Remond's dark eyes, merciless and unwinking, he seemed to be staring straight along the edge of the blade to its very point which was aimed at his heart.

The deafening roar of carronades was terrifying and broke the spellbound watchers into confusion. *Phalarope* had crossed the French flagship's stern and was firing through the windows and along the lower gundeck from transom to bows.

The ship felt as if it were falling apart, and Bolitho saw splinters and fragments of grape bursting up through the deck itself or ricocheting over the sea like disturbed hornets. One such fragment hit Remond before he could make that final thrust.

He realized that Allday was helping to get him to his feet, that Remond had fallen on his side, a hole the size of a fist punched through his stomach. Behind him a British seaman came out of his daze, and seeing the dying admiral, lifted his cutlass to end it.

Allday saw Bolitho's face and said to the man, 'Easy, mate! Enough's enough.' Almost gently he prised the old sword from Remond's fingers and added, 'It don't serve *two* masters, mounseer.' But Remond's stare had become fixed and without understanding.

Bolitho gripped the sword in both hands and turned it over very slowly. Around him his men were cheering and hugging each other, while Allday stood grim-faced and watchful until the last Frenchman had thrown down his weapons.

Bolitho looked at Stirling who was staring at him and shivering uncontrollably.

'We won, Mr Stirling.'

The boy nodded, his eyes too misty to record this great moment for his mother.

A young lieutenant, whose face was vaguely familiar, pushed through the cheering seamen and marines.

He saw Bolitho and touched his hat.

'Thank God you are safe, sir!'

Bolitho studied him gravely. 'Thank *you*, but is that what you came to say?'

The lieutenant stared around at the dead and wounded, the

scars and bloody patterns of battle.

'I have to tell you, sir, that the enemy have struck to us. All but one, which is running for the Loire with *Nicator* in full pursuit.'

Bolitho looked away. A complete victory. More than even Beauchamp could have expected.

He swung towards the lieutenant. He must think me mad. 'What ship?'

'*Phalarope*, sir. I am Fearn, acting-first lieutenant.'

Bolitho stared at him. 'Acting-first lieutenant?' He saw the man recoil but could only think of his nephew. 'Is Lieutenant Pascoe . . . ?' He could not say the word.

The lieutenant breathed out noisily, glad he was not in the wrong after all.

'Oh *no*, sir! Lieutenant Adam Pascoe is in temporary command!' He looked down at the deck as if the realization he had survived was only just reaching him. 'I fear Captain Emes fell as we broke through the French line.'

Bolitho gripped his hand. 'Return to your ship and give my thanks to the people.'

He followed the lieutenant along the gangway until he saw a boat hooked alongside.

Phalarope was lying hove to close by, her sails punctured, but every carronade still run out and ready to fire.

He remembered what he had said to Herrick after the Saintes, when he had spoken of others' ships.

Bolitho had replied then, 'Not like this one. Not like the *Phalarope*.'

There would be no need to tell Adam that. For like Emes before him, he would have discovered it for himself.

He saw Allday rolling up the captured French flag which had outlived its admiral.

Bolitho took it and handed it to the lieutenant.

'My compliments to your commanding officer, Mr Fearn. Give him this.' He looked at his old sword and added quietly, 'We can all honour this day.'

Epilogue

Richard Bolitho studied his reflection in a wall mirror with the same scrutiny he would offer a junior officer who had applied for promotion.

He said over his shoulder, 'It was good of you to stay with me, Thomas.' He turned and looked fondly at Herrick who was sitting on the edge of a chair, a half empty goblet clutched in one hand. 'Although in your present state of nerves I fear we will be of little use to one another!'

It was still difficult to believe he was home in Falmouth. After all that had happened, the squadron's slow return to Plymouth, the work involved in caring for the battle-scarred ships, the goodbyes, and the memories of those who would never set foot in England again.

How quiet the house was, so still he could hear the birds beyond the windows which were closed against the first October chill, so very quiet, like a ship before a fight or after a storm.

Herrick shifted uncomfortably in his chair and looked down at his new uniform.

'Acting-commodore, *they* said!' He sounded incredulous. 'But I'd lose even that when peace was signed!'

Bolitho smiled at Herrick's discomfort. Whatever the Admiralty's official attitude was to be about the French invasion fleet's destruction, their lordships had shown honest sense where Herrick was concerned.

Bolitho said quietly, 'It has the right ring to it. Thomas

Herrick, Rear-Admiral of the Red. I'm truly proud of you, and for you.'

Herrick stuck out his jaw. 'And what about you? *Nothing* for what you achieved?' He held up his hand. 'You can't shut me up any more! We're equal now, you said so yourself, so I'll say my piece and there's an end to it!'

'Yes, Thomas.'

Herrick nodded, satisfied. 'Right then. It's all over the West Country, everyone knows that peace is everything but signed, that fighting has ceased, and all because the French are the ones eager for an armistice! And *why*, do I ask?'

'Tell me, Thomas.'

Bolitho looked at himself in the mirror again. He felt worried and unsettled now that the moment had arrived. Within the hour he would be married to Belinda. What he had wanted more than anything, what he had clung to even in the worst moments in France and at sea.

But suppose she had inwardly changed her mind. She would still marry him, he had no doubt about that, but it would be on his terms and not hers. Herrick's anger at the Admiralty's attitude on his future seemed unimportant.

Herrick said, 'It is because of what you did, make no mistake on that! Without those damned invasion vessels the French can only make a noise. They could no more invade England than, than . . .' He groped for some suitable insult. He ended by saying, 'I think it's petty and unfair. I'm promoted, when God's teeth I'd rather remain a captain, while you stay where you are!'

Bolitho looked at him gravely. 'Was it hard for you at Plymouth?'

Herrick nodded. 'Aye. Saying farewell to *Benbow*. It *was* hard. I wanted to explain so much to the new captain, tell him what the ship could do . . .' He shrugged heavily. 'But there it is. We paid our formal respects, and I came here to Falmouth.'

'Like that other time, eh, Thomas?'

'Aye.'

Herrick stood up and placed the goblet firmly on the table.

He said, 'But today is a special day. Let's make the most of it. I'm glad we're walking down to the church.' He looked steadily into Bolitho's eyes. 'She's lucky. So are you.' He grinned. '*Sir.*'

Allday opened the door, their hats in his hands. He looked very smart in his new gilt-buttoned jacket and nankeen breeches, a far cry from the man with a cutlass on the French flagship's quarterdeck.

'There's a visitor, gentlemen.'

Herrick groaned. 'Send him or her packing, Allday. What a time to arrive!'

A tall shadow moved through the door and gave a stiff bow.

'With respect, sir, no admiral attends his wedding without his flag-lieutenant.'

Bolitho strode across the room and grasped both his hands.

'Oliver! Of all miracles!'

Browne gave his gentle smile. 'A long story, sir. We escaped by boat and were picked up by a Yankee trader. Unfortunately, he was unwilling to put us ashore until we reached Morocco!' He studied Bolitho for several seconds. 'Everywhere I've been I have heard nothing but praise for your victory. I did warn you that authority might take a different view if you succeeded with Admiral Beauchamp's plan.' He glanced at Herrick's new epaulettes and added, 'But some rightful reward has been made, sir.'

Herrick said, 'You've come at the right time, young fellow!'

Browne stepped back and then patted Bolitho's coat and neckcloth into shape.

'There, sir, fit for *the* day.'

Bolitho walked through the open doors and looked at the empty grounds. The wedding was to be a quiet, personal thing, but it seemed as if every servant, Ferguson his steward, the gardeners and even the stable-boy had gone on ahead of him.

He said softly, 'Your safe arrival has done more good than I can say, Oliver. It is like having a weight lifted from my heart.' He turned and looked at his three friends and knew he meant it. 'Now we shall walk down together.'

As they arrived in the square and moved towards the old church of King Charles the Martyr, Bolitho was surprised to see a great crowd of townspeople waiting to see him.

As the three sea-officers, followed cheerfully by Allday, approached the church, many of the people began to cheer and wave their hats, and one man, obviously an old sailor, cupped his hands and yelled, 'Good luck to ye! A cheer for Equality Dick!'

'What is happening, Thomas?'

Herrick shrugged unhelpfully. 'Probably market day.'

Allday nodded, hiding a grin. 'That might well be it, sir.'

Bolitho paused on the steps and smiled at the expectant faces. Some he knew, people he had played with as a child and had grown up with. Others he did not, for they had come from outlying villages, and some all the way from Plymouth where they had seen the squadron arrive and anchor.

For although the politicians and the lords of Admiralty could say and do as they pleased, to these ordinary people today was something important.

Once again a Bolitho had come home to the big grey house below Pendennis Castle. Not a stranger, but one of their own sons.

A clock chimed and Bolitho whispered, 'Let us enter, Thomas.'

Herrick smiled at Browne. He had rarely seen Bolitho at a loss before.

The doors opened, and one more surprise waited to disturb Bolitho's emotions.

The church was packed from end to end, and as Bolitho walked to meet the rector, he realized that many of them were officers and sailors from the squadron. One whole line was taken up by his captains and their wives, even their children. Inch, with his arm in a sling and his pretty wife. Veriker, his head to one side in case he misheard something. Valentine Keen whose *Nicator* had chased the last French ship under the guns of a coastal battery before he had decided to give the enemy best. Duncan and Lapish, and Lockhart of the *Ganymede*, obviously enjoying the twist of fate which had made him one of Bolitho's captains. Nancy, Bolitho's younger sister, was there beside her husband, the squire. She was already dabbing her eyes and smiling at the same time, and even her husband looked unusually pleased with himself.

Some would be remembering that other time seven years ago when Richard Bolitho, then a captain himself, had waited here for his bride.

Bolitho looked at Herrick. Allday had melted into the mass of watching sailors and marines, and Browne stood beside Dulcie Herrick, her hand resting on his cuff.

'Well, old friend, we are alone again it seems.'

Herrick smiled. 'Not for long.'

He too was remembering. In this place it was hard to forget. The line of plaques on the wall near the pulpit, all Bolithos, from Captain Julius Bolitho who had died right here in Falmouth in 1646 trying to lift the Roundhead blockade on Pendennis Castle. At the bottom there was one plain plaque. 'Lieutenant Hugh Bolitho. Born 1752 . . . Died 1782.' Nearby was another, and Herrick guessed it had been placed there only recently. It stated, 'To the memory of Mr Selby, Master's Mate in His Britannic Majesty's Ship *Hyperion*, 1795.'

Yes, it was very hard to forget.

He saw Bolitho straighten his back and turned to face the aisle as the doors reopened.

The organ played, and a rustle of expectancy transmitted itself through the building as Lieutenant Adam Pascoe, with Bolitho's bride on his arm, walked slowly towards the altar.

Bolitho watched, afraid he might miss something. Belinda was beautiful, and Adam like a picture of himself from the past.

He saw Belinda raise her eyes to his and smile, and reached

out to guide her the last few steps to the altar.

She gave his hand a gentle squeeze, and Herrick heard him say, 'Peace. At last.'

Herrick stepped up beside them. He doubted if anyone else here today would know what Bolitho had meant, and the realization made him feel like a giant.

The Only Victor

Alexander Kent

FEBRUARY 1806

The frigate carrying Vice-Admiral Sir Richard Bolitho drops anchor off the shores of southern Africa. It is only four months since the resounding victory over the combined Franco-Spanish fleet at Trafalgar, and the death of England's greatest naval hero.

Bolitho's instructions are to assist in hastening the campaign in Africa, where an expeditionary force is attempting to recapture Cape Town from the Dutch. Outside Europe few have yet heard of the battle of Trafalgar, and Bolitho's news is met with both optimism and disappointment as he reminds the senior officers that, despite the victory, Napolean's defeat is by no means assured. The men who follow Bolitho's flag into battle are to discover, not for the first time, that death is the only victor.

arrow books

With All Despatch

Alexander Kent

SPRING 1792

England is enjoying a troubled peace, with her old enemy France still in the grip of the Terror. In harbours and estuaries around the country, the fleet has been left to rot, and thousands of officers and seamen have been thrown unwanted on the beach. Even a frigate captain as famous as Richard Bolitho is forced to swallow his pride and accept a minor appointment to the Nore. With his small flotilla of three topsail cutters he sets out to search for the most brutal gang of smugglers England has known, the Brotherhood – a gang with men of influence behind them and a secret, sinister trade in human misery.

'One of our foremost writers of naval fiction'
Sunday Times

arrow books

Form Line of Battle

Alexander Kent

June 1793, Gibraltar

The gathering might of revolutionary France prepares to engulf Europe in another bloody war. As in the past, Britain will stand or fall by the fighting power of her fleet.

For Richard Bolitho, the renewal of hostilities means a fresh command and the chance of action after long months of inactivity. However, his mission to support Lord Hood in the monarchist-inspired occupation of Toulon has gone awry. Bolitho and the crew of the *Hyperion* are trapped by the French near a dry Mediterranean island. The great ship-of-the-line's battered hull begins to groan as her sails snap in the hot wind.

'One of our foremost writers of naval fiction'
Sunday Times

arrow books

Man of War

Alexander Kent

Antigua, 1817, and every harbour and estuary is filled with ghostly ships, the famous and the legendary now redundant in the aftermath of war. In this uneasy peace, Adam Bolitho is fortunate to be offered the seventy-four gun *Athena*, and as flag captain to Vice-Admiral Sir Graham Bethune once more follows his destiny to the Caribbean.

But in these haunted waters where Richard Bolitho and his 'band of brothers' once fought a familiar enemy, the quarry is now a renegade foe who flies no colours and offers no quarter, and whose traffic in human life is sanctioned by flawed treaties and men of influence. And here, when *Athena*'s guns speak, a day of terrible retribution will dawn for the innocent and the damned.

'One of our foremost writers of naval fiction'
Sunday Times

arrow books

Relentless Pursuit

Alexander Kent

It is December 1815 and Adam Bolitho's orders are unequivocal. As captain of His Majesty's Frigate *Unrivalled* of forty-six guns, he is required to *'repair in the first instance to Freetown Sierra Leone, and reasonably assist the senior officer of the patrolling squadron'*. But all efforts of the British anti-slavery patrols to curb a flourishing trade in human life are hampered by unsuitable ships, by the indifference of a government more concerned with old enemies made distrustful allies, and by the continuing belligerence of the Dey of Algiers, which threatens to ignite a full-scale war.

For Adam, also, there is no peace. Lost in grief and loneliness, his uncle's death still avenged, he is uncertain of all but his identity as a man of war. The sea is his element, the ship his only home, and a reckless, perhaps doomed attack on an impregnable stronghold his only hope of settling the bitterest of debts.

'As ever, Kent evokes the blood and smoke of battle in crimson-vivid prose'
Mail on Sunday

'A splendid yarn'
The Times

arrow books

Success to the Brave

Alexander Kent

Spring, 1802

Richard Bolitho is summoned to the Admiralty to receive his orders for a diffcult and thankless mission . . .

The recent Peace of Amiens is already showing signs of strain as old enemies wrangle over colonies won and lost during the war. In the little 64-gun *Achates*, Bolitho sails west for the Caribbean, to hand over the island of San Felipe to the French.

But diplomacy is not enough . . .

'One of our foremost writers of naval fiction . . .'
Sunday Times

arrow books

TO FIND OUT MORE ABOUT

Alexander Kent

Visit www.bolithomaritimeproductions.com
or you may wish to subscribe to
The Bolitho Newsletter.

To join our mailing list to receive *The Bolitho Newsletter*,
send your name and address to:

The Bolitho Newsletter
William Heinemann Marketing Department
20 Vauxhall Bridge Road
London
SW1V 2SA

If at any stage you wish to be deleted from *The Bolitho Newsletter*
mailing list, please notify us in writing at the address above.

*Your details will be held on our database in order for us to send
you *The Bolitho Newsletter* and information on Alexander Kent,
Douglas Reeman and any of our other authors you may find
interesting. Your personal details will not be passed to any third
parties. If you do not wish to receive information on any other
author please clearly state so when subscribing to the newsletter.

arrow books

Praise for James Rollins

'Nobody – and I mean nobody – does this stuff better than Rollins'
Lee Child

'Rollins combines real-world science with high-octane action to create rousing stories of adventure that are as exciting as any movie'
Chicago Sun-Times

'A spiralling, high-octane adventure . . . Rollins is clearly at the top of his game'
Steve Berry

'Rollins excels at combining action and history with larger-than-life characters . . . A must for pure action fans'
Booklist

'An adventure in the grand manner. Rollins takes the reader through the horror and intrigue . . . like no one else. The action never relents'
Clive Cussler

'Action-packed with hair-raising adventures' *Oxford Times*

'With this book, Rollins's writing, as ever, dispenses pacy and colourful fare'
Good Book Guide

'A non-stop thrill-a-minute ride'
Tess Gerritsen

'A breakneck thriller'
Glasgow Herald

'The modern master of the action thriller'
Providence Journal-Bulletin

C334027156

James Rollins is the author of several bestselling novels and series, including the Sigma Force series, a string of standalone thrillers and the novelisation of the cinema blockbuster *Indiana Jones and the Kingdom of the Crystal Skull*. His books are sold in more than thirty countries and have sold more than ten million copies worldwide. An amateur spelunker and scuba enthusiast, he also holds a doctorate in veterinary medicine from the University of Missouri. He currently lives and writes in Sacramento, California.

To find out more about James, visit his website www.jamesrollins.com, find him on Facebook www.facebook.com/sigmaforce or follow him on Twitter @jamesrollins